Berkley Sensation titles by Eileen Wilks

TEMPTING DANGER
MORTAL DANGER
BLOOD LINES

continued . . .

BLOOD LINES

EILEEN WILKS

BERKLEY SENSATION, NEW YORK

THE BERKLEY PUBLISHING GROUP
Published by the Penguin Group
Penguin Group (USA) Inc.
375 Hudson Street, New York, New York 10014, USA
Penguin Group (Canada), 90 Eglinton Avenue East, Suite 700, Toronto, Ontario M4P 2Y3, Canada
(a division of Pearson Penguin Canada Inc.)
Penguin Books Ltd., 80 Strand, London WC2R 0RL, England
Penguin Group Ireland, 25 St. Stephen's Green, Dublin 2, Ireland (a division of Penguin Books Ltd.)
Penguin Group (Australia), 250 Camberwell Road, Camberwell, Victoria 3124, Australia
(a division of Pearson Australia Group Pty. Ltd.)
Penguin Books India Pvt. Ltd., 11 Community Centre, Panchsheel Park, New Delhi—110 017, India
Penguin Group (NZ), Cnr. Airborne and Rosedale Roads, Albany, Auckland 1310, New Zealand
(a division of Pearson New Zealand Ltd.)
Penguin Books (South Africa) (Pty.) Ltd., 24 Sturdee Avenue, Rosebank, Johannesburg 2196,
South Africa

Penguin Books Ltd., Registered Offices: 80 Strand, London WC2R 0RL, England

BLOOD LINES

A Berkley Sensation Book / published by arrangement with the author

PRINTING HISTORY
Berkley Sensation mass-market edition / January 2007

Copyright © 2007 by Eileen Wilks.
Cover illustration by Don Sipley.
Cover design by George Long.
Interior text design by Kristin del Rosario.

ISBN: 978-0-425-21344-5

BERKLEY SENSATION®
Berkley Sensation Books are published by The Berkley Publishing Group,
a division of Penguin Group (USA) Inc.,
375 Hudson Street, New York, New York 10014.
BERKLEY SENSATION is a registered trademark of Penguin Group (USA) Inc.
The "B" design is a trademark belonging to Penguin Group (USA) Inc.

PRINTED IN THE UNITED STATES OF AMERICA

10   9   8   7   6   5   4   3   2   1

Dear Reader,

It's been a little over three months since I met Rule. It seems a lot longer. I could turn all mushy and say it feels as if my life began when our eyes met that night at Club Hell, but I'd be lying. I had a life before him—bumpy and imperfect, but a life.

Just about everything in that life has changed, though. That is why it feels like a lot more than three months have passed.

I was a homicide cop back then. That's all I'd ever wanted to be—at least since the age of eight, when I learned that the monsters are real and look a lot like the rest of us. Now I'm working for the FBI, Unit 12 in MCD—that's the Magical Crimes Division—and I'm bonded for life to the prince of the Nokolai Clan.

Two months ago I was investigating the first West Coast killing in decades by a werewolf—excuse me, a lupus. Rule Turner looked to be my prime suspect. I realized pretty quickly he couldn't be, but it took longer to find out who was behind it all. A nutty telepath, a charismatic cult leader, and an ancient goddess–wannabe had teamed up to destroy all lupi in the United States, and they didn't object to killing a few humans along the way to taking over the country.

We stopped them. By "we" I mean Rule and me and a few others, like my grandmother—who's gone to China, dammit, on some sort of personal pilgrimage. She left about a week before I ended up in hell. Literally.

See, I killed the telepath. She was doing her damnedest to kill me at the time, so I didn't have much choice. But the cult's leader got away, and he took her staff with him. Or maybe I should say *Her* staff, because it was tied to the goddess we don't name. We had to find and destroy the staff, which meant tracking down Harlowe, the cult leader.

We found him. It didn't turn out well for any of us. Harlowe got dead, along with some others. I got split in two, with half of me blasted into the demon realm.

Rule went with me. That part of me, anyway.

Don't ask me to explain this split business. Cullen—

that's Rule's friend, the sorcerer—might be able to, but you'd be making a mistake to ask. The man looks like walking sin, but he turns into the nutty professor when he starts talking spellwork and theory.

It gets pretty confusing after that. Neither part of me knew the other one existed. The one in hell—or Dis, as the natives call it—had no memory. She did have Rule, but he was stuck in wolf form. The me still on Earth knew Rule wasn't dead because of the mate bond, but finding him was another story. Eventually some of the lupus priestesses— they're called Rhejes—plus Cullen managed to open a small hellgate, which is only a little less illegal than mass murder. Me, Cullen, Cynna, and an obnoxious gnome named Max went after Rule.

Dis is split into regions, each ruled by its prince. The goddess-wannabe had infiltrated one of those regions by sending her avatar—think of an avatar as a sentient cup, with most of the person poured out to make room for some of the goddess—to make a deal with its prince. They had a falling out. The demon ate the avatar and went nuts, and both sides of me found ourselves in the middle of a war in hell.

Both of me were very surprised by the dragons.

The Other Me and Rule had been scooped up by a dragon early on. This hadn't seemed like a lucky break at the time; more like a nasty way to die. But in the end it was a dragon who knew how to get us back—get me back with my Other Me, that is, and get all of us back to Earth . . . including him and about twenty of his huge, beautiful, and deadly buddies.

We didn't escape unscathed. The authorities decided to pretend it wasn't possible to open a hellgate, so we weren't in trouble for that. After all, the gate vanished as soon as we returned. But Rule nearly died, and I . . . I know things I never thought it was possible to know. Death isn't the absolute I used to believe it to be.

And the dragons? They vanished so thoroughly that some people are talking about Hollywood publicity stunts. It did happen in California, after all.

This is the story of what happened after we all came

home, sort of like Dorothy & Co. after Oz. I'm betting you thought everything was peachy for Dorothy once she got home.

We forget that Kansas is no safer than Oz. After all, that's where the tornado hit.

Lily Yu

PROLOGUE

2:52 A.M., December 20 (Greenwich)

JUST outside Miller's Dale, Derbyshire, two budding naturalists snuck out of their cottage. Julie and Marnie weren't supposed to be out at night, of course, but they had every hope their mother would never know. She always slept very soundly after one of her "girls' night out" parties. They meant to find and photograph the pair of *Mustela erminea* whose tracks they'd spotted yesterday.

At least, Marnie was convinced they were stoat tracks. Julie kept annoying her sister by pointing out that they might have been made by *Mustela nivalis*, known to the Latin-impaired as the common weasel. Both left five-toed tracks and were largely nocturnal, though weasels often went about in the daytime, too.

But they'd also found a tuft of white fur nearby. "It could have come from a hare," Julie said for the fifth or sixth time.

"That was not hair from a hare."

"How do you know?"

"I just do." Privately Marnie had to admit she couldn't be sure, but it would be ever so lovely if they could find the weasel's beautiful white-coated cousin.

It was possible. Stoats weren't that uncommon, and Miller's Dale was blessed with not one, not two, but three nature preserves nearby: the two belonging to the Derbyshire Naturalists' Trust at Priestcliffe Lees and Station Quarry, and the National Nature Reserve at Monk's Dale. Being in the Peak District, the area was also lousy with hiking trails, not to mention tourists and other pests.

No hikers now. The moon was a lumpy golden goblin hanging low on the horizon, just over half-full. There was plenty of light for the girls to keep to the road that tracked the River Wye. Their breaths puffed pale in the still air. Marnie tucked her hands in her pockets, feeling the bulky shape of her new Nikon. She'd taken about a hundred pictures, trying to get the shutter speed, f-stop, and ISO right for night pictures. She'd preset everything. If they saw a *Mustela erminea*, all she had to do was point and shoot.

Some plans are never fulfilled. The girls made it less than halfway to the area where they'd spotted the tracks when they saw a soft glow coming from a small copse off to the left.

"Some stupid bugger has left a fire burning," Julie said.

"Maybe." The light wasn't flickering, like a fire would. "Looks more like a torch."

"Not moving, is it? C'mon. We'd better check."

Marnie jigged from foot to foot, wanting badly to pursue her stoats . . . but if that light did come from an abandoned campfire, it needed to be put out. "All right. But keep it quiet, in case it's just teenagers."

The girls were good at moving quietly so as not to alarm wildlife, but it was much darker beneath the trees. Still, they reached the small, circular clearing at the center of the copse without making too much racket. And stopped dead—then ducked behind a tree.

There were *fairies* in the fairy ring.

That's what Marnie thought they were, anyway, though no one had seen a fairy in . . . well, forever. But they were little, so little they probably wouldn't have come up to her knee if any of them had been standing . . . which they weren't. Plus they had great, huge, butterfly wings. And they *glowed*. As if they were made out of LEDs, a soft light radiated from all over their pale, perfect little bodies.

Which she could see quite clearly because they were naked. And what they were doing . . . well, she'd seen animals do that, but never anything that looked so much like people.

Marnie yanked her camera out of her pocket and clicked it

on. She pressed the shutter button and prayed. Pressed it again. Again.

"They're doing *sex*!" Julie whispered, shocked.

Marnie pinched her to make her be quiet, but it was too late. One of them—a female with yellow wings with big brown spots—stopped what she was doing to the male with reddish wings. Her little head swiveled as she looked around. She twittered something.

Marnie gaped. The little fairy had *teeth*. Pointy teeth, like a cat.

Several of them laughed. One chirped more words, and they looked all around as if they were spooked. A bitty little man with blue wings cried out and pointed right at the tree where Marnie and Julie were hiding.

The biggest female, a slender redhead with wings the color of dusk, raised her hands over her head. She cried out some words real sharp, like she was bossing someone around. She was loud, too, louder than someone that little ought to be. Her teeny hands closed into fists.

They all vanished, and it was very dark beneath the trees.

The girls did get in trouble for sneaking out, but it was worth it. Marnie sold her pictures to the local newspaper and then to a wire service. Eventually she even forgave her sister for opening her big mouth and scaring the fairies off.

8:52 P.M. December 19 (local);
2:52 A.M. December 20 (Greenwich)

LOS Lobos perched precariously on the mountainous coast of Michoacán, Mexico, where the peaks of the Sierra Madre del Sur crowded the coast so tightly they all but fell off into the Pacific. The tiny pueblo straddled one of the few roads into the mountains, a bumpy cement snake that shed its paving seven kilometers up to wriggle off in happy obscurity, becoming a dirt trail usable only by donkeys or those with no regard for their vehicle's undercarriage.

There was no inn or hotel in the village, but Señora de Pedrosa, old Enrique's widow, had an extra bedroom once she booted out her third-oldest grandson—who, after all, was well able to stay with his brother and sister-in-law for a few days. She'd rented that room to the stranger who slept there now, dreaming of darkness.

Cullen awoke with a start. For a second he didn't know where or when he was, but there was light. He could see.

Not that there was much to see. He'd fallen asleep at the little table his hostess had provided, dozing off with his head on his arms.

Gah. Tedious dream . . . though not as tedious as the other one. He'd hoped that one would quit squirming up from his unconscious now that he was Nokolai, but no such luck.

Cullen straightened, scrubbed his face with both hands, and twisted to stretch the kinks out of his spine. Apparently his recent late nights, added to tramping through the jungle, had caught up to him. What time was it, anyway?

He picked up the phone that served better as a clock than a communication device this far from any cell towers. The glowing display informed him it was a ridiculous hour to be asleep. Well, he was awake now.

What had woken him?

He frowned. The dream? But it had never woken him up before. He listened, sniffed, but didn't hear or smell anything unusual . . .

Then he felt it again. Soft as the brush of a feather, something tickled his shields.

Instinctively he snapped them tighter. What the hell—?

Then he smiled. Of course. Someone had noticed him, was trying to turn him aside. Who else but the one he sought?

His hand went to his chest, where the longer of his two necklaces dangled. He opened the pouch—leather, covered with silk— and removed the contents. For a moment he simply savored it, turning it over between his fingers.

It was hard and smooth as glass and shaped like a large flower petal. The edges were sharp enough to make him careful how he handled it. In daylight, he knew, it would be dark gray with an opalescent sheen, as if coated by oily water. At the moment his eyes could barely make it out.

But Cullen didn't rely only on his eyes to see. And his recent blinding, now healed, had only made his other vision sharper. With that vision he saw color: alive, glittering color. Blue for water, silver for air, brown for earth—red sparks, yellow, green—all the colors of magic danced across it. But underneath . . . ah, underneath them all, it was the deepest purple, a purple darkened nearly to black.

Purple, the color of those of the Blood. What he held had come from the oldest of the magical species, the one made more purely from magic than any other. Chances were, Cullen thought as he smoothed his thumb along the glassy surface, that no one on Earth had held one of these in four or five hundred years.

A dragon's scale, so recently shed that the magic of its former owner still lived in it.

A dragon who might be looking for Cullen, as Cullen was looking for him—though for different reasons. He grinned into the darkness, his hand closing around the sharp edges of his prize.

10:52 A.M. December 20 (local);
2:52 A.M. December 20 (Greenwich)

EIGHTY kilometers outside Chengdu in Sichuan Province, China, an old woman was climbing a mountain—quite a short mountain, actually, though the trail was steep. Few took that trail in winter, but today both land and sky were clear of snow. The sun was a shiny pebble overhead.

She wasn't alone. Five others lagged behind, perhaps not as keen as she on reaching the Taoist temple at the trail's end. The cold annoyed Madam Li Lei Yu, bringing as it did intimations of age and mortality. But then, her pilgrimage was itself a reminder of those states: both the immediate pilgrimage up this blasted mountain and the larger one that had brought her back to her homeland.

After arriving in Chengdu she'd learned that the man she'd come here to see—a monk—had died last year. She was annoyed with An Du. Couldn't he have waited a little longer? She would make the trip to his grave, but there was a strong flavor of "get it over with" to her climb.

She was twenty feet from the top and out of sight of the others when it hit. Not dizziness, though she lost track of up and down. Not blindness nor deafness, though her vision went gray and her hearing faded. Something strong and *other* blew through her, snuffing out her senses like candles, sending her sliding across reality as if it were ice.

She came to lying on her back with the sun still shining, the rest of the climbers still on the other side of the bend, and a name on her lips that hadn't been spoken aloud in four hundred years.

Li Lei didn't speak that name now, either. But it sang inside her, opening vistas of terror and joy, memory and change. For several breaths she didn't move, letting her heart settle back into its usual steady beat. Letting her thoughts settle, too, around the new shape of reality.

"So," she whispered in the language of her birth, "he has come back."

And just how long had he been back before the wind blew through and whispered his name? She scowled.

The sound of voices all too near made her push to her feet, wincing—since there was no one to see—at the pain in her hip. There was a time when a little fall like that . . . well, no matter. She was old, and the Maker had for some unfathomable reason chosen to include decrepitude as part of the package. Railing against it did no good.

Nonetheless, she was muttering under her breath to whomever might be listening as she walked back along the trail.

The others came around the bend, following their guide. He was a small, agile man of about forty who had not liked it when she went on ahead. He had actually thought he could prevent her. The married couple just behind him were from Beijing, the two young men from somewhere in Guizhou.

Li Lei Yu neither knew nor cared why the others had decided to climb a mountain today. She was interested in only one person of the party: the middle-aged woman at the rear. She ignored the guide's questions and expostulations as she made her way to her companion.

Li Qin's dear, ugly face was placid as ever, her voice as surprising in its beauty as it had been when they first met. "Have you reached the top and returned to show us the way, madam?"

That was Li Qin's notion of humor. Obviously there was only one way to the top. "I have lost my taste for gravesite conversations. They are too one-sided. We will leave now."

Obediently Li Qin turned around and started back down the trail. "We return to the hotel?"

"No. We are going home."

"Ah." Li Qin followed in silence.

"You are doing it again," Li Lei muttered. "It is most unattractive."

"I have said nothing."

"You think very loudly." They descended in silence for several minutes before she spoke again, grudgingly. "I will admit it. You were right. China is no longer home."

Li Qin answered gently, "That was not what I said."

Not precisely, no. She had said that Li Lei would not find what she sought in China. But it came to the same thing, for home was what Li Lei ached for. Home, and reunions that could never be, for so many were gone.

But not all. Not all. She stopped, turning to meet her old friend's eyes. "I have found something I didn't seek. Or it has found me." She took a slow breath, let it out. "The Turning. The Turning has come, Li Qin."

Li Qin's breath sucked in so softly even Li Lei's ears barely caught the sound. Her eyes went wide . . . and not placid at all.

ONE

9:52 P.M. December 19 (local);
2:52 A.M. December 20 (Greenwich)

THE National Symphony's performance of Handel's *Messiah* had started at eight thirty, so the choir was winding up the "Hallelujah Chorus" when the lead tenor turned into a wolf.

Until then, Lily Yu had been enjoying the evening. She hadn't expected to, not after getting the news about the investigation. And before that, there had been the problem of clothes. Lily liked clothes. She owned a fair number, too—mostly on-the-job jackets and such, but she'd brought her few dressy things to D.C., too. The assignment called for them. So she'd had her favorite black silk dress with her, and if she'd worn it four times already, so what? You couldn't go wrong with black, especially when it fit like it had been made for her.

Which it had. Her cousin Lynn was trying to get a dressmaking business going.

What she'd lacked was a coat. A dressy coat, to be specific. She'd bought a Lands' End jacket the day after her plane's wheels touched down at Reagan International Airport, but she couldn't very well toss it on over black silk.

Lily was in Washington, D.C., temporarily, taking a special version of the usual FBI training at nearby Quantico during the day and going to parties at night. The parties were work, not play. She was an FBI agent now, part of the secretive Unit Twelve within the Magical Crimes Division, but on loan to the Secret Service. The case she'd been brought in for was beyond the usual scope of that agency: a Congressman had been offered a deal by a demon.

He'd reported it. They'd been fairly sure others in the same position hadn't.

There was no denying they needed to know if any congressional critters or highly placed bureaucrats had signed in blood on the dotted line, but Lily had hated her part in the investigation—mainly because she hadn't been allowed to really investigate. Nor had she been told much of anything. The Secret Service took the first part of their name far too seriously, and most of them did not like or trust the Unit.

Lots of people felt that way about magic, of course. That's one reason Lily had kept her own Gift a secret so long.

Lily was a touch sensitive, one of the rarest Gifts. Magic didn't affect her, yet she could feel it on her skin, could identify its type and sometimes its source. For years sensitives had been used to out the Gifted and those of the Blood who were passing as normal. Supposedly the days of persecution were over, but prejudice hadn't evaporated with the lifting of official sanctions.

Lily did not out anyone. Period. The work she'd been doing for the Secret Service came close to that, but there was a difference between making demonic pact and practicing the craft or turning furry once a month or so. Lily understood that. Besides, The Powers That Be hadn't wanted a whiff of this investigation reaching the press, and she has a dandy cover for her partying. Rule spent time in D.C. often, lobbying for his people. His current cause—or his father's—was the Species Citizenship Bill, still bogged down in committee, but not dead.

So she'd shaken hands, smiled, and found one aide, a Representative, and a highly placed bureaucrat whose flesh carried a hint of orange. They'd been questioned, and though she hadn't been part of those interviews, it had looked like they were going to find whoever had brought the demon over to offer those deals.

This afternoon, she'd been told the investigation was closed. The perp had confessed by killing himself. He'd even been thoughtful enough to leave a note, so it looked like she'd be able to fly home for Christmas.

That ought to have pleased her. Pity she could so seldom feel the way she ought to.

Home was San Diego, where the weather made sense. Water didn't get hard in San Diego unless you put it in your freezer. It didn't fall from the sky often, either—certainly not as icy pellets, which it had done here the night before last.

That had been a shock. She'd always thought of Virginia as *warm*.

Yesterday when she returned from Quantico, a coat had been spread across her bed; a long, black coat in a sumptuous blend of wool, silk, and cashmere. An extravagantly warm and luxurious coat with a cheap red bow sitting askew on the collar . . . and a fat orange cat shedding all over it.

She'd removed Dirty Harry immediately, much to his displeasure.

Harry was one of Rule's extravagances. They hadn't known how long they'd be in Washington, so Rule had insisted on paying for a plane ticket for the cat. The funny thing was that he and Harry didn't much like each other, but Rule regarded Harry as Lily's dependent. So Harry had flown first-class with them, little though he'd appreciated the honor. He'd been in his carrier, of course, and sedated, the latter being as much for their sakes as his.

"I didn't have time to wrap it," Rule had said, coming into the room behind her.

"I thought we agreed to exchange presents on Christmas, not before." She'd tried to sound stern, but the way she'd been petting the coat probably gave the wrong impression.

His mouth had twitched. "I grew impatient. Forgive me. It isn't so much that I mind watching you shiver and shake and complain about the weather. I've gotten used to that, and your lips are really quite attractive when they turn blue. But I know how you hate waste, and since it seems we'll be back in California for the big day after all—"

She'd rolled her eyes and interrupted him with a kiss. Then she'd given him the tickets to tonight's shindig, her early Christmas present for him, which destroyed any chance of complaining that he'd jumped the gun with his gift.

She hadn't really wanted to complain. It was a gorgeous coat.

The gorgeous coat was draped over her shoulders at ten minutes before ten as the chorus wound up into the climactic strains of the "Hallelujah Chorus." She glanced at the man beside her.

He was a pleasure to look at. Lily was getting used to that. She cleaned up okay herself, but Rule Turner in a tux turned heads. It wasn't any one thing about him, she thought. His features were striking but imperfect: the lips a little thin, the nose a little crooked, like his smile. His cheekbones were sharp, with eyebrows parked along the same slant above eyes as dark as his hair.

At the moment he sat perfectly still, his head lifted slightly, his entire being focused on the music.

Ah, good. Good.

The magic that let lupi heal so fast was especially strong in Rule. He'd mended quickly from the surgery that put him back together after a demon ripped him apart, but something inside him hadn't healed. He was too often silent, too slow to smile.

Was he grieving? Did he miss *her*—the other Lily? The one who both was and wasn't gone?

The singers' voices pounded through her, the song that claimed there was no loss. That death, as the Buddhists held, was an illusion. Lily wished she could turn loose and go where the music wanted her to, but this wasn't her kind of music.

It was Rule's, though.

He'd told her his people were fond of music, but that was like saying Texans are fond of football, or cats of tuna fish. She'd learned that most lupi played at least one instrument, and all of them sang. Perfect pitch was more the norm than the exception.

That's why she was here, why she'd bought the tickets. She hadn't seen Rule this intent outside of bed . . .

. . . not since we sat on the rocky beach, listening to the dragons sing.

She blinked. Elation, grief, the pinch of envy—all twisted through her as the memory wisp faded. She could never hold on to them, those whispers from another self. Like dandelion fluff, they drifted across her mind sometimes, teasing her with the not-quite-lost.

Almost, she could summon the sound of dragons singing to the coming night. Almost.

She jolted.

Magic shivered and sparked across every inch of exposed skin—a rush of raw power, as if a door had opened and let an invisible wind blow through. Her heartbeat jumped and her breath sucked in, and magic prickled down her throat with her in-drawn breath—and *that* had never happened before.

Then it was gone, a magic dust devil that had blown on past. She turned to tell Rule.

His eyes were black. All the way black, not just dark, with no white showing. Beast-swallowed. A muscle jumped in his jaw, and his hands gripped the arms of the chair so tightly it was a wonder he hadn't squeezed them in two.

"Are you okay?" she whispered urgently.

He looked at her with those blind, black eyes. "Give me a minute," he managed through gritted teeth.

Someone screamed. For a second she thought it was because of Rule, but a second scream came on top of the first, and from the stage.

She looked—and caught the last few seconds of the Change.

Probably no one else in the audience knew what they were seeing. It was impossible to describe, a shifting slit in reality where forms seemed to slide elsewhere and back like a Möbius strip on speed.

But Lily had seen it before. She knew what was happening. They were about to have a werewolf onstage. If she was guessing right, a confused and frightened werewolf. Not a good mix with a lot of confused and frightened humans.

Lupus, she reminded herself as she stood and sidestepped past the people seated along her row. Not werewolf. Nowadays you had to call them lupi in the plural, lupus in the singular. "Police," she snapped at a beefy man who'd stood and was trying to see what was happening. "Sit."

He did. She emerged into the aisle. There was pandemonium onstage: singers tripping over each other trying to get away, mu-sicians deserting. The conductor hadn't budged. He was yelling at them, though not in English.

She glanced back quickly at Rule. He hadn't moved. The Change was riding him too hard, she guessed—if he let his con-centration slip, he'd lose the battle. Then they'd have two wolves scaring people.

She didn't have her weapon. A shoulder holster didn't make the right fashion statement for a night at the Kennedy Center, so she'd left it in the car, dammit.

This probably wasn't a problem a gun could solve, anyway.

She jogged up the aisle to the stage. Others in the audience were standing now. It wouldn't be long before confusion built into panic and they mobbed the exits.

"Police!" She shouted it this time. "Everyone sit down, stay calm. You are not in danger." At least there wasn't an orchestra pit. She heaved herself up onto the stage—an ungraceful procedure in a short skirt, but it couldn't be helped.

The choir had been perched on risers behind the orchestra. Most of those risers were empty now, though a few people were still scrambling off. A woman lay sprawled on the floor at the end of the highest tier, moaning.

But the area around the wolf had cleared. He stood at the bottom of the risers—a big beast, but smaller than Rule was in wolf form. Reddish fur. Hackles raised. Teeth bared.

The conductor was yelling at him.

"Idiot," she muttered under her breath, stomping up to seize him by the shoulder. "Shut up."

He turned, eyebrows flying up, his mouth pursing in a startled O.

"You're yelling at a wolf. He doesn't like it." Though there was a man inside the fur and snarls, the wolf seemed to be in charge right now.

"But he's ruined the performance! Ruined everything!"

"Not his fault. What's his name?"

"What? His name? Why?"

"Just tell me his name."

"Paul. Paul Chernowich."

"Okay. You've got people panicking, one injured." She gestured at the woman on the floor. "Get her some medical help. You." She turned to a lone woman who stood staring, slack-jawed, at the wolf, apparently too stunned to flee. She was young, dark-haired, at least half Asian. Her violin dangled from one hand, her bow from the other. "Play something."

The woman turned to her. "Wh-what?"

"Play something. Anything. It'll calm people down." Including the wolf, she hoped. "Lupi don't hurt women," she added. "You're safe."

The woman glanced at the wolf, out at the crowd, and back at Lily, comprehension leaking into her eyes. The corners of her mouth turned up. "A solo," she murmured. "Why not?" She stepped up to the front of the stage, tucked her violin under her chin, poised the bow for a dramatic moment—and began to play.

The sweet strains of a Bach violin sonata drifted out.

Lily faced the wolf. He was looking around, hackles still raised but no longer growling. Good. She wondered why he hadn't just run off. Wouldn't that be the natural thing to do? "Paul." She spoke firmly, not loudly. He'd hear. "You're upset. You don't know what happened, right?"

He glanced at her, then away, scanning the area.

What was he looking for? Whoever did this to him, maybe. "I don't know what forced the Change on you, but there's no immediate threat." She took one slow step closer. Where was Rule? Was he still fighting the Change? "We haven't met, but I bet you've heard of me. I'm Lily Yu, Rule's Chosen. Rule Turner of Nokolai."

He looked right at her and growled.

"Okay, maybe you're not Nokolai. But you wouldn't hurt a Chosen." She said that firmly, though the sight of all those teeth, not to mention the lowered head and raised hackles, had her heartbeat racing. She lifted the little charm hanging around her neck. "You know what this is. Your Lady—"

A shot rang out. She spun, her hand automatically going to the place where her gun wasn't.

A uniformed cop stood in the aisle, feet spread, weapon aimed.

The wolf raced past Lily almost too fast to see—straight for the idiot with the gun.

Rule landed on top of him.

Lily didn't know where he'd come from. He seemed to drop out of the air. And he was two-legged, dammit, in no shape to play tackle with a couple hundred pounds of wolf! The man-wolf tangle rolled, ending at the very edge of the stage with Rule on the bottom. The wolf's jaws opened as it lunged at Rule's throat—

Which Rule obligingly offered by tilting his head back. Someone screamed.

Maybe it was her this time.

The wolf froze. His teeth were on Rule's throat, but he wasn't moving. After a terrible pause, he removed his mouth. He sniffed Rule's chin and down his chest, and then looked at his face. She could have sworn he looked suspicious.

"Ni culpa, ne defensia," Rule said.

Slowly the wolf backed off, allowing Rule to stand.

Lily's breath shuddered in. The violinist glided from one sonata to another, slowing from allegro to adagio, her music drifting out across the stage and audience like foam from a retreating wave.

And the uniformed asshole with the gun took aim again.

TWO

~

CYNNA Weaver stood on a corner in Washington, D.C., that would never be featured on visitor tours or political photo ops. The temperature was supposed to be above freezing, but her fingers suspected it had dropped below that mark. She jammed her hands into the pockets of her bomber jacket. She'd remembered her jacket, her room key, phone, wallet, and weapon. No hat or gloves. Dumb.

She didn't know where she was. That was more than a little embarrassing, considering the nature of her Gift. Somewhere in Southeast D.C.—she'd switched to the Green Line at some point—but she couldn't for the life of her remember where she'd gotten off. Or why.

Probably Anacostia, Cynna thought, looking around. Which just showed how little she could trust her subconscious, but her conscious mind wasn't coming up much except *Get out of here*.

She chose a direction at random and started walking.

Her current lodgings weren't much different from a hundred other hotel rooms she'd stayed in since jumping sides in the law-and-order game seven years ago. The room had a decent bed, cable TV, plenty of hot water, and no trace of personality. Midway through a room service hamburger, she hadn't been able to stand it anymore.

Not that she knew what "it" was. The impersonal room? The too-personal dreams plaguing her? Or the dreams that had died . . . *Stubborn sons of bitches*, she thought, scowling. Those long-dead dreams kept throwing ghosts.

Whatever the cause this time, the feeling itself was familiar. She never had been able to put a name to it. She just knew that when it hit, she had to *do* something. Anything. Back when she was young and stupid, that had usually meant partying. Nowadays she tried to work it off physically.

Tonight she'd hopped the Metro, then started walking. Unfortunately, she'd been too busy chasing her thoughts round and round their hamster wheels to pay attention. When she'd finally woken from her stupid-induced trance . . . Well, this wasn't the worst street she'd ever been on, but it came close. And she'd been down some pretty badass streets.

A lowrider truck cruised by, windows down, stereo up, the bass thrumming the soles of her feet through her Reeboks. One of the wits in the backseat leaned out the window to make her an offer easy to refuse. She did, using sign language that would be recognized in any high school in America.

Not exactly professional, but she wasn't here professionally. She was here because . . . nope, couldn't come up with a single good reason.

Just ahead, a neon sign saying simply Bar fizzed over a scarred door. The door opened, spilling rap music, the scent of weed, and two young brothers in cargo pants onto the sidewalk. One of them staggered, giggling. The other one looked straight at her.

Uh-oh.

"Hey, ho," he said in a soft voice. "What you be doin' heah? Dis not yo' block."

It wasn't a friendly inquiry. Not with his eyes set on empty that way.

Middle-class people made a lot of assumptions about neighborhoods like this. They thought everyone did drugs, the only occupations were pusher, pimp, or hooker, and if you set foot in the hood, you'd be mugged, raped, or worse.

Like most assumptions, those were wrong. The people who lived here weren't assaulted every time they walked down the street, and many of them hated the crime and violence a lot more than any soccer mom watching a condensed version on CNN. But a woman alone, after dark, who wasn't from the hood . . .

Cynna stopped, rolling her shoulders to loosen them. She trickled a little power into one of the tattoos on her forearm, but left her jacket zipped so she wouldn't be tempted to draw on these idiots. Ruben would shit if she shot someone. "Bone out, bogart." *Get lost, tough guy.*

"Lissen dat!" Giggles straightened, still grinning. "White Cheeks here be talkin' flash. She a mud shark, fink?"

"Mebbe she white, mebbe banana." Dead eyes took a slow trip up and down her body. "Hard to say, all dat scribblin' on her face."

"I'm plaid." She sent more power to the spell on her right arm. "Your mamas know you're out this late, boys?"

He took a step forward. "Mebbe I find out what you are."

Wanted a fight, did he? Cynna's blood hummed. She settled her weight on the balls of her feet and opened her shields.

And staggered at the sudden onrush of power. *What the hell—?*

The bar's door opened again. Another young black male stepped out. He was snake-skinny and taller than the first two. "You blockin' traffic, man," he said, giving Giggles a shove. "Move it."

Giggles stepped aside obligingly. "Jo-Jo's gonna check out White Cheeks, see if her snatch is pale like her hair. Can't tell 'bout her skin wif all dat magic marker on her face."

The newcomer glanced at her. Then he pimp-slapped the back of his friend's head. "Fool!"

Jo-Jo spun, ready to explode. "What the fuck?"

"She's Dizzy."

Giggles snorted. "Dem Dizzies be old news. Dey all show, no blow."

"Some had juice." The tall young man looked at her. There was someone living behind these eyes, someone with a working brain. "She do."

Jo-Jo scowled. "You readin' her tea leaves, bro?"

"Asshole. Lookit her. You ready to jump her, yeah? Well, she waitin', not shakin'. She *wants* you to try it." He spoke to her directly for the first time. "Jo-Jo's assed-out, an' Patch here don' mean nothin'—he jes' dumb. No harm?"

She held his eyes a moment, then she gave a small nod. "No harm."

The three of them made room for her to pass—Tallboy and Jo-Jo quietly, Giggles with a flourished arm. She walked on by, not looking at them—confidence was half the battle—but with every sense alert in case the hopped-up Jo-Jo changed his mind.

Nothing happened.

Just as well, she told herself. Normally, her hands-off spell would give anyone who touched her a nasty jolt. Somehow, though, she'd pulled in a lot of extra juice. If she'd used the spell, she might have seriously injured one of those idiots.

Speaking of extra juice . . . She made another block and stopped. A few muttered words, a moment of focus, and some of the extra power crawled along her skin to a pattern that served as a storage cell. Couldn't keep it all there, though. There was too much.

She pressed her palm against the old brick of the nearest building and gradually discharged the rest. It made her think of Cullen. Wouldn't he have just loved to be around to soak up all that free magic?

Annoying man. Equally annoying was the way thinking about him gave her a sexual buzz. Which would really have pleased that big, fat ego of his, wouldn't it? If he knew about it, which of course he couldn't. Though he was conceited enough to think she'd get hot thinking about him, except he wouldn't, because she undoubtedly never crossed his mind at all. But if he did . . .

Shut up, she told her brain. Better to think about where that power had come from. Magic didn't just float around loose, ready for anyone with a bit of a Gift to suck up.

Not that Cynna had only a bit of a Gift. She tried not to be smug about it, but she was the strongest known Finder in the country. She was also pretty good at spellcraft. Theoretically, any Gifted could use spells, but most didn't. Some couldn't find a decent teacher. Others lacked the interest, the patience, or the knack of it, just like some people couldn't do math to save them.

Like her. Cynna sucked at math. But when it came to spellcraft, she had the knack, the desire, and the patience.

The air had broken out in a cold sweat, emphasis on the cold. There wasn't enough precip to call it a drizzle, just a clammy dampness that fuzzed the streetlights and numbed her cheeks.

Great weather for staying inside. That's where respectable citizens were, no doubt—comfy and cozy at home, maybe with a fire burning in the fireplace and a glass of wine in hand.

Well, she couldn't manage the fire, but wine sounded like a fine idea. Something fizzy, maybe. Another two blocks, and she'd hit a busy intersection. She'd get a cab, get back to the hotel, and order something from room service. Even after years of prosperity she got a kick out of room service. Maybe that would wipe out this stupid, let-down feeling.

For God's sake. Let down? Had she wanted a fight?

Yes. She had. That's why she'd headed for the worst neighborhood in Washington.

Dammit, dammit, dammit. When was she going to learn? Cynna scowled at her feet and walked faster.

Some people had the whole good-and-bad thing down. She was working on it, but when the shit hit the fan and there wasn't time to think things through, she didn't have the right instincts. Her default setting hit a lot closer to *kill the bastards* than *turn the other cheek*.

Not that she went around killing people. That had only happened twice, both times in self-defense. The Bureau had agreed she'd handled the second situation correctly. They didn't know about the other.

Well, Abel Karonski did. He was a friend as well as a fellow agent, and she'd spilled the story to him years ago. He might have told Ruben. But the deets weren't in any official file. She'd checked.

But she did like a fight. Especially on nights like this, when the nameless feeling clawed its way up from her gut and wrapped her in its barbed-wire coils, there were only two things she really wanted to do: fight or fuck.

That wasn't the way good people dealt with a bad mood.

She stopped at the light, scowling. The neighborhood had improved some in the last three blocks. The four corners at this intersection were held down by a Mexican food place, a car wash, a resale shop, and a convenience store.

Okay. She took a deep breath, let it out slowly. She couldn't control what she wanted to do, so she'd settle for controlling what she did. And what she was going to do now was get back to the hotel. Skip the wine, get some sleep. She could borrow a phone book at the 7-Eleven, call a cab, and let the driver figure out how to get from here to there.

Halfway across the street she noticed the church.

It was on the other end of the block, separated from the 7-Eleven by a couple of small stores and a big parking lot. *Bound to be locked up this time of night,* her reasonable side pointed out.

It wasn't that late, though. Just after ten. And there were cars in the parking lot. As soon as she hit that side of the street, her feet veered that way.

Probably isn't a Catholic church, the voice of reason said.

Probably not. Couldn't hurt to check, though. It wasn't like she had something important to . . . hey, look. People.

The side door had opened. An older couple and a younger one emerged, followed by another small knot of folks—Hispanic, looked like, though with everyone bundled up for the weather, she wasn't sure. The last one out wore a black cassock.

Sure looked like a priest. And . . . yes, she was close enough to read the sign now: Our Lady of the Assumption.

Ha. Take that, voice of reason.

People called cheerful good nights; car doors slammed and cars backed out of their parking spots. But one older couple seemed uninterested in leaving. They stood on the narrow porch by the side door, and the woman was talking a mile a minute to the priest about flowers and tables and the number of guests.

Wedding rehearsal. That's why they were here at this hour. Damn, she'd make a detective yet.

As Cynna drew near, the husband told his wife to let Father Jacobs go inside—it was freezing out here. One by one, they noticed her and fell silent. The woman clutched her husband's arm, eyes wide. He rose to his role as protector by giving Cynna a go-away frown.

At least this bunch wasn't likely to jump her. "Father Jacobs?" she said tentatively.

Despite the cassock, he looked more like an altar boy than a priest. He was a true towhead, with white-blond hair and skin the color of an old parchment, slightly reddened now from the cold. His smile was surprisingly sweet. "Yes? May I help you?"

"I was hoping . . . I know it's late, but can you take my confession?"

INSIDE, the scent was wood, incense, flowers. The kneeler was hard. Cynna could have gone around the screen to sit in an upholstered chair, but she'd take sore knees over face-to-face confession any time.

She crossed herself, wishing she'd waited and gone to her home church in Virginia. This priest didn't know her history.

His voice came quietly from the other side of the screen. "In the name of the Father, and of the Son, and of the Holy Spirit, may the Lord be in your heart and help you to confess your sins with true sorrow."

Start with the easy stuff. "Bless me, Father, for I have sinned. It's, uh . . . it's been five weeks since my last confession, and I've missed five Sunday Masses. The first one couldn't be helped because there wasn't a church there." No duh. Hell was seriously short on houses of worship. "The others . . . I've been busy. Okay," she admitted. "That's lame. But I like to be confessed when I take communion, and I guess I've been putting this off."

He waited.

"Uh . . . I lusted after a man. Two men, really, but one of them is taken, so that doesn't count. I just have to get over it, you know? But the other one . . ."

"Have you acted on your lust?"

"No. But I want to. I'm not married or otherwise committed," she added. "Neither is he." Another understatement. "So we wouldn't be breaking any vows if we did, uh, you know."

"Sex can be a joyous expression of love within the sacrament of marriage. Outside that union, it's an inherently selfish act, the pursuit of pleasure for selfish reasons."

This was one of those areas where she and the Church disagreed. Cynna couldn't see what was so wrong about sex. Back a zillion years ago, yeah, sex outside marriage had led to lots of ugly consequences, so abstaining had made sense. But now?

Of course, Father Michaels said it was hubris to put her own reasoning above the collected wisdom of God's holy Church. He was probably right, but Cynna figured she'd have to come to her own understanding in her own way. "I've been guilty of pride. And anger. And . . ." Her heart jumped in her chest and started pounding hard, as if she were pushing something uphill. "This is hard to say."

"Do you have a specific act in mind? Something you did that troubles you?"

"Yeah."

"Was this act a venial sin or a mortal sin?"

"I don't know." That was the problem.

"I couldn't help noticing your tattoos. You were once a Dizzy?"

Like most people, he referred to the street-born cult by its nickname. Not many had ever heard of the movement's real name: the *Msaidiza*. In Swahili, it meant helpers.

"Not since I came to the Church."

"Have you practiced other forms of forbidden magic or otherwise been drawn into superstition?"

That was a hard one. Father Michaels said the Church's stance on magic was so tangled you practically had to call a conclave before casting a spell. He'd advised her to consider her skills in the same light she did her weapon—to use her Gift and her spellcrafting only for self-defense or in pursuit of her duties, and only when it clearly served the greater good. "I think I'm clear there," she said after a moment. "That isn't what's bugging me."

He waited.

She took a deep breath and got it said. "I've killed."

Silence.

"Not humans. Shit. Sorry, Father. I'm saying this all wrong. What I mean is, I killed demons."

The silence was longer this time. Finally he said, "You are quite sure these were demons you killed?"

At least he hadn't told her she was nuts. She didn't blame him for asking, though. Everyone knew demons couldn't cross unsummoned, and accurate summoning spells were as rare as hens' teeth these days. Had been since the Purge. Like a lot of things "everyone knew," that was wrong, but this priest wouldn't have any way of knowing that.

Of course, demons were common as hell in hell. "Um . . . I'm with MCD. You know, in the FBI? And . . . look, I'm sorry, but I can't talk about the details, not even with a priest. But it involved killing demons."

"There is no sin in that, if the act was without malice," he said kindly. "Since Vatican II, destroying them hasn't been considered an act of grace in and of itself, but they are soulless creatures."

She sighed. That's pretty much the reaction she'd expected. "Thanks, Father."

He talked with her a little more and assigned her penance. He added that he'd be in his office a while, so the sanctuary would be available.

Cynna could take a hint. She sat in one of the pews to get started on her Our Fathers, but her attention kept drifting.

The thing about killing demons was that they stayed dead. The ones she'd shot had been planning things even nastier for her and the others, so she didn't regret killing them. Not exactly. But the whole thing didn't seem right to her. No souls meant they were morally blind. They didn't know they were being evil, so they couldn't choose good. No souls also meant no shot at an afterlife.

Didn't that make it worse to kill them?

And why had God set things up that way?

She shifted. Questioning the Almighty probably wasn't something good Catholics did, but she'd come late to the Church, and partly for selfish reasons. Believers were protected against possession.

Of course, possession was another thing everybody knew didn't happen anymore.

Damn. Still chasing her thoughts instead of paying attention to her act of contrition. Maybe she'd do better with her Hail Marys. She felt more comfortable with Mary than with the omnipotent Father.

"Hail Mary, full of grace . . ."

"Child."

The voice was church bells and wind, the lap of waves at night and the hunting hoot of an owl. And yet it was utterly human. Female. It was an actual voice, too, air vibrating to produce sound, not mindtalk . . . yet it seemed to happen inside her as well.

Awe. For the first time Cynna fully understood the meaning of that word. For a long moment she neither moved nor breathed, hoping the voice would speak again. Finally she said, "M-Mary?"

"No." The presence was amused, but so gently. "I have been many, but not that one. I am yours already, Cynna. Are you mine?"

There was no thought to her answer, but neither was there fear. "I don't know. Who are you?"

"When you know, you will choose. For now, Find your friends. Go quickly. You are needed."

THREE

WASHINGTON wasn't round-the-clock busy like New York or L.A. Even on the main arteries, traffic thinned out by midnight. But it didn't evaporate entirely. Lily watched the scattering of headlights on the other side of the median, the way they seemed to merge in the curve of the windshield with the reflections of taillights and neon. Her fingers tapped impatiently on her thigh.

They were in the Mercedes Rule had rented, not her government-issue Ford. It wasn't a convertible like his own car, but it had the same bells and whistles.

Lily still didn't get why Rule hadn't wanted to bring his car to D.C. Sure, it would have taken longer, but he hated flying. A touch of claustrophobia he liked to pretend didn't exist made anything but first class impossible for him. Maybe that was why he'd insisted on flying. He'd prefer fighting a weakness to working around it.

That, she understood.

There'd been no question that he would come with her to Washington. Even if they'd been okay with a long separation, the mate bond wouldn't have let them stay on opposite coasts.

The mate bond. That's what she'd referred to earlier when she'd said she was Rule's Chosen—not that he'd chosen her, or vice versa. According to Rule's people, their Lady had tied the knot for them—a till-death-do-us-part bond she'd fought like

crazy at first. But then, at first she'd thought of it as entirely physical. Sexual.

But mind-blowing sex was only part of it. There was a limit to
how much physical distance they could tolerate; put too much
space between them and they'd pass out. If that limit varied mad-
deningly according to no rules she could fathom, she was learning to live with it. Plus she always knew where Rule was—his
direction and roughly how far away he was.

There might be a spiritual aspect to the bond, too, but Lily preferred not to think about that. Religion made her uneasy, and dying
hadn't provided as many answers as you might think.

She glanced at the man behind the wheel and smiled, thinking
of the way he'd woken her that morning. Whatever the mate bond
had brought to their relationship, she'd fallen in love with him on
her own.

She loved him. He loved her. It was that simple, and sometimes that scary.

Rule had so many nooks and crannies, so much that remained
a mystery . . . but she knew the important things, didn't she? He
was smart and often kind. He could laugh, and he could listen.
Mostly he was reasonable, though there was an autocratic streak
in him.

No surprise there. Rule was the heir, the Lu Nuncio, of his
clan. When his father died, he'd be the big cheese, the Nokolai
Rho. Lily hoped Isen Turner lived a long, long time.

Which he might. One of the more unsettling things she'd
learned recently was that lupi aged roughly half as fast as humans.

Another thing she knew about Rule: at the moment, he was in
a major snit. "All right," she said. "Let's talk. All that silent, simmering anger is interfering with my thinking."

"Should I be flattered?"

"What's got your tail in a twist?"

"If that's your colorful way of asking why I'm angry—"

"That's me. Colorful."

"You stepped between a shooter and his target." Rule didn't
get loud when he was angry. He turned quiet. His voice lowered
now until it thrummed like an overloaded power line. "That cop
was ready to pull the trigger, and you put yourself in his line of
fire."

"It worked, didn't it?"

Rule growled. It was an honest-to-God growl, not a sound human throats accommodate well.

"Look, the cop pulled an idiot act. Paul wasn't a threat until someone tried to shoot him, and firing a normal load at a lupus is more likely to annoy him than stop him. Not a good way to live to collect your pension. But most cops don't know enough about lupi to handle them right, and he'd had good training otherwise. It showed in his stance, the way he handled his weapon. I figured he wouldn't shoot with someone in his line of fire. I was right."

"If you expect me to applaud your decision to risk your life because you won your gamble—"

"I expect you to trust my judgment! What about you? You jumped an angry wolf, for God's sake, and invited him to rip out your throat!"

"It was a brave act, and an honorable one," the man in the backseat said. "Especially under the circumstances. You want the next exit, sir."

Lily didn't quite jump, but she came close. Their passenger hadn't spoken since telling Rule how to get to his apartment. She'd nearly forgotten him.

It wasn't easy for a lupus to Change back to human quickly after going wolf. Paul Chernowich had managed it an hour after turning down his chance to kill Rule. By then the place had emptied of audience and most of the performers, and refilled with cops.

It had taken another hour for the locals to accept that Paul hadn't actually violated any laws and let him leave. The soprano who usually gave him a ride home was among those who'd left, so Rule had offered to drop him off.

Rule signaled and pulled into the exit lane. Lily twisted to look at Paul in the backseat. "What do you mean, 'under the circumstances'?"

He shrugged. He was a young man—at least he looked young— with a gangly build, a hooked nose, and straw-colored hair. "Just the obvious. He's the Nokolai Lu Nuncio."

"And you don't care for Nokolai." She'd had a clue about that earlier, but it was hard to read a wolf's emotional reactions.

They'd left the elevated highway for the stop-and-go of regular city streets. Here the late hour was more obvious. There was little traffic. She looked at Rule as he slowed for a light. "Something you want to tell me?"

He was silent a moment. "Paul is Leidolf."

Her jaw dropped. "Leidolf? As in, your clans are hereditary enemies? The Hatfields and McCoys of the lupus world? Leidolf would be the ones who nearly killed your father not long ago. *And you offered him your throat?*" Unlike Rule, she did get loud when she was mad.

Paul spoke stiffly. "The assassination attempt on your Rho was not sanctioned by our Rho."

"Oh, well, that's all right, then! And if you'd killed Rule, that would have been okay, too, I guess, as long as your Rho didn't order it!"

"No. It would have been greatly dishonorable." He gave the back of Rule's head a puzzled glance. "She does not understand *ni culpa, ne defensia*?"

"The Lady brought us together only recently. Lily is learning our ways, but the past two months have been . . . busy."

There was an understatement. "What Paul just said . . . Isn't that what you said when you invited him to rip out your throat?"

"It is."

"So clue in the ignorant human. What does it mean?"

"Literally, 'if not guilty, don't defend.' To prove innocence, we submit without offering any defense. Guilt has a scent," he added, slowing as he took the off-ramp.

"Your mate did me great honor," Paul told her earnestly. "I'm not alpha, but my blood was up enough that I didn't realize at first that he'd allowed me to pin him."

"Allowed." Her finger began tapping on her thigh again. She looked at Rule. "You jumped him so he could pin you?"

"It was the quickest way to control the situation. Paul wasn't beast-lost, but he was too deeply into the wolf for reason to be effective. Instinct would have been pressing him to find his enemy, the one who'd exposed him by forcing the Change."

She thought of the way the wolf had stayed onstage instead of seeking cover. "He was looking for you."

"But not overhead." Paul sounded sheepish. "With no breeze and everyone's scents jumbled together, I couldn't pick out Rule's clearly enough to locate him. But I should have remembered to look up."

"You were rattled," Rule said. "The Change had been forced on you."

Paul was clearly disgusted. "Forced into Change like a pup."

"You couldn't help it." Rule stopped for a light. "I damned near Changed, myself."

"You? But you're—"

"Too old for such loss of control, normally." Rule's face looked grim in the uneven light of the dash and the traffic light. "What happened tonight wasn't normal. Something hit us both. I'd give a good deal to know what, and who did it."

"Maybe no one," Lily said.

"What do you mean?"

"I don't think it was aimed at anyone. It just swept through—something raw and powerful, not like anything I've ever touched before. Like . . ." She struggled to find words for a sensation others never experienced. "It reminded me of the sorcéri Cullen uses. You know, the loose bits of magic that leak from nodes? Unworked stuff. Only this was a zillion times more powerful than any sorcéri I've ever felt."

"It didn't have any of *Her* taint?"

She shook her head.

Rule drummed the steering wheel once. The light turned green and he accelerated quickly. "This was a hell of a time for Cullen to run off."

Looking for dragons. Ever since they came back from hell, Cullen had been obsessed with finding the dragons who'd returned with them. But Sam and the others had vanished so thoroughly that Cullen wasn't having much more luck finding them than the U.S. government was. "Didn't he take a phone with him?"

"Yes, and if he's in an area with coverage and hasn't turned it off, he might even answer . . . if he wants something."

Cullen's attitude toward phones reminded Lily of her grandmother.

"Take a left at the next light," Paul said. "Who's Cullen?"

"A knowledgeable friend," Rule said.

That was one way to put it. Cullen Seabourne was a lupus, a friend of Rule's who'd been clanless until Nokolai adopted him two months ago. He was also a sorcerer.

Sorcery was illegal. Cullen claimed that was the result of envy and ignorance, that lawmakers had long ago banned sorcery without having a clue what they were writing laws against. People either associated it with death magic or believed it had died out after the Purge. Some claimed it had never been real—that there had never been adepts or sorcerers, just a lot of clever charlatans and a few witches willing to use death magic to augment their inborn Gifts.

Lily turned the conversation away from their friend, the sorcerer. "Can you tell me what it felt like?" she asked Paul. "Was the Change different in any way from usual?"

"It hurt." Paul grimaced. "Hurt like hell, actually. There's always some pain, more if you aren't earthed, but this was like being yanked backward through the proverbial eye of a needle. If there was any other difference, the pain blotted it out."

"I understand that young lupi—adolescents—can't resist the Change at the full moon. Is that what this was like?"

He considered that a moment. "Not exactly. When the moon's full, you hear her calling. Adults can resist the call or go with it, but teenagers are just too enthralled to see it as a choice, you know? But this . . . I wasn't feeling her call, yet something made me Change."

"So Changing without the call isn't normal?"

"It isn't possible," Rule said. "The moon is never wholly silent. Her call ebbs as she wanes, growing louder as she waxes toward full. That's how we're able to Change at will, rather than only at the full moon. We learn to release ourselves to the call even when it's a whisper."

"I didn't hear her," Paul insisted.

"I did." Rule slowed the car. "And still do. How old are you, Paul?"

"Twenty-six."

Rule nodded as if that proved his point. Lily supposed it did; the clans considered a lupus an adult at twenty-five, so by their standards Paul was barely old enough to live on his own. "Have you learned to hear her call when the moon isn't full or nearly full?"

Paul obviously grudged his answer. "Sometimes I can."

"First you were focused on your performance. Then you were distracted by the pain of the Change. I'm not surprised you didn't notice the moon's call, but it's just as it always is at this point in her cycle."

"If you say so. That's my place on the next block. The Belleview Arms."

"The one on the other side of the skin flick joint?" Lily asked dryly.

"Rent's cheap, and no one bothers me."

No, lupi generally weren't bothered much, even in the worst neighborhoods. Which this one wasn't. On the seedy side, but she'd seen worse. Patrolled worse, for that matter.

"See if I've got this right," she said. "The door to the Change is always open—wide open at the full moon, barely a crack when the moon's new, but never shut tight. When that blast of magic blew in, it didn't open the door any wider. It just huffed and puffed Paul through the crack, while Rule—"

"Grabbed the frame and held on tight. Good analogy," he added as he pulled to a stop in front of a self-service laundry and shut off the engine. "The Change is rather like stepping through a doorway."

They were still a block from the misnamed Belleview, but the curb was packed nose-to-tail with cars, probably courtesy of the all-night Triple-X Theater down the street. "Um . . . are we getting out?"

Paul opened his door. "Rule will want me to revoke the *susmussio*. We'd both like privacy for that."

She looked at Rule. "Meaning?"

"I'll explain as we walk."

"Pop the glove box first."

He gave her a lifted eyebrow but did as she asked. She retrieved her SIG Sauer. "Pass me my shoulder holster, would you, Paul? It's on the seat next to you."

"You don't need a gun." Paul was indulgent. "I know this isn't the greatest area, but you've got two big, strong lupi to protect you."

She reminded herself that he was young. "Not your decision. Pass me my shoulder holster."

But Rule had twisted around and snagged it for her. "Paul wasn't trained by Benedict."

Benedict was Rule's older brother, a warrior who was something of a legend among the clans. He did things that really weren't possible, even for a lupus. But what Rule meant by the reference was that Paul, being Leidolf, wouldn't have had the usual lupus distaste for guns trained out of him.

"Point taken." She was probably locking the barn door after the proverbial horses had escaped. She didn't care. Weird stuff kept happening, and she had no intention of wandering around without her weapon.

She had to slip out of the wonderful coat in order to strap on the shoulder harness. She did that standing next to the car and scowling at the cold. "So what's a *susmissus*?"

"*Susmussio.*" Paul paused to yawn. "It's a fancy word for submission. Lord, but I'm tired. Changing twice like that takes a lot out of you."

She gave Rule a sharp look. He was wearing his imperturbable face. "But wasn't that just a ritual thing? A token submission so you could smell that he wasn't your enemy?"

The two men exchanged glances. Rule answered. "Even a token submission carries meaning. Think of it as a debt. Since no terms were set beforehand—"

"Terms?" He was holding her coat out, so she slipped her arms in. Warmth, blessed warmth.

"When used in a planned ritual, the *susmussio* has conditions attached. It's how we make treaties between clans. But this was personal, with no terms set. I owe Paul, not his clan."

He started down the street. She fell into step beside him, with Paul slightly ahead. "Owe him what?"

"A certain level of loyalty."

"And with him being Leidolf, that's awkward."

"Yes. Added to that, while the *susmussio* is in effect, his actions affect my honor, and my actions reflect on him."

"Plus we're out of balance," Paul said. "Rule submitted, but he's alpha, older, and higher status. And yet I'm sort of responsible for him. It's . . . unsettling. And," he added over his shoulder, a grin flashing, "it's probably bugging the hell out of him."

It would. "How do you cancel it?"

"Easy enough." Paul seemed cheerful now, but tired, like a kid who'd been allowed to stay up late with the adults. "We agree to some basic terms that cancel the first submission. Then I submit to him. Which is why we want a bit of privacy. That looks a bit odd to—holy shit!"

It shot out of a narrow alley between the skin flick place and Paul's apartment building. It was big, red-eyed, and ugly—sort of like a hyena on steroids, only hairless, with arms growing out of its chest. The arms had too many joints and ended in claws. It ran straight at them.

It was a demon.

"Get down!" she shouted at Paul, even as the air beside her shimmered and reality danced for a second time that night.

Lily felt that happen. She didn't look. Before her shout cleared her throat, her gun had cleared its holster. She flowed into position—legs spread, arms outstretched, left hand supporting the right.

Paul didn't drop, dammit. He crouched as if he meant to spar with the thing. She cursed and stepped aside so he didn't block her line of fire.

The two men who came out of the adult theater did, though. One of them had a second to see the demon coming at them and threw himself to the ground. The other didn't. The demon didn't bother to swerve. It swiped the man out of the way with a clawed arm and left him howling and bleeding on the sidewalk.

Clear target. Lily squeezed the trigger, ignored the slap of sound on her eardrums, corrected her aim, squeezed again—

And the demon blurred itself into heat waves—a demon-shaped shimmer rushing at them. Would a bullet go right through it? More people had come out of the Triple-X—more stupid bedamned innocent bystanders, who she'd probably hit if she fired at an immaterial demon.

At ten feet away, it turned solid again. And leaped.

So did the wolf beside her.

Rule's wolf form was big, but the demon was bigger, stronger, and those clawed arms gave it a pair of formidable natural weapons Rule lacked. His only real advantage was speed. Lupi could move like the wind—faster than any terrestrial creatures or any they'd encountered in hell.

He went in low—to deflect, not to engage. They collided in midair and Rule somehow twisted his body to send the red-eye sailing off at an angle. It hit the street with a thud. Rule landed more neatly, rolling and coming up on his feet.

Lily fired again before it could dissolve. Blood spurted from the demon's haunch. It screeched in rage and charged again.

Charged Rule, not her. She'd shot it, but it went after Rule.

Rule dodged, but barely, coming away with a bleeding flank from one of those claws. He was trying to stay between her and the demon, she realized. "It's after you, not me!"

He acknowledged that with the flick of an ear. Then began a fast, deadly tarantella, with the demon lunging, grabbing, leaping, and Rule dancing aside just in time. Rule was drawing it away, she realized. And keeping it solid—apparently it couldn't engage him while in the shimmer-state.

Good tactics, even if it did make her sick with fear. "Not too far, dammit! I'm not Annie Oakley!"

A second wolf arrowed at the demon. Paul. "Don't close with it!"

He didn't. Instead he darted in, nipping at it, and whirled away before it reacted. God, but lupi were fast.

She circled, staying out of the wolves' way, trying to find a clear shot. A head shot, if possible. That was the only way to kill one with a handgun. She had to redistribute the brains.

Dimly she heard cries from down the street. She hoped someone was helping the man the demon had wounded. She hoped they'd had the sense to call this in. Backup would be good—say, a SWAT team or two.

Rule lunged in close and got a mouthful of demon—shit, shit, it nearly had him that time! But he broke away when Paul attacked from the other side, and Lily managed another shot. And missed.

At least she'd missed the wolves, too.

Up the street, a car turned in. Brakes squealed. *Good idea,* she thought. *Go away.* All they needed was more civilians underfoot.

She couldn't get a clear shot. The wolves moved so fast she could scarcely track them—darting in, distracting, herding—and her reactions were too much slower than theirs. She didn't dare pull the trigger. But the wolves couldn't stop, couldn't slow down, or they'd be dead.

How long could they keep it up? Paul had already been tired when . . . What was that?

Feet pounding on pavement. Running toward them, not away. Lily flicked a glance that way. *Cynna? How the hell—?*

Cynna shouted some nonsense syllables without slowing. She flung out her hand.

A gruesome mix of sounds snapped Lily's attention back to the demon. It had a wolf in its jaws—a wolf with reddish fur. Paul. He was making a high, terrible sound. Rule leaped, his jaws closing around as much of the demon's thick throat as possible.

The demon dropped Paul and fell onto its back, hind legs coming up to try to gut Rule, who released it and rolled away. Lily's finger tightened on the trigger, but the demon moved too fast.

It stuck its snout into Paul's gut and slurped.

Rule jumped on its back. It screeched in rage and threw him off.

Cynna stopped and her voice rose: *". . . aerigarashiPAD!"* Light snapped between her outflung hand and the demon, light thin and cold and colorless. The demon jerked.

And died.

Lily ran up to the big, ugly body, pressed her gun to the skull, and pulled the trigger. Her ears echoing from the shot, she called to Cynna. "Have you got your phone?"

Cynna stood motionless, her expression masked by the tattoos. Her hand fell, limp, to her side. "Yes."

"Call it in." She turned to Paul.

Some of his guts hung out the hole in his middle. The smell was rank. Rule sat on the other side of him and touched his nose to the red wolf's muzzle.

She knelt. Lupi healed so much faster than humans, but this . . . there was so much blood. Too much. It pumped out in spurts, but weakly. "Shit. He's bleeding out. There's an artery torn open somewhere . . ." She had to try, had to reach into the bloody cavity and try to find that torn artery.

His eyes opened. Then . . . it was like shaking the chips in a kaleidoscope to make them fall back in another pattern. The second she touched the ripped and slippery flesh, magic hummed along her fingertips like tactile music. And the cells of his body jiggled like agitated dust motes and fell back in place.

It was a man lying on the rough pavement of the street, not a wolf. A man naked and gutted and dying.

His eyes met hers. She saw confusion there, not pain. His mouth opened as if he would speak, but no sound came. Instead, blood did—filling his mouth, staining his lips, dribbling down his chin. His eyes cut to Rule and held there for a long moment. He exhaled . . . and left. Just like that, there was no one home anymore.

Rule lifted his nose to the sky and howled.

FOUR

OVERHEAD, the sky was shit-brown. City lights reflected off low-hanging clouds, tossing back light without heat.

Things were mostly shit down below, too.

Police spots punctured the darkness. The street was cluttered with vehicles at both ends of the scene: squad cars, a government-issue Ford like Lily's, an ambulance, the crime-scene van, the cars that had delivered reporters from the *Post* and the AP. For the moment, local and federal officials were playing nice with each other, with the uniformed cops keeping the press and other nuisances away while FBI techs recorded the scene.

One ambulance had already departed, carrying the man who'd left the Triple-X Theater at the wrong time. He should be in surgery by now.

The red pulse of the lights on the remaining ambulance reminded Lily of Paul's blood pumping out, beat by beat.

Cynna knelt beside the demon's body, one hand stroking the air above it. Her form of spellcraft didn't look like much from the outside. Rule was across the street, talking on his cell phone. He'd needed to call his father.

So had Lily. Her own father, that is, and for different reasons. He was expecting to pick her up at the airport in a couple days, and she wouldn't be on that flight. She might not make it back for

Christmas. She'd left him a text message, hoping to delay the explanations.

"Cynna told you she had a premonition?" Croft asked as Lily finished a quick summary.

"Yeah." The man beside her was the only familiar face in the bustle of strangers working the scene. Martin Croft was a special agent, one of the two who'd recruited her. He was brown, too, but a lot friendlier shade than the sky—cinnamon without the sugar. There was a touch of Hah-vahd in his voice, a high gloss on his shoes, and no trace of a Gift in his makeup.

Despite that lack, he was one of the Unit's top agents. She'd been glad when he showed up. Lily knew how to handle a crime scene. She didn't know what to do with a dead demon.

Besides, if Croft was in charge, he'd have to talk to the press, not her. "She said it hit her suddenly that she needed to Find us."

"Hmm." Croft looked at Cynna, still making passes over the demon's corpse. "Yet she tests in the low teens on precognition."

"Low teens?" Lily's eyebrows went up. "Some of the unGifted score higher than that."

"Exactly. We'd better have a word with our Cynna."

Cynna stood as they approached. She was a tall woman with an Amazon's build: strong shoulders, miles of legs, and breasts any centerfold model would covet. Her hair was blond and brutally short; Lily suspected nature got a chemical assist in the coloring. Her features were the most ordinary thing about her, once you looked beneath the indigo tattoos that covered most of her face and body. She had a crooked nose, strong jaw, and eyes the color of whiskey. Her mouth was wide and prone to smiling.

Not tonight.

Cynna wore jeans, a thin black sweater, and an unzipped bomber jacket. Looking at her made Lily feel even colder. "Anything?"

Cynna shook her head. "Nothing. Like I figured, the bindings slipped off when it died. I couldn't trace its master."

"But you're sure it had a master? It didn't just show up on its own?" Lily's toes were going numb. She curled and uncurled them inside her shoes, hoping to get some circulation going.

The Evidence Response Team—that's what the FBI called their crime-scene techs—was standing by. Their boss broke in. She was an older woman with an unfortunate resemblance to Lou

Grant, only with more hair. "You finished with the woo-woo stuff?"

Cynna waved at the demon. "Have at it."

They'd already taken photos, both film and digital, so the next part was hands-on. It turned out two of the three were a mite reluctant to put their hands on a demon.

One—a short white guy with a mustache—shook his head. "I dunno, Marion. Jesus. Look at that thing. Just look at it. You ever seen anything like that? Seventeen years I've been doing this, and I've never seen anything like that."

"Now you have," his boss said. "Get your gloves on."

"Maybe this is a dumb question," said the third tech, "but are we sure it's dead?"

Lily supposed even jaded federal crime-scene officers weren't used to dealing with three hundred pounds of fanged and clawed demon. "See the brains spattered outside the skull?" she said. "They're a clue."

"Yeah, but demons—"

"Need brains to live," Cynna drawled, "same as everyone but politicians."

That brought a couple chuckles. D.C. cops loved jokes about politicians. "So what do we look for?" the one with a mustache asked, pulling on his gloves.

"Same as usual," Croft said. "Anything and everything." He collected Lily and Cynna with a glance, and the three of them moved away to let the techs do their job.

Not that Lily expected much to come of it. Cynna said there was a physical component involved in binding a demon, but they'd need an autopsy to find it. The demon would have eaten it.

Croft repeated Lily's earlier question. "Do you think the demon was sent? Bound to its task?"

"Well, yeah. You know they don't act like that normally."

"Pretend I don't know what you're talking about," Lily said. "Since I don't."

"Oh. Okay. First, it's supposed to be impossible for a demon to cross unsummoned. We now know that's not true, but the ability is damned rare. But mostly I'm going by the way it behaved. It went straight for Rule, even though you were the more immediate threat. An unbound demon wouldn't do that."

"It seemed to lose that focus on Rule after it attacked Paul."

"It got a taste of blood. Demons love blood, especially the

human variety. Makes them drunk. I don't know what lupus blood does to them, but it might have gotten enough of a charge from the victim's blood to resist the binding briefly."

"They get a magical zing from blood?"

"Oh, yeah. Blood carries power. That's why it's been used in so many spells and rituals over the centuries."

Even she knew that much. "Black magic."

Croft shook his head. "Not necessarily. Many practices ban blood magic, but that's mostly because of the temptation it presents, not because using blood in a spell is inherently evil. The Catholic Church—pretty much the expert on good and evil—tacitly acknowledges that. Their transubstantiation doctrine is based on the power of blood."

"Keep translating," Lily said. "Transubstantiation?"

"The belief that the communion wine literally becomes Jesus's blood." He nodded at Cynna. "No offense."

"None taken." She looked at Lily. "I wish I could've gotten here faster."

Croft's voice was very dry. "You had a premonition, I understand."

"Ah . . ." Cynna shoved her hands in her pockets. "Not exactly."

"What *exactly* happened, then?" Lily's voice was sharp. Too sharp, maybe, considering that Cynna might have saved Rule's life.

"It's complicated. Make that weird. Majorly weird." She puffed air through pursed lips, annoyed. "And it doesn't have anything to do with finding whoever sent the demon."

Croft shook his head. "You know you can't leave it at that."

She gave him a dirty look. "All right, all right. I, uh, was contacted by someone. She told me I'd better Find you quick, which turned out to be right."

"Who? Who told you that?"

"She didn't give me a name, but I think maybe it was . . . you know. *Her.* The one the lupi talk about. And now I'm going to call it a night, so—"

Lily grabbed her arm. "Wait one minute. If you were contacted by the goddess who wants to destroy the lupi—"

"Not that *Her*!" Cynna shook off Lily's hand. "Holy hell, but there's too many unnamed deities messing around lately. There's the one we don't name because it might draw Her attention, and the one the lupi call the Lady—that's who I meant. She showed up . . . well, not in person, but there was this voice. It was . . . I don't know how to describe it, but I've never heard anything like her voice. I was in a church," she added, aggrieved. "Praying, or trying to. And *not* to her."

Lily stared. "The Rhej was right."

"She was not, and I'm not talking about it anymore."

"Rhej?" Croft's eyebrows lifted. "Who is that, and what was she right about?"

Lily felt Rule drawing closer. "There's no real human analogue, but a Rhej is like a clan's priestess or historian. The Nokolai Rhej thinks Cynna is her successor. Which sounds crazy, but if the Lady has started talking to Cynna—"

"I don't know that's who it was," Cynna insisted. "I'm just guessing. And it doesn't matter anyway. I'm not Nokolai. I'm Catholic."

"The two aren't necessarily at odds," Rule said as he joined them. He'd pulled his clothes back on after resuming the shape they were made to cover. His slacks and shirt were wrinkled, his tie missing, and he was probably exhausted.

On him, it all looked good. Slightly debauched, maybe, but sexy.

Cynna shot him an angry look. "I suppose you heard what I said."

He nodded. "I'm not going to pressure you. The matter lies between you and the Lady. But you should know she speaks very, very rarely, and only to those who are or will become a Rhej."

Cynna hunched her shoulders as if she could deflect his words that way, jamming her hands deeper in her pockets. Or maybe she was just cold. Lily sure was.

Not as cold as Paul. At least they'd covered him now.

"Damn," Croft said, looking off to the side. "The TV people found us." He grimaced. "I'd better see if I can get this spun right before they have demons attacking people all over the capital."

"Better you than me," Lily said.

"I'll tell the EMTs they can get the body loaded. If they do it while the press is busy hounding me, maybe the ghouls won't get any good shots."

It was a small dignity to offer, but Lily was glad he'd thought of it. As he walked away, she looked at Rule. "You reached your father?"

"I talked to the Rho." Rule sometimes spoke of Isen Turner as if he were two people—the man who'd fathered him, and the one who ruled his clan. "He's not pleased."

"Because his son was nearly killed? Or because the one who did get killed was Leidolf, and that will complicate things?"

"Yes. To both."

The muscles of Rule's face were drawn too tightly over the elegant architecture beneath. His eyes were unhappy. If Paul's death weighed on her, how much heavier did it sit on Rule's shoulders? The *susmussio* had still been in place.

She laid a hand on his arm. "How many bodyguards is he sending?"

His smile was quick and brief. "You surprise me, *nadia*." He didn't say whether he meant by her question or her touch. Maybe the latter. She usually tried to keep the touching down in public. "I don't know yet how many will be shadowing my every footstep, but you're right. He insists on guards. Benedict will call me later with the details."

When he wasn't busy being a legend among the clans, Benedict had charge of Nokolai security. "Every once in a while your father and I agree." Reluctantly—for the contact comforted her, too—she let go of his arm.

"You're tired," he said.

Once the adrenaline drained out, tired was inevitable. "What about you? That thing got in one good swipe. Are you sure the paramedics shouldn't have a look?"

He waved that notion away. "It's a big scratch, that's all. Will you be much longer?"

It wasn't a scratch by human standards, but the demon's claws hadn't ripped deeply into the muscle. Rule would heal it quickly. "Hard to say. Croft can handle the scene, but . . ." She shrugged.

"But you want to be here if they find anything."

"Don't you?"

He looked aside. The EMTs were loading Paul's body on a gurney. "What I want is for that damned thing to be alive again so I can kill it." Abruptly, he walked away.

Cynna said tentatively, "The guy who was killed was a friend?"

Had Paul been a friend? His clan was Nokolai's enemy. She'd only known him for a few hours, yet she'd saved his life once. Then she'd watched a demon drink his blood. He'd fought for them. Died helping them. "It's complicated," she said at last. "But he mattered."

"Complicated." Cynna's head tilted to one side. "Seems like that's what I said earlier."

"You switched to 'majorly weird.'" But Cynna was right. She deserved a description of the night's events, if not a full explanation . . . which Lily didn't have. "We were at the Kennedy Center when some kind of magic swept through the place. It was strong and . . . different. It forced the Change on Paul . . ." Her throat tightened around a wad of emotions.

If only she'd *hit* the damned thing more than once! Another bullet or two in its body might have slowed it, and if it had been a little slower . . . "He was onstage, one of the performers. A tenor. After we sorted things out there, it was late, so Rule offered him a ride home. That's how we ended up here."

Cynna frowned. "When did this magical surge happen?"

"Just before ten."

"I felt something around then—a jolt of power, way more than any stray *sorcéri*. I had to drain some of it off."

Lily's brows rose. "Where were you?"

"Maybe fifteen blocks from here. Nowhere near the Kennedy Center."

A magical wind that covered the whole city? "What could have caused that?"

Cynna shrugged. "I'm not a theory person. You need Cullen. He's nuts for theory."

"I don't have him. Cynna . . ." There wasn't a tactful way to ask, so she might as well spit it out. "Do you think your old teacher might be involved? The one you knew when you were with the Dizzies?"

Cynna looked unhappy. "Can't say. You've been investigating another summoning."

"I've been connected to an investigation," Lily said dryly. "I wouldn't say I'd been allowed to investigate. But yes, it's quite a coincidence, only I can't see any connection. Except . . ." She wasn't supposed to discuss the case's conclusion, but she knew Cynna could keep her mouth shut. "They did find out who did it."

Cynna's eyebrows shot up. "Yeah? How come I haven't read about the arrest?"

"You won't, if the suits have their way. He's dead, an apparent suicide." She had her doubts about that, but no one was listening.

"And he's not a U.S. citizen, so the big boys cut a deal with his government to keep it all quiet."

"And your point is . . . ?"

"He's from an African nation."

"Shit." Cynna's former teacher followed ancient African traditions, too. She studied the demon's corpse. The techs didn't seem to be making much progress. Marion was arguing with the youngest one, who kept shaking his head. "Part of me hopes Jiri wasn't behind this. Part of me hopes she was."

Jiri had been Cynna's teacher in the *Msaidizi* movement, commonly known as the Dizzies. The movement sprang up in slums about fifteen years ago, spread like crazy for a few years, then fizzled. Most of its members had known next to nothing about the magic they tried to harness.

Not Jiri. The FBI had a file on her, but it was ninety percent speculation, precious little fact. But she was thought to be African, not African American—from Senegal or Gambia, maybe.

Or maybe not. "Why?"

"Summoning a demon is one thing. Not many can do it, but the knowledge isn't as lost as people like to think. But binding a demon—not riding it, binding it—that's high-level shit. Master level. I don't like to think there's more than one person running around with that kind of knowledge."

"What's the difference between riding and binding?"

Cynna jammed her hands in her pockets and looked away. "When you ride, you're in the demon. You control it from inside. Binding means you control it outside a summoning circle without being in the demon. Jiri could do that. If she didn't do this, there's someone else who knows way too much about demons."

"Could you do it—control without riding?"

"I'm not *shetanni mwenye*."

"But could you be, if you'd wanted to?"

Cynna looked back at her. "Yeah. Probably, if I were willing to pay the price. Am I a suspect?"

"No!" A couple of people glanced their way. "No," Lily repeated more quietly. "Even if I thought you were capable of sending a demon to kill someone, that someone wouldn't be Rule."

The other woman's mouth crooked up. "You don't buy into the woman scorned bit?"

Lily smiled back. It wasn't hard to smile about it now. Rule and Cynna had been involved several years ago. That prior history had been a problem for her and Cynna both, at first. Nice to know they were past that. "No. You might pout over being turned down—"

"I don't pout!"

"You did," Lily corrected her. "But you got over it."

"Don't be silly. Big, mean Dizzies never pout. Even former Dizzies," she added as Lily's smile widened. "Um . . . can I ask you something?"

"Sure." She owed Cynna more than the answer to a question or two.

"Why did you shoot the demon after I—"

"After your spell stunned it? To make sure, of course. I had no way of knowing how long it would be out."

Cynna shook her head. "You know better."

Exasperated, Lily lowered her voice. Death spells carried the death penalty. Technically that meant a spell that killed people, not demons, but . . . "The record will state that my bullet killed the demon."

"Gotcha. But there's no problem. The spell I used only works on demons."

"Are you sure?"

Cynna had never acquired a cop face. Maybe she thought the designs covering her skin were enough concealment. Probably they were, most of the time, with most people. But Lily had literally been through hell with this woman. The inky swirls didn't distract her from the emotions swirling across Cynna's face: confusion, doubt, some conclusion reached. Finally she said, "Not one hundred percent. It would have to be modified, but maybe . . . uh, thanks."

She nodded. "I'm trying not to do any assuming here, but I can't help thinking my main suspect is a pissed-off goddess. Or Her avatar, who was recently eaten by a demon prince."

"Who promptly went nuts, according to informed sources."

"That about sums it up. Tell me something," Lily said. "Is there any way our enemies in hell—or Dis, or whatever you want to call that realm—could have sent a demon to kill Rule without someone on this side helping?"

Cynna chewed on her lip. "I hate to say something's completely impossible. The line keeps moving, you know? But on a scale of 'sure' to 'no way, no how, not ever,' that hits pretty close to 'no way.'"

"Glad to hear it. Goddess, avatar, crazy demon prince—any of them would be tricky to bring in on charges." She paused, considering her options. "I don't have Cullen around to help with theory, but I do know someone with firsthand experience of what is and isn't possible for demons."

"You don't mean . . . hell. You do. You're going to bring it here?"

"Her," Lily corrected absently, trying to catch one of those will-o'-the-wisp memories. "Not it, not anymore. But she might not come." Might not be willing, might not be able. Lily wasn't even sure she'd be able to reach her. "I have to try."

"The Bureau won't like it."

Lily looked at where Rule stood, motionless, at the edge of the law enforcement bustle. He watched as they loaded Paul's body into the waiting ambulance. He had his expression locked down, nothing showing . . . but every inch of his body spoke to her of tension and pain. "The Bureau isn't my only worry."

FIVE

"**YOU'RE** *what*?"

"Going to get in touch with Gan, if I can. Bring her here, if she can come."

It was one thirty in the morning. They were headed for his car, parked a block away from the bloodstained concrete where Paul had died. Rule tried taking a slow breath. He needed to calm down. "I don't suppose it occurred to you to ask my opinion."

"Not necessary," she said dryly. "I knew what you'd think."

"After what it did to us? You don't remember, but it—"

"She," Lily said, her voice cold. "Not it. And maybe I don't remember the details, but I know enough. I know what I need to do. Think about it, Rule. Where else can I learn so much about demons but from one of them?"

Lily's soul had been split in two when Gan tried to possess her. Rule didn't understand how she could forgive the demon for that, even if she didn't remember what happened to them afterward, in hell. At least, it had happened to one of her—the one she couldn't quite remember.

He did. He remembered everything about that other Lily . . . what she'd said and done, the sheer courage of her, the companionship and the caring. The one thing he couldn't remember was her death. He'd been unconscious. He hadn't seen her sacrifice herself for him.

Rule's hip throbbed. He ignored it. "You don't have a way to reach her."

"Max does. Open the back door, will you? I need my laptop."

He grimaced and clicked the locks.

Max was Rule's friend . . . and a gnome. A half-gnome, actually, though Rule thought he was the only one outside of Max's own people who knew that. When they returned from hell with one unanticipated addition to their party, Max had agreed to let the little demon stay with him while they figured out what to do with her.

Max had come up with his own solution. Two weeks ago, he'd called to tell Rule that Gan was "going under" for a while—a term Rule understood to mean she would be living with one of the gnomish peoples. "Can't stay a demon, can she?" he'd demanded. "Growing a soul now. Gonna have to make up her pointy little head what she wants."

Typically, Max had hung up then.

"Just because she's growing a soul doesn't mean she's one of the good guys," Rule said as he slammed his door.

"She doesn't need a highly developed moral sense to be useful."

"She'll trick you." Demons couldn't lie outright, but they prized the ability to deceive.

"I'm pretty good at questioning people who want to trick me. Not that I think she'll try. She likes me." She opened her laptop and powered it up. "I'm going to work on my report."

Irritation flickered into anger. "You don't care to discuss your plan to bring a demon into your investigation?"

She gave him a level look. "You mean argue, not discuss, and I'm too tired for it."

Guilt bit. He took a slow breath and pulled out into the street. Needs coiled in his stomach, a restless serpent with the sweetest of venom. The hairs on his arms stirred with the serpent's breath, and its tail wrapped round his heart, controlling the beat.

He needed to Change. Still. Again.

Hell has no moon. Rule had entered that realm in wolf form, so wolf he'd remained. But lupi who stay too long in wolf form eventually lose the human in the beguiling simplicity of the beast. Rule hadn't been lost, not quite. But returned to Earth and his human form, he wasn't the man he used to be. The balance between man and wolf had shifted, and the control he'd spent his life building had thinned to tissue, easily torn.

Tonight it had torn.

The demon had come at them from upwind, and in damnable silence. He'd had no warning until he saw it—and in seeing it, he'd lost the power of choice. Instinct had ruled, and instinct craved teeth and claws for that enemy, four legs for speed and senses keened to a pitch no human could know. Not even a part-time human.

Twenty minutes, he told himself as he pulled into the traffic on I-295. It should take no more than twenty minutes to reach their temporary home. By then he'd be back in control.

Rule's father had been pleased when the Bureau sent Lily to Washington. After the Supreme Court put an end to centuries of legal persecution of the lupi, Nokolai had joined with two other clans to purchase a row house in Georgetown. Isen had wanted a presence in the capital, both for show and for lobbying.

Most of the time, Rule was that presence, the public face of a people accustomed to the shadows. To put it another way—as Lily once had—he was the lupus poster boy, the safe, almost tame image they presented to the public. He understood the image, how to use it, what was needed. A whiff of danger made him exotic, intriguing enough to be invited to all the best parties.

All the best beds, too, though he no longer accepted that sort of invitation.

Rule glanced at the woman beside him. The tilt of her head toward her laptop swung her hair forward, hiding her face. Her hair was beautiful, black and lustrous by day, keeping its secrets at night. Absently she lifted a hand and tucked a strand behind her ear, gifting him with her profile. The glow of her skin in the monitor's light reminded him of the moon—cool and pale.

She smelled of blood. Paul's blood.

Rule gave his attention to the road once more.

Lily had fought for him tonight. The demon had come to kill him—a fact she'd recognized before he did. He thought of the way she'd moved, weapon ready, focused on her target. If she'd felt fear, she'd ignored it.

It wasn't the first time he'd seen her fight. It wouldn't be the last. The thought terrified him. She was small, easily damaged, and slow to heal. Yet mixed with the fear was pride. That, he would never have expected.

Who would have thought a warrior would suit him so well?

Lily closed her computer. "You okay?"

"What do you mean?"

"You're obeying the speed limit. You've got to be either vastly preoccupied or exhausted."

He smiled because she'd expect it. "A bit of both, I think. When will—"

"There's something—" she said at the same time.

They stopped, exchanged a smile. His was more genuine this time. "Ladies and federal agents first. You have questions." Questions were the way she dealt with the world's cruelties and confusions.

Lily said, "Yes, and my first one is, what were you about to ask?"

"I should have seen that coming. All right. When will Paul's body be released?"

"Hard to say. The lab won't be able to learn much, but they have to go through the motions."

Rule nodded. Those of the Blood—lupi, gnomes, and others—had magic woven into their cells, which played hell with laboratory results. That didn't mean the authorities would omit one jot from their usual procedures. "When it is, I'll escort it back to his people."

"But . . . you? They won't release it to you. His family will have to claim the body."

"Isen is arranging matters with the Leidolf Rho. He'll see that your legalities are observed, and I will take Paul's body to his clanhome. You'll have to accompany me, but you won't be in any danger. Leidolf is ruled by a cur, but even he doesn't make war on women."

"Well, that was certainly my first concern." She shoved her hair back with both hands. "Why? Why do you want to do this?"

"The *susmussio*." That was part of the serpent in his belly, the coils of need and rage and ragged ends. "Paul died because of it. Because of me."

"You don't know that! He might have helped us even without the, uh, *susmussio*. Or he might have figured the fight was too good to miss, or that the demon would come after him anyway. Or that he had to protect the female—your crowd is bent that way."

Rule shook his head. "It doesn't matter. Even if I'm wrong about his motives, his actions were those of an honorable lupus who'd accepted submission in combat. He was exhausted, ill-equipped through training or experience to fight a demon, yet he came to my aid." Rule bit out the next: "He felt *responsible* for me."

"But . . ." She was silent for a long moment. Rule knew the problems she'd be ticking off in her head: the investigation, the enmity between Nokolai and Leidolf, the enemy who'd apparently reached out from hell to attack them.

To attack *him*. It was her poor luck to be nearby . . . but that wasn't something either of them could change.

Her voice was quiet. "You don't feel you have a choice."

"No more than you could choose not to hunt whoever sent the demon that killed Paul."

"All right, then." She took a deep breath, let it out. "We'll work something out."

He touched her hand briefly, a thank-you. "You're in luck on one count. Our trip won't take long. Leidolf Clanhome is in Virginia."

"How far is it from Halo?"

Halo, North Carolina . . . where his son lived. "It doesn't matter. You know I can't go there."

"I know you're convinced of that. We'll have to ditch the press anyway so they don't follow us to Leidolf 's Clanhome."

"The press are only part of the problem. Any of his friends or neighbors could recognize me. His grandmother agrees. She doesn't want me there."

"Toby does."

A muscle jumped in his jaw. Toby had come up to spend the weekend with them shortly after they arrived in D.C. They'd spent their time together indoors, unable to see the sights together. Toby hadn't liked that. "He's a child still. He doesn't understand what the consequences would be if he were known to be my son."

"The clans don't harm children."

"His neighbors might. Some of those he thought were friends suddenly wouldn't be, or their parents wouldn't let them be. His life would never be the same. It would be different if . . ." If he could be raised at Clanhome, surrounded by his clan.

Rule shut the door quickly on that thought. Toby's mother would never agree. She might not want to raise their son herself, but that didn't mean she'd let Rule have him.

"His life won't be the same anyway," Lily said quietly, "once he hits puberty."

"That's years away still. Leave it alone."

She said nothing, but held out her hand. After a second's hesitation, he took it. For a time they were both silent.

She spoke again as they passed the Arlington exit. "About this *susmussio* thing . . . you didn't get to undo it. What does that mean? Are there consequences for you or for the clan?"

She was learning, he thought with a flick of pleasure. She was beginning to think of the clan. As his Chosen, she was Nokolai, too, though she sometimes forgot. "Though things are never simple between Leidolf and Nokolai, there should be few consequences to the clan." As long as he handled things correctly, that is. "For myself . . . there are two rituals that may be observed. One is part of the burial service. Normally I would be expected to present an account of Paul's death in a formal response to questions."

"Normally?"

"Paul's people may not want Nokolai present."

"You mean his clan won't want you there."

"Not precisely. The Leidolf Rho would probably like to bar me from the ceremony, but the decision belongs to Paul's father, if he's alive. If not, his other male relatives will make the decision."

"Male?" she said sharply. "What about his mother? His sisters, if any?"

"Leidolf's customs are different from Nokolai and most of the other clans." He paused, choosing his words. "You won't care for some of their ways."

"That's two."

"Two?"

"Topics you'll need to go into more later. You said there were two possible rituals. What's the other?"

"If Paul's father is alive, I owe him a son's duty. I will offer it. He may not accept. Pride could hold him back, or a desire to shame Nokolai. Or pragmatism. In accepting, he would also take on certain responsibilities."

"What do you mean, 'a son's duty'? What sort of duty?"

"Nothing so different from what you probably feel you owe your father. Not obedience, but respect, financial support if needed. My presence, if he wishes it, at certain occasions."

"Since your presence means my presence, too, I'd like to know . . ." She stopped to frown at her purse. Her phone was buzzing from its depths. She retrieved it, glanced at the caller ID, and sighed. "Of course." She thumbed it on. "Hello, Dad. It's after one in the morning here, you know."

Rule smiled faintly. Lily's father was well aware of the time difference. He was a stockbroker, and the Street was in their time zone. "Tell him we'll still try to fly back for Christmas."

She shot him a frown. "Yes, that was Rule. He'll be—I know she is, but with what happened tonight . . ."

They were nearly home. The street was quiet, the area thoroughly urban but more upscale than where Paul had lived. Here the row houses were brick or board or stone, the window boxes tidy, the Christmas lights tasteful. The tiny restaurant on the corner served decorative little seafood entrées with mango chutney or saffron aioli.

In some ways, Rule preferred Paul's neighborhood.

"Tell Mother we'll try. That's the best I can do." Lily paused. "Well, how can I? She isn't speaking to me."

While Rule was trapped in hell with another Lily, something had gone wrong between this Lily and her mother. She'd told him little about it. He'd been patient, thinking their return to San Diego would shake things loose, but if they didn't go home for the holiday . . .

"You know I can't tell you much," she was saying. "You'll read about it, though. There was a demon, and—no, no, I'm fine." A pause. "He's okay, too, but someone else was killed. That's why . . . no. No one you know."

Rule passed the elegant little bed-and-breakfast where he'd spent a few pleasant nights on other trips to D.C. Whether here or in San Diego, he'd seldom brought women home. A few, yes—those few who'd become friends as much as lovers.

That life was over. There was only Lily for him now. After a lifetime of many women, there was only Lily. He wouldn't have changed that if change were possible, but tonight . . .

He felt it still. The moon's song throbbed through him, a bass drumming played on his bones, carried by his blood.

He shouldn't have. She was nowhere near full, and though he'd fought the Change once—and won, by a margin so small it shamed him—in the end he had Changed. That should have diminished the pull. Yet power still pooled in his belly, tangling with the other needs, and the wolf was close. So close.

He wanted sex.

The house where they were staying had a detached garage at the back of its narrow yard. He didn't look at his mate as he turned down the alley. What he wanted now had nothing to do with love or tenderness. He wanted a body to pound into, the smell of an aroused female filling him, the mindless rush to release.

Sex dissipated the strength of the Change need. Nettie called that "evolution in action," encouraging behavior likely to result in more children. Considering the low fertility rate of his people, Rule supposed that could be true, though he wasn't sure evolution applied to those of the Blood. Whatever the reason, though, sex worked. Even in adolescence, when control was all but nonexistent, a bout of hot, sweaty sex could reseat a lupus firmly in his human form.

But it was risky if the wolf was too close. A wolf in rut didn't care about the female's pleasure . . . or even consent. With true wolves, an unwilling female could keep a male from mounting her. Men, however, had been raping women since the species arose.

He wouldn't risk Lily that way. He had to regain control on his own.

"Sure," she said into her phone. "I'll let you know." She disconnected and sighed. "I should have known he'd call. Unlike Mother, Dad actually reads his e-mail and text messages."

"He's upset that we might not be back for Christmas."

"He claims it's Mother who's upset. No matter what, I'm still supposed to show up so she can refuse to speak to me in person. God knows my job is no excuse."

There was too much bitterness in her voice . . . and he was more sledgehammer than scalpel tonight. Too preoccupied with his own needs, he admitted, to deal with hers with any delicacy. "That's one," he said, reaching up to hit the remote for the garage door.

"One?"

"Topic you're going to fill me in on later."

"Oh." She gave a slow nod. "That's fair."

The garage door slid up, the lights inside came on, and he turned in.

The garage smelled like most—of oil, hot metal from the car, exhaust. There were mice here, too, which pleased Dirty Harry. The cat spent a fair amount of time in the garage.

Rule breathed in more deeply as they left the garage to walk to the house. Though city smells still dominated, humus and cedar sweetened the air, too, and the hint of a breeze carried the scent of the old tom who'd been engaging in territorial disputes with Harry. He smelled the German shepherd next door, too. The dog was following them along the fence line.

Rule wanted to pace the darkness on four feet, too. To tip his nose toward the moon and join her song, mourning a life cut off young. So very young.

"Are you coming in?"

Until Lily spoke from the doorway, Rule hadn't realized he'd stopped. He mentally cursed his inattention. "Of course."

"You don't have to, you know."

He couldn't read her expression. Sadness? Pity? Something solemn and annoying, he decided, and moved abruptly toward the house.

She didn't step aside when he reached the doorway. He stopped, scowling. "I thought you were inviting me in, but if you prefer to bar the door—"

"I'd say it's the other way around. You've been shutting me out."

"Is my every thought supposed to be joint property? Move aside, Lily. I'm in no mood for hand-holding."

"Good, because I'm running low on sympathy. Why are you working so hard at pushing me away?"

"I'm not—"

"Especially since you'd like to toss me on the floor and rip my clothes off."

Her bluntness stripped him of words.

She rolled her eyes. "Jesus, Rule, do you think I'm blind? You aren't *that* different, you know."

"Except that I might suddenly develop very large teeth and the appetite to go with them."

"So we add turning furry to your list of ways to cope with stress."

"Stress?" he echoed in disbelief. "Is that what you think this is about?"

"You're right. Discussion is a bad idea." She moved up to him, put her hands on either side of his face, and brought his head down to hers. She didn't kiss him. Instead, she rubbed her cheek along his.

He went still. The smells of her flooded him—citrus from her shampoo, the slightly tinny scent of her cosmetics. Blood. Arousal. *Lily.* He shuddered. "I'm not . . ." *Safe,* he wanted to say. Not safe, not whole, not in control, not . . .

"It's okay," she whispered, her fingers threading his hair. "It's okay."

It wasn't okay. Nothing was . . . nothing but this. He scooped her close, some thread of sanity warning him to mind his strength. She was small, crushable . . .

Fierce. Her hands roamed him. Her mouth demanded his.

He gave it to her. And took hers in return.

Taste joined scent, tangling with touch and heat to burst inside him in kinesthetic pinwheels. He turned with her in his arms—once, twice, spinning the two of them inside the darkened house. He slapped the door, shutting it. The lock clicked. Her purse slid from her shoulder. Her coat spilled to the floor.

Within seconds, he forgot everything he knew about a woman's needs, how to tend them, build them. Her breath, her hands, told him he could, that she neither needed nor wanted tending. She wanted him.

He needed her. Needed inside. Beneath the black dress she wore panty hose. Damnable stuff, but it ripped easily.

The sound of it tearing nearly hid the catch of her breath, but he caught it. He flung his head up, nostrils flared, searching her face. No, that was hunger he saw, not fear. *Good, yes, good . . .* He kissed her again to thank her. Her hands gripped his shoulders, her fingers digging in hard.

A tremor shook him. Here. He could do it here, standing. Her weight meant little with need riding him so hard. But he wanted, craved, the feel of her beneath him. For that he needed softness beneath her.

He cupped her bottom, lifting her so that her heat met his.

The living room. The couch there was soft. He could make it. He could get that far. He began to walk. She wiggled, wrapping her legs around his waist. He made it out of the kitchen. Using touch, memory, and luck, he passed through the windowless dining room into the muffled charcoals of the front room, where a crack in the drapes leaked city light.

The couch was five paces away. Four.

His phone chimed. Without missing a step he unclipped it from his belt and flung it aside. The crack of plastic meeting brick told him it hit the fireplace.

He laid her down on the couch, propped himself over her, one hand at his belt. But his hand shook. Her hands joined his, helping with the button, the zipper. He kissed her, finding some ease in the intimacy of joining their mouths, scents, breath . . . *"Mon fleur,"* he whispered, finding her with his fingers. "So beautiful . . . *ton pétales comme une rose,* so soft . . ."

Then he was in and moving, and lacked both air and mind enough for words. It was a short, hard climb to the top, bereft of finesse but joined, joined, with her matching him thrust for thrust. The world became musk and motion, sensation too keen to sustain.

He reached between them, found the bud hidden in her petals, and she cried out. Her body arched. The ripples of her climax pulled him over after her.

An aeon later, with the world resettled into more ordinary shapes, with her breath warm on his skin and his chest still heaving, she murmured, "What . . . was that . . . you said? It was French."

"I praised your flower." He touched her to show her what he meant.

"Oh." Her sigh mixed happy with sleepy. "It sounds better in . . . damn."

It was her phone ringing this time. "Telemarketers," he said.

"At two in the morning? Off." She pushed at his chest.

"I'll get it." He forced himself to move.

"I might as well. It's either my father again or something about the case." She rolled off the couch, stood, and frowned. "My legs don't work right after you've vaporized the bones."

It was easier to smile now, so he did. She padded back through the darkness toward the kitchen, naked and untroubled by it. He followed. The demon's claw mark was burning after all that exercise, but otherwise his muscles were warm, loose. He felt comfortable in his body again.

Lily bent to get her purse, presenting him with a pleasant view. He wondered if she realized how clearly he could see in the dim light.

"Mr-r-row," said Harry.

The big cat was sitting by the refrigerator, glaring at him. Harry liked to blame Rule for any disruption: rain, closed doors, an empty food dish. This time, though, Rule conceded that the cat had a point. He *had* delayed Lily. "I'll tend to your beast." He opened the refrigerator, spilling chilly white light across the floor.

Lily grinned. "You already did." She thumbed her phone. "Hello?"

He felt something damp and warm on his leg and glanced down. A thin trail of blood dripped down his leg from the wound. He frowned, puzzled. It had been scabbed over earlier.

Lily was close enough for Rule to hear his father on the other end: "Good. You weren't asleep. I trust my son is around."

Her eyebrows went up. "He is. Just a moment. Calm down, Harry," she said to the cat, who stropped her leg vigorously, purring like a furry chain saw. She held out the phone.

"Yes?" Rule pulled out the carton of milk.

A deep bass rumbled in his ear. "You screening calls now, or is something wrong with your phone?"

"I need to replace it." The pieces weren't likely to go back together correctly.

"Damn technology. Always breaking or getting bugs. Get a new phone first thing; we'll need to stay in touch. I've spoken to Leidolf."

"Yes?" Rule was puzzled. What about the conversation with the Leidolf Rho could be so urgent that Isen needed to call at this hour?

"I've also spoken to Szós, Kyffin, Etorri, and Ybirra, and I've got calls in to the others. Should hear back soon. You weren't the only heir attacked tonight."

SIX

>〰

THE inhabitants of Los Lobos didn't see many visitors from *los Estados Unidos*. U.S. tourists went to the province's capital, Morelia, or to Pátzcuaro, near the beautiful lake of the same name. A few made it down to Playa Azul for surfing. But there was little to draw them along the highway that skirted the coast to a tiny fishing village, so the pale-skinned man sitting on the patio in front of the village's only café attracted a lot of attention.

He was probably used to that. No one who looked the way he did could have passed through life without drawing many eyes. Especially female eyes.

Pity he was crazy.

His Spanish was very funny, so at first they weren't sure if he meant what he said, but he'd drawn a picture for Jesús Garcia, who owned the café. He really was looking for *el dragón*. But his money spent as well as anyone else's, so they shrugged and indulged him. If it made him happy to hunt for creatures that did not exist, why spoil his pleasure?

At the moment the crazy man was scowling at his map as if he could make the little lines move into patterns more to his liking. He had a cup of coffee near his elbow, and his plate held the remains of his breakfast. He'd eaten four eggs and several tortillas, but he'd ignored the sliced mango.

The two old men at the other front table who'd observed and

commented on his breakfast sniggered when the waitress approached the stranger's table. Carmencita put so much sway in her hips it was a wonder she didn't hurt herself. But the man was busy disapproving of his map. He didn't notice.

"¿Le gustaría más, señor?"

The tone of voice, more than the words, pulled Cullen's attention away from the topographic map. His smile was an automatic response to that husky purr asking what more he wanted, but it tilted into real appreciation when she removed his plate and wiped the table—a process that seemed to require her to bend over a lot. He looked where she meant him to and admired the view.

"Ah . . . *ahora, no. Pero más tarde* . . ." He let his expression say what his limited Spanish couldn't. She understood well enough. She gave him back a torrent of words he couldn't untangle, though it seemed to involve setting a firm time. He laughed, told her *no comprendo*, and eventually she had to settle for the ambiguous *later* that he'd promised.

Considering how well things weren't going, he might be here a while. No point in being standoffish, was there? Or depriving himself.

Cullen had stopped in Los Lobos for two reasons. The name tickled his fancy, of course. And his curiosity. The village was farther south than he'd thought wolves ranged, even when there had been plenty of his wild cousins in North America. Why name it for animals the natives had never seen?

If he understood the locals right, the place had been named for a pair of peaks, oddly denuded of forest, visible from the village. They, too, were called Los Lobos. From this angle, Cullen supposed they looked a bit like a beast's gaping jaws. That didn't explain why they'd been assigned to a wolf rather than a panther, which this region did have. Maybe the village had been named by the Spanish. Spaniards would have thought of wolves.

The bigger reason he'd stopped here, of course, was that his trail did. Dammit.

A soccer ball bounced into the street, followed by a gaggle of screaming children. Boys, mostly, though one gap-toothed athlete wore braids and a dress. She was the one whose knee connected with the ball, sending it flying straight at him.

He grimaced, stretched up a hand, and punched the ball. It sailed over their heads, hit the cement-block wall of the *mercado* across the street, and rebounded into the stomach of the tallest boy, who landed on his butt on the cracked pavement. The under-age mob erupted in hoots, jeers, and a few shouted comments aimed at Cullen.

"Little monsters," Cullen muttered. They ought to be in school. Why weren't they in school? It wasn't Christmas yet, was it? He checked in with the moon, knowing it wouldn't be full until the thirty-first.

Barely half-full. Not Christmas yet, then. So why didn't their parents chain them up somewhere?

To his relief, the soccer players chased their ball down the street. He returned his attention to the topographic map in front of him.

Before leaving California, Cullen had spent three days en-spelling his maps: a large one to give him the general direction, with successively smaller maps to pinpoint his target. He was no Finder, but he'd gotten the spell from one, a luscious and annoy-ing Amazon who'd gone with them into hell, where they'd found plenty of demons, as expected. And a war, which they hadn't ex-pected.

Also dragons. Dragons who'd returned with them to Earth to escape the war. Dragons who had, in fact, made their return possi-ble because one of them knew more about magic than any Faerie lord.

And that damned dragon had flown off before Cullen could ask him one single damned question. Flown away and vanished from sight, radar, second sight, and scrying.

And now from his map. Cullen scowled and moved his coffee out of the way.

He hadn't tried to trace the dragons directly. They knew too much about magic—at least the one who called himself Sam did. Sam could block any direct search Cullen might devise. He'd blocked Cynna, and Cynna, however irritating she might be, was a powerful Finder. So Cullen had been tracking where they'd been, not where they were now.

Cullen was very good with fire, and fire elementals exist partly in the present, partly in the past and future, so he'd tied the spell to a small salamander. Dragons being of the present, like men, they shouldn't be able to block the past.

Until five days ago, the spell had worked. The thin gold band on his map, invisible to those who couldn't see magic, flowed along the coast, turned in to the mountains near this little village . . . and vanished.

Just like those damned dragons.

Since then, he'd been trying to find them by more ordinary means: asking about missing livestock or sightings of strange creatures. As a result, his hosts thought he was insane. Not that he cared, but they told him whatever they thought he wanted to hear, not what they'd actually seen or heard of.

But he was close. He knew it. There was that tickling at his shields last night—which didn't, he admitted, prove anything. But when he'd tramped well up one of the mountain trails yesterday, he'd hit a spot where magic was damped. That proved he was in the right area. Something about dragons smothered or absorbed the magic in their vicinity. Today he would—

The soccer ball came sailing at him again.

"Dammit!" This time he stood and snatched it out of the air. The herd of children swarming toward him stopped. The girl giggled. The tallest boy—the one who'd ended up on his butt earlier—shot a babble of words at him.

It didn't sound like an apology. Or a polite request to have his ball back.

Cullen smiled at him in a way that had been known to make grown men nervous. He passed the ball back and forth between his hands. *"¿Este es su pelota?"*

"Sí. ¡Démelo!"

Cullen gave the kid credit for guts. Instead of stepping back, he puffed out his skinny chest and tried to grab the ball—and fell back, nostrils flared, shocked eyes huge in his thin face.

"Brujo," he whispered. Witch.

No, Cullen thought, *and neither are you. Though you may not have a clue what you really are.* For he had caught the boy's scent, just as the boy had caught his.

To make sure, though, he *saw* the boy.

Sorcerous vision didn't involve the eyes, or even some arcane third eye that could be opened and closed. Cullen saw magic all the time, but the vividness of ordinary vision obscured it until he paid attention. Some sorcerers had to close their eyes to see magic. For Cullen, it was a matter of changing his focus—something that came easier for him now, after spending three weeks without eyes.

The boy's aura was bright, lively . . . and shot through with streaks of purple. Oh, yeah. The skinny brat was definitely of the Blood, though not full-blood.

Add that to what Cullen's nose had told him, and the riddle of the village's name was solved. "Boy," he said softly, "we need to talk."

The boy, of course, didn't understand English.

Jesús came waddling out of the cramped interior of the café, scolding away in rapid-fire Spanish.

Cullen smiled pleasantly, tossing the ball idly from one hand to another as he listened, catching maybe one word in ten. How should he handle this? The boy hadn't hit puberty yet—both his scent and his aura confirmed that—but it wouldn't be long. He couldn't be left to face his first Change alone. Who should he . . .

An odd, unpleasant scent made him turn his head.

To his regular senses, it was the barest shimmer in the air fifty feet away, a whiff of a carrion stench. To his other vision, it was a nightmare striding down the street.

It walked upright on two great, clawed feet. The haunches were huge, making the lumpy body look too small. There were no upper limbs. The head—shaped like a cross between a crocodile and a rhinoceros, with the teeth of the former and the horn of the latter—quested forward on about five feet of thick neck and still topped the tin roofs on either side of the road. A naked woman rode on its back, her skin the black-brown of the mask on a Siamese cat.

No, he realized a split second later. The astral form of a woman. The demon was dashtu—physically present but slightly out of phase with this realm. The woman wasn't really here at all.

"Shit. Double shit. I don't guess any of you see that?"

"¿Señor? ¿Qué dijo usted?" The café's owner tapped his arm, jabbering at him. The boy talked right over his elder, glaring at Cullen and gesturing. Three of the kids were sitting in the middle of the road, playing some stupid game with a bit of string. The others shoved each other, chattered, or watched Cullen and the boy.

And the demon was coming, one slow stride at a time. Its head swung from side to side—and zeroed in on Cullen. The eyes glowed red.

So did the woman's eyes. She smiled at him and raised one lazy hand.

Instinctively he reached for the diamond hanging on a chain

around his neck. That single, flawless carat, lab-certified, was the reason he was on a cash-only basis these days. Visa still didn't understand why its computers had allowed him to go so far over his limit, and they weren't happy about it.

The stone was only about half-full, since he'd used some of the stored magic in his search. Didn't matter, though, did it? No arcane duels with all those kids in the line of fire. "Shit!" he said again, with feeling. And moved.

Cullen wasn't as strong as some of his kind. He could fight, of course, but he wasn't trained. But he was fast—faster than anyone he knew, except Rule's supernally skilled brother, Benedict. Fast enough that the humans around him would later deny what they'd seen.

So he ran . . . toward the demon, not away. Running away would draw it after him, right over the underage mob. He didn't know what would happen if a dashtu demon stepped on a kid, but he wasn't minded to experiment.

He'd surprised the demon's rider. The glimpse he caught of her expression as he barreled straight at her and her nightmare pet told him that. Not enough for her to lose focus, though. Her raised hand still directed the magic she'd gathered, an energy loop spinning over her head in slow circles, like a lasso.

Fortunately, her mount had less control. It stopped, jerking its head back, and hesitated briefly before thrusting those toothy jaws at the idiot charging it.

Cullen dodged.

One huge foot lifted as the demon tried stomping on him. He threw himself aside, rolling as he hit the ground, and came up running. No point in hanging around to fight, not when there was a good chance he'd lose.

He made for the church. It was tiny and crumbling, but those consecrated walls should repel the demon. He felt rather than heard the thing's feet thud against the ground behind him. So why he could feel that, when the thing wasn't present enough to be seen or heard? He knew damn little about the dashtu state, but—

Damn! That thing could *jump*!

Cullen skidded to a halt. The demon had leaped over him, landing less than ten feet away. Its snout darted toward him even as the rider sent the glowing loop she controlled his way.

No time for a spell or to draw down from his diamond. Cullen did the one thing he could without weapons or spells. He flung fire at it.

The creature bellowed as flames crawled up its belly and chest. It tossed its head, staggering back so fast its rider lost control of her lasso. The glowing loop snaked wildly through the air.

Cullen was already running the other way when the loop whizzed over his head. The demon was annoyed, not stopped. Not enough of it was physically present for normal fire to do real damage, and Cullen needed a boost from the diamond to call mage fire.

Probably just as well. Mage fire was the devil to control.

He ducked between two houses, where the demon's bulk wouldn't fit. Unless, that is, it could slip deeper into dashtu so its mass could overlap with—

A glance over his shoulder told him it could.

He popped into a yard overrun with chickens, which squawked and fluttered and generally got in his way. And kept running—into the trees and up a winding mountain path.

An hour later he perched in a gnarly oak tree surrounded by thousands of others. His chest heaved. The muscles in his thighs jumped and twitched, and his shirt was soaked with sweat. The legs of his jeans were wet to the knees.

A butterfly with wings the color of sunrise drifted past like a scrap of tissue paper. Monkeys screeched nearby. He was maybe eight or nine miles from the village and at least a thousand feet higher.

Time was on his side, he told himself. Eventually the woman would have to give up. Legend said that some adepts had been able to sustain an astral body for nearly a full day, but he was damned if he'd credit that bitch with an adept's abilities. Another hour or three, and she'd have to return to her physical body.

He just hoped she took her demon with her when she left.

As the sweat cooled on his body, he shivered, but not really from the chill. Twice he'd thought he'd gotten away; twice the demon and its rider had found him.

How? That was the twenty-thousand-dollar question.

Not psychically. He was sure of that; his shields were locked down tight, and they'd kept out a crazy telepath assisted by an ancient staff. Nor did he think the demon was using scent, not after he'd splashed along that damned creek. Hearing was theoretically possible, he supposed. In his wolf form, he could distinguish between one beating heart and another, but he had to be pretty damned close. He didn't think his heartbeat was giving him away.

That left vision or magic. Maybe the demon was Davy Crockett on steroids and could spot Cullen's traces whether he went down a creek, over boulders, or made like Tarzan through the trees.

Or maybe the demon's rider had some kind of magical fix on him.

Last night something had brushed against his shields. He'd assumed it was Sam. Too bloody sure of himself, he thought now, bitter at finding himself a fool. He should have been warned. Instead he'd been smug, knowing nothing could get through. He . . .

Cullen blinked. How did he know nothing could get through?

Dumb question. He tested everything. When he'd devised his shields . . .

The flush of vertigo hit so suddenly he nearly swayed right off his perch. He grabbed the trunk, sweat popping out on his forehead.

When he'd devised his shields. That's what he'd thought just before falling off into . . . nothing. Because he couldn't remember testing the shields. He couldn't remember coming up with them in the first place.

Them?

Cullen's fingers dug into the bark. He stared out at the jungle, seeing nothing. A beetle as big as his thumb investigated his hand. He ignored it.

He had a shield. One shield, singular, that protected him from any sort of mental attack. And he had no idea where it had come from, or why he kept thinking of *shields,* plural.

Someone or something had messed with his mind, swallowed part of his memory.

He began tracking his memories, plucking at one, then another, trying to figure out when he'd acquired his shields. When had he first begun relying on them?

It didn't take him long to turn up an answer. That day wasn't one he was likely to forget. He could make a good guess about the culprit, too, though not the motive nor the man's current location. Lucky him, though—he knew someone who could help. Someone with access to all sorts of information.

Gradually, the silence penetrated his concentration. No birds called, no monkeys fussed and chattered. The forest was quiet . . . and drifting faintly in the air was the stink of rotting flesh.

Son of a bitch! He didn't have *time* to play hide-and-seek. He needed to be out of this damned jungle and onto a plane.

When the demon's questing snout preceded its ungainly body up the path twenty feet from Cullen's tree, he was standing on the ground at its base. He waited with one hand closed around the little diamond at his throat, the other outstretched.

"All right, sugar," he murmured. "Have it your way. You want to play? I'm ready."

SEVEN

CYNNA skidded into Headquarters at two minutes after ten o'clock. Elevators never come when you're late, so it was 10:07 when she arrived, only slightly breathless, at his secretary's desk. "He's expecting me."

Ida Rheinhart was older than God and a lot meaner. She looked at Cynna over the top of bright red reading glasses and handed her a folder. "He was expecting you at ten. Everyone else is here already. Conference room B-12."

She started to explain—Ida had that effect on her—but closed her mouth. What was the point? Ida had never been late in her life. But that was easy for her, because she never left her desk. Cynna was pretty sure she curled up beneath it at night, waiting to snatch unwary agents or cleaning people who trod too close to her lair.

Cynna tucked the folder under her arm and hurried down the hall. She hadn't expected they'd use a conference room. Apparently this was a bigger meeting than she'd thought.

That worried her. The news this morning had been decidedly odd.

The demon she'd killed had been given a big play, of course, but that was only one of last night's oddities. The *New York Times* online edition reported all sorts of sightings—of lupi, yeti, banshees, even fairies. Of course, people claimed to see things they hadn't really seen all the time, but what about that brownie reservation in Tennessee? Supposedly it had doubled its population overnight.

A school bus in Texas had disappeared on the way back from a football game; drivers around it claimed they'd seen it vanish. A well-known medium had announced the end of the world. So had an infamous terrorist organization. Not that Cynna put any stock in end-of-world bullshit, but something was up.

She shoved open the conference room door and stopped dead. Two dozen people sat around the dark wood table. Every one of them turned to look at her.

"Sorry. Car died." Jesus. She'd never seen this many of the Unit's agents in one meeting before. And it wasn't just Unit agents at the table. Not even just FBI.

Sherry O'Shaunessy, the high priestess for the oldest and largest Wiccan coven in the country, sat beside a short, dark-haired man in a clerical collar. Cynna was pretty sure he was Archbishop Brown, a fiery Catholic with reformist leanings. She didn't know the old guy with Einstein hair or the bald man built like a pro wrestler, but she recognized the woman sitting on Ruben's right.

Cynna swallowed and hurried to sit down. She'd never met the president's senior adviser, but she'd sure seen pictures.

Ruben sat at the head of the table. Nothing about his appearance explained the respect he commanded. He was painfully thin, making the custom-tailored suit a necessity. His nose was large, and Cynna knew for a fact that his wife cut his hair. He'd mended his glasses with duct tape again. On his good days, when he could walk with a cane, he was slightly above average height.

Cynna hadn't seen him on a good day for over a year. Today, as usual, he sat in his motorized wheelchair.

Ruben gave her a nod. "Gentlemen and ladies, this is Cynna Weaver, one of my best agents. Her particular Gift is Finding, but she's trained in spellcraft and demonology as well. Cynna, Agent Yu just finished summarizing two of last night's ASEs—ah, excuse me. Some of you aren't familiar with our jargon. ASE stands for *apparent supernatural event*, which is the designation given to events that meet our criteria for investigation."

"Two?" Cynna repeated, zeroing in on the important part. "How many ASEs were there?"

"Since ten o'clock last night, we've received fifty-seven

reports of ASEs from official sources and two hundred forty-two reports from unofficial sources."

Cynna's jaw dropped. That was beyond unprecedented. It was . . . scary as hell, she decided.

She wasn't the only one shocked. Ruben had to quiet the questions and exclamations with a raised hand before continuing. "This is more than ten times our usual load. Since we can't suddenly acquire ten times our usual personnel, we're forced to apply triage. Only the most critical incidents will be handled by Unit agents. For the rest, some investigations will be delayed, some will be left to local authorities, and some will be turned over to our non-Unit colleagues in MCD. I realize," he added with a brief smile, "that will displease some of you."

No duh. In Cynna's opinion, most of MCD—the FBI's Magical Crimes Division—was staffed by pencil pushers and exterminators. The pencil pushers were useless. They wouldn't know a spell after it turned them small, furry, and fond of carrots. But the others were worse—MCD agents who'd tracked down lupi and others in the bad old days, before the Supreme Court changed the rules.

Exterminators wasn't Cynna's nickname for that bunch. It was what they'd called themselves.

"However," Ruben was saying, "because these events lie within our jurisdiction, we will retain some control. MCD agents will be loaned to us and will report to Special Agent Croft."

Cynna's eyebrows shot up. How had Ruben pulled that off? On paper, the Unit looked like part of MCD. In practice, Ruben operated free of the nominal chain of command, which did not endear him to the rabidly territorial head of MCD.

She glanced at the presidential adviser. Had she leaned on MCD? What was going on here?

Ruben shifted in his chair. "So far I've referred only to ASEs within our borders, but the United States wasn't the only country affected by what happened last night. For example, in Dublin a pair of banshees—"

The bald guy snorted. "If I had a dollar for every Irishman who claims to have seen a banshee, I could pay off the federal debt."

Ruben nodded politely. "Perhaps, though I believe there are somewhat less than eight trillion Irishmen. But irrelevant. This sighting was witnessed by the Japanese prime minister—you may recall he's on an official visit to Great Britain—as well as three journalists and two members of Parliament. And that was a single example. Ms. Pearson brought me a report, which I'm unable to share with you due to security constraints, but it confirms my gut feeling that we are dealing with a worldwide phenomenon."

Holy shit.

"Perhaps all of the consequences of this unknown phenomenon have already occurred. Perhaps not. My strong feeling is that we've seen only the first wave—that more will follow."

One of the Unit's agents said quietly, "One to ten, Ruben?"

Ruben gave him the faintest of smiles but spoke generally to all of them. "Sean's in the habit of asking me to pluck a number from thin air to back up my hunches. On a scale of one to ten, he's asking now how certain I am that I'm right." He looked at Sean. "I'd give this one a ten."

Cynna shivered suddenly. She knew about Sean's scale, including the part Ruben hadn't mentioned. Ten meant Ruben was slightly more sure of this hunch than he was of gravity.

"Yet we need more than my gut feelings. We need to know what happened, whether it could happen again, what the consequences might be. The president has asked me to create a task force to answer these questions. Dr. Fagin will head this task force."

Einstein-hair was doodling on a pad of paper. He looked up to smile vaguely at them.

"Archbishop Brown and Ms. O'Shaughnessy have also agreed to serve, and Hikaru Ito will be joining them soon. Dr. Fagin has the authority and the budget to add to his staff as needed. They will require your utmost cooperation and have been granted security clearances that will allow you to freely answer any questions."

He shifted again. Cynna hoped he wasn't having one of his bad spells, when his muscles ached constantly. He'd probably been up most of the night.

"Some of you have already received your assignments and are eager to be off. I think you understand now why I delayed your departures for this meeting. Before you go, you need to know two more things. First, I will be unable to monitor individual investigations as I normally do, nor can even one of my Gifted agents be pulled from the field to assist with coordination. We have too many fires to put out. Therefore, for the duration of this emergency, field agents will operate with full field authority. Get your codes from Ida before you leave."

Full field authority. For *all* of them. That slid down Cynna's gullet and settled in her stomach with all the comfort of a lumpy rock.

"Second, you are to consider this morning's briefing highly confidential. Full field authority permits you to reveal classified information if such revelation is essential to your investigation. It does not allow you to discuss it around the water cooler."

There was a bustle of papers and movement as Ruben dismissed those agents who had their assignments. Cynna was so busy assimilating the morning's shocks that she didn't notice Lily until she felt a tap on her shoulder.

"Come on. You're with me on this one." Lily grimaced. "Though we'll have to use your office. They haven't assigned me one yet."

EIGHT

LILY felt short, tense, and awkward as she kept up with Cynna's longer legs. She needed to explain that she hadn't asked to be put in charge; that was Ruben's doing. But they couldn't discuss that or any of the morning's shocks in the corridor.

When they reached the elevator she thought of a way to break the silence. "Car trouble?"

Cynna grimaced. "Son of a bitch turned belly-up on I-235. I should've taken the Metro, like usual. Cars hate me."

The doors whooshed open and they joined three others. Lily didn't know any of them, but Cynna exchanged nods with an older man. After that, they followed the usual elevator protocol, pretending they didn't see the others trapped in the little box with them. "All cars?" she asked. "Or just that one?"

"Any of them I drive too often. Computers hate me, too. So do cell phones and remote controls, and I gave up wearing a watch years ago."

"Wait a minute. You use a cell phone."

"Sure. And most of the time it works. But if I leak, it doesn't."

"Leak?" Lily said. "Leak magic, you mean? I know some of the Blood don't deal well with technology, but I hadn't heard of any Gifted having problems."

"Most don't, but—"

The doors opened. Cynna finished explaining as they left the elevator for a long hallway. "I wear a lot of my magic on my skin. It's locked up in the *kilingo* and *kielezo*—the two kinds of what you'd call tattoos—but sometimes there's a discharge, like static electricity. Then things go wacko."

"Magic can interfere with technology?"

"Sure, but the little bit that floats around loose is weak, not enough to . . ." Cynna fell silent as the implications sank in. "Holy shit."

"Yeah." Loose magic hadn't been a problem before, but if last night's phenomenon hit again . . . Lily added that to her list of things to worry about when she had time. "What's 'full field authority'?"

"Scary." Cynna stopped in front of a door that looked exactly like the others spaced with metronomic precision along the hall.

"I was hoping for a more precise definition," Lily said dryly.

"Just a minute. Put your hand here, next to mine." Cynna flattened her palm on the door above the knob. "I want to key it to you."

Puzzled, Lily did.

"There," she said after a moment, and moved her hand to turn the knob. "You'll be able to open it if I'm not around."

"Most people use keys."

"So do I."

Not the usual sort, obviously. Lily followed her into a small office made smaller by a cacophony of objects: a desk bearing the expected computer and such, yes, but also a sitar, two dead plants, a human skeleton, a bookcase crammed with peculiar objects—the shrunken head was an eye-grabber—piles of baskets and files and papers, and a little fountain.

To her surprise, the fountain was burbling away. "Where do you pace?"

That brought a grin. "It's a challenge. Full field authority," Cynna said, grabbing a stack of files from the visitor's chair and dropping them on the floor, "means you can commandeer just about anything, no forms to fill out, no questions asked. Supplies, personnel, weapons, airplanes . . . technically you could call in the army, but I don't think anyone's ever done that."

Cynna was right. That was scary. "Ruben said something about a code."

She nodded and plunked herself down on the corner of her desk. "On the rare occasions when a Unit agent is granted full field authority, he or she gets a code number. That's the authorization, but it's only good for a short time. Ida will tell us how long our codes are good and what the procedure will be to invoke them."

There was plenty she needed to tell Cynna, plenty she needed to ask. But Lily wanted to clear the air first. "Cynna, I told Ruben you should be in charge, but—"

"Whoa!" Cynna held up both hands. "Is that what has you as stiff as if rigor had set in? I don't *want* to be in charge. Ruben knows that."

"I've only been an agent for two months. You've got the seniority, the knowledge—"

"Not to mention the rap sheet." She grinned. "Didn't know about that, did you? Penny-ante stuff from when I was young and stupid, but I did some time. It would disqualify me for any part of the Bureau except the Unit. As for my seniority, that's bullshit."

"Experience isn't bullshit."

"No, but your experience counts more than mine. I'm a Finder, not an investigator. The only cases I've handled on my own are missing persons. Kids," she added, her voice turning soft and sad. "A lot of the time, Ruben sends me to Find kids. Sometimes they're just lost. Sometimes . . . too often . . . they've been kidnapped, raped, hurt. Killed. But even then, someone else puts together the case. I'm not trained for that. You are."

Lily drew a breath, let it out. "So we're okay."

"We are. Sit, if your body will bend now."

"I've been sitting all morning." Besides, if she sat in that chair, she'd get a crick in her neck looking up at Cynna. "We're working the case we started last night. The demon summoner."

Cynna nodded, obviously expecting that. "You should know that I tried to Find Jiri before I left the scene. Bombed."

"You told me your Gift can only reach a certain distance."

"About a hundred miles, given a tight, fresh pattern. Which I don't have for Jiri," Cynna admitted. "I haven't seen her in years, so my pattern for her is old. But I still should have been able to Find her if she'd been close enough to control that demon."

"Did she have to be close? You said summoning and binding were two different things."

"They are, but you still have to bring the demon here, to our realm, which means bringing it into a summoning circle. There's no way to do that from a distance."

That's what Lily had thought. It wasn't what she'd wanted to hear. "There were five demons last night, not one. Five demons who attacked the lupi heirs to their clans—three here in the United States and two in Canada. Three of the heirs were killed. So were at least two of the demons, counting the one we killed."

Cynna stared. "Holy Mother Mary. Five summoners?"

"And maybe three demons still around." Lily gave her a moment to absorb that. "From what I was told, one of the demons vanished after killing its target. But that doesn't mean it's really gone, does it? The one last night mostly vanished, too. It turned shimmery. I almost couldn't see it."

"Almost?" Cynna was surprised. "You shouldn't have been able to see it at all when it was dashtu. I wonder if that means dashtu is part illusion?"

"I'm not following you."

"A dashtu demon is out of phase with our realm—not quite here, not quite gone. They can't go dashtu in hell," she added. "That's one reason they like to come here. I thought dashtu made them completely invisible, but if you saw something, there must be a degree of illusion involved. Illusion wouldn't work on you."

"I saw Gan when she was invisible to others. No shimmer."

"Huh." Cynna considered that a moment. "There's a lot I don't know, but Gan's a really young demon. Maybe she can't phase out as completely as the older ones, so she relies more on illusion. What kind of demons attacked the others? Did you get a description?"

"Only of two of them. They match the one we killed last night: big, built like a hyena with a broad chest and short rear legs, red eyes. A third pair of limbs attached at the chest that end in claws."

Cynna nodded. "Like the ones we fought in Dis, then."

"Except for the claws on the forelimbs." Which made a difference. Lily took a slow breath to steady herself. "Five demons means we're looking for five people who can summon and bind demons. That suggests a strong, organized conspiracy."

Cynna frowned. "Maybe not. Give me a minute." She stared at the fountain, jiggling first one foot, then the other, as if trying to pace sitting down. "Five summoners were needed," she said slowly. "We can't get around that. But maybe only one did the binding."

"How?"

"Theoretically, at the master level—and with binding, that's what we're talking about, a demon master—at that level you start getting into demon politics. Politics in hell," she added, "make the UN look good."

"I can believe that, but I don't see where you're going."

"It's because of the way demons are bound to their higher-ups, see? You bind enough low-level demons, or reach for one of the more powerful ones, and you're treading on some powerful toes. See, the one you're hooked into is hooked into a more powerful demon, and so on, right up the feeding chain. So your deal can end up involving some of hell's big muckety-mucks." She took a deep breath, let it out. "The short version is that our perp could've cut a deal with a demon lord, who can bind multiple demons, no problem. Though distance still could be a problem . . . but if the deal involved a demon prince, it wouldn't be."

Sickness settled in the pit of Lily's stomach. "Xitil."

Cynna nodded.

Xitil was the demon prince who'd made an ally of *Her* avatar, then fought her, then eaten her—and promptly gone insane. Demons didn't just eat the flesh of those they consumed. They absorbed something of the essence.

How much of the lupi's ancient enemy now lived inside a demon prince? Had someone here allied with that prince?

Lily pressed her fingers into the hollow where neck met skull, trying to dig out an incipient headache. "It makes too damned much sense. Xitil is controlled or strongly influenced by *Her.* Killing lupus heirs would suit Her. The one thing I can't figure is how She was able to track her targets. She's not supposed to be able to see lupi with her X-ray vision—or whatever it is She uses to see into our realm."

"Maybe the human perp has a strong farseeing Gift."

Lily frowned, mentally running through what little was in the dossier on Jiri. "What's Jiri's Gift?"

"I don't know. No one did, though we all tried to guess. I can say for certain it's a strong Gift, and it isn't Finding. I always thought she might be a precog—it was uncanny the way she could make things work out the way she wanted. But her Gift could be farseeing."

Lily heard the reluctance in Cynna's voice. "You don't want our perp to be Jiri."

"She wasn't . . . when I knew her; she wasn't a person who could do something like this."

"But you left."

"Yeah." After a moment Cynna shrugged. "I left, and I don't know what she's like now. If half the street talk about her is true, she's turned into a major badass."

Lily's brain felt sluggish, unable to keep up with the thoughts skittering around in it. She'd only gotten about three hours of sleep. But she could see Cynna was hurting.

New subject. "You don't have a coffeepot in here."

"Never touch the stuff, but there's a pot down the hall. You need a cup?"

Yes. "It can wait. Ruben is proceeding on the assumption the demons who weren't killed are still around. He's informed the authorities in Canada."

"What about the U.S. attacks? Where were they?"

"Montana and Virginia. The one in Montana occurred on federal land, so the Billings FBI office will handle it with some help from MCD. At least, Ruben hopes they can handle it." Lily was glad that call wasn't hers to make.

"And in the one in Virginia?"

"Near a little town called Nutley, on land owned by the Leidolf clan. That one's ours. Actually, it's yours for now, but I'll be joining you there as soon as possible."

Lily told Cynna about Leidolf and Nokolai and Rule's duty to escort Paul's body home. There was plenty for her to do while she waited for the body to be released—Dr. Fagin wanted to ask her some questions, and she had some for him and the other task force members. And she needed to pry some information out of the Secret Service. They'd traced some of Jiri's former associates in the course of their investigation—people who'd been students, hangers-on, or lovers, according to Cynna. Not apprentices. As far as Cynna knew, she'd been Jiri's only true apprentice.

Cynna seemed to think Lily's delay was reasonable, even necessary. And it was, dammit. But reason didn't ease her guilt. All those good, solid reasons weren't the only thing holding her in D.C.

There were details to settle: the need for a warrant if the Leidolf Rho didn't cooperate; the type of weapons to take; the type of backup. Cynna tried to argue about that. She didn't have a high opinion of MCD agents, and no one from the Unit could be spared.

Lily wasn't having it. "You're not going without backup. You need someone who can shoot an M-16. If they can use a rocket launcher, even better."

"They won't be much help if they get themselves possessed."

"You can't be the only Catholic with the Bureau. Or the only person of faith. That's what counts, right? Anyone with a strong, personal faith is protected."

"Yeah, yeah, but—"

"You mentioned coffee down the hall."

"And you'd like me to shut up and quit arguing." Instead of being offended, Cynna grinned. "See? This is why you're in charge, not me. Who'd I argue with if I was heading up the case? Come on. Let's get you some caffeine."

The break room smelled of old, burned-to-bitter coffee. Lily felt right at home. The cops she used to work with never made fresh, either. "In Virginia, I've notified the local police chief and the state cops, as required. But I told the state troopers not to go in yet."

"Good." Cynna nodded emphatically. "The last thing we need is a possessed state trooper."

"Which could happen if the demon's still there. Also, Rule says Leidolf is pretty territorial. If a dozen gun-toting heroes charge into their clanhome—"

"Could be a bloodbath."

"That was my thinking." She blew on her coffee, then took a sip. Tasted as bad as it smelled. "You'll need to check in with Chief Mann in Nutley when you get there. When I told him of a possible demon outbreak in his jurisdiction, he was inclined to doubt my sanity, but he did agree to speak to the Leidolf Rho."

"I guess the lupi didn't report the attacks."

"Good guess," she said dryly. Lupi weren't exactly known for cooperating with the authorities. "If the Virginia demon is still there, how hard will it be for you to Find it?"

"My range will be limited—probably closer to ten miles than a hundred. The pattern I got last night will let me Find other demons of the same type, but it won't be an exact match."

"Because they're different individuals?"

"Mostly because I took it from a corpse. Death doesn't res- onate strongly with life, even when the patterns match otherwise."

That made a grisly sort of sense. "There's one more thing you should know before you leave."

"What's that?"

"These demons are different from the red-eyes we tangled with in hell."

"Yeah, we covered that. They've got claws on those stubby little arms."

"That's right. They may . . ." Lily had to stop, take a breath. "Those claws seem to carry some kind of poison. Rule's wound . . . it isn't healing."

NINE

~

CYNNA insisted on going home with Lily before leaving for Virginia. Lily didn't argue as much as she should have.

Rule hadn't told her, dammit. She'd found out the wound wasn't healing when she saw blood on the sheet this morning. Not until then had he admitted something was wrong, and he still refused to see a doctor. He didn't think traditional medicine would help.

He was probably right. When she'd touched the ripped flesh, she'd touched magic. Orange magic, coating his wound like sticky syrup. Demon magic.

"The stickiness reminds me of a curse I touched once," she said as she climbed out of her car.

"You think it's a curse, then?" Cynna shut the passenger door.

"Gan doesn't think so." Unlike a lot of the others in Lily's life, Gan liked talking on the phone. The little demon had returned her call that morning.

Cynna followed her out of the garage. "So you talked to it? Ah—her, I mean. Do you believe her?"

"She can't lie." Yet. That was one of the treats in store for Gan if she converted to a more terrestrial body.

"Demons may not be able to lie outright, but they love to deceive."

"I don't see any advantage for her in deceiving me about this."

"So what did she say?"

"She says the . . . I can't pronounce the word she used. It's all consonants. But she meant the red-eyes. They're foot soldiers, bred to fight in demon wars. A few of them—the elite troops, like Special Forces—have something extra. Their claws exude . . . call it a poison. It interferes with magic, which blocks healing. She said . . ."

"Huh," Gan had said when Lily told her about Rule's wound. "You mean he isn't dead yet? I would've thought he'd have bled out by now."

Gan was nothing if not tactless.

Lily jammed her key in the back door. "The magic poison is fatal for less powerful demons. The stronger ones eventually throw it off. She thinks it probably works differently in a lupus, because your magic is different from a demon's. Or even," she added neutrally as she swung the door open, "that Rule's Lady is blocking some of it."

Lily preferred to ignore the subject of religion, but to Gan the Lady was fact, not belief. So were souls. Demons didn't understand souls, but they were fascinated by them.

She and Gan had that much in common. Lily didn't understand souls, either, though she knew now that something continued after death. Might as well call it a soul. She supposed the Lady was real, too . . . but she could think about that later.

"Back, Harry." She blocked her cat with her foot and edged inside, juggling messenger bag and laptop so she could punch the code into the alarm system.

Rule was upstairs. She didn't call to let him know she was home. He'd know.

"Even though the magic isn't a curse, it might work enough like one to be lifted that way. Or antihex spells might work." Cynna bent to give Harry a rub behind his ears. "Hey, big guy. These folks treating you okay?"

"Never well enough, in his opinion." Lily set her burdens on the table, slipped out of her coat, and draped it on the back of a chair.

"What did you mean about hexes and curses?"

"Hexes have a physical component. Curses don't. So if this poison is partly physical, it might respond to the same techniques that remove a hex. Any decent Vodun priestess can lift a hex—I can give you someone to call. If it's more like a curse, though, you want a faith-based practitioner like Abel or Sherry."

"Both of whom are going to be busy. Who else could do it?"

"Well, some Catholic priests are trained in removing curses, but these days it's rare. And I think their method works best if you're Catholic."

"What about Nettie, then? Or the Rhej? If faith-based healing works—"

"Isen is going to speak to her about it," Rule said from the doorway. He wore khaki slacks and nothing else. Even his feet were bare. Lupi didn't much feel the cold. "She may have something in the memories that will help."

"Will she come here if she does?"

The Rhejes were pretty much laws unto themselves, and the Nokolai Rhej in particular was known for never leaving Clanhome. She had reason for that, though, being over eighty and blind.

He shrugged. "We'll find out. Hello, Cynna."

"Hey, Rule. Would you believe Lily wants you to take off your pants for me?"

His eyebrow quirked up. "You do like to live on the edge."

"That's me. Edgy." Cynna grinned. "So drop 'em."

What flashed through his eyes wasn't as obvious as temper. "I appreciate the offer, but it isn't needed. I'm inconvenienced, not incapacitated . . . as I've pointed out more than once. If my body can't clear the poison on its own, in a week or so Nettie will fly out." He looked at Lily as if the subject were closed. "How did the big meeting go?"

"It turned out to be even bigger than I expected. I'll tell you about it, but first you tell me why Nettie can't leave Clanhome for a week."

"She's in Oregon, not Clanhome."

Lily's breath sucked in. "The twins?"

"Their mother went into labor last night . . . about the time the Change hit Paul."

There could be no arguing with Nettie's priorities. The entire clan had been worried about the fate of twins due to be born to a Nokolai man this month. The babies would need every ounce of skill the shaman—who was also a Harvard-trained physician—could offer. On the very rare occasions when a lupus sired twins, one or both babies almost always died right after birth.

Lupi kept more than one secret from the humans around them,

but the one they guarded most closely was the effect their innate magic had on their fertility. Some were completely sterile; many were nearly so. This was the reason for their promiscuity, their taboo against marriage, even the way their leaders derived their authority. A Rho and his heir had to be fertile.

Technically, Rule was fertile. He had a son. But Toby was the only child he'd sired in a lifespan almost twice Lily's, and he'd not play the bumblebee anymore, flitting from flower to flower to scatter his seed. Toby was probably the only child he'd ever have.

"Okay." Lily nodded. "I see why Nettie can't come. That makes it even more important to let Cynna see if she can help."

His eyebrow did that little lift that turned his expression mocking. "And is Cynna taking up healing now?"

Lily looked at Cynna. "You'll have to excuse him. I think the poison is leaking into this brain—testosterone poisoning, that is. He's turned all male and I'm-fine-don't-fuss."

Then again, he could mock without budging a brow. "You wouldn't know anything about that sort of thinking, of course."

"I'm no healer." Cynna was cheerful, as if she could ignore his sarcasm out of existence. "I probably can't fix this magical poison, or poisonous magic, or whatever it is. And Lily can tell quicker than anyone if it starts spreading, just by touching you. But I'm well-stocked with holy water, since I'm heading off to hunt a demon. It might work."

"I'm not Catholic."

"But I am, and I'm the one who will use it, so we've got the faith thing covered. Now, it's true that holy water doesn't work on all demons, so it might not work on demon poison. But it's worth a try, right?"

"I learned this morning," Lily said quietly, "that the demon's other victim—the man from the adult theater—died on the way to the hospital. They couldn't stop the bleeding."

"I believe he was human."

"Which is probably why he's dead and you're alive. But you're not healing."

His mouth flattened. For a second she thought he'd refuse, but he shrugged one shoulder. "Very well." His hands went to his belt.

Rule had about as much inherent modesty as her cat. He stepped out of his slacks as casually as Lily would slip off her shoes. At least he'd worn boxers today. "Do I need to remove the bandage?" he asked.

"Probably better." Cynna put her satchel-sized purse on the table and began rooting through it. "I need to get holy water directly on the wound."

So much for the boxers.

The demon had clawed his flank. Translated to this form, the wound ran from the top of his buttock diagonally across his hip, ending a few inches down his thigh. Awkward to bandage. She'd taped a pair of sanitary pads over it, that being the most absorbent thing she could find at six A.M.

There was only one pad now, taped on differently than before. And it was bright red, saturated with blood. "How many times have you had to change the bandage?" she asked quietly.

"Once. Which does not mean that I'm bleeding to death. Even a human wouldn't be bothered by such a small blood loss."

Lily bit her lip to keep back the sharp words she wanted to use and bent to pick up the slacks he'd dropped on the floor. Fear didn't bring out her best side.

Maybe he was afraid, too. Maybe that's why he was being such an ass about this.

He removed the pad. The wound looked fresh, with no trace of a scab. Blood welled up and trickled down his leg. A drop hit the floor.

"Question," Cynna said. "Is the poison carried by blood? If so, I'd better wear gloves. I'd rather not pick up a little demon poison accidentally."

"I didn't notice." When she'd inspected the wound earlier, it hadn't been bleeding this freely. "I'll check."

She went to him and bent to touch the rivulet of blood running down his thigh. "It's clean. While I'm here, though . . ." As gently as possible, she touched the flesh near the wound. Her breath hitched. "The contagion is spreading. I'm picking it up in the flesh around the wound now."

Rule touched her cheek. She looked up. His eyes were very dark, opaque to her. "Then it's a good thing you and Cynna thought of holy water. I apologize for my churlishness."

She swallowed. Nodded. And moved aside to make room for Cynna.

"You shouldn't feel anything other than wet," Cynna said as she came to stand in front of him, carrying a small glass vial. "But we're in experimental territory here."

He gave her a single nod.

She frowned, looking down at his bare hip. Her lips moved, but if she was praying, Lily couldn't hear it. She uncapped the vial and poured its contents directly on his wound.

Rule's face contorted. His hand swung out so fast it was a blur. And Cynna went flying backward.

TEN

HORROR froze Rule in place. Lily scrambled over to Cynna, who lay crumpled on the floor. Acid ate at his hip and thigh, a screech of pain shouting *enemy* and *hide, run, fight* . . .

"I'm okay," Cynna muttered. With Lily's help, she sat up. She gave her head a careful shake as if checking that it was still attached. "But, Jesus! You do pack a punch."

A punch. He'd hit her. He'd hit a woman.

"Good thing you slapped instead of making a fist," she went on, "or I'd probably be . . . Rule?"

He'd lurched to his feet. The burning in his hip made him unsteady, or maybe it was guilt spinning him into vertigo. He couldn't look at the woman he'd struck or at the one he loved. Quickly he left the room.

His ears weren't interested in what he could or couldn't deal with. They continued to report to him. He heard the two women talking as he moved blindly into the parlor—Lily asking where Cynna hurt, Cynna telling her, "Go on. I'm sore, but nothing's broken. I'm not so sure about him."

Broken. She was right. Something inside was broken, and he couldn't make it work right anymore.

Lily came up behind him. Without saying a word she put her arms around him. He stiffened. He didn't deserve comfort. She ignored the implicit rejection, laying her head on the bare skin of his back. And then she did nothing at all.

Her scent made the air sweet to him; the beat of her heart and the soft susurration of her breath were the only sounds. She didn't question or accuse or excuse. She just stood there, letting her body say things he wouldn't have listened to had she spoken them aloud.

His body listened. "It was pride," he said, not having planned to speak at all. "Pride. I didn't want to admit how little control I have. The wolf is always close now—too nearly in charge, too much of the time. I shouldn't have let Cynna near me. A wounded animal is dangerous."

"You tried to avoid it. We wouldn't let you."

"Because I hadn't told you what the real problem was."

The silk of her hair moved against his skin as she nodded. "You should have told me, yes. Now you have."

Something unlocked inside him and settled. He wasn't sure if he should call it acceptance or despair. "No questions?"

"Dozens," she assured him. "Think of this as the lull before the storm. The holy water hurt more than Cynna expected."

"Yes," he said dryly. Though the first shrill shriek of pain had faded to a steady throbbing, his hip certainly hurt more now than before she splashed him. "If we want to be optimistic, we can assume that means it accomplished something."

"The hell with optimism. I want to know." Her hand slid down his side.

Rule tensed. But when her fingertips traced the wound it was only pain he felt, simple physical pain. No instinctive rush to defend drowning out reason.

But he should have known instinct and reason would agree this time. The wolf was as bound to this woman as the man.

"It's scabbing over," she said.

He'd have felt more relief if she'd sounded happier. Rule turned to face her. "But . . . ?"

"The contagion isn't gone. The holy water diminished it. Diluted it," she corrected herself, as if precise speech could limit the danger. "It doesn't cover as much area, but there's a hard knot of it still, and . . . look. Look at your leg, Rule."

He did. His eyebrows rose. "Is it forming a scar?"

"Looks like."

Most of it was scabbed over, though the deepest part still oozed blood. The shallowest part of the scratch, on his thigh, was closed entirely . . . in a thin line of shiny skin. "Interesting. I've never had a scar."

"Adds to the machismo."

She was trying for humor. He helped. "Should be good for the image. What do you think? Should I take *Cosmopolitan* up on their offer?"

"What offer?"

"I believe it involves a bearskin rug. At least, something was mentioned about bare skin."

She rolled her eyes. "Speaking of which, maybe you could put your pants back on now."

He looked toward the kitchen. Humor drowned in a rush of need and guilt. "There's something I must do first."

"You need to do this naked?"

"Actually, yes." He detached himself gently and headed for the kitchen.

Cynna sat at the table, holding a bag of frozen peas to her jaw and scribbling on a pad. She looked up. "How'd we do? Is it gone?"

"Diminished. Repeated doses may eliminate it entirely."

"I've got more. We can—"

"No, we can't. Someone else will administer any further doses." He knelt in front of her, bowed his head, and closed his eyes.

"What are you . . . get up, Rule. Rule?" She smelled upset. Her voice shifted as she turned her head. "What is he doing?"

"It looks like he's submitting to you," Lily said.

"Kinky. But so not necessary. Rule, get up."

He spoke quietly. "My regret is not enough. My apology is not enough. I submit myself to punishment, payment, or penance."

"You're forgiven, all right?" She sounded panicky. "No payment or punishment or anything."

"Cynna." That was Lily. "I agree that punishment isn't called for, since he's beating himself up pretty well already. But you're Catholic. You understand the need for penance. His need, not yours."

"Oh." She took a deep breath. "From where I stand, we all made a mistake, not just you, but I can tell you're not ready to be reasonable. Only I'm clueless. I don't think assigning you an Our Father or two will help."

He'd allowed himself to be ruled by instinct. Again. A moment's thought, and he would have known to explain before he knelt; he wasn't supposed to speak once the ritual began. But that was unfair to Cynna, who was understandably confused.

"Lily," he said. "I can't speak to Cynna now, but you're clan. You may speak to her, if you wish."

Lily's voice was cool and thoughtful. "Am I allowed to ask you questions?"

"Yes." Though he'd have to be careful that his answers didn't suggest a particular response.

"If the Rho were here, what would he do?"

"He would ask, as I did, that Cynna choose penance, payment, or punishment."

"And if she chose penance?"

"He would ask if she wished to assign it herself."

"If she didn't?"

"If the Rhej wasn't present, he'd summon her." And that, he realized, was why instinct had led him to begin the ritual of contrition without explanation. Like the Rhej, Cynna was Lady-touched. For the first time he felt that in her, an indefinable stir of recognition.

Lily still had questions. "What would the Rhej do?"

"Assign penance."

Cynna snorted. "Oh, that's helpful, seeing that the Rhej is in California. I know—let's put off the penance bit until she can handle it."

Good try, but not an option. Once the ritual of contrition began, it had to be followed to completion.

"He's not moving," Lily observed. "I think we're going to have to wing it. Do you want me to ask him anything else?"

"I don't know. I can't think of anything." Cynna sighed. "This is like being called on in class when I didn't do the assignment."

For several moments no one spoke. Cynna broke the silence, her voice closer by a breath. She'd bent her head toward him. "It seems like you want forgiveness, but from yourself, not from me. So it isn't me you need to hear from." Her voice changed subtly. "Very well."

Her hand came to rest on the back of his neck, warm and dry. "For ten minutes a day, every day for a month, you will be wolf. While you are wolf, you will lie quietly, not moving, and consider the man who is also you. At the end of ten minutes, you will Change back."

Rule swallowed. He'd expected . . . he wasn't sure what he'd expected. Some version of a hair shirt, he supposed. But this reached deep inside, rasping against fears already raw. Changing every day would bring the wolf closer. If he couldn't relearn control . . .

He'd asked for this, though, hadn't he? Insisted on it. "I accept the penance."

Her hand left his neck. "Are we done?" Cynna's voice was back to normal. "I really need to hit the road."

"We're done." He flowed to his feet. "What made you choose ten minutes?"

She shrugged. "It just sounded right."

"That's the shortest time possible between Changes."

"Shit, did I do it wrong? I can make it—"

"No," he said. "No. I can accomplish the Change twice in that time." But most couldn't, and it would be painful. He supposed he'd gotten his hair shirt, after all. "You touched my neck."

Cynna grinned. "If I'd touched anything else, Lily would've swatted me. And she wouldn't have apologized afterward, either."

"That's part of the ritual."

Her eyes widened, then narrowed in a frown. "Don't go reading anything into that. The way your head was bent, it was the natural thing to do."

He smiled. Cynna did not want to believe she was Lady-touched.

Lily tapped him on the shoulder. "Here." She handed him his slacks. "I realize I'm the only one bothered by you running around naked. Humor me."

"Spoilsport." Cynna tucked her writing pad back in her over-size purse, which she slung on her shoulder. "I'll call and let you know where I end up staying. You suppose Nutley, Virginia, is big enough for a Holiday Inn?"

"It isn't," Rule said. "But Harrisonburg is close. Who's going with you? Abel?"

"No one you know. No one I know, for that matter. He's one of MCD's God-I-hate-magic types. He won't like me," she added, "but I probably won't like him, either, so that's fair. He's sup-posed to be a good shooter."

Rule shot a hard, questioning look at Lily.

"The Unit's stretched thin," she said. Her scent shifted—not to the pungency of fear, but to a more subtle mingling that signaled distress. "There's a lot I need to tell you, but it can wait until Cynna leaves. Is there anything she should know about Leidolf or its Rho?"

"Leidolf is . . . difficult," he said, stepping into his slacks. The movement pulled on his wound, but the scab held. "They're the largest clan, and the most feudal. Their Rho is Victor Frey—tall, fair, looks about sixty. Smart. Mean. Unpredictable. If you speak to him, be very polite. Victor isn't the sort of tyrant who respects those who stand up to him."

Lily shook her head. "Somehow *polite* isn't the first word that springs to mind when I think of Cynna."

"Hey, I can be respectful," Cynna said. "Especially if it was this guy's son who was killed last night."

"It was." Rule zipped carefully, since he hadn't bothered with underwear. "I didn't like Randall, but I wouldn't have wished such a death on him. And it creates problems. Cynna." He held her gaze with his. "I'd feel better if you'd wait to speak with Victor until Lily and I can join you. He can be unpredictable. I don't know how grief will take him."

"Unless he's crazy along with smart and mean, he won't mess with a federal agent. He may not cooperate, but a warrant will take care of that."

"We hope. Here." Lily tossed a key ring at Cynna. "Be careful."

Cynna caught the keys one-handed, included them both in a cheeky salute, and left.

Rule watched her go, then turned to Lily. He saw shadows beneath her eyes, but the shadows trapped inside them worried him more. Her face was calm, but she smelled of distress.

What was wrong? He helped the one way he could think of. "You have questions."

ELEVEN

"**THEY** can wait. I need to tell you about the meeting." Lily's chest felt full, as if inside the cage of ribs a storm was brewing, a cloudburst of words that might break any second. Yet she didn't know what she needed to say. To ask.

Something about the wolf . . .

Rule's eyes were dark and grave. And though he remained human, though his face and form and voice were calm, wildness seemed to shimmer inside him. She could almost glimpse the wolf hiding behind bone and sinew the way a wolf in the wild might peer out from the trees.

Was she seeing him differently because he'd admitted his wolf was close? Or had something changed inside her?

His words were prosaic enough. "Cynna is taking your car?"

"Hers broke down, and she needs to get to Nutley as quickly as possible." Though right this moment that seemed less urgent than the imminence in her chest, she didn't know what else to say. *Help me? I've swallowed my words and they're swelling up inside me.*

"Tell me." He was unaccountably gentle, as if he knew about the cloudburst and was asking for it rather than facts.

But facts were all she had. "Last night's power surge wasn't a local phenomenon. It happened all over the world, causing all sorts of problems and oddities. As I said earlier, the Unit's stretched to capacity and beyond. Goblins showed up in Missouri, brownies in Tennessee, and there may be a golem in Vermont. A school bus is missing in Texas. And, of course, we have demons to chase."

"That's why Cynna's going to Nutley with someone she doesn't know. There's no one from the Unit to send with her."

"Yes. Ruben has put together a task force to come up with an explanation and make guesses about the implications. He believes last night's power wind will happen again. That something fundamental has changed."

For a long moment he looked at her, the dark slashes of his brows drawn down in thought. Finally he spoke. "Have you eaten?"

She was telling him about the disasters stalking their world, and he wanted to know if she'd had lunch? "I'm not hungry."

"Healing burns a lot of calories. I need to eat whether you do or not. You talk. I'll put together sandwiches." He moved to the refrigerator and began pulling out the fixings. "Extra, extra, extra pickles, right?"

"You're going to make me a sandwich whether I want one or not, aren't you?"

He smiled at her over his shoulder. "Of course."

For no reason at all, that smile popped a bubble in her throat and words spilled out. "I missed pickles."

Rule, of course, looked puzzled.

"Not . . . me. The other me, the one who was with you while you were a wolf. I—I think she's trying to tell me something. Or maybe . . ." *Something about the wolf.* "She needs to tell you something."

Rule crossed to her, put his hands on her shoulders. "She *is* you."

"Sort of." Same soul, different memories. "I can't get it to come up to the top, but it feels important. If—"

The doorbell rang.

"I'll get it."

"Lily—"

"I'll get it," she repeated. And fled for the front door.

The house was familiar to her now. She knew where things were, could navigate the furniture in the dark. Most of the time she was glad to be here instead of in some bland and crowded hotel. And sometimes she felt as if the place were choking her.

These rooms held too much stuff. Beautiful stuff, of course: a Jacobean chest in the entry, a dining table whose dark wood gleamed beneath a crystal chandelier, a pair of Queen Anne chairs facing a plush sofa in the parlor. Excellent prints hung on the walls. Elegant arrangements occupied all the various surfaces—silk flowers, leather-bound books, candlesticks, brass or crystal whatnots.

Her mother would love it.

As Lily passed through the dining room she resisted the urge to sweep her arm along the sideboard and knock the cut-glass decanter, the shiny glasses on their silver tray, onto the floor.

Less stuff, she thought. *More plants.* She longed for at least one blank wall and air that smelled of the ocean.

She was homesick?

Maybe she wanted to be home so she could pull the covers over her head and hide from monsters, responsibilities, and change. Life was very simple with a blanket over your head.

She had to go up on tiptoe to see through the peephole in the front door. Whoever had installed it thought the whole world was at least five foot six.

What she saw had her rearing back in surprise.

The alarm was still disengaged. She unlocked the door, swung it open, and was hit with a second surprise.

The two people at her door must be planning to stay awhile. Each had a large duffel bag. The one she'd seen through the peephole was a man of average height with light brown hair. Those were the bits that looked normal. He was completely abnormal otherwise—head-turning, heart-stopping gorgeous, the most physically beautiful man she'd ever known.

Cullen Seabourne smiled at her. "Hello, luv. Look what I found."

The other person on her doorstep was much shorter than Cullen, too short to be seen through the peephole. He was cute, not sexy, and his smile lacked the cocky confidence of Cullen's.

He was eight years old.

"Hi, Lily," Toby said, his voice as wobbly as his smile. "Is my dad home?"

SO far, Toby's interrogators hadn't gotten any more from him than Cullen had.

Rule and Lily sat at the kitchen table with Rule's surprising son. Dirty Harry had plunked his fat ass next to Cullen, who'd taken over slicing roast for sandwiches.

"It wasn't hard." Toby's set jaw made him, for a second, a miniature of his grandfather. "I went on the Internet an' booked the flight. There's a box to check if you're a minor, so I checked it."

"How alarming," Cullen murmured. Toby looked so much like Rule, and Rule so little like his own father, that he'd never noticed the resemblance before. It was a matter of expression rather than bone structure, he supposed. And scent. No question about it—Toby was a dominant.

"What?" Rule snapped.

Cullen appeased the beast at his feet with another scrap of roast, then used his knife to point. "Look at him. Can't you see Isen's ghostly image floating over that cherubic young face?"

Toby joined the adults in frowning at Cullen. "My granddad isn't a ghost."

"It's a metaphor." Cullen turned back to the cutting board to send the knife whizzing through a tomato, leaving a tidy pile of slices. "That's when you say a thing is something else to make a point. Like saying it's raining cats and dogs when, in fact, nothing more amazing than water is falling."

"But why's it alarming if I look like Granddad?"

"Isen kept going back for seconds when they handed out stubborn. Got way more than his share." Cullen dealt tomato slices over the meat heaped up on the sub rolls. "I'm thinking you did, too."

"We've wandered off the subject," Rule said. "How did you book the flight, Toby? I'm unaware of any companies that issue credit cards to children."

Toby looked down. "I used yours," he admitted. "The numbers of it. I had them 'cause . . . 'member when you let me order that music?"

"I see." Rule's voice was utterly level. "Two months ago, you memorized my credit card number so you could use it again without permission."

"No!" Toby sat up straight. "I didn't . . . I mean, the computer 'membered the number, not me. I didn't know I'd need it. I mean," he said again, correcting himself meticulously, "I didn't *plan* on being bad. Only then I had to."

"Which brings us back to the original question," Lily said gently. "Why?"

Toby shrugged, kicked the table leg, and wouldn't look at any of them.

Poor kid. Wasn't it obvious? Cullen grabbed two plates and crossed to the table. "Me and my mum got along fine," he said. "It was my dad who couldn't deal with what I was."

Toby's serious face swung up toward him. "But your dad was a lupus! He knew what you were."

"He wasn't a sorcerer. Or even a witch, like my mother. Mum wasn't thrilled when I accidentally burned something— my Gift was greater than my control when I was young—but she didn't think I was too weird for words because I could see magic." He set a plate in front of Toby. "My father couldn't handle it."

Toby's eyes, dark and intent, fixed on Cullen's face. "Your dad didn't like you?"

"He didn't trust me." He said that as if it didn't matter, though after all these years that simple truth still stuck in his throat. "I possessed a power he didn't understand. He thought I ought to be able to give that up to fit into his world. And I couldn't."

Lily and Rule exchanged glances.

The house phone rang. "That's probably your grandmother," Rule said, standing.

Mrs. Asteglio hadn't been home when Rule called, but that wasn't surprising. She didn't think her grandson was missing; she thought he'd flown to D.C. to spend Christmas with his father. Exactly true, of course. She just didn't know it had been all Toby's doing, not Rule's.

Quite an achievement, really, Cullen reflected as he delivered two more plates to people with no interest in food. The boy possessed unsuspected talents.

Toby's lower lip jutted out. He opened the sub roll and gave full attention to removing the tomato Cullen had just placed there. "She's gonna be mad. I don't see why we can't just tell her you want me here."

Rule stopped in midstep, swung around, and knelt on one knee in front of his son, putting their faces on a level. He gripped Toby's shoulders. "I want you here." His voice was low and fierce. "I have always wanted you with me. You know that."

Lily looked at the two of them and went to get the phone.

"Hello? Yes, Mrs. Asteglio, he arrived just fine. The problem is that we didn't know he was coming."

Cullen took his own plate to the table and listened to both conversations—Lily explaining to the grandmother that they hadn't sent for Toby, and Rule explaining to his son the difference between wanting him here and allowing him to show up on his own initiative.

The boy certainly had shown initiative. Cullen took a bite of his sandwich. Toby had planned his adventure well, right up to the moment the stewardess expected to hand him off to a waiting parent. The jig would have been up then if Cullen's plane hadn't landed when it did—just enough ahead of Toby's for Cullen to be making his way down the concourse and hear a familiar voice.

What are the odds? he thought, taking another bite. Then he put his sandwich down, his eyes narrowing in thought.

Coincidences happen all the time. People run into someone from their hometown while thousands of miles away, or stand in line behind a stranger with the same last name. Statisticians worked their own sort of magic to show that these events were less remarkable than they seemed. In a country of 280 million people, you could expect a one-in-a-million event 280 times a day.

But the odds of encountering one specific person at an airport far from home at one specific moment . . .

Cullen *looked* at Toby.

No, that wasn't it. The boy's aura looked much as it always had—the magic a little stronger, maybe, but that was to be expected as he grew older.

It had been a wild notion, anyway. Patterning was a damned rare Gift, and as far as Cullen knew, he was the only Gifted lupus on the planet.

Lily promised to call Mrs. Asteglio back and hung up. Rule asked with a lift of his brows what she'd learned.

"She's upset, of course." Lily wore her just-the-facts-ma'am face, void of opinion. "We need to call her back when we've decided what to do so she can adjust her plans, if necessary."

Rule's eyebrows crunched down. "What plans?"

"Toby's mother was transferred to her wire service's office in Beirut. She flew there yesterday, so she won't be able to make it home for Christmas. Mrs. Asteglio decided to spend the holiday with her son and his family in Memphis. Toby . . ." She cast him a glance. ". . . objected. She thought he'd contacted you, and that you'd booked the flight for him."

A beat of silence followed. Rule looked at Toby. "I understand you were disappointed that your mother won't make it home for Christmas. But you *didn't* call me. Why not?"

Toby studied his shoes. "I dunno."

"You know I can smell it when you lie."

When Toby looked up, his stubborn expression reminded Cullen of a mule—or Toby's grandfather. "Grammy says Mom loves me, but she doesn't. She doesn't want to be around me 'cause I'm lupus. I want to live with you."

"Toby." Rule's voice held a helpless ache. "Your mother has refused several times to share custody, much less cede it to me. Changing that would mean a court battle, and I'm not in a good position to win."

"You think the judge won't like you 'cause you're lupus, but so am I."

"Which would become public knowledge if I sued for custody."

"I don't care! You love me. She doesn't. An' we could prove that to the judge, 'cause you're with me a lot more'n she is. And I know you have to go places sometimes, but during school I could stay at Clanhome with Granddad, so you could still do clan business."

"What about your Grammy?" Lily said softly. "She loves you."

Toby's lip jutted stubbornly. "She could come to Clanhome, too."

Oh, that was likely to happen. Cullen had only met the woman once, but once was enough to know she didn't like lupi any better than her daughter did. She did seem to care about the boy, which must set up a colossal inner conflict or two . . . richly deserved inner conflicts, in his opinion.

Rule sighed and stood. "We aren't going to settle this now, and, given recent events, it may be just as well for Toby to stay here for a while. We'll have bodyguards soon."

"Oh, God. I hadn't—" Lily broke off abruptly, shutting her mouth on whatever she'd been about to say. She and Rule exchanged another glance.

"It's possible," he said, just as if she'd asked a question. "Lord knows *She* is capable of any abomination."

Cullen's eyebrows rose. "I'm feeling sadly uninformed."

"Later." Rule was curt. He looked down at his son. "We've a matter of clan discipline to deal with first."

Lily shook her head. "This isn't about the clan."

Cullen had a feeling she was going to be difficult. He stood and headed for her.

Rule didn't look away from his son. "It is, and Toby knows that. Toby." His voice was hard now, as hard as his own father's would have been. "You came here hoping to force my hand."

He hung his head. "I—I guess so."

"By using my credit card without permission, you stole. You disobeyed and deceived those who have charge of you. You understand that there are consequences for your actions."

Toby gave a single, small nod.

"Kneel."

"Wait one minute!" Lily burst out. "He's—"

"Lily." Cullen took her arm. "Shut up."

She rounded on him. "He's a little boy!"

"Yes," Cullen said softly. "A little boy who, in another five years or so, will be capable of ripping out throats. Who will sometimes *want* to rip out throats, including, on occasion, his father's. Adolescence is trying for anyone. For a lupus, it brings perils you do not understand."

Lily opened her mouth. Shut it again. She aimed her frown at Rule, who hadn't taken his gaze from his son.

Cullen grabbed his plate. "Come on," he told her. "You and I need to talk about what brought me to your door." And Toby didn't need an audience.

In the parlor, Cullen plopped onto the couch—a fussy Victorian thing with a curvy back and too many pillows—and pointed at the painted armoire in the corner. "Is there a TV in that thing?"

Lily stared. "You want to watch television?"

"No, I want some sound. Toby's hearing isn't as good as it will be, but it's not a large house. He can probably hear us from the kitchen."

Lily stalked to the coffee table, picked up a remote, and pointed it. A rolling guitar arpeggio flowed from the armoire—Spanish flamenco, he thought, and took a bite of his sandwich. Either the channel was set to a radio station, or Rule had installed a CD player instead of a TV. Whichever, it ought to do the trick.

Lily paced the length of the room, turned. "That bitch."

It wasn't the subject he'd expected her to jump on first. "Which one?"

"Alicia. Toby's mother." She paced. "Two weeks ago, Rule asked Toby's mother if he could spend Christmas with us. She wouldn't even discuss it, but she doesn't feel any obligation to spend it with him herself."

He shrugged. "Alicia never should have been a mother. She hadn't planned on it, and I give her points for letting her mother raise him instead of botching the job herself."

"She could have let his father have him."

Lily's intensity roused his curiosity. He hadn't thought she was much more interested in motherhood than Alicia. "Is that what you want?"

She waved that away. "We're talking about what Toby wants. What he needs. Alicia doesn't seem to care about that."

"To be fair, Alicia believes she's doing what's best for Toby by limiting his exposure to our perversions. If her mother hadn't insisted that Toby be allowed to spend time with Rule, he wouldn't get even the brief visits he does."

"Alicia doesn't approve of lupi, but she went to bed with one?"

"Amazing. After working homicide, you still think people are consistent."

She lifted one hand, palm out. "All right, point taken." She brooded over the situation a moment, then asked, "Tell me why discipline means that Toby has to kneel to his father."

Still not the subject he'd expected. Maybe he didn't know her as well as he'd thought. "Toby's alpha. Rule has to remain his dominant, so when the boy hits his first Change and hormones collide with the moon's song and his brain shuts down, he'll still obey."

"But to make him kneel—"

"Quit being so damned human. Submission isn't humiliating. It's instinctively right for us, but humans do it, too. Does a sergeant feel humiliated because he has to salute his colonel?"

Her voice was dry. "He might, if the colonel made him prostrate himself first. How would you feel about kneeling to Rule?"

"Wouldn't do it," he said promptly. "But I'd kneel to my Lu Nuncio."

She looked at him a long moment, then shook her head. "Men don't make sense. Men who are lupi really don't make sense."

Her frown tightened down another notch. "Rule was uncomfortable after submitting to Paul, but I guess the act itself didn't bother him."

Cullen's eyebrows climbed. "Who's Paul?"

"It's complicated, and I'm getting things out of order." At last she sat, tucking one foot up on the chair with her. "It started with the power surge last night."

"Are we talking electrical power?"

"Magic. A big, fat whirlwind of it, unleashed at the same time all over the world, from what we can tell. You didn't feel it?"

He frowned. "The dragons were probably closer to the node than me when it hit. Greedy bastards must have soaked it all up."

"They can do that?"

"Like sponges. Remember how hard it was to work magic in their territory in Dis? Tell me about this power surge," he said, picking up his sandwich again. "I'll eat."

TWELVE

CULLEN did eat, but he didn't taste a bite. Demons, demonic poison, and the Great Bitch indulging in cross-realms assassination . . . the Lady speaking to an outclan know-it-all . . . a top secret task force investigating a mysterious power surge, and a top-notch precog who thought that was just the beginning. Even if he hadn't interrupted with questions here and there, the tale would have taken awhile.

Cullen's ears being better than a prepubescent boy's, he'd heard Rule assign Toby his punishment and send him upstairs, where he was to play on the computer until further notice. That wasn't the punishment, of course; Rule wanted to hear the game's sound effects so he'd know Toby hadn't snuck down to eavesdrop.

Harry joined them, staring at Cullen's sandwich with a twitching tail. Rule followed, though he gravitated to Lily, not roast. He settled on the floor next to her chair, and she rested a hand on his shoulder without pausing in her tale.

Cullen doubted she even knew she'd done it. The mate-bound were touchy-feely that way. He passed Harry a bite of roast.

When Lily finished, the *boing-boing* of Toby's game was still competing with Pepé Romero's guitar. For the first time since joining them, Rule spoke. "You didn't tell him everything."

"All that concerns him." Their eyes met. After a moment she said, "It's your decision."

He smiled, it evaporated when he looked at Cullen. "When Cynna dosed my wound with holy water, I hit her."

"Shit."

"Pretty much. My control has suffered ever since we returned from Dis. You need to be aware of that. You should also know that I submitted to the ritual of contrition."

His eyebrows flew up. "With Cynna? Bet that confused her."

"It did, but she handled it well. She's Lady-touched, Cullen."

Rule seemed certain. Cullen wasn't, but if the Lady had spoken to her . . . He frowned. He didn't like that, but for the life of him, couldn't see why it would matter to him.

Lily spoke. "Pretty much everything I've told you is highly secret. Repeat any of it and I'll have to pull out your tongue."

"I adore secrets. I'm fond of my tongue, too, as you would be if you'd let me—"

"I may pull it out anyway."

He grinned. It was fun to flirt with Lily. She disliked it so much. "Will you be in trouble if they find out you've told me all this?"

"Not unless you abuse the confidence." Her fingers drummed once on her thigh. "You said the dragons must have been closer to the node than you were. You're assuming this magic wind came from nodes?"

"That's where all magic comes from. Not that your friend Sherry will agree," he said, bending to put his plate on the floor so Harry could nose out any scraps of roast. "Wiccans believe the Earth inherently possesses magic, but they're wrong."

"Explain."

"I can't. The realms connect at the nodes, but I don't know enough about the way they connect to devise a coherent theory. But I've watched magic. They haven't. It comes from nodes, then dissipates in air and is absorbed by earth or water."

"If you didn't come here because you felt the magic wind, what made you abandon your dragon hunt?"

"Postpone, not abandon. I had a spot of demon trouble myself. Different model—"

"You were attacked?"

"Chased. I don't know what she had in mind if she caught me, though I'd wager I wouldn't have liked it. *She* meaning, in this instance, the demon's rider. No doubt, left to its own devices, the demon would have just killed me."

Lily's eyes widened. "Someone was riding it?"

"Not physically. What I saw was her astral form. That's drawn from the physical state, but it's not an exact mirror of the body. For example, amputations and most scars aren't reflected in one's astral form, and age is fluid. You won't project an astral body that's older than you are, but your projection might look a lot younger. Within those parameters, I can give you a description, if you like."

She did.

"Tall, very dark skin, thin but with wide shoulders and a prominent rib cage. No boobs to speak of."

"You're sure it was a woman, though?"

"There's another thing about the astral state—no clothes. I'm sure. Her hair was buzzed off close to the skull, and she looked about thirty, so she's at least that old. Tattoos everywhere."

"Then . . . but I thought scars didn't show up."

"These weren't regular tattoos. I'm thinking our Cynna knows her."

Lily didn't look happy. "It sounds like her old teacher, Jiri Asmahani. Which is *not* her real surname, just something she made up—and that's about all we know. We don't have a social security number, place of birth, parents. We don't know what her Gift is. Cynna's sure it isn't Finding, but other than that . . . it might be one of the elemental Gifts." Earth, air, fire, water. "Those are less formed, so they work best for spells, and Jiri is apparently hell on wheels with spells. But we don't know."

"A dark Athena, sprung whole from Zeus's brow," he murmured.

"What?"

"Never mind. I think I singed her, by the way."

"But she wasn't really there. She was, ah . . . what would you call it? Astrally present?"

"Mage fire reaches farther than ordinary fire."

"Cullen," Rule said.

That was all he said, but Cullen knew a rebuke when he heard one. He flung a frown at Rule. "I was being chased by a damned demon! What was I supposed to do—call my lawyer?"

"I thought you weren't going to use mage fire anymore."

"I agreed not to experiment with it. This wasn't an experiment."

Lily rolled her eyes. "We'll examine your verbal contract

later. I need to know the rest of the story. Where were you? And when did this happen?"

"This morning, at a little village called Los Lobos in Michoacán, Mexico."

Her eyebrows lifted. "The other attacks all occurred about the same time, shortly after the power surge."

"I'm special." When she rolled her eyes, he grinned. "Actually, I did experience something last night that might be connected to your magic wind—a tickling at my shields. I assumed it was one of the dragons, probably the one who calls himself Sam." He was still annoyed about it, too. "That would be when Cynna's Jiri got a fix on me. I'm betting she used the power surge to give her search a boost."

"But she didn't come after you then."

He shrugged. "Maybe she was busy coordinating the other attacks. Maybe she was sleeping or having sex or never misses *American Idol.* All I know is, around ten the next morning she showed up riding a demon the size of a tyrannosaur. They chased me into the mountains and kept finding me and finding me. Since running wasn't working, I decided to fight."

"You think you hurt her?"

"Maybe. She winked out the second the mage fire hit. The demon was slower to leave," he said with satisfaction. "I know I burned it."

"But did you kill it?"

"Probably not, but it's gone."

"Not necessarily." Lily leaned forward. "They can turn invisible, or very nearly so."

"Yeah, I know. You're talking about dashtu."

"That's the word Cynna used. The one that chased you might have turned dashtu. It could still be around."

"It's gone," he repeated patiently. "Dashtu doesn't affect my other vision." He chuckled, remembering. "I was talking with a couple of the locals when Jiri and her ugly pet sauntered up the street. I'll bet the village is still talking about the crazy American who took off as he were being chased by demons."

He remembered something else and looked at Rule. "I said that the village is called Los Lobos. That puzzled me at first—it's pretty far south for wolves. I figured out where the name came from just before I left. There's a lost one there, almost surely a throwback."

"Shit. How old?"

"Hasn't hit puberty yet, but he's close. We need to tell someone. Ybirra?"

Rule nodded and stood. "I'll take care of it. You have his name?"

He shook his head. "When I went back to the village for my things, I asked about him, but either my Spanish wasn't up to the job or they didn't want to tell the crazy man about one of their kids."

"Describe him."

"Five feet or thereabouts and skinny as a post. Probably had a recent growth spurt—his pants don't reach his ankles. Black hair, skin the same color as Sarita's . . . you remember her, don't you? Used to dance with me? Had the prettiest little ass, and—"

"Cullen," Rule said.

"Right. He's mestizo, of course, but looks pure Indian. You can't see the European side of his heritage in his face, though it shows in his height."

Lily was looking from one to the other of them. "Someone want to tell me what you're talking about?"

"Cullen can explain. I need to call the Ybirra Rho." Rule left the room.

Cullen looked at Rule's Chosen, the stubborn cop who'd been to hell and back for her mate. He felt a twinge of . . . something. Not jealousy, nothing so obvious or demeaning, but . . . *Never mind. It will go away.* "Basically, a lost one is a lupus who doesn't know what he is."

She frowned. "I thought the clans made sure of their children. Since you always know if you've sired a child—"

"We do, but there are two ways a lupus child can be born without the clan knowing. First, the father might die before registering the conception. Second, a lupus can be born to apparently human parents." A gossamer glow drifted by near Cullen's foot. He snagged it.

"Quit playing with your invisible friends and explain. Lupi can't be born to human parents."

"Apparently human." The sorcéri clung to his palm, but he couldn't hold it there long. Sorcéri were cobwebby strands of pure magic usually generated by a node, though the ocean or a storm could throw them, too. This one would either dissipate or soak into him in another couple seconds.

He wrapped his hand around his diamond. "Just a sec. If I don't feed it in right, I'll get dissonance."

"As in something might blow up?"

"Not yet." Blasting the demon had emptied his diamond, and it took days to refill the thing one wisp at a time. For that he needed raw magic; mage fire turned treacherous if fed by filtered magic. "There. Recessive genes," he said, looking up. "You know that only our male children are lupi. The girls still carry that heritage in their genes, however."

"Ah. I get it. You called that boy a throwback—the product of some recessives meeting up. But why doesn't anyone know this is possible?"

"Oh, you think we should make it public knowledge? Then they could develop a test, and mothers-to-be who didn't want occasionally furry offspring could abort any fetuses that—"

"You know very well that's not what I meant. Never mind. I assume this doesn't happen often."

"It's rare. The descendants of female clan are seldom fertile with each other. But if they do manage to get a zygote started, there's a decent chance the offspring will be lupus. These days we keep track of our children's children, but the conquistadores settled Los Lobos long before anyone knew about recessives."

"The Inquisition," she said suddenly. "Mexico was conquered before the Purge, but the Inquisition was getting going about then."

Her apparent non sequitur made him raise his brows. "Very good. You've been studying our history."

"I'm Nokolai now. I'm supposed to know this stuff." She drummed her fingers on her thigh. "Not that it's easy. Your people don't keep much written history. But the Rhej gave me an English translation of a sixteenth-century journal, and the lupus who kept it was worried about the Inquisition."

"With good reason," Cullen said. "Nokolai was centered in France then, but the inquisitors stuck their big noses in everywhere. The Spanish Inquisition was the worst. Spain mostly deported Muslims and Jews who wouldn't convert. Us, they killed. Extra points for burning us alive."

"They killed the Gifted, too," Rule said from the doorway.

Cullen didn't jump. He hadn't heard Rule—the son of a bitch was almost as good as his big brother at silent sneaking—but he'd caught Rule's scent. "And anyone else who was a little odd, on the chance they might be Gifted, but both Spanish clans were essentially wiped out. The boy?"

"Ybirra will see to him."

Cullen exhaled in relief. Harry jumped up on the couch and informed him with a head bump that petting was now allowed. Cullen complied.

"Wait a minute," Lily said. "If they had killed all the Spanish lupi, there wouldn't have been any to sire a lost one in the New World."

"Not all the lupi," Rule said. "Many, but not all. But somehow the Church learned the identities of the Rhos. They killed them and their sons—all of their sons, not just the heirs. Without a Rho, there is no clan, only lone wolves and a scattering of packs."

Lily's brow creased. "Packs. Wouldn't they be just small clans?"

"Packs are unstable. Without a Rho, most lupi go feral."

"Surely you have some system for a new Rho to be chosen in an emergency."

"Rhos aren't chosen," Rule said patiently. "They simply *are.* Each clan has some not in the direct line who can claim the clan's founder among their ancestors, but if the Rho and all his line are killed, those of collateral lines are unlikely to withstand the death shock."

"The *what*?"

"We're bound by blood to blood," Cullen said. "Didn't Rule explain that when I was brought into Nokolai?" *You are called to Nokolai by blood, by earth, and by fire . . .* The ritual words flamed in Cullen's mind, igniting a spasm of memory and emotion he fought to keep from his face.

Simplest to change the subject, and there were so many juicy ones to choose from. "You think that's the Great Bitch's goal?" he asked Rule. "Kill enough heirs and the clans are in trouble."

"So far, no Rhos have been attacked, however. And you aren't an heir."

"But I'm handy to have around."

Amusement glimmered in Rule's eyes. "True. Isen believes Her main goal is to block the All-Clan he's called."

"Isen sees everything in terms of his own goals. Doesn't mean he's wrong, of course. The Rhos aren't likely to risk their people by gathering so many of us in one spot for Her to attack."

A grim silence fell. Harry broke it to complain that Cullen had stopped petting. Rebuked, Cullen rubbed the beast's jawbone, and Harry cranked up his buzz saw.

Rule's eyebrows lifted. "That cat actually likes you."

"I'm a charming fellow."

Rule shook his head and settled on the floor beside Lily again. She laid a hand on his shoulder as she spoke. "There's still one Spanish clan, though, right? The one you just contacted. Ybirra."

Rule leaned back against her chair and rested a hand on her foot. "Ybirra is our newest clan. It wasn't recognized until long after the Spanish diaspora. Tomás Ybirra proved his claim at the 1882 All-Clan."

Touching. The two of them kept doing that. And why would that bother him? It didn't, he decided, and carried on with the history lesson. "Tomás Ybirra was born Leidolf. He was a full alpha who disagreed frequently with his Rho, especially over the need to gather the lost ones. Rather than Challenge, he went lone wolf until he'd collected enough strays to form his own clan."

"A lone wolf?" Lily said, surprised. "I thought—"

"We don't all go mad," he snapped.

"Don't be in such a rush to read my mind. You aren't good at it. I was about to say that I didn't know lupi ever voluntarily left their clans."

"It's . . . uncommon," Rule said quietly. "And *voluntary* isn't the best word, perhaps. But it does happen."

About once every century or so, Cullen thought. And no, *voluntary* wasn't the word he'd choose, but Tomás had been given a choice: submit to your Rho's will, Challenge, or be expelled.

So had Cullen, thirty-five years ago. "Returning to our own era, has it occurred to you that she may not be able to continue her demonic harassment?"

"I'd like to think so," Rule said dryly. "But what's stopping her?"

"Her agents acted at or right after the power surge. I'm no expert on summoning, but it's reasonable to assume they needed the extra juice."

"That would be more reassuring," Lily said, "if we knew the magic wind wouldn't blow through again next week. Or tomorrow."

"There is that." Cullen had some ideas about the cause of the power surge, but they weren't ready for prime time. He frowned. "Have you talked to the Rhej about this?"

She blinked. "Nokolai's Rhej? No. She doesn't have a phone, and I don't have time to fly back for a chat."

"But she's got the memories." About three thousand years' worth. If anything like this had happened before, she'd be able to access a memory of it.

"You're right," Rule said. "Isen was going to ask her about the demon poison. I'll ask him to question her about the power surge, too. But . . ."

"Rhejes don't always tell everything they know," Cullen finished. "It's one of their more annoying traits. I'll bet she'd speak to her chosen apprentice, though. We need to get Cynna to—"

"Can't," Lily said. "Not right away. She's headed for Nutley."

"Shit. She's gone after that demon."

"Someone had to, and she's qualified. I wish . . ."

"What?"

"Nothing. It's just that I don't know these people. But the backup I sent with her is supposed to be a good shooter and a good Baptist."

"Gifted?"

"Not even from the Unit. He's MCD. We've got too many fires and too few Gifted to put them out."

Pepé Romero ceased strumming. In the silence as the CD ended Cullen heard the frenzied pinging from Toby's video game. He thought about a tall woman with a butch haircut and ornate skin who thought too highly of her own abilities and too little of his.

But she sure smelled good.

Rule stood and headed for the armoire. "While I put some more music on," he said, "why don't you tell us why you're here? I'm thinking you didn't come running because a demon pestered you."

Cullen grinned. "You think right. I'm here because of what I realized while I was dodging Jiri and her pet. Someone's tampered with my memory."

"What?" Lily sat up straight. "But your shields—even Helen couldn't get past them with that damned staff to help her."

Cullen did not have fond memories of the former leader of the Azá, the cult devoted to the Great Bitch. Helen had been a powerful telepath; she'd also proved the dictum that insanity follows close on the heels of that particular Gift. Among other things, she'd had his eyes put out. "It must have happened before she got hold of me. Not long before, though. Probably the same day. I was her default choice, remember? They were hunting another sorcerer, one who'd visited me earlier that day. We quarreled—at least, that's the way I remember it. He left rather abruptly." Left Cullen unconscious, actually, but that embarrassment he preferred not to mention.

"So what did he do to you?"

"I don't know. That's the problem." Cullen brooded on that a moment. "I wouldn't have agreed to meet with him at all, but a friend vouched for him."

"Molly, wasn't it?" Rule said dryly.

"Molly's okay." Memories that hadn't been altered made him grin. "In fact, she's damned good, even for a succubus. But—"

"Wait a minute," Lily said. "You didn't say anything about a demon being there."

"Molly isn't a demon. She started out human. Now . . ." He shrugged. "Whatever she is, she got there by being cursed by the one we don't name, which seems to put her on our side." Though he wasn't as sure of that as he used to be. "Anyway, she wasn't there for sex that day. She set up a meet between me and this guy she'd hooked up with. Called himself Michael."

Greed had played a part in his agreeing to the meet, he admitted. He seldom had the chance to learn from another sorcerer. There were damned few of them, for one thing. And those few tended toward a high level of mutual distrust.

With good reason. "Anyway, the gap in my memory shows up right after Molly and her friend left, and right before the Azá came calling. Before then, no shields. Afterward, I had shields that could stop a high-powered telepath backed by an ancient artifact."

"But that's good."

"Sure, the shields are great. Not so great is that I can't remember how I came by them."

Neither of the others spoke for a moment, then Rule said, "You think this other sorcerer gave you these shields, then tampered with your memory? Why?"

"He'd have to have done it the other way around, but yeah. And I've no idea why. I've dug up some other snatches of memory—stuff that had been . . . overwritten, not erased. It's not complete." In fact, the memory bits were tooth-grindingly fragmented. "But I think Molly brought her friend to see me because they needed help. There's something about an active node and the FBI taking an interest." He flashed Lily a grin. "Which brings me to you, luv."

"You want me to find out what the Bureau knows about him, or her, or both."

"Yep. Molly Brown, Galveston, Texas. She isn't there now—I checked—and she's probably changed her name. The nodal activity would have been on or shortly before the seventeenth of October." He stood and stretched. "Lord, but all that flying, followed by all this sitting, has me stiff. Do you still take care of the clan's finances?" he asked Rule.

Rule hiked his eyebrows. "I do."

"Invest in silk. The price is bound to shoot up—it's a magical insulator. Gold and silver probably will, too, but—"

"Those aren't insulators," Lily said.

"No, they conduct or carry magic, which is why those won't shoot up in price for a while. Well." He twisted, ridding himself of the kinks. "Guess I'd better be going. Get that poison removed," he added, nodding at Rule. "Nasty stuff."

"Wait a minute," Lily said. "You just got here. Where are you going?"

"To give you a hand with your little demon problem, of course. That's fair—you help me, I'll help you."

She huffed out a breath. "I haven't agreed yet. What will you do with any information I pass on about Molly Brown or Michael no-last-name? Assuming there *is* something to pass on."

"Bound to be a report—bureaucracies thrive on 'em. Cross out anything too terribly secret and pass it on to me. Shouldn't take long. As for what I'll do . . ." His frown came and went. He shrugged. "I don't know yet. Find him, obviously. Don't you want to know the whereabouts of a sorcerer the Azá—and, by extension, our enemy—were interested in?"

Lily didn't speak, but he could almost hear her busy little mind totting up possibilities. "All right," she said at last. "I'll see what I can find out. In return, I want your promise that you won't take off on a vendetta."

"I'm not after revenge." A flash of honesty mixed with anger made him add, "Not major revenge, anyway. I wouldn't mind bloodying the bastard's nose, but anything more would depend on his reasons for messing with me, then taking off to leave me to deal with his chums." A yawn overtook him.

"You can have the west bedroom," Rule said.

"Thanks, but I'd rather borrow your car."

"I need my car."

"Then Lily's."

"Cynna's using it," Lily said. "I thought you were going to give me a hand with my little demon problem."

His eyebrows flew up in surprise. "I am. I'm off for Nutley. Cynna might be up to handling a demon, but a demon *and* Victor Frey? And maybe Brady. He could be around, too." The woman didn't know half as much as she thought she did, and her much-decorated skin smelled too good to let a demon rip it up.

Or anyone else.

There was a beat of silence. "I'll rent a car for you," Rule said.

THIRTEEN

"**WELL,** now, if there is a demon around, it's the quiet type." Chief Mann leaned back in his creaky office chair and laced his hands over a stomach Cynna could have used for an ironing board. If she ironed, that is. He treated them to a laid-back grin. "Hasn't stirred up any trouble."

Nutley was small. The town boasted a single traffic light; the speed limit was twenty-five. Jail and cop shop shared space in the basement of the courthouse, a stout redbrick building that held down one end of Main Street.

Cynna felt as if she'd accidentally wandered into Mayberry.

Not that Chief Mann resembled Andy Griffith. No, he was a manly Mann, six feet of the sort of sculpted muscle body builders love to see in the mirror. But he had the folksy bit down pat, and he was sure white enough for Mayberry. So was every other cast member she'd seen so far. Kind of weird in a little Southern town. "Aside from killing Randall Frey, you mean."

"Don't know exactly what happened to Randall. His father didn't say."

Agent Timms snapped, "And you didn't think it was worth asking."

If Nutley's boss cop was Andy, then Cynna had brought Opie with her—a quarrelsome, grown-up version of Opie, that is. On uppers. MCD Agent Steve Timms was short, wiry, and wired.

His boyish face, complete with red hair and freckles, clashed with his passion for weapons. She'd heard more than she ever wanted to know about the properties of the M72 LAW they'd borrowed from the Army—LAW being one of those cute acronyms government types adored. This one stood for Light Anti-Tank Weapon.

But he also knew how to use a dart gun. He used to shoot lupi with one, back before the Registration Act was ruled unconstitutional—and he'd survived, which said a lot for his skill. Darts were their fallback weapon. If the demon had possessed someone, they'd need to tranq the host.

Cynna didn't think they'd need it. Some demons loved the opportunities afforded them by possession, but if this one was like the one she'd killed last night, it was all fight, no stealth.

She'd been wrong about one thing, though. Timms didn't dislike her. Not when she was his ticket to the biggest, baddest quarry he'd ever sighted down on. He was all aquiver over the prospect of bagging a demon.

Chief Mann shrugged those impressive shoulders. He wore an old flannel shirt, jeans, and boots. "None of my business. The law's got nothin' to say about what happens to a wolf."

"So Randall was killed in wolf form." Not surprising; Rule had Changed, too, when faced with a demon. Still . . . "Did you see the body?"

That amused him. "Yes, ma'am, I did. It was pretty torn up, but a torn-up wolf doesn't much resemble a human."

Cynna fought the urge to tell him to quit calling her ma'am. He'd probably just start calling her honey or sugar, and then she'd have to hit him. That was not the way to get along with the locals, and besides, she had a headache.

She was no healer, couldn't do a thing about her swollen jaw. But she did have a nifty little spell that blocked pain, though it only worked on her. Had to be careful with it, since pain was nature's way of saying, "Watch out," but a little more power should be okay. She upped the trickle feeding the spell. "Did you ask Victor Frey who or what killed his son?"

"Course I did. Told that other FBI agent I would, didn't I? Victor said he didn't know."

"Did you get a description?"

"He didn't see the killer."

Cynna nodded as if he'd said something reasonable. "Did you

ask any of the others? Like, say, someone who'd actually witnessed the killing."

"Appears Randall was alone when it happened."

Timms snorted. "And you believed that."

Chief Mann looked at him. "They're always alone when one
of 'em kills another one, son. Doesn't pay to get your panties in
a twist about it."

Timms leaned forward, all but vibrating with intensity. "It
seems to me you've got a pretty cozy relationship with this werewolf, Chief. Makes me wonder if you're getting paid to look the
other—"

"Hey." Cynna tapped his arm. "Chill. You're out of line."
She'd never been the one to put on the brakes when it came to
harassing the local cops. Wouldn't Abel just bust something
laughing if he could see her now?

Timms gave her a hard look, but he settled back in his chair.

"I'm hoping you can drive out to the Leidolf clanhome with
us, Chief," Cynna said, trying a big smile to see if that helped.

Ouch. Apparently big, wide smiles were out for the time being. She resisted the temptation to pump up the power into the
pain-blocking spell. "I'd appreciate being introduced to the Rho.
I've got a warrant, but I'd rather not use it if I don't have to. I'm
hoping he'll cooperate."

"Well, that's good thinking—Victor doesn't like feelin' pushed
around. But . . . clanhome? Rho? You speakin' English?"

Could he really know that little about the lupi living so close
to his town? "Victor Frey is the Rho or leader of the Leidolf clan,
which has its clanhome—uh, the land owned by the clan—just
outside Nutley."

"Victor's in charge, all right," he said, nodding. "And he owns
a few acres. I don't know about that clanhome stuff, but I can take
you out to see Victor." He reached for the Stetson hat on the corner of his desk, unhooked the bomber jacket draped over the
back of his chair, and shot a glance at Timms. "Y'all be polite,
though. He's suffered a loss."

Cynna snagged her tote and followed. The tote held several
vials of holy water packed in a foam wedge. The vials were specially made, designed to shatter on impact. It was usually best to
apply holy water to a demon from a distance.

Pity she hadn't done it that way with Rule.

They stepped outside into light burnished to gold by the setting sun. The air was chill and dry, and winter-bare trees and white clapboard buildings dragged long shadows behind them. Somewhere a dog barked, over and over, in tired repetition. On three sides of the little town a rolling stack of browns and greens climbed the mountains to a lumpy blue horizon. In the west the hills were dark, blackened by the glare of the descending sun.

Dammit. It was nearly five o'clock. The drive down here had only taken a couple hours, but before leaving D.C. she'd had to change into something better for hunting demons than her got-a-meeting clothes, pack a bag, and collect Timms and his arsenal. By the time they finished talking to Victor Frey, it would be fully dark. Cynna wasn't crazy about chasing a demon at night.

Maybe she wouldn't have to. So far she hadn't Found any lurking demons. Surreptitiously she raised a hand and did a cast, not putting all her power behind it, just running a quick check. Even with only a partial pattern, she ought to Find it if it was within a mile or three.

"You tryin' to flag a taxi, ma'am?" Manly Mann was amused.

"No." Still no trace of a demon. Maybe Timms was destined for disappointment. "We'll follow you out," she said, "if that's okay."

He gave an amiable nod and headed for his cop car in the middle of the reserved spaces in front of the courthouse. Cynna spoke firmly to Timms as they made for the public lot across the street. "We're not here to investigate the chief."

Timms scowled. "If he's in bed with those werewolves—"

"Our assignment is the demon," said Cynna, who had been in bed with a werewolf and had liked it very much, thank you. "If it's still around, we kill it. Whether it's here or not, we need to talk to those who saw it, check out the scene, examine the victim's body . . . you know. Investigate. We'll need Victor Frey's cooperation for that, and the chief can help us get it."

Timms muttered something under his breath Cynna pretended not to hear.

A few courthouse employees had jumped the gun on quitting time. A dumpy woman was cranking up her shiny red Mustang as Cynna and Timms reached the parking lot; two men carrying briefcases got into matching SUVs. A battered pickup pulled out of the lot.

One car was arriving, not leaving. A white, late-model Camry with D.C. plates turned into the lot and parked in the empty spot two spaces down from the Ford Cynna had borrowed from Lily. Cynna glanced at the driver as he climbed out, then stopped dead. Her hormones did the Snoopy dance.

Cullen Seabourne stood there grinning at her. His T-shirt was old and tight, his denim jacket in worse shape than hers, and his jeans worn threadbare in interesting places. Two days of stubble decorated that impossibly gorgeous face, and he'd needed a haircut at least a month ago.

At least one person here was dressed worse than she was, even if shabby looked a lot better on him than it did on her. She parked her hands on her hips. "Well, hell."

"Been there, done that," he said cheerfully. "You going to introduce me to your sidekick?"

"What are you doing here?"

His eyebrows climbed. "Isn't it obvious? I'm going to help you bag your demon."

"It's not my demon, and you are not—"

Timms spoke right over her. "Who is he?"

She rolled her eyes. "Agent Timms, Cullen Seabourne. Cullen's a lupus," she added, not sure which of the two men she wanted to needle but figuring they both deserved it.

Timms narrowed his eyes at Cullen. "You don't look like part of the Unit."

"Oh, no," he said blithely. "I help out when I can, but the FBI isn't interested in my professional skills. I take my clothes off for a living."

CYNNA told Cullen he wasn't going with them to speak to the Leidolf Rho. She told him to go back to D.C., where he might be of some use. She was firm. She let him know his help was not needed.

So why was he sitting next to her in the backseat of Lily's Ford while Timms drove?

Well, she did know why she'd let Timms get behind the wheel. She wanted to be free to do a cast every so often. But how, exactly, had the man with the face of a god and the morals of an alley cat ended up in the car with them?

Surely she hadn't caved in to her body, which really appreciated being close enough to reach out and touch. Because she was so not touching him. No way, no how. She was working, dammit.

Besides, he was a jerk. Oh, not an all-around jerk. She admitted that. Cullen had risked everything to rescue Rule, so he had friendship potential. But where women were concerned, he set off her jerk-o-meter.

Cynna knew a jerk when she lusted after one—which was usually, she admitted. Rule was the single, shining exception to her lousy taste in men. Not that she was looking for Mr. Right. She couldn't imagine pledging to live with one person for her entire life. It boggled her brain that people did this regularly. How could they possibly *know*?

But she was tired of waking up with yet another Mr. What-Was-I-Thinking. She meant to change that, even if her stupid hormones hadn't yet signed on with the plan. "Victor Frey may not allow you on his land."

"Victor thinks I'm scum," he agreed. He sat in a comfortable sprawl that took up more than his share of the seat, with his knee nearly touching her thigh. "But that means he'll think he can use me. Victor gets off on using people."

"Guess we'll find out soon." The cop car ahead of them turned off on a dirt road marked by a small sign that read, Private Property. Keep Out. "Don't they have guards, like at Nokolai Clanhome?"

"You won't see them unless they decide to stop us. You haven't picked up any trace of the demon that killed Randall?"

She shook her head. "My range is limited, though, because the pattern's from a dead demon, and I'm looking for a live one. Also, I haven't done a full cast yet—just quickies."

They turned onto the dirt road. Its ungraded surface trended mostly upward, winding through a slew of trees.

Cynna was a child of the city. She didn't really approve of trees. Not *wild* trees, anyway, and not in such numbers, and especially not when they held hands overhead as if they wanted to be ready to drop a branch on intruders.

Enough with the trees, she told herself. "Uh . . . I guess Lily and Rule briefed you."

"Thoroughly enough that she felt obliged to threaten my tongue. That's her gentle way of suggesting I don't discuss top secret secrets in front of those who lack my wisdom and discretion." He wiggled his eyebrows at the back of Timms's head. "Speaking of being briefed, did Rule warn you about Victor Frey?"

"Said he's mean, smart, and hard to predict."

"That's one way to put it. Victor's a treacherous son of a bitch. He'll try to charm you."

"I'm hard to charm."

"Pretend, then. He doesn't expect much from women, so you can lull his suspicions that way, and you're going to need every advantage you can get. If you'd sleep with him, too—"

"What?"

"Okay, that's out. Not that I blame you, but for some reason a lot of women have slept with Victor—or not slept, as the case may be, but I'm trying to be tactful. Did Rule mention that Victor's surviving son and possible heir is crazy?"

Her eyebrows shot up. "You're talking figuratively?"

"No, I'm pretty sure that's the literal truth. Brady Gunning is a sadistic sociopath."

"Gunning? Isn't he a Frey, too?"

"Not unless he's named heir. Mummy and Daddy don't marry when Daddy's a lupus—you know that. So we carry our mother's surname."

"Rule doesn't."

"An accepted heir usually adopts his father's surname."

So Rule hadn't started out as a Turner. Maybe that's why the FBI had never been able to dig up much about him before he "came out" as the Nokolai prince. "Will this Brady Gunning be there today?"

Cullen shrugged. "If not, he'll show up soon. Leidolf Clanhome is smaller than Nokolai Clanhome. Not many clan actually live there, but most are close by. They'll be descending on their clanhome for the naming."

"The naming. Of the new heir, you mean?"

He nodded, frowning into space as if he'd half forgotten she was there.

Which was another good reason not to touch. Cullen Seabourne was fantastic fling material, and she'd been tempted to pursue that option when they first met. But then she'd gotten to know him. In between hot, sweaty bouts of sex he was likely to forget you existed.

Not that it mattered, since she wasn't going to have hot, sweaty sex with him. She dragged her thoughts back to business. Cullen hadn't answered her question about why he was here instead of chasing dragons, but Timms was listening. She'd ask again when they were alone.

In the meantime, she might as well see if anything nasty was hiding in all those trees. Cynna trickled power into the *kielezo* for the dead demon, letting it itch there a moment as it built. Then she held up her hand, and—"Ow!"

They'd bounced over a rut so hard she'd hit her head on the roof.

"Sorry." Timms didn't sound sorry.

Cynna scowled at the back of his head. The headache she'd already started on ached in earnest now. "Slow it down. I can't do a cast if I'm bouncing off the roof."

"What does it matter? You haven't found anything."

Sitting in the driver's seat seemed to have gone to his head. "Slow. It. Down."

"Rebellion in the ranks," Cullen said sympathetically. "Want me to bite him for you?"

Timms's shoulders twitched.

"Better not," Cynna said. "He'd shoot you, and Lily would be pissed if we got blood all over her car."

Cullen grinned. "No, he wouldn't. Not before I—"

"Cullen—"

"Shut the fuck up," Timms said.

She swung toward him. *"What?"*

"Him. Not you. I'm not working with a damned werewolf. A damned werewolf *stripper.*"

"Yes, you are. You know why? Because I'm in charge." Good Lord. Had that just come out of her mouth? If she didn't watch it, she'd be telling him she was the decider, and then she'd have to wash her mouth out with soap.

"I know I can't be possessed," Timms said. "You say you've got faith, too, so you're safe. But him?" Timms snorted. "If a godless heathen of a werewolf gets possessed, he's gonna take us both down."

"No worries," Cullen said, leaning back at his ease. "This particular godless heathen can't be possessed."

"You know that, Timms," Cynna said, exasperated. "At least you should, since I told you on the way out. Lupi claim they can't be possessed. You'd better hope that's true, since we're going to be around a number of lupi, and it would be real inconvenient if the demon was in one of them. And while we're there, you're going to be very, very quiet. I don't want your prejudices screwing things up."

Timms breathed his way through a few moments of silence. He sounded more grumpy than truly pissed when he spoke. "If I slow down, I'll lose sight of the chief's car."

"Not a problem," Cullen said. "The road leads to Victor's place. Can't miss it."

Cynna looked at him. "You've been here before."

"Not lately, but yeah, I have."

He didn't signal discomfort—no frown, tensed muscles, averted eyes. His voice didn't go flat or sharp, and every luscious inch of his body stayed easy, announcing how little the subject mattered. So why was she struck with the notion that this rutted tree tunnel was memory lane for him, and damned unpleasant memories at that?

She thought of a neighborhood in Chicago and how she'd feel if she returned there accompanied by people from her new life. People who thought she was basically okay. The last thing she'd want would be for anyone to notice her reaction. "Is it normal for there to be this many trees?"

He blinked. "You've heard of forests?"

"I've even been in one." They'd been looking for an eleven-year-old girl . . . She pushed that memory aside. "But it had space between the trees, and those trees were a lot taller. These are all tangled up together. They lean out over the road."

"Leaving aside whether we can call this a road—" They hit another bump for emphasis. "This is a deciduous forest that's been logged in the past. What you're seeing is new growth, which includes a lot of shrubby stuff. Older forests, especially conifer forests, have less competing growth."

"Yeah, these trees are so into competition they've decided to take on the road. They're trying to push it right out of here."

"Oh, please. Don't tell me you're one of those idiots who personifies everything."

"Hey, personification is a tool in some magical systems. And Wiccans and other pagans say plants do possess intent, so—"

He snorted. "You've been watching Saturday morning cartoons. Plants lack the sense of self it takes to form independent will, though en masse they sometimes develop an accreted version of consciousness. But it's ridiculous to ascribe human motives to them."

She settled in to enjoy the argument. "I'm a simple kind of a gal. Even if these trees aren't aware in the sense we understand it, they might have a dryad or something guarding them."

"A dryad?" he repeated, disbelieving. "In a new-growth forest this close to civilization?"

She waved a hand. "Okay, not likely. But a number of African, Celtic, and American Indian traditions claim trees have spirits that people can communicate with, right? There are tons of legends about it."

"Legends are mostly allegorical. Which means," he explained kindly, as if to a three-year-old, "that they're not meant to be taken literally."

"I kind of get the difference between symbolic and literal truth. Hard to work a spell without some grasp of symbolism, isn't it? But maybe the tree spirit bit is literally true. I know a shaman who sacrifices to the oak in his backyard every new moon by burying tobacco leaves at the roots."

"Shamanic practices connect the practitioner to major and minor earth spirits or gods, not individual trees."

"*He* says he's contacting the tree, not some all-purpose spirit."

"He's mistaken. Oh, his oak probably does have power. Trees soak up a fair amount of magic over the years, but not everything that possesses magic is sentient. Or do you think crystals are alive and plotting against you?"

She rolled her eyes. "Sarcasm doesn't prove anything. Don't you feel something menacing about these trees?"

Not only did he not sense any menace, he thought she was an idiot. Which she was perfectly willing to debate, too.

Cynna had known Cullen wouldn't need much encouragement to argue. That's what they usually did. It made for a nice distraction the rest of the way to the clanhome, and not just for Cullen. Timms was so busy eavesdropping that he drove slower and didn't say a word.

Maybe she wasn't completely inept at the in-charge thing, after all, even if her methods were unconventional. They reached their destination without a drop of blood being spilled.

Leidolf's home territory didn't look much like Nokolai's version. The road took them to a clearing about the size of two football fields laid end to end. She saw four buildings, total: a barn, a long, one-story structure like a bunkhouse, and two houses. The first house was small and built from gray stone. Smoke trickled up from the chimney. Across from it, three pickups and a car were parked in front of the bunkhouse-type building.

They were headed for the larger of the two houses, a two-story structure at the far end of the clearing. Two vehicles sat in front of it—a two-year-old Bronco and the chief's cop car.

"Are there any more houses?" she asked Cullen. "Hiding back in the trees, maybe?"

"Not that I know of. Leidolf is poor compared to Nokolai, but they could afford more housing here. Victor doesn't want that. He doesn't trust the mainstreaming movement, doesn't want his wolves coming out of the closet, and anyone living here is admitting he's lupus."

Victor Frey's house had all the charm of a big, white box. The wide front porch was its only grace note. There was a detached garage on the near side, and she caught a glimpse of a swing set on the other side before they pulled to a stop.

Chief Mann was leaning against his car, chatting with another man—tall, blond, and bony, with a tidy mustache and old jeans. No shirt, no shoes, nice chest. He looked about thirty. Had to be a lupus, but not the one she'd come to see.

"Shit," Cullen said.

"What?" She paused with her hand on the door handle.

"That's Brady, the local sociopath. Timms—"

"What?" Timms snapped.

"Brady's nuts, but he knows how to hold a grudge. If he can't get you now, he'll get you later, and he thinks an eye for an eye isn't nearly enough. Don't insult him."

"I'm a federal agent. He'd better be polite to me."

Cynna shook her head. "So does testosterone make fools of you all. Behave, or at least be quiet."

Cullen cocked an eyebrow. "You've read Shakespeare?"

"Hey, I'm not illiterate. No warnings for me?"

"You're a woman. His expectations will be different. But if he asks you for sex and you turn him down, do it with regret."

She snorted and opened the door.

FOURTEEN

CHIEF Mann turned to nod at her, still leaning casually against his car. "Brady, this is the federal agent I was telling you about. Agent Weaver, this here's Brady Gunning. He's the brother of the deceased."

"I'm sorry for your loss, Mr. Gunning."

"Randall's no loss to me. Couldn't stand the bastard." He gave her a thorough once-over. "I never saw anything like you before. What are you?"

"An FBI agent." Cullen and Timms got out. "And this is—"

"My, my. Cullen Seabourne, and on Leidolf land." Now he smiled.

Nasty, she thought. Maybe Cullen hadn't exaggerated. "I'm here to speak with your father, Mr. Gunning."

Gunning's head turned toward her slowly, as if he were reluctant to take his eyes off Cullen. But he didn't look angry. Instead, his face was snake-empty.

A second later he'd slipped on a smile, as if remembering that was what people did. "But does he want to speak with you?"

"Why don't we find out?" She started for the porch.

He stepped in front of her, moving a little too fast for a human. His smile was warmer now, frankly sexual. "I didn't hear you say 'pretty please,' pretty lady."

She raised her brows. He was a full head taller than her, which was unusual and annoying. Made it hard to look down her nose at him. "It's my understanding that this property belongs to your father, Mr. Gunning. Not you."

"So?"

"So I don't need your permission." She stepped aside to go around him.

"*He* does." Gunning didn't look at Cullen, but it was obvious who he meant. "He needs my permission to go on breathing."

"Brady," Chief Mann said mildly, "you see anyone here who isn't shaped like a human?"

"I smell something that—"

"The law doesn't take account of what you smell." He straightened, moving away from the car. "You remember that. Agent Weaver, is this one of your people?" He nodded at Cullen.

Great. If she said no, she could ditch Cullen now . . . leaving him out here with a sociopath who didn't like the way he smelled. "Mr. Seabourne's a consultant."

Chief Mann sighed. "Wish you'd told me about him ahead of time. Let's go see if Victor's up for company." He headed for the house.

Cynna and the others fell in behind him. She was conscious of the blond lupus standing perfectly still, watching them with those dead-empty eyes. *Stone killer,* she thought—the kind that scared her worst, because you couldn't handle them, reason with them, get on their good side. They didn't have one.

She told herself that big, tough FBI agents didn't break out in a sweat when they walked within grabbing distance of death. But death reached for Cullen, not her.

Only Cullen wasn't there.

She'd never seen anyone, human or lupus, move that fast. She wasn't sure she'd seen it now. Cullen stood three feet away, smiling. "No touching, Brady. You're not my type."

"From what I hear, anything's your type, if it stands still long enough," Gunning said. "Stay away from the dogs while you're here."

Cullen kept smiling. *"Vesceris corpi."*

Gunning lunged for him.

It was like trying to track a hummingbird. Cullen slid aside so fast he seemed to teleport. "You want to Challenge, Brady?"

"Boys," Chief Mann said from the porch, "I don't think Victor would appreciate your squabbling right now."

Cullen looked at him incredulously.

Gunning spat in the dirt. "I don't Challenge a cow turd if I accidentally step in one. I just scrape it off my boot." He turned and stalked off.

Cynna remembered to breathe. The manly Mann had gone up in her regard.

"Think Gunning will try something?" Timms sounded hopeful. No doubt the possibility of shooting something cheered him up.

"Oh, yeah," Cullen said. "But not here and now. Too many witnesses."

"Come on," Cynna said, starting for the house. As Cullen fell into step beside her, she muttered, "Be polite, he says. Don't insult the crazy man. Remind me to kick your ass later."

"Sure. Did you say kick, or lick?"

"Maybe I'll do it now." That was just talk, of course. This wasn't the time for ass-kicking. Or for questions, and she was accumulating a goodly pile of questions for Cullen Seabourne.

As they reached the porch she caught the tune Timms was whistling: "The Battle Hymn of the Republic." Just the thing to endear him to Southerners.

Maybe she should shoot them both.

The porch was painted, wooden, and empty. "Sorry about that," she said to the chief. "I didn't realize my consultant had a history with Gunning."

Chief Mann pressed the doorbell. Dimly she heard it chime inside the house. "You want to watch out for that Brady," he told her seriously. "He's a bit wobbly."

A bit?

"As for you," Mann said to Cullen, "I don't know who you are, but I don't want you provoking Brady anymore."

It was one of those man-to-man moments, with Cullen and the chief holding each other's gazes without speaking. Cynna could almost smell the testosterone. She knew Cullen was about to say something flip and insulting, and then she really would have to hurt him.

Instead, he asked, "You the sheriff?"

"Chief of police."

He nodded. "I'll do my best not to make your job harder, Chief."

Huh. Who would have guessed Cullen could actually show some respect?

The door opened. The middle-aged woman who stood there wore her dark hair short, her June Cleaver dress belted, and flip-flops on her feet. Her voice went with her expression—soft and sad. "Hello, Chief. Did you wish to speak with Victor?"

He nodded. "Brought someone who needs to talk to him."

The woman gave Cynna a disinterested glance, let her gaze linger a bit on Timms—and then she saw Cullen. Her eyes widened. "Oh, my."

"Hello, Sabra," Cullen said gently. "It's been awhile."

"I . . . yes." Her hand flew to her chest and fluttered there uncertainly. "Yes, it has. Uh . . . come in. I'll let Papa know you're here."

They were left standing in a large foyer while Sabra retreated down the hall, her flip-flops slapping the wooden floor. A staircase faced the door; on the right a closed door suggested a coat closet. On the left an arched opening led to the living room they hadn't been invited into.

Everything was very clean and about sixty years out of date. Cynna was getting a real lost-in-the-fifties feeling.

She turned to Cullen, keeping her voice low. "She's Victor's daughter?

"One of three. The youngest girl married out—caused quite a fuss. The oldest one died several years ago. Suicide."

Chief Mann shook his head. "If you're thinking of Marybeth; she was Victor's sister, not his daughter. Happened better'n twenty years ago, and Marybeth was over forty when she died. Sad story. She drove herself onto the train tracks one night, then just waited for the train."

"Sounds like I had some of the details confused," Cullen said. "I'm surprised you've heard about it."

Cullen smiled. "We're great gossips. Talk about each other all the time."

Cynna gave him a curious look. Cullen had many faults, but his memory was excellent. Shouldn't he have known how many children the Leidolf Rho had had? Seemed like that was the sort of thing all the lupi would keep track of.

Cullen didn't notice her quizzical glance. He was looking at the wall. "I'll be right back," he said suddenly and reached for the door.

"Wait a—" Too late. He was gone. Some consultant he was, taking off like that. If he didn't . . .

A board creaked on the stairs. She looked up.

A young woman—really young, Cynna thought, maybe late teens—descended slowly, holding on to the rail. Her smile was shy, her eyes blue, her hair a soft brown. She wore low-slung jeans with a snug blue sweater.

Interesting fashion choice, considering she was at least seven months pregnant. Didn't all that exposed belly get cold?

"Merilee. Aren't you supposed to be resting?"

Cynna jumped. The man who'd spoken had come up the hall so silently she'd had no idea he was there.

Victor Frey looked more like a professor than a tyrant. Maybe it was the old sweater with leather patches at the elbows, or the wrinkled slacks. He was tall—well over six feet—and skinny, with bony wrists and big hands.

The girl smiled down at him uncertainly. "I wasn't sleepy."

Sabra came up behind her father. "I could use some help in the kitchen, Merilee, if you're feeling up to it."

"Of course." She finished her descent at the same careful pace.

Victor watched her as if he weren't sure of her balance. He'd probably been as golden as his wobbly son when he was younger, but his hair had faded to white-streaked straw. His eyes were the pale blue of a winter sky, and his face bore a friendly assortment of lines. Right now, the lines drooped with weariness, and he looked older than the sixty Rule had mentioned.

Grief can do that.

"You doin' all right, Merilee?" Chief Mann asked.

"I'm okay." Now that she was closer, Cynna could see that the girl's eyes were red and puffy. "Half the time I can't believe he's gone. He'd be . . . he was so proud . . ." Her hand went to her swollen stomach, and her lip quivered.

"Come on, sugar," Sabra said, putting an arm around the slim shoulders. "Staying busy helps, and I've got a bushel of apples that need to be peeled."

As the two women left down the hall, Victor Frey turned to the chief. "I thought we covered everything yesterday, Robert. What now?"

"I'm just here to introduce you to this young lady. Agent Cynna Weaver." He nodded at her. "She and Agent Timms are with the FBI, and they believe it was a demon killed your boy. She needs to talk to you."

The door opened, and in came Cullen.

Victor Frey's face went from tight to furious. "What the—"

"*Accipiaris in pace,*" Cullen said.

The old man looked at him a long moment. The anger didn't so much drain out as get packed up, put away. He smiled a hard little smile. "*Accipio in pace.* I didn't expect to ever see you on Leidolf land again."

"Life confounds us all," Cullen murmured. "I'm helping our lovely demon hunter—who, by the way, is also the chosen apprentice of the Nokolai Rhej, though not yet formally installed."

Several heartbeats passed while Cynna considered once again the need to kick Cullen's butt. He had no business revealing that. Finally Victor spoke, his tone precise, though his words were oblique. "She's an FBI agent."

Cullen smiled. "Life confounds us all."

Victor turned his attention to Cynna. "Agent Weaver." There was an old-world courtliness to his nod that somehow suggested a bow. He barely glanced at Timms. "Agent Timms. Excuse me for failing to greet you right away."

"No problem." Dammit, Lily would've known how to talk to this guy, how to use the formal courtesy his manner seemed to require. Cynna didn't. "I'm sorry for your loss, Mr. Frey."

He nodded again. "Our Rhej will wish to meet you. Perhaps after you've fulfilled your official duties, you'll visit her." He gestured at the living room. "We might as well be comfortable. May I offer you something to drink?"

"No, thanks."

"I won't be staying, Victor," Chief Mann said. "You let me know if I can do anything to help, though."

"Thank you. Ah . . . Agent Weaver?" He waved again at the arched doorway.

The living room was huge, maybe twenty feet by thirty, with an oversize stone fireplace and three big windows that let in what was left of the daylight. It held two couches, a love seat, a piano, and an assortment of chairs. Overall, the decor looked straight out of *Leave It to Beaver.*

Cynna sat in a big, square armchair upholstered in a nubby beige fabric. "Mr. Frey, I know this is a difficult time for you. I'll try not to take long. I mainly need permission to check out your land. There's a chance that the demon that killed your son is still around."

The Leidolf Rho chose a wooden rocker about five feet away. It creaked gently as he sat. "You're very sure a demon killed Randall." He looked at Cullen, sprawled next to Timms on the closest couch. "Rule Turner's Chosen works for the FBI, doesn't she?"

"Yes."

Frey nodded and returned his attention to Cynna. "I don't mean to be rude, but I'm wondering about the designs on your skin."

"I used to be a Dizzy. Now I'm FBI, but things I learned then will help me Find and deal with a demon, if there's one around."

"There isn't."

"I'll have to confirm that, I'm afraid. That young woman—Merilee—she's family?"

"Not the way you would define it. She's carrying my son's child."

Timms quivered with indignation. "She can't be old enough to—"

"She's of legal age," Victor said without looking at him. "Is this what you wished to question me about, Agent Weaver? My grandchild?"

Cynna gave Timms a quelling look and promised herself she'd check with the chief about the girl's age. "I'm told Randall was alone when he was attacked."

"Randall likes—liked—to range for a while in wolf form most evenings. Sometimes someone goes with him, but last night he was alone. It apparently happened very quickly. He didn't . . ." His breath hitched almost imperceptibly. "He didn't have time to cry out, to call for help."

"The attack took place on Leidolf land?"

"Your consultant keeps you well-informed. Most people would have spoken of it as my land, since it's registered in my name. Perhaps you've begun learning our ways, even though you aren't formally apprenticed yet?"

He was fishing, and she had to decide how to play this. Cullen could have let her in on his intentions ahead of time, dammit.

Keep it simple, she decided—and the truth is usually simplest. But there was no need to offer a lot of details. "I know a little more than the average person, but not much. Think of me as ignorant and you won't go wrong. Was Randall attacked on Leidolf land?"

"Yes. We're careful where we travel in wolf form."

"Understandable. How did you learn about it?"

"He was my heir. When he died, I felt it." His eyes, Cynna realized, were totally opaque. He moved slowly, like a man weighed down by grief; the very lines on his face seemed to sag beneath the emotion. But his eyes gave up nothing. "You may find that difficult to credit."

"That's why she has a consultant," Cullen said. He looked at her. "That part's true. If a Rho loses his heir, he knows."

Either Victor Frey didn't notice the innuendo in Cullen's phrasing, or he didn't care to react. He'd reverted to silent mode. Time for another question. "Did you smell the demon—try to track it? They have a distinctive odor, I'm told."

His eyebrows lifted. He still didn't speak, just looked at her out of eyes that gave back nothing.

"I'm not interested in arresting anyone for failure to report—too much paperwork for damned little result. Besides, it would piss you off, which would make my job harder."

"A practical woman." His smile was small and tight. "I did follow a scent I didn't recognize that led away from the scene of the attack. Perhaps that was your demon. After a mile the trail evaporated. If there was a demon, it's gone."

"I'm hoping you're right. Do I have your permission to search your lands to make sure?"

He sat, thinking. The rocker creaked. "We are a private people," he said at last. "Nor have the authorities been our friends. But you'll get a warrant if I try to keep you out, won't you? Very well. You may look for your demon."

"Thank you. Could I—"

"Leave now."

"What?"

"Time to go," Cullen said, standing.

"I'm not—"

"Yes. You are." He took two steps, tugged her to her feet, put his hand over her mouth, damn him! And spun her to face the Leidolf Rho.

Frey was sitting perfectly still in his rocker, yet she still heard it creaking. She blinked. His eyes were blank, giving up nothing, but his hands gripped the arms of the chair so hard the wood squeaked in protest.

Shit.

Cullen's hand fell away from her mouth. "Thank you," she

told the paralyzed Rho again and let Cullen propel her from the room. Timms followed, glancing over his shoulder several times.

"That was weird," she said, low-voiced, in the hall. "What—"

"Shut up. He can still hear you." Cullen reached for the front door.

"You're leaving?" Sabra said.

Cynna jolted. The woman had ditched the flip-flops. Without them, she moved as quietly as a lupus.

"Victor is unwell," Cullen said. "No, don't check on him. He's having some trouble balancing the *heres valos*."

Sabra glanced in the living room, paled, and turned and walked quickly back down the hall. Cullen grabbed the doorknob and dragged Cynna onto the porch—which was now occupied.

FIFTEEN

TWO men stood at either end of the porch. So did a pair of wolves. The men were bare-chested and held knives as long as her forearm. The wolves were big. Really big.

Cullen's hand flashed, knocking Timms's hand away from his jacket. "Don't draw on them, fool. They'd kill you before you touched your weapon."

Timms scowled. "I'm not going to—"

"Do anything. Right. Good decision. These are the Rho's personal guard," he said, putting his hand on the small of Cynna's back and pushing. "They'd like us to leave now."

"You've taken up mind reading?" she said, but she obeyed the urgent hand at her back. "No one needs to speak, you just know what we all want. Handy."

He ignored her. Once they were off the porch and a few feet away, he looked up at the older of the two guards. "This woman has permission to search on your land. I'll accompany her, as we discussed."

Was that why he'd ducked while they were waiting for Victor Frey? He must have heard the guards show up. What had he told them?

The man he addressed was grizzled, just under six feet, and built like a pro wrestler. He was also the first nonwhite she'd seen, with skin the color of burnt toast. He gave a nod so small it might have been an optical illusion. "Very well, Nokolai whelp. The other man will leave. He won't be allowed back."

"Excuse me," Cynna said. "You need to speak to me about that, not the Nokolai whelp. Your Rho gave permission for us to search for the demon. That includes Agent Timms."

Dark brown eyes met hers. "I heard him. He gave *you* permission, not the FBI. That one"—he nodded at Cullen—"gave proper greeting and was accepted in peace. The Rho didn't restrict his guesting, so it's within my authority to allow him to accompany you. The human will leave."

She sighed. "Timms, wait in the car. Just for now," she added before the protest forming on his face could erupt in words. "I need to consult with my consultant. Privately." She gave Cullen a lift of her eyebrows to ask *where*.

"Center of the meeting field," he said, nodding at the middle of the clearing. "If we keep our voices low, they shouldn't be able to hear us."

"The human will leave," big, bad, and burly insisted.

"Hey, there are two humans here. The one with the Y chromosome is named Timms, and your Rho didn't say anything about him one way or the other, so I think you're exceeding your authority by trying to kick him out. I'm considering a compromise. You do the same."

"The *male* human will leave."

She rolled her eyes. "Temporarily. Timms—the car."

Timms shot her a look fraught with meaning, but—lacking telepathy as she did—she had no clue what meaning. He did obey, so she and Cullen headed for their designated private area in full view.

Maybe she could get through a few of the questions piling up. "What did you call him?"

"Who?"

"Gunning. You called him something in that bastardized Latin you use."

"Is that what you wanted a private consult about?"

"We're not private yet." She was sure the guards and their wolf comrades could still hear them.

"True. The phrase translates literally as *eater of corpses* and implies taking a certain carnal pleasure in the act."

"Jesus. You warn everyone else to play nice with the nutcase, then accuse him of some weird-ass version of necrophilia."

"Brady can't hate me more than he already does."

Her curiosity was itching fit to kill. She wanted to know when Cullen had been here before, what had happened, why the nutcase hated him, why he'd thought the long-ago suicide was Sabra's sister instead of her aunt.

It wasn't nosiness . . . well, not entirely nosiness. If Brady was likely to come after Cullen while she was standing beside him, she should know that. But she'd have to sit on it for now. They'd reached the center of the field, and the light was fading.

She stopped and faced him.

What was left of the sunlight loved Cullen's face. It lingered on the crests of his cheekbones, played over his forehead, and tucked shadows around the contours. His lips looked like a sculptor's version of the sensual ideal. When he frowned in thought, the beauty of his face lent him an air of gravitas she knew was false.

But oh, he was lovely to look at. She forgave herself for the little hitch in her breath. At least her voice stayed level, since she kept it low enough she barely heard herself. "What's wrong with Frey?"

His frown deepened. "The Rhej has already shared one of our most closely guarded secrets with you, even though you haven't accepted her offer of apprenticeship. I'm taking that as permission. But you are not to speak of this, ever, with anyone outside the clans."

"I made Timms wait in the car, didn't I?" Something occurred to her. "Lily's Nokolai, though. I can tell her."

"Rule needs to know, so yes, tell her. But don't say much over the phone—just that Victor's having trouble with the *heres valos.*"

"Keep going with that explanation."

"I'll give you the short version, but bear in mind I'm oversimplifying. Part of a Rho's mantle is invested in the Lu Nuncio, or heir. If the heir—"

"Wait, wait. Mantle?"

"The power that makes a Rho. When a Rho dies, the full mantle automatically descends on the heir, since he's already carrying part of it. Among other things, this protects the clan from death shock. But if the heir dies first, the Rho has to reabsorb the *heres valos*. That can be difficult, and grief makes it worse, but anyone who becomes Rho is a hardheaded son of a bitch. Normally they manage it okay."

"But Victor isn't."

"No. He must have invested more than the usual amount of the mantle in his heir."

"Why would he do that?"

"Ill health is the obvious reason."

"I thought lupi didn't get sick."

"You want the long explanation after all?"

She glanced at the sky. The sun was out of sight, and the shadows were beginning to blend together. "Just tell me what the danger is with Victor."

"He's likely to be testy."

She rolled her eyes. "Testy? You hustled me out as if he were about to rip out my throat."

"Testy enough to rip out the throat of anyone who seems a threat to his authority, male or female."

"You're saying he's crazy. That this *heres valos* makes him insane." That's what Rule had told her, long ago—that an adult lupus who attacked a woman was considered insane.

But Rule had struck her. She hadn't thought that was possible in either of his forms. *A slap isn't an attack,* she told herself, but there was a tight, unhappy feeling in her stomach. "Or else the 'lupi don't hurt women' thing isn't true."

"Rule's problem isn't the same as Victor's."

"What?" He'd sounded kind. Cullen, kind?

"That's what you were thinking about, wasn't it? Rule slapped you, so you're wondering if he's gone nuts or if he lied about lupi not hurting women."

She scowled. What was the world coming to if Cullen Seabourne could turn perceptive on her? "I can't believe he told you. He felt so bad about it."

"Of course he wanted me to know. Part of his hair shirt is exposing his shame. But like I said, Rule's problem is very different from Victor's. Victor is a tyrant at the best of times. Right now, he's only intermittently rational. There's nothing wrong with Rule's thinking—he just doesn't trust his wolf enough."

"Maybe he has reason? It wasn't his human side that socked me."

"He was injured. The wolf reacted to the pain you caused, but even with reason out of the loop entirely, he was careful with his strength. Or did you think a little slap is the way he'd respond to a real threat?"

"Little?" she said, indignant. "You think it's okay to hit a woman as long as you don't damage her too much?"

"No, I think you're deliberately misunderstanding me."

She looked away. Her stomach still felt unhappy. She was making a big deal out of this and didn't know why. Time to change the subject.

Over at the house, the guards—human and wolf—were watching them. "You heard the bodyguards show up. Why weren't they out front earlier? And why did you go talk to them?"

He snorted. "I already knew they were around—Frederick's good, but the breeze wasn't with him."

"That wasn't what I asked."

He waved that off. "Personal business. Victor's a great believer in passing for human as much as possible, and knife-wielding toughs don't fit the image, so he kept them out of sight at first and had Sabra answer the door. I'm sure Merilee was supposed to stay in her room."

"You heard her? Yes, of course you did. But I still don't get it. I knew Frey was a Rho. I was expecting guards."

"Most humans don't even know the word *Rho*, much less what it means. He was expecting a regular FBI agent who'd buy the scene he set—a nice old man, grieving but handling it well enough. No threat. Then I showed up, and it turned out you might become the next Nokolai Rhej. Blew his stage-setting all to pieces. He kept to his role, but he'd lost control of the situation, and he knew it. When he realized he had to let you hunt on his land, he crashed. He's down to a fingernail's worth of sanity, and gnawing on that."

"You could have warned me ahead of time about this *heres* thing."

"Am I a precog? I didn't know Victor was in trouble until we got here. Smelled it then, but that was a bit late for warnings."

She thought of the way Frey's daughter had turned pale and left when she learned he was having trouble with the *heres valos*. "He's a danger to those around him."

"We can't help them. What are you going to do about Timms?"

She chewed on her bottom lip. If she served her warrant she could insist on Timms's presence, but that challenge to his authority might push Victor over the edge. "Who gets hurt if Victor goes round the bend? Us, or the people around him?"

"Anyone. Everyone. It's impossible to predict."

Great. "I'm going to do a full cast, see if the demon's anywhere near."

"There's a node here," he warned her. "Keyed to Leidolf, so it's not usable by anyone else, and it's small. But we're standing close. Will that distort your cast?"

"Shouldn't. If I don't pick up anything, we'll come back tomorrow, get someone to take us to the site of the attack. We don't have a description of this demon. Maybe it wasn't like the dead one, and that's why I can't Find it."

"And if you do pick up something?"

"We hunt." She glanced at the car. "All of us. Timms is an ass, but he's a top shooter and those things are hard to kill. I've got a spell that works, but it takes everything I've got. I'd like backup."

"What am I, Swiss cheese? Alex and company won't let Timms out of the car."

"Alex is the boss guard? Well, he might not like it, but what can he do?"

"Kill us, if Victor tells them to."

"So we don't tell Victor."

"Alex will."

Shit. This was why she didn't like being in charge. Sometimes there weren't any good options, and you had to pick one anyway. "Can you fire an M72 LAW?"

"Does it have a trigger?"

"Never mind. Are you armed?"

"With my wits and charm. I hate guns."

"But you can use one if you have to. Guess what? You have to. We've got an M-16 in the trunk, and it does have a trigger. What about your diamond?"

"Not recharged yet."

Yet? She mentally added one more question to the "when we're alone" list. "I'm going to do a full cast now."

He nodded and turned his back on her.

It wasn't rudeness. He was facing out while she faced in, watching her back so she could concentrate on her cast. That was one of the things she actually liked about Cullen. She didn't have to explain herself when it came to magic. He knew.

Working magic typically requires three things: knowledge, focus, and power. Power could be innate, pooled with other practitioners, drawn from natural sources, or stolen—though that was dark magic, what most people thought of when they thought about sorcery. Focus was learned. Knowledge usually meant knowing the spell to be performed; with a Find, that meant using the *kilingo* for the target.

With a quick cast, Cynna just had to give her attention to the object she sought. Doing a full cast meant putting a lot of power into her search. For that, she needed her focus crystal clear.

She said a quick Our Father, bent, untied her shoes, and removed them and her socks.

The ground was cold and prickly with dried grass. She closed her eyes and shook her arms until her fingertips tingled. She sent that tingling up her arms, down her spine, tracing the magic that coursed over her skin, attached yet never entirely still. Like fur, she thought, always ruffling a bit in the breeze.

Some of the intricate tattoos stored spells. Those were the *kilingo*, and they took days or weeks to perfect and imprint, and would take at least as long to alter or remove. Most were *kielezo*, patterns lifted from something or someone she'd Found or might need to Find. *Kielezo* were much quicker to imprint, change, or remove.

The *kielezo* for the dead demon was on her right shoulder blade. The skin there felt tight with residual power from the cast she'd started in the car and never finished. She fed more power into it . . . and began to move.

Only her feet at first. She flexed her knees and lifted one heel, then the other, keeping the balls of her feet earthed. Slowly, then faster, her heels thumped out a rhythm as old as Africa, letting it build, catching her power up into it and lifting the essence of the *kielezo* from her shoulder to thrum in the air all around her. Her arms began to lift, too—hip high, waist, chest. She breathed the pattern in.

When her arms were over her head, with her heels still pounding the earth, she searched. And Found.

Not an exact match, but the click of connection was unmistakable. She felt it in her stomach, her palms, the lifting of all the tiny hairs on her arms. Her eyes opened.

She was facing the house.

SIXTEEN

"**Shit!**" Cynna snatched up her tote and kicked into a run, not taking the time to put her shoes back on.

"Where?" Cullen demanded, loping along easily beside her. "Where is it? How far?"

"The house. It's in the house."

"Can't be. Even if I didn't smell it when we were inside, Victor or his guards would have. Behind the house, maybe."

"No. It's on the second floor." That's what made her so sure it was in the house—it was *that* way, and the right distance, and well above ground level. "The connection feels odd, but it's clear enough."

"What kind of odd?"

"Finding is kind of like tying a rope between me and what I've searched for. The texture of this rope is funny, a little like when I search for a living person and Find a ghost. But not exactly, and anyway, demons don't throw ghosts."

"Maybe it's dashtu. That might explain . . . no, it wouldn't," he said, arguing with himself before she could. "I still smelled the one that chased me when it was dashtu."

"You were chased by a demon? When? Where?"

"Later. They aren't going to let us in." He kept pace with her even as he told her it was pointless. "They won't believe you.

Demons stink. Even a human could smell one if you were close enough."

"Maybe this one's using deodorant."

"I'd have seen it. I think. If it were in someone, I should've seen it."

"So maybe it's in someone you didn't see. Get Timms."

"They for damned sure won't let him in. If that odd texture you mentioned . . ." His voice trailed away. He stopped. "Holy Mother."

She stopped, too, though it made her twitchy. "What?"

"I'm stupid. I'm a fool. There are humans in that house. *We* can't be possessed, but there are humans in that house."

"Oh, God." She stopped and tossed him the car keys. "M-16 in the trunk." She took off running.

He ran with her, damn him. "Go get a weapon!" she shouted.

"And shoot who? It's in a woman!"

The car door slammed. Timms started for them, .357 in one hand, submachine gun slung over his shoulder. "Get the dart gun!" she called.

He paused, spun, and went back for it.

The guards, human and lupine, massed in front of the door. "Stop."

That was the one with African blood. Alex. Boss guard. "You heard us, dammit!" She skidded to a halt at the steps. Her heart was pounding, and not from the short run. *The back of the house. The demon is upstairs, at the back of the house. It can't hear us. It has only its human host's senses.* "There's a demon inside. We need in. Now."

"The Rho is resting. He's not to be disturbed."

"He'll be damned disturbed if that demon gets hold of him!"

Timms slid into place beside her. "What's going on?"

She answered without taking her eyes off the guards. "The demon has possessed one of the women. That's why the lupi didn't sniff it out. Look," she said to the boss guard. "I'm Dizzy and a Finder. I know demons, and I know Finding. You've got a demon in the same house as your Rho, and there's a good chance it wants to kill him. *She* sent the demon, and *She* may be trying to decapitate the clans."

"*She?*" he repeated, brows snapping down in a scowl.

"The Great Bitch," Cullen said. "The Lady's enemy."

"You can prove this?"

"Not from out here," Cynna snapped, "but I have holy water. If one of the women reacts to it, will you accept that as proof?"

He thought about it longer than she liked, but at last nodded. "Wait here. I'll wake the Rho."

"I need in *now*. I have the authority. If you don't—"

Cullen put a hand on her arm, then said something Latin. At least she thought it was Latin. He spoke so softly she barely heard him.

Boss Guard heard just fine. He looked at Cynna, astonishment mixing with skepticism, then back at Cullen. "All right. Gary, go get her." One of the wolves—the one with reddish fur—leaped over the porch railing, landed on the ground, and hit high speed in a blink.

"Where's he—"

Boss Guard spoke right over her. "If you've lied, Nokolai—"

"You'll pull me apart and feed me to the pups. Fine." Cullen leaped onto the porch without bothering with the steps. "Lead on," he told her.

One hell of a leader she was. She should have planned for this possibility. Lily would have.

She'd have to wing it. "Timms," she said, "we treat this as a hostage situation, only the hostage may try to kill us or take other hostages. We have to restrain her, not kill her. I want to surprise her if possible, so hang back, try not to let her see you. Be ready with the dart gun." And pray the dose they were using worked. "Cullen, burning things won't help. What else have you got?"

"I'm more of a brute force kind of guy, but I do have a sleep charm."

"Good. That's good. How long will it hold her under?"

He shrugged. "It'll put a human to sleep for up to a week if left undisturbed, but I haven't tried it on a demon. And it has to be activated while touching her skin."

Okay, the demon might not stand around quietly for that. "We may still need it. If Timms darts her, the anesthetic should have an effect, but we don't know how much, or how long it'll last." It was getting hard to stand still—this close to a target, the Find pulled at her.

Boss Guard shook his head. "You aren't shooting anyone unless you prove she's possessed."

"You'll have your proof. How many women are in the house?"

"Three adults and two children."

Oh, God. She hadn't thought of that. Never mind *The Exorcist*; demons seldom possessed a child. Kids were too constrained by size, social roles, and the lack of a Visa to be much fun for them. But she'd already been wrong about this demon once. "Timms, if it's in a child, you can't dart her. That dose is for an adult."

"If I don't dart her, how will we hold her long enough for an exorcism?"

"We'll think of something." Oh, that was lame. She looked at Boss Guard again. "How many of you are coming with me?"

"Me. David." He nodded at a man-shaped guard, then told the wolf to hold the door.

"Okay. Keep in mind that she'll have demonic strength— more than you've got—but she won't be as fast as you."

"If there *is* a demon."

He worried her. Doubt could make him hesitate, and hesitation could get him killed. But she didn't know what else to say. "Here's the plan. I Find her, splash her with holy water. She'll react in a way that proves she's possessed." Except that not all demons were hurt by holy water . . . but this demon matched the pattern of the one she'd killed. The poison from that one had definitely been affected by holy water, so the demon should be, too. Shouldn't it?

Never mind. She didn't have time for second-guessing. "Soon as she reacts, I'll get out of the way." She shifted from foot to foot, wanting to get moving, to follow her Find. "If she's an adult, Timms darts her, and you big, strong lupi can finish subduing her, if necessary. Then Cullen puts a sleep on her."

Boss Guard and Cullen exchanged a glance. "Well," Cullen murmured, "it does have the virtue of simplicity."

Boss Guard grunted. "And if this alleged demon is in a child?"

"There's three of us," Cullen said. "We might be able to hold her long enough for my charm to work."

Or not, in which case . . . dammit, she couldn't think of any other options. Cynna took a deep breath, made the sign of the cross, pulled a vial of holy water out of her tote, and opened the door.

No one in the entry, the hall, or on the stairs. She gave the living room a quick scan. Empty. Couldn't hear any voices, but music was playing upstairs—something longhair, with violins. She started up.

The Find yanked hard now. She had to consciously mind her pace or she'd have sprinted up the stairs. *Stealth,* she reminded herself, and kept to the outsides of the risers, hoping to avoid any creaky spots.

The music grew louder as she climbed but remained muffled. Someone was listening to it in a bedroom, she thought, and hoped it was the Leidolf Rho, and that he wouldn't pop out of his room to make trouble. Then she hoped even more he was alone in his room.

Close. So close. Fourteen feet away, and up. Thirteen.

Cynna gestured at those behind her: wait. She eased up the last few steps.

The pregnant Merilee was in the middle of the hall that ran the length of the house. So was Victor Frey. She was bent over her big belly, hands braced on the wall, her sweater bunched up beneath her breasts, jeans and panties MIA. His pants hung at his knees, stopped in their descent by his spread legs. He was fucking her from the rear, quick and hard.

Merilee turned her head and met Cynna's eyes. Her face was flushed, her mouth smiling, her eyes wild. She liked it.

Typical damned demon. Cynna drew her arm back and pitched the vial.

Frey saw her. His face contorted in rage, his hips kept pumping, and his hand flashed up—and caught the vial before it struck.

Damned lupus reflexes! Cynna dug out another vial, dumped the tote, and raced down the hall. "Timms—dart her!" she cried, cursing herself for telling the others to stay back. "Frey, she's possessed! She—aw, shit!"

Still smiling, still fucking, Merilee had twisted around impossibly to loop one arm around Frey's neck, and squeeze. Frey's eyes bulged.

Vial in hand, Cynna threw herself into a tackle.

And Cullen, who'd never heard an order he didn't disobey, hurtled right past her.

He arrived first, ducking as Merilee swung at him with her free hand. He grabbed the arm clamped around Frey's throat and threw himself back, pulling all of them off balance.

They'd just started to topple when Cynna collided with a confusion of legs. She glimpsed shaved skin on a shapely calf and smashed the vial against it.

Merilee howled. A heavy weight landed on Cynna's back, smashing her to the floor. Her breath whooshed out. Someone yelled. Feet thudded down the hall. A sledgehammer hit the side of her head, and everything went black.

SEVENTEEN

THAT afternoon, Lily developed a deeper appreciation for the problems of working parents.

Right after Cullen left, she did, too, heading for the Secret Service's headquarters on Murray Drive. She wanted everything they had on the perp they'd tagged for demonic dealings. She wanted copies of whatever they'd learned about Jiri and the others on the list Cynna had given her, too.

She struck out. The two men she'd worked with still wouldn't tell her a damned thing, so she insisted on being passed up the food chain to the assistant chief muckety-muck. He made her wait, then made vague promises of cooperation, claiming he wanted to help but had to clear it "at the highest level" first. But his face and body language said he'd die and rot before he gave freaks like her and the others in the Unit one jot of information.

She wondered if the presidential adviser would take her phone call, maybe goose the jerk a bit. Didn't hurt to try, she decided, so she called Ida on the way back to the row house, requesting the number. Ida wouldn't give it to her.

So Lily wasn't in the best of moods when she headed back to the row house. Next up was a meet with the task force at five, and she wanted Rule there. They'd have questions about the lupi's ancient enemy and *Her* role in the demons sprouting up like spring flowers. Plus he needed to get the last of the poison removed, and at least two of the task force members should be able to handle that.

But Toby was there—scrubbing the kitchen floor, at the moment, as penance.

"I don't see why he can't come with us," she said for the second time.

"To FBI headquarters." He was incredulous.

"It's secure."

"And what do you plan to do with him? You don't have an office to park him in—not that I'd recommend that, anyway. The number of things a kid his age can get into—"

"Like an airplane, but he managed to get here okay, didn't he? He's a bright kid."

"He's a bright eight-year-old. Last summer he decided to make a pair of wings modeled after da Vinci's sketches. I found out before he tested them, thank God."

"Maybe we can find someone there to keep an eye on him while we talk to the task force."

"Ruben, maybe?"

"Very good." She nodded. "You don't have anything reasonable to say, so you use sarcasm."

"Reasonable. You think it's reasonable to insist I leave my son—"

"Have I once said you should leave him?"

"—with strangers because you're determined to manage my life. You don't trust me to take care of my leg. You don't trust a solution you haven't come up with yourself, so—"

"Waiting is not a solution!" That's what he'd suggested—that he wait until the bodyguards arrived to deal with his wound.

"—you want to drag me with you and make sure it's done on your schedule."

She flushed. "I do have other priorities, like trying to find out how these demons are being summoned and who's behind it. Plus the task force needs to know about the conclusions we've drawn and the goddess we don't name."

"So go."

She stared at him a long moment, then shoved her hair back with both hands. "Why are we arguing? Do you even know why? I don't."

"I'm arguing because my hip hurts and I'm an ass. You're arguing because you're worried about me. And because I'm an ass."

"At least there's a good reason." She went to him and wrapped her arms around his waist. He put his arms around her, too, and rested his cheek on the top of her head. Within a few breaths, they were okay again.

"You didn't mention the other reason we were fighting," she said.

"Which is . . . ?"

"The way I turn into a control freak when I'm scared."

"Oh, that. I was being tactful."

She snorted. "If we don't—" The doorbell chimed. She repressed a sigh. The world never gave them much time before poking its nose in. "Guess we should see who that is."

"We should," he agreed without moving.

Feet thudded on the stairs. "I'll get it!" Toby called.

"No, you won't," Rule said, disengaging and starting for the stairs.

Lily headed for the door. "Have you told him what's going on?"

"Not yet. I will as soon as I see who our caller is. Toby, go back upstairs."

Lily didn't listen to the argument that followed. She'd applied her eye to the peephole again and received an even bigger shock than finding Cullen on her doorstep. After a stunned pause, she unlocked and opened the door.

This time it was two women who stood there, both Chinese.

One was middle-aged, plain, and wore a simple dark-blue pantsuit with a wool jacket. The other was old, tiny, and as proudly erect as a queen. Her black hair was winged with white and drawn into a ruthless bun; her dress was crimson and reached her ankles; her jacket was quilted silk of many colors.

Lily sighed. "Grandmother. Of course you would show up now."

"You are not moving aside so we may come in," Li Lei Yu pointed out severely.

Automatically Lily complied.

Grandmother brushed past. "Our bags are in the car. Your Rule Turner may see to them. Do you still have that cat?"

Grandmother was using English instead of insisting Lily speak Chinese. No doubt that was meant to convey some sort of message, but Lily was in no mood to decode it. "Harry's around someplace. Grandmother, why have you—"

"Not now," she said, giving the living room a disapproving eye. "Ugly. I suppose that is not your fault, however."

Li Qin paused on the threshold to give Lily an apologetic smile. "The limousine driver can bring in the bags, Lily. Are you well?"

"Mostly." She watched, resigned to her fate, as her grandmother seated herself on the sofa. Her feet didn't reach the floor.

"I will need a footstool," the old woman announced, "but later. I have been in airplanes and airports for seventy-two hours. You have no Christmas tree."

"We expected to go home for Christmas, so we didn't put one up. Grandmother—"

"Your plans have changed? Ha! I am not surprised," she said darkly. "Later you will tell me. Now you may tell me where my room is. Li Qin will wish to go to her room, also. We have eaten. Abominable food, but we do not require a meal."

Lily's conscience nipped at her. It was easy to forget that Grandmother was *old*. She sat as erect as ever, but the skin around her eyes looked bruised with fatigue.

But why exhaust herself so? Why had Grandmother cut her trip short and flown here instead of home to San Diego? "Upstairs," she said automatically. "Your room will be upstairs. But, ah, we weren't expecting you, and we have to—"

"Madam Yu," Rule said, entering with Toby trailing behind. Toby hung back in the doorway while Rule crossed the room. He bent, taking the old woman's hand to press a kiss there. "You honor us. May I present to you my son, Toby Asteglio?"

Grandmother gave an approving nod. "You may. You are Toby," she informed the boy. "You may greet me."

Toby gave his father a panicky glance but came forward a few steps, offered a jerky little bow, and said, "Madam Yu. H-how do you do?"

"I am well, thank you. Do you stay here, also?"

He nodded uncertainly. "I wasn't supposed to, and I'm in trouble about it."

"I will teach you to play mah-jongg. You will not enjoy it at first because I will win, but you will like it later, when you find players you can defeat. Lily." She turned imperious black eyes on her granddaughter. "I have much to say to you and Rule Turner, but I will rest first. Why are you not at work?"

"I'm trying to work," she said dryly. "People keep showing up, expecting to stay here."

A gleam of amusement brightened the tired eyes. Grandmother enjoyed being outrageous, but at least she knew she was doing it. Mostly. "You require a Christmas tree."

Oh, Lord, she was right. With Toby here . . . "Maybe you'd like to take care of that for us."

"I will call," she announced, as if making a great concession. "You want one with candy. Sugarplums. No Santas. I do not like Santas. Someone will deliver it." The painted eyebrows arched. "I think you have much to tell me."

They shared a look of understanding affection. "As you say, later. I've an appointment I—"

"*We* have an appointment," Rule said smoothly. "Madam Yu, I have a great favor to ask of you."

"**SHE'S** not a stranger," Lily said as she punched the elevator button. "But do you really feel good about leaving Toby with Grandmother?"

Rule grinned. "He may consider it part of his punishment, but he's safe with her."

She couldn't argue. Grandmother was a real tiger when it came to protecting children.

A *real* tiger.

No one outside the family knew about that, of course . . . well, aside from two members of the Unit, and they would keep the secret. And even the family didn't know how Grandmother had come to possess her unique ability. She discouraged questions. Sure, there were stories of adepts in pre-Purge times who'd been able to take a beast form or curse someone into an animal's body. But who knew if those tales were true? The days of the adepts were long over. Today the only werebeasts were the lupi . . . and Grandmother.

"I expect Li Qin will do any actual work," Lily said as they climbed into a little box already nearly full of people she didn't know.

"You forget. She's going to teach him mah-jongg."

She grinned. "That's a mark of high approval. She normally refuses to play with anyone not up to her standards." If Lily hadn't known him so well, she wouldn't have seen the tension in Rule's body. He didn't like elevators. He didn't like anyone noticing his discomfort, either, so she kept talking. "We should do something for Li Qin as a thank-you."

"A vacation? Without your grandmother, that is."

"Surprising as it may seem, Li Qin is devoted to Grandmother. I doubt she'd go. But Christmas is nearly here."

"Yes, and it looks like we'll have family around for the holiday, after all. Not to mention a Christmas tree. With sugarplums."

"But no Santas. I hope you realize you're paying for that. Grandmother will feel she's done more than her share by condescending to use the phone."

"I certainly wouldn't let her pay for it. You need to call your mother."

That had sure come out of left field. It took her a second to recover. "She'll just refuse to talk to me."

The elevator doors opened on someone else's floor. Two men got off. "Then leave a message. You know better than most that we aren't guaranteed the time we think we need to mend fences with those we love."

She stared at the closing doors. "Wrong time, wrong place. Nag me later."

He lowered his voice. "You haven't told me what's wrong between the two of you. But does it matter? Does it matter as much as spending the holiday without speaking to her? She's difficult, but she loves you."

Lily didn't answer. He meant well, but so did her mother. Every time she told Lily how she ought to be running her life, Julia Yu meant well.

Almost every time. When Lily had desperately needed her support . . . "This is our floor," she said, as glad as Rule must be to escape the crowded elevator.

Before she and Rule left San Diego, Lily had gone to her parents' house to say goodbye to her father and her younger sister . . . and to apologize to her mother. She owed her that much, though she'd known damned well she'd get no apology in return.

She'd managed two out of three. Her mother hadn't been home.

Five weeks ago Lily and her younger sister had both been in the emergency room. Lily had been injured physically; Rule was missing and presumed dead, and Lily's Gift had been reft from her. She'd needed her mother, and Julia Yu had come . . . to hover over her youngest daughter and blame Lily for everything.

"Your sister could have been killed! And why? Because of

him! Him and your job, the stupid job you insisted on, no matter
how many times I told you I didn't like it. And now you've
brought hurt to your family, you and that—that wolf man you're
sleeping with. I'm glad he's dead! I—"

That's when Lily had slapped her.

"Lily," Rule said.

Yanked back to the present, Lily noticed the woman hurrying
toward them—fortyish, with dust-colored hair, glasses, and a bright
pink shirt straining over generous breasts. Sandy McPherson was
an analyst in data collection with a wicked sense of humor, and
one of the few people Lily knew in Headquarters.

"You sleepwalking?" Sandy said. "I called you twice."

"Sorry. What's up?"

"Ida is looking for you."

"Is it urgent?" Lily glanced at her watch. "We're due in a
meeting in two and half minutes."

"She didn't say, but . . ." Sandy shrugged. "It's Ida."

"Right." Ruben's secretary wasn't likely to make a fuss if it
wasn't important. "Thanks, Sandy."

"You can thank me by introducing me to the sexiest man I've
ever seen."

She was looking at Rule with a familiar expression on her
face. Lily grinned. "Mine."

"I can still drool, can't I? You're Rule Turner. Not only can I
read your visitor's badge, I read the gossip mags, and . . . no, better not go there. I'm supposed to be somewhere myself as of . . ."
She checked her own watch. "Twelve minutes ago."

"It's good to almost meet you, Sandy," Rule said.

She grinned, sighed, and bustled off down the hall. They
headed for the next intersection in the maze, took a left, and arrived at Ida's lair.

Ida was speaking into her headset, tapping away at a key-
board, and passing a file to the woman standing by her desk.
"Take that in to Ruben," she said without missing a keystroke.
The other woman hurried to the door on the far wall.

Lily waited a moment, but Ida didn't look up. "Cynna sus-
pects she's an alien," she whispered, "but I think she has three
brains. Has to, to multitask that way."

"I heard that," Ida said without looking away from the screen,
adding—presumably into the headset—"You're booked on the
4:30 flight. Yes. I'll ask. For now, use the Morrison ID."

"She also has supernaturally keen hearing," Lily said in a normal voice. "I can't figure out why I don't get a buzz of magic from her."

"Call Jules. No, not yet—I'll let you know when we do. All right. Goodbye." Ida stopped typing long enough to remove her headset. She spared Lily a glance. "The report you wanted is in the blue folder. I thought you might need it before your meeting."

"And she's supernaturally quick with flashes of omniscience." Lily picked up the folder. "Thanks, Ida."

"You've got thirty seconds to make it to the conference room." Lily hurried.

"Friendly soul," Rule said.

"Maybe not, but she's devoted to Ruben and the Unit—"

"How can you tell?"

"—and she's got a better memory than my computer. You're miffed because she didn't drool."

"I don't expect drool. A glance, maybe, some hint of awareness . . . Do you think she's a robot?"

Lily grinned and pushed open the door.

They walked in on a fierce argument. Sherry O'Shaunessy was stabbing her finger in the air at a man Lily didn't recognize, who scowled back at her. The archbishop was nowhere in sight.

Sherry didn't look like either of Hollywood's versions of witches—the cackling crone or the nubile young Wiccan. Aside from the hair, that is. Her hair flowed in a gray and silver cascade to her hips, held out of her face by a silver headband. Otherwise she might have been someone's suburban grandma: short, chubby, with rosy cheeks and blue eyes set off by plenty of smile lines. She wore tailored slacks and a sky-blue twinset.

Not that she was smiling now. The object of her stabbing finger was a man of about forty: skinny, wide mouth, rimless glasses, and thick eyebrows. Japanese or Korean descent, probably; wrinkled white dress shirt, conservative haircut, no tie, brown slacks.

The third person in the room, Dr. Xavier Fagin, wore cargo pants—an interesting sight on a man of his age and girth—a black T-shirt, and a tweed jacket. His white hair poked up in all directions like dandelion fluff. He was leaning back in his chair, fingers laced together over a comfortable paunch, smiling on the others like an aging hippie, still stoned after all these years.

"We can't possibly accept the Dante Protocols as the basis

for inter-realm transcorporation," the unknown man insisted. "Its provenance is riddled with flaws. Flaws and outright deception."

The high priestess threw up both hands. "Then where do we start? Because we have to make a start. Xavier . . ." She turned to Dr. Fagin.

"We have company," the professor said mildly.

Sherry blinked, then smiled at them. "Sorry. We get intense. Since you're Lily," she said, her gaze flicking between them, "you must be Rule."

He gave her back a smile. "I am. And you must be Sherry O'Shaunessy. Though we haven't met, I've heard of your beauty."

Rule could get away with saying things like that because he meant them. Lily wasn't sure what his standards for beauty were, but they didn't match with the usual ones. Maybe he just found women beautiful, period.

Dr. Fagin unlaced his fingers and pushed to his feet, holding out a hand. "Rule Turner? Pleased to meet you, sir, and glad you survived last night's encounter. I'm Xavier Fagin."

The older man kept right on talking as they shook. "One of our members is absent—Archbishop Brown—but he should rejoin us shortly. You've now met Sherry, who insists on calling me by my first name when everyone else calls me Fagin . . . among other, less repeatable things. Sherry's co-combatant is Hikaru Ito. Ms. Yu, you won't have met him, either. He arrived this afternoon."

The name was Japanese, as were his features—second generation, probably. No accent, but a traditional first name.

Rule turned to Ito, smiling. "I've read your book on substitutionary symbology."

Ito was still simmering over inter-realm transcorporation, but he made an effort to be civil. "Have you, now. And what did you think?"

"That it was way over my head. I passed it to a friend of mine who understands the lingo."

"And did he offer an opinion?" Ito's tone made it clear he doubted that anyone Rule knew could have understood his work.

"He called you brilliant but misguided."

Ito snorted. "That's better than many of my critics will concede. Fagin thinks I'm—"

"Brilliant but misguided," Fagin said, chuckling. "About the Pythagorean linkage, that is. Liked what you did with Hambly's translation. Neat. Very neat. Dr. Ito," he added with a sleepy smile aimed in Lily's direction, "is a symbolist, specializing in prophecies."

Lily had no intention of letting the handshaking part of the introductions lag. Several people had summoned demons. It would be a bitch if one of the perps turned out to be on the task force. She held out her hand. "Pleased to met you, Dr. Ito. You've worked on Nostradamus's prophecies as well, I think?"

He looked surprised but accepted her hand. "My one and only attempt at writing for the popular market. Didn't sell well, I'm afraid."

The tingle of magic was very faint, almost nonexistent. Lily dropped his hand and turned to Sherry, smiling. "We didn't exactly meet earlier. I'm glad you're here." She extended her hand.

Sherry's eyebrows lifted. "Checking us out?"

"Any reason I shouldn't?"

"You sound like a cop." But that was observation, not complaint. Sherry took Lily's hand.

Good grip; the magic was strong, cool, flowing—a major water Gift. No trace of the demonic. Lily released the woman's hand just as the door opened.

It was Archbishop Brown, looking intense. Lily suspected that was his usual expression. "I've cleared my calendar for two days," he said abruptly. "That's as much as I can . . . oh. Hello, Ms., ah . . . sorry. I've forgotten your last name."

"Lily Yu," she said, moving forward and holding out her hand. "And this is Rule Turner. Rule, Archbishop Brown."

"Call me Patrick." The cleric's grip was firm, his palm dry. No magic. He gave Rule a sharp glance. "You're the Nokolai prince."

"Heir," Rule said mildly. " 'Prince' is the press's term, and not particularly apt."

He nodded once. "The press gets most things wrong. I've some questions for you about the demon you encountered."

"I have questions for you, too," Lily said. The archbishop was possibly the foremost demonologist in the Catholic Church. "Dr. Fagin?" She held out her hand again.

"Clean sweep, eh?" He wiggled his eyebrows as if she'd suggested something naughty. "Why not?"

His palm was wide, the knuckles prominent. There was

enough coarse hair on the back of his hand and fingers to have gotten him in trouble fifty years ago, when people still believed werewolves sprouted extra hair, even in human form.

She took it. For a split second she felt nothing, then magic itched along her palm. Which was weird. She'd never had any sort of delayed read before. What—

Dr. Fagin's eyes rolled back in his head. He toppled slowly, like an old elm.

EIGHTEEN

RULE grabbed Fagin on the way down, easing him to the floor. He looked over his shoulder at Lily. "You're—?"

"Fine." She knelt beside the fallen man, reaching for his neck to check the pulse.

Sherry grabbed Lily's arm, aborting the gesture. "Don't. He collapsed when you touched him."

Lily frowned over her shoulder at the woman. "It wasn't me. Sensitives can't do magic—black, benign, or anywhere in between."

Ito fidgeted beside Rule. "We should call someone. Call for help."

"No . . . no need." Fagin blinked up at them. "My. I'd wondered if that would happen."

"What?" Lily snapped. Anxiety tended to piss her off.

"Yes, Xavier," Sherry said. "What did happen?"

"Backlash. I'm a sensitive, too, you see."

After a beat of silence, Lily said quietly, "I've never met another sensitive."

"We are rare, aren't we?" He sat up, brushing aside the archbishop's protests. "No, no, I took no harm at all, thanks to Mr. Turner's quick action. Fascinating!" He sounded as pleased as a kid with a new video game. "I remained aware, you see, merely stunned, rather like having my breath knocked out. Ms. Yu, perhaps we could touch again, see how long it takes for the dissonance to—"

"No," Rule said.

"I don't think so," Lily said.

Ito frowned. "Is this appropriate? Our time is—"

"Fagin!" the archbishop snapped. "Pay attention! You can play with dissonance when the fate of the world isn't hanging in the balance."

"Of course." He looked sheepish.

Sherry spoke quietly. "We've known each other for years, yet you never told me you were a sensitive."

"No one knows," he said simply. "Lily understands, I'm sure. It's so tempting to put us to use. Not that I think you would have done so," he said kindly to Sherry. "But silence becomes a habit. Would someone give me a hand up?"

Rule did that. The old man's scent made him think of soda crackers and cream cheese: sweet and salty mixed. No whiff of fear.

"Well." Fagin smiled vaguely at them. "I believe this is my coming-out party. I should have warned you, but I do love a surprise, and I wished to test my theory. I didn't realize how dramatic the results would be."

Rule was not happy. "Lily could have ended up on the floor instead of you."

"Oh, no. Evidence—anecdotal, but sufficient—indicated hers was the greater Gift, though I didn't realize how much greater. You are quite amazing, my dear."

Lily didn't look flattered. "So what happened?"

"Why, our Gifts duked it out, and yours won."

"Is that supposed to be an explanation?" Sherry asked dryly.

"Come, Sherry, you aren't thinking. You know what makes the sensitive Gift unique, don't you? It cannot be controlled in any way."

"Telepaths can't control their Gift, either," Ito said. "Or they wouldn't go insane so often."

"Fernando Baccardi, Ito?" Fagin's eyebrows bounced up and down. "Yes, I see you know what I mean. Baccardi was a telepath in the last century," he explained to the others, "who remained stable well into his forties because he could dial his Gift down. His ability supports my thesis that, before the Codex Arcanum was lost, it was possible to erect psychic blocks or shields."

"Actually," Lily said, "that's still possible."

"Is it? Is it, indeed?" His expression was all astonishment, but the eyes beneath those bushy eyebrows turned sharp. "I hope you'll tell me more about that later. For now, I attempt to cling to the subject at hand. As I was saying, my Gift and Lily's cannot be controlled—not consciously or unconsciously, not by ourselves or any outside agency. Intriguing, isn't it? In addition, sensitives are said to be completely impervious to magic. That's obviously not true, so—"

Lily broke in. "Wait a minute. What do you mean?"

"We know when we touch magic, don't we? We may even know what kind of magic we're touching—you do, I suspect . . . yes?" He was pleased by her nod. "I can't always tell, myself. Still, this makes it clear there is some slight interaction between what we touch and our own magic, yet we remain untouched ourselves, so to speak. I've devised two models to explain this. First, we may possess a sort of permeable film of magic overlying an impenetrable core. The interaction would take place in that film. Second, we might be absorbing a tiny bit of power from whatever we touch and transmuting it, making it purely ours."

Lily frowned. "Transmuting it, not blocking it?"

"You see the difference, don't you? I'll confess I'd favored the first model, but my reaction today tends to support the second one."

The archbishop shook his head. "Fagin, try to remember that not all of us are familiar with your field."

"Of course. Sorry. If the transmutation model is accurate, when I touch someone who possesses a fire Gift I suck up a tiny bit of fire magic and turn it into my own type of magic. I affect it—it doesn't affect me. You can see why I preferred the other model."

"This one raises as many questions as it answers."

"Just so. Yet when I touched Lily, it seemed that my Gift tried to take in a bit of hers and couldn't, because hers is so much stronger. My power snapped back at me like a rubber band." He beamed at her. "What was it like for you?"

Rule bent his head closer to hers to murmur, "It was good for me. Was it—" The quick pinch on his ass stopped him, as she'd meant it to. It also made him grin.

She pretended not to notice. "Static. As if music was playing, but I couldn't get the station tuned in."

"Ah! So my—but no. I'm so easily moved to digressions! Let us sit down, and perhaps you will tolerate a few questions."

There were more than a few questions, and they ranged all over the place. Had either of them experienced any unusual sensations or thoughts during the demon's attack? What did the demon's poison feel like now? How much holy water had Cynna used? How strong would Lily rate the power wind? Did she associate it with a color? A sound? Had Rule smelled anything when it hit? Why did the lupi not name this so-called goddess? What kind of powers were attributed to Her? How did they know Her avatar had been eaten by a demon prince?

Some answers were simple. They didn't name the goddess because names held power, and She might be drawn to the namer. Cynna had used about six ounces of holy water. The demon's poison felt, to Lily's touch, like a rotted orange.

Other answers took longer, and some they simply couldn't give.

When the others weren't asking questions, they were arguing about what the answers meant. At least, three out of four of them argued; Fagin looked on, a dreamy Buddha contemplating the isness of being, or maybe a nap.

Rule grew twitchy as the discussion dragged on. The wolf was bored, and his hip hurt. Not with the sharp pain of a fresh wound, but a tired sort of ache, as if the muscle were weary of the battle going on inside it. He was getting hungry, too; healing burned calories like crazy. The wolf didn't see the humans as food—only the feral or the very newly Changed lost their humanity to that extent—but he wanted to explore, even if he couldn't hunt.

Rule glanced at the door for the second or third time.

"Uh-uh," Lily whispered, leaning close. "If I can't escape, neither can you. Kind of like being around triplet Cullens, isn't it?"

"At least none of them are burning anything," he murmured.

The human in him recognized the method beneath the apparent disorder, however. Fagin might claim to be prone to digression, but he let the others have only enough time to see if a debate was going anywhere productive, then sighed and, professing regret at the necessity, pulled them back on topic.

Which apparently *was* the fate of the world.

When Lily asked, it turned out that all four of them did agree on one thing: the world teetered on the cusp of great change. Ito saw that change in terms of various prophecies; Sherry spoke of a trembling in her bones and a vision experienced by a member of her coven. The archbishop simply agreed that if the power winds continued, the level of magic in the world would rise.

And that could change everything.

Fagin grounded his explanation in his own specialty. "There are two schools of thought concerning pre-Purge history. The first school, accepted by the majority of the Western world, holds that early accounts of great magical events and abilities were the product of propaganda, exaggeration, hysteria, and superstition. Yet many of those accounts come from men who were hardly charlatans or credulous fools."

"It's the winners who write history," Sherry said.

He awarded her a delighted smile. "Precisely. Those who conducted the Purge were the winners, and their view is enshrined in our culture. We teach it to middle school students and expound upon it in countless doctoral theses."

Ito snorted. "It's not the first time a lot of crap has been taught at Harvard."

Sherry's eyes twinkled. "Hikaru, don't you teach at Harvard?"

"That's how I know."

Fagin nodded at Lily. "You've undoubtedly guessed that some of us do not share the accepted view. We believe there was once much more magic in the world, and that the failure of magic to deliver as it once had caused the Purge."

"You're right," Rule said quietly.

"Ah!" The bushy brows drew down in the first frown Rule had seen on the man's face. "I've heard that your people have a particularly vital oral history. One you don't share with outsiders."

"True on both counts."

Fagin regarded him a moment. "I may attempt to change your mind about that, but later. Interesting, isn't it, that your Mr. Brooks assembled his task force from academics and practitioners who don't subscribe to the conventional wisdom about the Purge?"

Lily leaned forward. "So what do you unconventional thinkers think?"

"Basically that during the sixteenth century the quantity of available magic began to decline. Perhaps people depleted it, just as any natural resource may be depleted. Perhaps the decline was part of a purely natural cycle, an ebb and flow of magic that produces occasional barren periods, just as the cyclical nature of global temperatures results in periodic ice ages. That is my own theory."

"Or perhaps," Ito said, "when the Codex Arcanum was lost or destroyed, it took much of the world's magic with it."

Fagin smiled. "And that is Ito's theory, based on his interpretation of Nostradamus. In any case, what we are seeing now suggests that our magical ice age is drawing to an end."

For a moment no one spoke. Rule thought about the power grid, the stock market, the banking system . . . air traffic control. The Internet. Cars. Buses. Medical technology. Laboratories. All of them vulnerable to sudden surges of magic. "How well does silk insulate against magic?"

It was Sherry who answered, her voice soft. "Not well enough."

No one spoke for a moment. Then Ito scraped his chair back. "I'm sorry to leave, but my wife is flying here to join me, and I need to pick her up."

Lily checked her watch. "It's later than I thought. If you're through with me for now, I'd like to see if Ruben's still here. I need some help prying information out of the Secret Service."

"I don't think he goes home much." Fagin pushed his chair out. "I'd like a word with him myself. Shall we hunt him up? We can compare notes on our mutual Gift on the way."

She looked at Rule. She didn't say a word. He knew what she wanted.

He sighed. "About the poison . . ."

"Yes." Sherry's frown was sharp. "We need to talk about that. Patrick?"

Lily touched Rule's shoulder lightly, then rose. "Have you ever touched a magic that seemed—well, evil?" she was asking Fagin as the door closed behind them.

Rule soon decided he might as well have left with Lily. Sherry and the archbishop didn't seem to require his presence. Patrick Brown paced, paused, threw up his hands. He spoke of souls, demonic intrusion, and quasi-magical energies, while Sherry just kept talking, wearing away at the man's arguments the way water wears away stone.

After five or ten minutes of that, Rule agreed with his wolf. He'd sat here long enough. Abruptly he stood. "I'm going in search of vending machine calories and some of the sludge they call coffee here. Would either of you care to risk your stomach lining on a cup?"

Sherry chuckled. "I don't heal as well as you do. No, thanks."

The churchman stopped moving and grimaced. "We've ignored you. Sorry. I get caught up . . . but I have a question for you. You said the holy water caused pain. How much?"

"Like cauterizing a wound."

His eyebrows shot up. "Have you experienced that? Never mind—none of my business. A high level of pain, then." He didn't look happy about that. His eyes flicked to Sherry. "How quickly can you call a coven?"

"Maybe by tonight. Tomorrow night at the latest. We won't need to work full-coven, and my healer is a local."

He nodded reluctantly. "Then I'll defer to your technique. We'll try my method if yours doesn't work as well as you expect."

"That's what I've been saying." She was brisk as she reached into the large purse by her chair and pulled out her phone. "I'll start calling."

"Wait a minute," Rule said. "You're calling a coven? Isn't that overkill?"

Her gaze lifted to him. "It may have sounded like Patrick and I can't agree on the color of the sky, but we do agree about one thing. It is vitally important to get that poison out of you as soon as possible."

"Most of it's already gone, and more holy water—"

"Is unlikely to work on its own," the archbishop said. "I'm surprised it worked at all, frankly. You must have a great deal of trust in the woman who used it, and she must possess a great deal of faith."

"Cynna?" Rule hoped he didn't sound as incredulous as he felt.

"Holy water does have some intrinsic power, but it's slight. Mostly it acts as a conduit for faith. Since you aren't Catholic, her faith would have to be unusually strong for the holy water to affect the poison."

Rule hadn't really adjusted to the idea of Cynna being Catholic. That she might be truly fervent unsettled him. "Why wouldn't more holy water eliminate the poison entirely?" Not that he was crazy about the technique. He'd probably have to be held down—a humiliating prospect—and that required lupus strength, which meant a delay until his bodyguards arrived. But at least it would be quick.

"It's complicated." The man frowned, tapping his fingers against his thigh. "We've been calling the substance in your wound poison, but that's misleading. It's actually a bit of the demon itself—a demonic artifact, or intrusion."

"That's why it's important to remove it as soon as possible," Sherry said, holding her phone to her ear. Rule could hear it ringing on the other end. "You may not be losing much blood now, but . . . Oh, Linda, hi. This is Sherry."

Patrick Brown took it from there as Sherry spoke to one of her coven members. "But there are potentially other problems. As I understand it, magic permeates your physical being. Yes?"

"Basically."

"You have demon magic lodged in your body, interfering with your innate magic to prevent your healing. That much we know. It's also quite possible that it's interfering in other ways we're unable to detect. Any such other effects could be negligible or serious. You might grow horns or tentacles, begin to crave blood, or fall down dead. We simply don't know. But the longer the demon stuff stays in your body, the greater the chance of additional adverse effects."

Rule was glad Lily had left the room. She was already worried about him. "All right, I'm picking up on the urgency. I still don't see why you won't try holy water again."

Brown sighed. "It seems you're strongly attached to your guilt."

"What?" His scalp twitched, trying to flatten ears that didn't lay down in this form.

"That wasn't an accusation. Being human means being subject to the ills of guilt and temptation. I assume that is true for a lupus, also."

Rule gave a tense nod.

"Demons lack souls, yet they can have a terrible effect on ours. Demonic intrusions act on us through magic but bind to us through spirit. The binding agents are temptation, guilt, or both."

"You're saying that I'm holding on to the poison myself."

"More that guilt creates a sticky place for it to adhere. If you were of my faith, I'd advise you to attend confession. Since you aren't, I suggest you search your conscience. If you can make peace with yourself and the Creator, however you think of Him—"

"Her." The wolf wanted to bare its teeth. He had no great sins on his conscience. "We worship the female aspect of the One."

"So do we," Sherry said, punching in more numbers on her

phone. "Male and female both, actually. Our healer wants to check you out first, but if she gives the go-ahead we'll hold the ritual at midnight."

"Midnight."

"Tradition has its . . . hello, Stephen. I need to know if . . ."

Patrick Brown was looking at Rule with a damnable degree of sympathy. "Guilt doesn't always exist for rational reasons, you know. We may feel terrible guilt for events beyond our control. Survivor's guilt, for example."

"This all has something to do with holy water, I presume."

"Through a mechanism involving guilt, your body has been fooled into accepting the demon's substance as part of it, rather the way a human body is fooled into feeding cancer cells. Holy water affects the demonic, but it would affect your body, too, because of this misidentification. If it worked at all, it could cause lasting damage. I'm surprised it didn't the first time."

Rule's hip throbbed quietly. After a moment he said, "There's a scar." A scar was nothing in itself, but was there other, less visible damage?

Sherry thanked someone, disconnected, and immediately punched in another number. Rule felt Lily drawing nearer. A moment later, he heard her and Fagin talking on the other side of the wall. At first their words were indistinct; then Lily's voice rose, incredulous. "You've got to be kidding."

Fagin's low rumble was soothing. ". . . just a theory . . . my family . . . old stories and folklore."

"But that's not—it isn't—it can't be physically possible. A dragon?" She was at the door. The knob turned.

Rule's left foot landed on gray carpet.

Vertigo struck. He staggered, righted himself, and looked around wildly. He—he was in a hall, one of the many hallways of the FBI building. He heard a copy machine humming, voices behind him and in the office to his left, the chime of the elevator up ahead as it stopped on this floor.

This floor? Which one? Where was he?

Lily grabbed his arm. "Rule? What is it? What's wrong?"

"We . . ." He turned carefully, looking back down the hall. Back the way he must have come. It was the same floor, he realized. The conference room was just around that bend.

Lily didn't seem to notice anything wrong, other than the way he was acting. Whatever had happened, it happened to him, not both of them. "I was in the conference room with Sherry and the archbishop. You and Fagin were about to enter. You'd just turned the doorknob. Then . . . then I was here."

Her eyes were wide with distress, her voice level. "You've been with me since I walked back into the conference room."

"What happened?" What could possibly have happened to rob him of himself for . . . how long? How much time had he lost?

Lily took the question literally. "Fagin and I came in. Archbishop Brown explained about the problem with holy water. He said Sherry's healer will have a look at you, then her coven will perform some sort of ritual. You didn't say much, but you were there. Present. I *felt* you as clearly as I feel you now. Then Cullen called, and—"

"Cullen called?"

"You spoke to him." The distress leaked into her voice. "He called on my phone to let me know what happened with the demon. It had possessed someone. They dispatched it, but Cynna was hurt. Then he talked to you—something about, uh, *heres valos.* Clan stuff. You—you were going to explain that, but wanted to wait until we were private."

"Cynna—"

"She'll be okay."

Would he? Rule knew he couldn't be possessed, and yet . . . "Are you sure it was me?"

"You sounded like yourself. I felt you there, beside me. You . . ." She stopped, swallowed. "I touched you. I didn't feel anything, no spell, no . . ."

"Demon." He searched for a scrap, a hint, any shred of memory that something had occurred between the moment he'd watched the doorknob turn and the one when he found himself in midstride on this hall.

Nothing. "I don't remember. I don't remember any of it."

Instinctively she reached for his arm. Her eyes widened—then narrowed. She stared at her hand, then deliberately reached up and touched the bare skin of his face.

"Well, shit," she said.

NINETEEN

SOMEONE was messing with her foot. It hurt. She jerked it away.

"Hold still."

That was Cullen's voice. He sounded peevish. Someone—Cullen?—yanked her foot back onto the warm place it had been resting and wiped it with the stinging stuff again.

"Ow!" Cynna's eyes popped open.

"Don't be a sissy. It's not much of a cut."

She blinked as memory seeped back in. She was lying on her back in a bed—pretty decent bed, too. Soft. The ceiling was white, and somewhere that longhair music was still playing. So she was still in Victor Frey's house, and not too much time had passed.

What had happened after things went black? Was the demon . . . *Check, fool.*

She did a quick cast. Okay, good. She was badly drained, but she was sure the demon wasn't nearby. And Cullen was all right. What about Merilee and Frey and Timms and the lupus guards? Had they come through okay? She propped herself up on one elbow.

Hey. Her head didn't hurt.

She was in a small bedroom with faded wallpaper and maple furniture. Very tidy, like the rest of the house. Cullen sat on the bed with her right foot in his lap. His hair was mussed, and his shirt was ripped and bloody. "You're hurt."

"No, dummy, you are." He finished what he'd been doing with the washrag and picked up a tube of antibiotic ointment.

"I guess I stepped on something." She didn't remember cutting her foot, but in all the excitement she might not have noticed. A dozen questions jockeyed for position. She plucked the simplest and asked it. "What happened?"

"You pissed off a demon." His voice was funny. He squirted ointment on her foot and smeared it around. "Remember that part?"

"Yeah. She clobbered me."

"She cracked your skull." Now he looked up, and she knew why he'd sounded odd. She'd never heard him flat-out furious before. "Of all the lamebrained, stupid-ass stunts—"

"Did it work?"

He shoved her foot off his lap and sprang to his feet. "I'm not believing this. Two humans and three lupi go after a demon. Do the humans let the lupi deal with the hand-to-hand? No, since you lack the common sense of a dung beetle, you—"

"Two humans? Is Timms okay?"

The door opened. A handsome woman with broad hips and shoulders and hot-cocoa skin came in. "Banged up some, but he'll mend. They're loading him into the ambulance now. He wouldn't let me set his arm—said he wanted a real doctor." She looked at Cullen. "Quit yelling at my patient."

She was a patient? Cynna gave her head a shake. Nothing rattled. "I'm fine. What happened with Frey and Merilee and the demon? Anyone else hurt?"

The woman turned a solemn face on her. She looked somewhere over forty but still downwind of old age; beyond that, it was hard to guess. "The Rho's well enough to heal on his own, thanks to you. Merilee . . ." She sighed. "Ah don't know about her. Her body's not hurt aside from a couple bruises, and the baby's fine, praise the Lord. But the poor child's mind is a mess."

Possession could do that to you. "Then the demon's not in her anymore."

The full lips tightened. "Ah got rid of it."

"You did? Oh—excuse me. It would be nice if Mr. Gorgeous got over his snit long enough to introduce us, but I'm not holding my breath. I'm Cynna Weaver."

A laugh rolled up from the woman's comfortable middle. She glanced at Cullen, who was leaning against the wall, arms crossed, scowling at both of them. "Ah think maybe I like you, Cynna Weaver. I'm the Leidolf Rhej, and I'm a healer, which is why you ain't in that ambulance with the other one."

Cynna knew the clans' holy women didn't usually offer their names, so she didn't ask. "You're also an exorcist, I take it."

"Not till today, but the Lady don't put up with demons messing with her people. Good thing someone had the sense to send for me. Ah had a few minutes to call up the right memory for the job."

"That was you," Cynna said to Cullen. "You had Boss Guard send someone to get her, didn't you?"

He just kept scowling. He didn't like Rhejes, she knew. Or maybe *grudge* was a better word than *dislike*—a grudge connected to the time he'd spent clanless. Which he didn't talk about, so she didn't know what the connection was, but maybe that was what was making him act like a ten-year-old who'd had his TV privileges taken away.

"He did," the woman said, " since it didn't occur to my bonehead brother to fetch me. That was a right mess I walked into— you an' the other human sprawled out like the dead, my brother and that David tryin' to hold down Merilee. She was pretty lively, too."

"Timms couldn't get a dart in her?"

Cullen condescended to speak. "Oh, he darted her. The tranquilizer didn't exactly make her tranquil, though, so he rushed her with the others. Idiot."

"The drug had some effect," the Rhej said judiciously. "Or else Alex and David couldn't've held her down at all. She did toss David off once—that's when she tried to rip open your Mr. Gorgeous's throat. Good thing she just had fingernails to work with, not claws."

Cynna's head swung toward Cullen. "That's your blood," she said accusingly.

"The cut's not deep. Be healed by tomorrow, which is more than you can say about your head."

He was wrong there. The Rhej must be one hell of a healer. "Did you use the charm? Did it work?"

Cullen shot her a withering look. "Of course it did."

"Still is," the Rhej said, her face creasing into trouble lines. "I didn't know what to do for Merilee after I got rid of that demon. When she came around, she was . . . well, I had Cullen use his charm to keep her asleep for now. Couldn't do it myself—putting your head back together took everything I dared tap, but we owed you that." She gave a nod. "Victor'd be dead if you hadn't jumped that demon. He may be an ass, but he's our ass. We need him."

There was plain speaking. Maybe a Rhej didn't have to be as respectful of the Rho as the rest of the clan. Cynna swung her feet off the bed. "Maybe I can help Merilee. I—"

"Hey!" For a big woman, the Rhej moved fast. She grabbed Cynna's shoulders and held her down. "I'm good, but I'm not that good. You don't need to be bouncin' around yet."

"I'm fine."

Her eyes narrowed. She placed her big hands on either side of Cynna's head and hummed quietly as her eyes lost their focus. Her palms grew warm. Very warm. Cynna began to feel sleepy.

All at once she dropped her hands and frowned. "What have you done to yourself? Something's stopped up inside you—some kind of spell, an' the tangle it's made is full to burstin' with your magic."

"I don't . . . oh, shit." The pain-block spell. She closed her eyes and mentally traced the *kilingo* for the spell. Yep, way too much power going into it. How did that happen?

Figure that out later. She turned it off . . . and nearly toppled off the bed. "Owww . . . oh, man. That hurts."

Cullen's scowl was back. "A depressed skull fracture is supposed to hurt."

Depressed skull fracture. Cynna felt cold and dizzy thinking about it . . . or maybe just thinking did that. Her head was throbbing like a bad tooth.

"Now, don't let him scare you," the woman said. "Your head was a big job, but Ah fixed it. Lifted up that bit of broken skull, got rid of the fluid, knit up the torn whatchamacallit—that stuff right under the skull—drained the blood clot an' healed the bruisin' on the brain. Got the skull started knitting, too, enough to hold, but I couldn't do it all in one whack. Your head's gonna ache for a couple days. But what was stopping up the pain before?"

Blood clot? Torn whatchamacallit? Bruising on the brain? "Ah . . . this spell I've got blocks pain, but it shouldn't have . . . I had a trickle of power going into it before, see. Somehow it got turned up on high while I was unconscious."

"How?" Cullen demanded.

"No idea." She might care about that later. Right now . . . "Any reason I can't use the spell? Not on full power, but enough to take the edge off."

"Sugah, that spell had your body thinking it wasn't hurt at all. It had quit healing."

Sounded like the answer was no. Cynna grimaced.

"I'd like to learn that spell, though," the Rhej went on. "See if it can be tinkered with, made to work so's it don't block the healing."

"It only works on me." Cynna rested the uncracked side of her head in her hand. "I've tried to modify it so it could be used on others, but nothing works."

"I'd like to take a look at it," Cullen said in a neutral voice. "With your permission."

She looked at him out of pain-narrowed eyes. Sorcerers had a real edge when it came to altering a spell. He'd be able to see it, see exactly how it worked. "Later, maybe. I'm—"

"Well, well, well." Brady stood in the doorway, blue eyes bright with pleasure. "Fancy meeting you again, Seabourne. I like the way your blood looks. Pity there isn't more of it showing."

The Rhej turned to face him. Cynna couldn't read her expression—she had the woman's profile—but her body language said, *watch out.* "What are you doin' in the house, Brady? Alex didn't let you in."

"My father's hurt. I wanted to see him."

"You aren't supposed to be here till after the naming. You know that. An' your father ain't in this room."

"You sure? Maybe I should check." He moved into the room, graceful as a snake. "Could be under the bed. I'll have a peek."

The Rhej stepped in front of him. "Don't you try to play your games with me, Brady Gunning."

"Better call your brother." He raised his voice in a falsetto. "Help, Alex! Brady's picking on me!"

Brady wasn't here to needle Cullen, Cynna realized with a jolt. It was the Rhej he was after.

Cullen uncoiled himself from his snit, straightening to stand with his arms loose at his sides. "Now that's interesting. She can't smell your fear, Brady, but I can."

"Fear?" Brady laughed, but it didn't come out right. "You think I'm afraid of a female too old to breed?" He looked over at the Rhej. "More like the other way around, isn't it? At least it should be."

Cullen moved—not too fast to see this time, but fast enough. He put himself between the Rhej and Brady. "You still scared of fire?"

Brady snarled. "This is Leidolf business. Stay out."

Cynna had never seen Cullen's face wiped so clean of whimsy or mockery. "You threatened the Lady's Voice. You'll beg her forgiveness."

The Rhej started to say something, but Brady spoke right over her. "Beg? Of a *female*?" He made the word sound like something nasty that had gotten stuck in his teeth.

Cullen flicked his fingertips. Sparks danced in the air. "Beg or burn. Your choice."

"Hey!" Cynna said. "FBI agent here. I hate to point this out, but burning people's illegal."

"Brady." Alex, aka Boss Guard, filled the doorway like a quiet mountain.

Brady turned slowly. "Yeah?"

"You'll leave now. You won't come back in the house until the naming."

The two men locked gazes. Cynna held her breath. Brady wanted to attack. No, he wanted to kill. He vibrated with that need, probably stank of it to the other lupi. But some thread of sanity or self-preservation prevailed. His posture changed subtly as the challenge went out of him. He dropped his eyes and nodded once.

Cullen spoke. "He threatened your Rhej."

The big man exchanged a look with his sister. "If that's so—"

"I meant no threat." Brady smiled as if he hadn't been a breath away from killing a moment ago. "If my words seemed a threat, I didn't mean them so."

Her face was stony. She gave a small nod.

Cullen didn't like it. "That's not—"

"It's enough," the Rhej said firmly. "I require no more . . . at this time." She gave Brady a look that ought to have had him tucking his tail between his legs.

Instead he smirked, offered a mocking bow, and walked up to the mountain, eyebrow cocked. Alex looked to his right and gave a small nod to someone out of sight in the hall, then stepped aside. Brady—thank God—left.

A large gray wolf trotted after him. An escort, Cynna guessed, to make sure he did leave.

Alex watched him go, then turned to the Rhej. "Sister . . ."

"I know." She rubbed her temple, looking about ten years older than she had at first. "But this is a bad time for it. They'd say I was interfering in the naming."

Cullen looked like he couldn't believe what he was hearing. "You can't let him get away with that, naming or no naming. Which is going to involve you anyway. The Lady's approval—"

"This is Leidolf."

Apparently that answered Cullen, who sighed. "He means you ill."

"You think I'm a fool? I know that. But the founder's line is thin."

"Sister." Alex specialized in one-word comments. This time his voice was heavy with disapproval.

She snorted. "You think Nokolai and the other clans don't know exactly who carries the bloodline?"

"She's right." Cullen tried to look apologetic. He wasn't good at it. "Not counting Brady—who, sadly, is a sure thing from this standpoint—you've got two from a collateral line who can almost certainly carry the mantle. Two others stand a fair chance. The rest are long shots."

"So we're thin," she said. "If Brady sires a child—"

"You want *that* to breed?" Cynna said, appalled.

"Don't judge what you don't understand." She straightened her shoulders. "And don't be playing with that spell of yours till you're mended. I'll check back with you in the morning, see how you're doing. Anything you need tonight, let Sabra know. You'd best stay in the room," she added to Cullen. "It's poor hospitality, but—"

Cullen broke in, polite but firm. "Serra, I've already called Rule." She stared at him, then looked at her brother, who nodded. He didn't look happy about it. She sighed.

"So I'll not stretch your hospitality at such a difficult time," Cullen went on. "And Cynna wants—"

"Cynna," Cynna said firmly, "wants to speak for herself. I appreciate the offer," she told the Rhej, "but I need to check on Timms."

The older woman shook her head. "He wasn't hurt near so bad as you. What you have to do, girl, is rest."

"I will, but after I see about Timms. I was in charge. He got hurt. I have to go to the hospital and see how he's doing, if he needs anything."

"She's right," Alex said unexpectedly. "Unless it will cause her grave injury, she must see to her man."

His sister rolled her eyes. "Lord help me. I expect macho bull-shit from you—now I'm gettin' it from another woman. All right, honey, you do what you're gonna do, but come back tomorrow and let me see how your head's doing. We need to keep the in-flammation down. Then, if you're up to it, maybe we'll talk a bit. Adriane—she's my apprentice—will want to meet you, and I'm a mite curious myself. Till now, I was the only Rhej who was out-clan before the Lady spoke."

"But . . . I'm sorry. Cullen has given you the wrong impression. I can't become a Rhej. I'm Catholic."

The woman smiled. "And I'm Baptist. Don't go to services as often as I ought to, but I still go. It don't matter, sugar. Didn't our Lord say it? 'In my Father's house are many rooms.' You an' me, we started out in one room, then it turned out we were needed in another one."

TWENTY

CULLEN carried her out of the house.

Cynna protested, of course. Maybe she'd gone a bit dizzy when she stood up—didn't mean she wasn't perfectly capable of walking. "This is ridiculous. Didn't I tell you to—"

"Shut up."

"Oh, like that's going to happen." It felt weird, being carried. Embarrassing, too, but he was really warm, and firm in all the places a man ought to be firm . . . though she was just guessing about one spot. That might or might not be firming up. She couldn't tell without groping him, which would be way tacky.

Especially since they had an escort. Alex had sent the big, reddish wolf with them—either making sure they didn't steal the silver, or that no one bothered them on their way out. Like Brady.

She felt the flex of his muscles as he started down the stairs, trailing the wolf. This was interesting enough that she decided to let the uncracked side of her head rest on his shoulder. He smelled good, too. She probably didn't, but there wasn't much she could do about that.

She'd hooked her tote on her left arm, which was curled around his neck. It thumped gently against his back as they descended. "So why did you try to make Brady apologize to the Rhej?"

"I thought I told you to shut up."

Rude as hell. Still pissed, too. But he was taking the stairs so carefully it didn't jar her head at all. That was as interesting as the hard chest she rested against. "You don't like Rhejes, but you wanted to burn Brady. I can see why you might, but why don't you like Rhejes?"

"None of your business."

True, but that didn't do a thing to ease her curiosity. Maybe he didn't want the wolf to hear, though. "Did you see the demon possessing Merilee, like you thought you would?"

"Yes."

He'd answered. Hallelujah. She dug into her question hoard for some that couldn't be answered yes or no. "You said another demon chased you. When? And where were you? How did you get away?"

"I burned it. In Mexico. Yesterday. And I didn't stop to ask for names, but your old friend was riding it in astral form."

"Jiri?"

He nodded.

Shit. "How'd you know it was her?"

"Lily has a description, remember? I saw a tall woman, African heritage, no boobs, strong shoulders. Good with demons. Oh, and her eyes glowed red. Sound familiar?"

They'd reached the bottom of the stairs. Three men—lupi, she supposed, but in human form—were in the living room. They watched, silent and unfriendly, as their wolf escort stopped at the door.

Cullen stopped there, too. "Someone want to open this? Or I could just drop her and get it myself."

"Let me." She stretched her free hand down and turned the knob.

It was fully dark now. Creepy-dark once the door shut behind them. She couldn't see the wolf anymore, but heard his claws on the porch. "Don't lupi believe in porch lights?"

"I can see." He proved it by stepping off the porch.

There must have been clouds overhead, because only a few stars were showing off their twinkles. It never got this black in a city. "How long was I out?"

"About forty minutes. Putting you down now," he said as they reached the car, suiting action to words. As soon as she heard the lock click, she opened the door, and in the spill of light saw not one, but three wolves sitting on the porch, watching.

She climbed in. Her heartbeat was making the kettledrum in her head act up. You'd think she'd raced across the yard instead of traveling in a beautiful man's arms, but her pulse rate might have something to do with those three pony-size wolves staring at them.

She slammed the door. "I need to call Lily."

He was already behind the wheel. "I called Rule, remember?"

"Rule isn't my boss. And what was that about, anyway? They acted funny when you said you'd called him."

"They'd rather no one knew about Victor's condition." He started the engine.

"And that explains something?"

He sighed. "Got to have it all spelled out, do you? Okay. You, they can't kill. Me, they might, though not here, since Victor made me guest. Once I leave their land, that doesn't apply."

"Yet here we are, leaving."

He pulled the car around in a wide circle, heading them back the way they'd come in. "If I don't leave now, they're apt to hold on to me until after the naming."

"Maybe they haven't heard? Kidnapping's illegal."

He shrugged. "We don't tattle on each other to the authorities."

"I am the authorities." Weird as it still seemed.

"Which is one reason they're not stopping us. The other is that I've already spoken to Rule. They aren't sure what I told him and might like to keep me around to find out, but they probably won't try anything with you by my side." He flashed her a grin, almost unseen in the darkness. "My bodyguard."

Lupus politics would have made her head hurt even without a half-healed skull fracture. "I still have to report."

"No, you don't. I spoke to Lily, too. She knows we found the demon and got rid of it. The rest can wait until tomorrow."

Or until they reached the hospital, anyway. She leaned her head against the headrest and gave the kettledrum a chance to settle down.

They left the clearing behind, and the trees loomed over them, twisty black hulks holding hands overhead. It was dusk here, with the belly of the sky hanging low and rain clouds dimming the day. There was no way to make the dirt road anything but bumpy, and Cullen liked to drive fast. She gritted her teeth on a couple bumps, but that hurt, too, so she tried to Zen out on watching the headlights bounce over the rutted road.

She wasn't good at Zen but did start feeling kind of spacey. And tired. Really tired. She let her eyes drift closed, shutting out the spooky trees, but she was still awake when they turned onto the smoother surface of the highway.

"Where's your hotel?" he asked, all curt.

"Harrisonburg, but I have to go to the hospital first, remember."

"The mental hospital, maybe?"

"What are you so mad about, anyway?"

"Why the hell do you think?" he snapped. "I started liking you. I don't like many people, so it pisses me off if one of them tries to get herself killed."

"Oh." *Friendship potential,* she thought. Hadn't she decided Cullen had that much going for him?

The tires hummed on the pavement. He didn't turn the radio on or put in a CD, and she wondered why. Lupi were nuts for music. A few moments later, the shushing sound of rain swept over them. *That's better than any CD,* she thought as a few more muscles quit bracing themselves against what-might-be and relaxed.

Maybe he liked the sound of rain, too. She listened to wet sheets of it rushing at the car and tried to remember . . . Why wasn't she supposed to be interested in Cullen, anyway?

Oh, yeah. Hormones. Jerk. Lousy track record. Those were good reasons, but her hormones weren't putting in a vote now . . . or if they were, it was drowned out by all the pain signals.

Friendship. She could work with that. "So, you want to have sex after my head quits hurting?"

"Hell, yes. You going to be mad when I remind you that you asked?"

Eyes closed, head throbbing, she felt her lips curve up. "Probably."

TWENTY-ONE

WHEN they arrived at the ER, the doctor was showing Timms X-rays of his arm—which, Cullen had said, Merilee had snapped over her knee like a stick. He'd lucked out. The bone was broken in two places, but they were clean breaks. No need for surgery or a hospital stay.

Timms was glad to see them. Even Cullen. Either the men had bonded during battle, or he was a lot friendlier with enough of Percodan zipping around his system. Then he opened his big mouth, asking about her head, and shouldn't she get that checked out?

The doctor—a young guy, real short hair, pierced ears but not wearing anything in them at the moment—wanted to do a CT scan. She explained that a healer had taken care of the injury.

This didn't soothe him at all. But Cullen did. He assured the doctor he'd monitored the procedure, tossing out phrases like "frontoparietal region," "shear force," and "subdural hematoma." He didn't actually claim to be a doctor, but he sure talked the talk.

It would have worked, too, if Timms hadn't stared at him more in confusion than suspicion. "I thought you were a stripper."

Cullen widened his eyes. "Medical school is expensive."

It was a slow night at the ER. The young doctor decided she really needed that CT scan and would not let up, apparently willing to wait indefinitely before setting Timms's arm if that's what it took to get her to agree. Cynna lost her temper.

Another doctor—this one older, blacker, and a lot more tired—followed the sound of her raised voice. "That's some fine cussing," he told her, "and you may be right about Dr. Farley's lineage, but there are other patients here. Keep it down." She sighed and agreed, and he went on, "You were injured out at Victor's. Is that where the healing took place, too?"

She nodded, hoping he wouldn't ask who'd done it. He turned to the younger one. "That'll be Leah's work, then. Don't worry about it. Set the man's arm."

Leah, huh? Cynna filed the name away. She wouldn't use it without permission.

Cynna adjourned to the waiting room while the doctor set and casted Timms's arm. Cullen headed for the men's room. She sank into an empty chair with relief. Eyes closed, she amused herself by matching the sounds and voices to the others in the room.

The wailing baby was easy. It belonged to the heavyset woman across the room, as did the little-girl whine—a toddler with many braids. The sharp-voiced complaints came from a skinny grandma trying to straighten out something to do with insurance, and the sneeze was from the old guy at the end of her row of chairs.

She was contemplating summoning the energy to get herself a Coke when someone sat beside her. She cranked her eyelids up, cut her eyes that way, and closed them again. "Medical school?"

"Very expensive," Cullen said. "Here."

She frowned at the Styrofoam cup he held. "I'm not a coffee drinker."

"Caffeine's a mild analgesic. Good for headaches."

She sighed and straightened and took the cup, frowning at the murky liquid. "Ibuprofin works better and doesn't taste nasty."

"You already took some. I dumped three packets of sugar in."

That might make it bearable. And if it would blunt this headache . . . She took a sip, grimaced. "People drink this stuff on purpose."

"Elixir of the gods." Cullen sipped from his own cup. "Though this particular brew might be for minor deities. Very minor. About that healing spell—"

"For chrissake, Cullen, not now."

"I might learn something from it that would help understand the demon poison in Rule."

"Huh?" she said cleverly.

"Rule's wound won't heal. Your spell blocks healing along with pain. It's worth checking out."

She thought about it, or tried to. The caffeine hadn't done much for her yet. "You're thinking you can reverse the spell and use it to restart his healing?"

"Maybe. Or just understand the action of the poison better by seeing how your spell works. May I see the *kilingo* for the spell?"

Hardly anyone knew the correct terms for Msaidizi magic, but he did. He knew she'd been a *shetanni rakibu*, a demon rider, too, and he had a pretty good idea what that meant.

She wanted him to go away. "I'm not supposed to use the spell, remember? You won't be able to see anything while it's inactive."

"The Rhej didn't know the spell was there when she was healing you, so its effect must be very minimal unless the power's turned up. Trickle just enough juice into it for me to see how it works."

She bit her lip. She wanted to help Rule, but this felt oddly intimate. "Okay, but try not to be overwhelmed with passion. I have to lift up my sweater."

"Goody," he murmured.

She was sure that was an automatic response. Lupi felt obligated to flirt with females—it was like please and thank you for them, a basic courtesy. Cullen might like the idea of having sex with her, but his real passion was magic. "It's on my stomach. Here . . . this area above my belly button." She showed him the outline of the spell, mentally adding a trickle of power to her moving finger.

Ah, that felt better. Even set on low, the spell worked great.

He bent, tilting his head as he studied her stomach. "This part"—he traced the skin of her belly with a fingertip—"looks promising. I take it you converted a spell that originally used physical components?"

"Yeah." Whoa. With her headache turned off, her hormones were rioting, and happy about it. His touch left heat behind. Actual heat, not just the sexual sort.

Wait a minute. Her headache *was* gone, wasn't it? Completely.

"That looks like the *signa* for marjoram."

"It is." She'd barely tapped into her power. Could a spell get better with use? Adjust itself somehow? "The spell's got four stages, moon-sequenced. Takes a month to set up. I just finished it last month."

"Hmm." He pulled his hand back, and she let her sweater fall down to cover her oddly warm skin. Then he looked in her eyes and smiled, and the heat was there, too. "I'm good with fire," he said softly. "Which means I can bring its gentler cousin to life, too. With a touch."

Was he saying he could . . . oh, yeah, he was. "Magic hands?"

"Pity I can't show you exactly what I mean, but . . ." He took her hand and put it in his lap, which was interesting all by itself. Then he drew a lazy circle on her palm with the tip of one finger . . . and heat. "This is a sample," he said, his smile turning wicked.

He was thinking about other spots he could touch with that heat. So was she.

He made more slow circles. Unlike most of her body, her palms were naked, unmarked. She hadn't thought of that as erotic until this moment. Her tongue darted out to moisten her lips. "Endorphins."

"Endorphins?" His voice was husky.

She nodded. "Better than caffeine."

"We could make lovely endorphins together." He sighed and closed her fingers up around the lingering warmth in her palm. "But not tonight. You need to turn that spell off again, and the Rhej told me in no uncertain terms that I wasn't to pester you for sex yet."

She was surprised. She'd once seen him obey the Nokolai Rhej, which had been pretty amazing. But this Rhej wasn't even of his clan. "You going to do like she says?"

"She threatened one of my favorite body parts. Besides, she's right. You need rest more than endorphins right now."

She needed to shut down the spell, too. With a sigh, Cynna closed her eyes and paid attention. "Hey." Her eyes popped open. "It's grabbing power."

"The spell?"

"Yeah. It . . . even in that little bit of time, it started pulling more power without my permission. I . . . ow. Shit." The second she shut down the flow of magic, the pain returned with a vengeance.

He was fascinated. "Where did you get this spell?"

"A Vodun priestess."

"For God's sake! Vodun magic is based on their pantheon. You can't strip the invocation and expect—"

"I'm not an idiot! Why do you always assume I'm an idiot? This is a *spell*, not one of their rites or incantations. No deities involved. She got it from her granny, who got it from her granny, and on back. She uses it herself."

"Any graveyard dust involved? Bones?"

"No and no."

"Blood magic?"

"Well, yes, but my own blood. Jesus, Cullen! Every tradition on the planet uses some blood spells."

"I'm not an idiot, either," he snapped. "I use blood spells myself. But using your own blood tied it to you. I don't know the process for transcribing a spell onto your skin—yes, yes, do close your mouth. I realize you aren't going to tell me—oath of secrecy and all that rot. But it must be similar to making a charm, only more personal, since it's inscribed on your body, not an inanimate object. The spell may be tied to you twice—through blood in the initial casting, and again when you absorbed it." He brooded on that a moment. "I need to see it. I need to watch what happens when it starts grabbing power."

Her head throbbed along with her heartbeat. "Not today, you aren't."

"No." He sounded regretful. "Tell me. Can you transcribe the spell onto someone else?"

"I . . . yeah, that's how I was taught, by having the first spell inscribed on me. I've never done it myself, but I think I could."

"That's what I hoped. We—lupi—need that spell. We can't be anesthetized for surgery, which increases the risk of shock."

She hadn't thought of that. "It's risky. Since the spell gobbles power, it could slow healing. But we'll look into it, okay? Just not tonight." She rubbed her head gingerly. "Speaking of healing, I don't see how I could have had a depressed skull fracture. Healers can help the body mend quicker, but they can't go lifting bits of skull. Is that a Rhej thing?"

He was sitting with his knees sprawled, leaning forward to rest his elbows on his thighs. He tilted his head to give her an odd look. "You were there when we opened the hellgate."

She glanced around. The crying baby two chairs over probably drowned out anything they said, but still . . . "Let's not talk about that."

He straightened. "Did you really think three women and one sorcerer had the power to do that on our own?"

"That's what the node was for. It was small, but so was the gate."

His foot started tapping restlessly. "You've got a good brain. I don't know why you don't use it more often. Power to power, Cynna. It takes power to use power, and we didn't have enough on our own to open the node. The Rhejes drew on the power of their clans."

She was appalled. "They can do that? Pull the magic from others and use it?"

"They generally don't, but they can. When the Leidolf Rhej talked about your healing she said 'we' owed it to you. We, not I. She used some of the clanpower to knit you back together."

Cynna didn't know if anyone ought to be able to use other people's magic without their permission. She was damned sure she shouldn't be given that kind of power.

The tapping foot stilled. "Did we ever eat?"

"Eat?"

"Supper. No," he decided, springing to his feet. "We didn't. There must be a cafeteria or something here." He looked around as if it might be tucked into a corner of the waiting room.

"What pushed your button?"

"Hunger. It's a wolf thing. We're all about five years old when it comes to mealtimes. Do you—never mind. You need to eat whether you feel like it or not."

No, she didn't. "Your phone's ringing."

He glanced down at the phone clipped to his belt, annoyed. "I thought I turned that off."

"You going to answer it?"

He grimaced but unhooked it and held it to his face. "I'm here, but I'm hungry. Can we keep this short?"

"Who is it?"

"Lily. No," he said into the phone, "I was answering Cynna. Yeah, aside from a helluva headache and her usual lunacy, she's fine. What about . . ." His voice drifted off into a frown.

A dark-skinned nurse wheeled Timms out of the treatment area. Cynna's eyebrows climbed. Timms had depths she'd never have dreamed of. He wore a brand-new sling and a brand-new cast . . . in flamingo pink.

He was going to be pissed once the painkiller wore off. She

grinned as she pushed to her feet and waved at the two of them.
"Over here."

There were a few moments of everyone talking at once.
Timms was soaring on Percodan and chatty; he wanted to talk
about demon tranquilizers. The nurse was upset about Cullen's
cell phone, so he went outside. Then she nabbed Cynna, determined to explain to someone about Timms's care.

Apparently he'd sprained his ankle, which explained the
wheelchair. Cynna persuaded Timms they'd go over their demon
drug strategy later, listened to the nurse, and pocketed scrips for
painkillers and crutches and a list of care instructions. They could
fill the prescription at the hospital but wouldn't be able to get the
crutches until tomorrow when a medical supply place opened up.

She was wondering if he'd mind sharing one of his pain pills
when Cullen came back in.

The nurse, the cranky granny, and the weary mother all forgot
their troubles for a moment to watch. Cullen was great eye candy
when he was still; in motion, he was music given form.

An up-tempo tune at the moment. He moved like he needed to
be somewhere else, and stopped in front of her, his face tight with
trouble. "Rule's worse. I'm heading straight back to D.C. Where
should I leave you?"

"Dumb question. I'm going with you."

"You need rest."

"Buy me a pillow. I'll sleep on the way."

He didn't argue, which worried her. "What about him?"

Timms blinked up at them fuzzily. "You've got my guns. I'd
better go, too."

Clearly Percodan didn't affect the man's priorities. "Dibs on
the backseat," she said.

TWENTY-TWO

RAIN had settled over eastern Maryland and Virginia like a broody hen. The storm didn't bother with thunder or lightning; it squatted patiently over the land, incubating grass, trees, and traffic accidents.

Cullen made good time on I-81 and I-66 in spite of his sedate pace—he'd held it under ninety pretty much the whole way. Too many humans cluttered the interstates, and they did the damnedest things behind the wheel. But D.C.'s traffic was constipated, as usual; once he hit the Parkway, it was more like an impacted bowel. Nothing was moving.

He drummed his fingers on the steering wheel, scowling at the cars ahead. He'd turned on the radio long enough to listen to the eye-in-the-sky traffic report; apparently some numbnuts had skidded his car across two lanes, causing a pileup.

Humans should not be allowed to drive when it rained.

He ought to be tired. He'd shorted himself on sleep for over a week now, and it was bound to catch up with him. But he was twitchy, wanting a run more than a rest—preferably four-footed. He'd been cooped up in a plane or a car for most of the past twenty-four hours.

"AK-47," Timms said suddenly. "Few bursts from that would make 'em move."

Cullen glanced at the man in the passenger seat, his lips

quirking. Timms had drifted in and out of a narcotic doze for most of the trip, but whenever he hit more-or-less awake, his comments were unabashedly bloodthirsty. "You might inspire the drivers, but when you kill cars, they don't get out of your way."

"True." Timms sighed heavily. "Couldn't shoot it with this damned arm, anyway."

There was a rustling in the backseat. "Shoot what?" Cynna asked.

"Timms is indulging in wishful thinking." Cullen felt a disproportionate sense of relief. She'd conked out after eating half of a hamburger and slept the whole way. He'd kept the radio turned off so he could listen to her breathing and heart rate, but medical school was a long time ago, and he hadn't paid attention to the parts that didn't interest him . . . which included much of the actual medicine. He hadn't attended with the intention of healing the sick. Only one of the sick, and he'd failed dismally there.

So he hadn't been sure if he should wake her or let her sleep, and he wasn't used to uncertainty. Or worrying. It was all damned annoying.

"What time is it?" she asked.

"Ten thirty. On the off chance we don't spend the night in this damned traffic jam, can I bunk at your place after we see what's up with Rule? Nokolai's house is running out of beds."

"Sorry. I don't have a place."

"You sleep in ditches?" The cars ahead finally eased forward, so Cullen did, too. Ten miles an hour was better than standing still.

"At a hotel. I'm on the go so much with my job—"

"You live in hotel rooms? All the time?"

"I had an apartment." She was defensive. "When it went condo I didn't want to buy, so I moved my junk into storage. I just haven't gotten around to finding another place, is all. Rent's crazy here."

"How long ago did your apartment go condo?"

"None of your business."

And he thought he lived a footloose life. She couldn't even commit to a rental contract. "I'd ask if your hotel room has a couch, but I don't trust me that much. I wouldn't stay on the couch." He sighed. "Maybe Rule has a sleeping bag."

"Rule's the one with demon stuff in him, right?" Timms said, frowning. "You sure you want to stay there? I don't have a spare room, but you could have the couch."

Amused, Cullen shot him a glance. "Thanks. I may take you up on that."

Cynna spoke. "Shouldn't we drop Timms off first?"

"He took one of his painkillers, which he seems to have a strong reaction to. He's flying. I don't think he'll mind waiting a little longer to go home." And he probably shouldn't be left alone until the medication wore off. He might shoot his neighbor's cat. Or his neighbor.

"But—"

"I'm okay," Timms said. "Uh . . . where are we going, again?"

Cullen explained one more time. You'd think the head injury victim would be the one with a short-term memory deficit, but Cynna remembered everything—including any number of questions she was forced to sit on with Timms around. She'd pointed that out during a brief period when Timms was asleep and she wasn't. She'd also pointed out that Rule wouldn't want to discuss clan stuff in front of Timms.

"I thought you felt responsible for him," he'd said. "What with him being wounded under your command."

That had pissed her off. He gave her points for knowing when he was dancing around the truth, but she jumped to the wrong conclusion. She thought he was using Timms to avoid her questions, but he didn't need the man around for that. He never answered questions he didn't want to.

It was five minutes after eleven when they finally parked on the street just down from the Nokolai house. Cullen helped his two wounded out of the car—at least, he tried to. Timms was wobbly, but not feeling any pain. Cynna insisted her nap in the car had done wonders for her headache.

"You think they're in bed?" she asked as they approached. "The porch light's off."

"Rule's bodyguards arrived. The ones outside won't want their night vision messed up."

"I don't see anyone."

"You wouldn't." Cullen had amused himself by using his other vision, so he knew his assumption was correct. The unmistakable aura of a lupus hovered faintly over the front seat of the two-year-old Mercury parked in front of the house.

He was surprised, though, at who opened the door. Surprised enough to stare.

The man facing him filled the doorway. His black hair was short and shot through with silver; his hands were the size of dinner plates. He had his mother's dark eyes and coppery skin, and he almost never left Clanhome.

"You coming in?" Benedict said.

"That's the idea." Cullen waved Cynna through. "Cynna Weaver, this is Rule's brother, Benedict. Rumor has it he does have a last name, but, like Madonna, he doesn't use it."

Rumor—or at least Rule—also claimed Benedict had a sense of humor, but Cullen had never seen evidence of it. He didn't tonight, either. "Come in, then. I don't want to leave the door open."

"She's a little slow tonight," Cullen said, using one hand to urge Cynna through the door. "It may be the depressed skull fracture. It may be your chest. Did you know that people in cities usually wear shirts?"

Benedict, of course, ignored the irrelevancies. It was as impossible to insult the man as it was to joke with him. He looked at Cynna. "Lily said the Leidolf Rhej performed a healing."

Cynna recovered from her startlement, which had probably been caused as much by what Benedict did wear as what he didn't. Benedict liked sharp objects. Twin knives were sheathed on his forearms, and a sword rode in its scabbard on his back. She shot Cullen an annoyed glance. "She did. I'm fine, aside from a bit of a headache."

Bit of a headache. Ha. "Who's watching over Isen?" he asked as Benedict secured the door.

"A number of people." Benedict turned to Timms. "I don't allow weapons in the Lu Nuncio's presence."

Cullen shook his head. "You won't part him from his gun, but I'll vouch for him." He looked at Timms. "No shooting my friend."

"That must be Timms," Rule said, entering the little hall from the rear. "I understand his arm was broken while fighting the demon-possessed. I'm not sure why . . ." He let that trail off, cocking an eyebrow at Cullen.

But it was Timms who answered. "Saved my life."

"I beg your pardon?"

"He did. Your friend." Timms nodded several times for emphasis. "I tranked her. Made her mad. The other two froze. Woman's body, you know? Threw them for a second. Seaboard didn't freeze. Pulled her off when she got hold of me. You're Rule Turner?"

"I am." Rule looked fascinated.

"Got demon stuff in you. Not your fault, but . . . thought I'd better come along, keep an eye out."

"I see." Rule was amused but hid it well. He crossed to Cynna—not limping, Cullen noticed—and took her hands in his. "How are you, really?"

That intent, caring gaze had flustered women more confident than Cynna. She didn't quite stammer. "I'm okay. Really. My head hurts, but it's no biggie. But are you okay?"

He grimaced and dropped her hands. "Let's adjourn to the kitchen. Lily's there."

Benedict didn't like it. "He's got a weapon."

"Cullen will see to it he doesn't shoot me." Rule waved them on, waiting until Cullen passed him to murmur, "Collecting strays again?"

Cullen felt the tips of his ears heat, dammit. "I always say you can never have too many FBI agents around."

Rule chuckled. "I'm not keeping this one for you."

The way the house was laid out they had to go through the parlor and dining room to get to the kitchen; Rule was still grinning as they reached it.

Lily was pacing, her cell phone held to her ear. Her eyes flashed up. She grimaced. "I know, but . . . no, I didn't. I didn't say that. Look, I'm sorry, but I have to go."

She disconnected.

Rule cocked an eyebrow at her. She gave a tiny shake of her head, then said to the rest of them, "My sister. My *older* sister," she added with a grimace, as if that explained something.

"Problems?" Cynna said, pulling out one of the chairs at the big, round table.

"Family. Problems." Lily flipped her hand once. "Two sides of the same coin, aren't they?"

Cullen watched Cynna's face. Nothing showed, but he wondered what she was thinking. He'd never heard her mention any family and suspected she didn't have one. "Lily, this is Agent Timms. Timms, Lily hangs out on your side of reality most of the time—her aka is Agent Yu of MCD."

"We've spoken," Lily started to hold out her hand, then realized the cast was on his right arm. She settled for a nod and gave Cullen a questioning look.

"Cullen vouches for him," Rule said dryly. He moved to the coffeepot. "Anyone care for a cup?"

Timms was the only taker—seems he thought the pain meds had his mind a bit fuzzy.

"Oh." Lily reached for a folder on the table. "This is a copy of that report you wanted." She handed it to Cullen.

Cullen's hand closed tightly on it. He needed to read it right now, needed to find the one who'd tampered with his mind. Instinctively, he hid the strength of that need, saying the first thing that came to mind. "What's Benedict doing here?"

Rule handed Timms a mug. "Isen believes I'm in more danger than he is right now."

Benedict spoke. "He also believes you won't argue with me. Hard to get one of my people to guard Rule properly," he added to the rest of them. "They have a bad habit of obeying him."

"Not a flaw you're prone to," Cullen said. "Tends to run the other way with you." Lily hadn't said a word about what was in the report. Was it useless? Or did she not want to comment in front of Timms?

"I'm sorry you raced back this way," Rule said, apparently addressing the coffeepot as he poured his own coffee. "I told Lily there was no point."

Cullen spoke sharply. "Don't give her grief about this. Rule, I can see it now."

Rule's head jerked up. He scowled at Cullen.

"It's in your aura. The change is slight, small enough that I wouldn't notice if I didn't know you so well. But it's there."

"I don't want to be pushy," Cynna said, "but what are you talking about? Cullen said you were worse, Rule—that something went wacky with your memory. But even he couldn't *see* that."

Lily answered, her voice low. "The demon poison. It's metastasized, or something like that. I knew it the second I touched him."

"What?" Cynna demanded. "What did you feel?"

"It didn't stay in the wound. It's spread throughout his body."

TWENTY-THREE

"**WOULD** you slow it down?" Cynna said.

"No." Cullen knew he was driving too fast. He didn't care. He was back in the Mother-damned car when he *needed* to run.

The Wiccan healer—one of Sherry's people, so she was among the best—had checked Rule out earlier that evening. She couldn't do anything, with or without the coven's backing. It wasn't a matter of power, but knowledge.

They had a Catholic archbishop in their task force. He couldn't do a damned thing, either. Whatever was happening to Rule, it wasn't possession. It wasn't anything anyone knew a goddamned thing about.

Including him. They rocketed around a corner, tires squealing.

"Déjà vu all over again. Every time I let a man behind the wheel today, he goes too fast. Slow down, Cullen. Now."

He glanced at her—and yelped. "You pulled a damned gun on me!"

The barrel of a snub-nosed revolver stared at him. So did a pair of tired but determined brown eyes. "I'm not in the mood to splatter all over the pavement tonight. I'm not in the mood for stupid men who won't listen. And I am so not in the mood to argue. Slow down."

He gave a quick bark of laughter and eased off on the accelerator until they were going a sedate forty. "Better?" he asked mildly.

"Much." She holstered her weapon. "Ah . . . you're pretty cheerful about being drawn on."

"I needed a good laugh."

"You find it funny to have people point guns at you?"

"You weren't going to use it. Shooting the driver at seventy miles an hour is a tad risky, even for you." He grinned. "Silliest thing I've seen in years. Got to love a woman who knows how to overreact."

"Glad I could improve your mood. Want me to brighten things even more and put a bullet in your leg?"

He chuckled. "You're pissed."

"You're just full of insight. That's my hotel."

"Right." He slowed further and pulled into the parking lot. "Where now?"

"Use the side entry—it's closer to my room." She twisted to check on his other passenger.

"Sleeping Beauty still out cold?"

She nodded. Cynna had the front seat this time, Timms the back. He'd fallen asleep the moment he curled up back there and didn't seem likely to wake for anything short of the last trumpet. Cullen marveled at his ability to sleep so soundly with a freshly broken bone, having experienced a few breaks in his time. Maybe the man had fewer pain receptors than most people.

Of course, Timms's body didn't flush out painkillers within minutes the way Cullen's did. There were advantages to being human, Cullen conceded. Not many, but a few.

He pulled to a stop near the side entry and shut off the engine.

"Cullen." Her hand on his arm was almost as big a surprise as the gun had been. "We're going to fix Rule. Just because we don't know how yet doesn't mean we can't do it."

"Right." He took a deep breath, let it out. He was too old to believe in fairy tales. Right didn't make might, bad things did happen to good people, and determination didn't always win the day.

But you didn't get far without it. "Right," he said again, meaning it this time, and opened his door.

"For crying out loud. I make it safely inside all the time, you know."

"I'm going to kiss you. I could do it here, but—"

"If you get any mushier I'm going to tear up." But she didn't object to the idea. She didn't object when he took her hand, either.

Weird. They were holding hands. He might wonder if he was going through a second adolescence, but he hadn't been much for holding hands in the first one. He wasn't even going to go to bed with the woman—yet. He just wanted a little taste. A kiss.

How long had it been since he stopped at kissing?

But it felt good to hold her hand. He'd forgotten how good a simple touch could be. He'd trained himself not to need it; a clanless wolf couldn't afford that need, because humans didn't understand. If you touched one of them, male or female, they thought it meant sex.

Or, in his case, they hoped it did. His lips quirked.

She dropped his hand to dig out her key card, which she needed to unlock the side door at this hour.

"How can you afford to stay here?" he asked.

"Hey, I negotiated. I get off-season rates year-round, and only pay for the nights I'm actually here, which averages about ten a month." She located the card and stuck it in. "There's a lot of demand for a good Finder. I fly all over the country, then when I come back, I get maid service, room service, laundry facilities, a gym, a pool, cable, Internet—"

"I get it. You like staying here."

"What's not to like? I guess someone who's into owning stuff wouldn't be happy, but it works for me."

The lock snicked. He leaned around her to open the door and hold it for her.

She gave him a funny look.

"I've got manners. I don't always bother with them, but they're around when I want them." His position put him close to her, close enough for her scent to stir him. Heady, familiar, and welcome, arousal began tightening his body.

It had been a long time since he took the time to anticipate going to bed with a woman instead of just doing it. He decided he liked it. He trailed his free hand down the side of her neck. "Besides, ladies first has always been my motto." He wasn't referring to doors.

She got that. Her eyes smiled at him—pretty eyes, he thought. The color of whiskey. The rest of her face stayed solemn. "Good motto, but some ladies like to go second and third, too."

"Greedy, aren't you?"

"When my head isn't hurting." She walked through the door, and he let it close behind them. "I guess you do know how to flirt."

"Meaning?"

She gave a one-shoulder shrug. "I didn't think you were interested. Until I asked about sex, you didn't flirt, didn't give me any looks . . . you know."

He'd hurt her feelings. Cullen considered that as they headed down a hall—hotel standard, with beige carpet, beige walls. Did she prefer to live someplace where nothing of her showed? "You're going to accuse me of being an arrogant ass."

"I already have, lots of times. Not always when you were around."

"Been thinking about me, huh?" He flashed her a grin. "Lots of women do."

"We're getting to the arrogant part already, I see."

He shrugged. He knew what he looked like. That was reality, not arrogance. "My looks tip the scales too much in my favor, so I have a rule. No flirting, no seducing, no come-ons unless a woman gives me the green light."

She stopped. "You're saying you're chivalrous?"

"Hell, no. Chivalry is sick—men pretending to moon chastely after ladies, when we all know there's no such thing as a chaste moon."

"Your own, twisted version of chivalry, then." She was delighted. "Is that why you're letting Timms hang around?"

"I can promise you he doesn't have designs on my body. Or vice versa."

She waved that off. "No, I mean he's like a feral puppy trotting around after you. I can't get over it. He couldn't stand you before."

"Timms doesn't know it, but he's looking for a pack. He's accepted me as dominant—not that he thinks of it that way, but he's not able to deal with other men as equals. He'll bully those beneath him and think of those above as his friends."

They'd reached her door, apparently, because she stopped in front of it—1014. She snorted. "He's not a lupus."

"Humans need packs, but you think you aren't supposed to, which is why you're all so confused—the XY half of you, especially. Drink, drugs, gangs, outdoing the Joneses—all symptoms of the need for a pack, and a defined status within the pack. The American cult of rugged individualism makes human men think they're all supposed to be alphas, but it doesn't work that way."

She leaned against the doorframe, crossing her arms and hiking her eyebrows. So skeptical. It made him smile. "Cult of rugged individualism?"

"Sure. It's a myth, a story people tell each other to make modern isolation more tolerable. America wasn't founded by rugged individualists but by people who didn't like the packs back home and wanted to form their own—religious packs in the northern colonies, wealth-based packs down South. They weren't a bunch of loners. They couldn't be—they needed each other to survive."

"What about all those rugged Westerners? Cowboys, wagon trains, frontiersmen—"

"The settlers relied on each other to survive, too. As for cowboys—rugged individualists, my ass. They're a perfect example of human-style packs. Ranch hands were sometimes misfits, but there were no real loners on a ranch. They banded together beneath a strong leader to tend cattle, care for horses and gear, and fight."

"Gunfighters—"

"Were outcasts, but still sought status, which is another way of saying they needed a place within the pack, even if it was based on fear. Trappers were the one exception. Some went native, living with one tribe or another, but others did live completely alone for months at a time. And they were often a little nuts." He shook his head. "Humans aren't loners by nature."

"Neither are lupi." She tilted her head. Her eyes met his. The cool curiosity he saw there was less abrasive than sympathy would have been. That didn't make it welcome. "You lived like that for a while, though, didn't you? As a lone wolf."

"Shut up, Cynna."

She gave that wry, one-sided smile, neither offended nor, he felt sure, accepting his suggestion to avoid the topic. He took her face in his two hands, running his thumb along the sensitive hollow just beneath the jawbone. Her skin was a soft surprise. The filigree covering it, so obvious to the eye, was invisible to the touch.

He lowered his head slowly, enjoying the droop of her eyelids as her body consented to the kiss. Her musky scent pleased him, though her hair products did not; a whiff of bleach clung to the short, spiky strands, its smell masked by that of industrial-strength gel. And another scent . . .

Blood. Close up, he saw flecks of rusty red at the tips of some of those spiky strands. Not her blood, since her skin hadn't broken when her skull did, but there wasn't enough for him to sniff out the original owner, not in this form.

Still, the reminder helped. She was injured. And while he might have decided anticipation was intriguing, he was unaccustomed to waiting.

Their breaths mingled. Their mouths met.

Cullen meant it to be a quiet kiss—a taste, a sampling, letting fire brush without burning. Nothing that pushed either of them. He'd forgotten how badly he needed to run.

The first skimming touch of lips made him smile. His tongue asked to be let in, and she did, and she tasted even better than she smelled. She put her hands on his waist and clamped her teeth on his tongue.

He pressed her back against the door. She was a tall woman, and he liked that. He could feel that strong-soft body all along his, the warmth and pressure delicious to him. Then she sank his good intentions. She cupped his butt, holding him firmly against her as she rolled her hips.

Wildness roared up and swallowed his brain. He forgot about asking and anticipation and all that rot. She was here and she wanted him.

He dove in. His hands needed to learn the feel of her—the curve of her hip, the welcoming fullness of her breast, the heat between her legs. His mouth wanted the taste of her throat, her jaw. And the rest of him—"

But her hand was pushing at him. Pushing his hand away from the zipper on her jeans. She got her mouth free. "The hall, Cullen. We're in the hall."

"Right." Slowly he pulled away. He expected to see smugness. It would be mixed with pleasure, because she'd been right there with him, but she'd drowned him, purely drowned him, and she knew it. "Sorry. I mean . . . your head. How's your head?"

"My head?" She blinked at him, her eyes dazed . . . with pleasure or pain? "Oh. It hurts, but . . ."

But she hadn't cared. For a few moments there, she'd forgotten or hadn't noticed. His smile started small and spread. "Oh, we are going to have us one hell of a good time, *shetanni rakibu*." He brushed her jaw with his knuckles. "Soon. But right now . . ." He took a deep breath and straightened. His jeans were much too tight.

Hell, his skin was too tight. "Sleep well," he said, giving her cheek a last touch.

She licked her lips. "You, too."

Not likely—not right away, at least. He badly wanted to read the report Lily had gotten him, but first things first. As soon as he got his feral puppy settled, he was going running.

"I told you earlier that I could be patient when I have to," he said, releasing her. "I lied. I'm not a patient man."

TWENTY-FOUR

SHETANNI *rakibu.* Demon rider.

Cullen knew. He knew and apparently didn't care what that meant. But *she* cared, and the reminder had splashed cold water all over Cynna's hormones, so she didn't need to turn the faucet to chilly when she showered. She got into bed with her hair still wet, her head pounding, and her body dissatisfied.

She didn't expect to fall asleep within moments of cuddling her sore head into the pillow, but she did.

She did not sleep well.

". . . too far for a little one like you to go alone," Mrs. Johnson said. *"Specially round here. Better you stay home an' hep your mama."*

"Amy Garcia's going with me and Sarita," she promised and hurried away before her neighbor could tell her more things she should or shouldn't do. Grown-ups were so full of shoulds and shouldn'ts. It made her glad she was a kid.

The air was chilly, and her last-year's jacket was missing some buttons and didn't go all the way down her arms anymore. Mama said they'd get her a new one real soon, but "real soon" didn't mean much. So she walked fast to stay warm. She knew the way. Even if she hadn't been able to Find the park, she'd know the way.

Cynna wasn't going there to swing or go down the slide. She

wanted the leaves—dead leaves, brown and crisp, that crunched when you walked through them. She loved that sound.

"Hey, Cynna!" Sarita called. "Wait up!"

Cynna waited, shifting from foot to foot, as a girl her age but shorter, darker, and plumper hurried across the street. "Are you ready?" she demanded. "Where's your sister?"

"Amy can't go. Won't go," Sarita corrected, making a face. "She's coloring her hair, and when Mama gets home from work she's going to be so grounded. Mama told her she couldn't dye her hair till she was sixteen, but she bought it anyway. Miss Clairol Sunset Red. So I can't go, not without Amy."

"But we have to go *today*." There was only a little time when the leaves crunched. After a while they'd get all soppy, and they weren't fun anymore.

Sarita rolled her eyes. "You don't ever want to wait. Amy said she'd take us Saturday. That's only two days."

"But if she's grounded—"

"Mama never keeps her grounded all that long. She cries at her, and Mama gets mad, but then she ungrounds her."

But Amy might not be ungrounded in time. It could rain, couldn't it? If it rained, the leaves wouldn't be any good anymore.

. . . no, don't. Don't go to the park. Not this time.

Like a swimmer running out of air, Cynna forced herself up, fighting to break the surface. *Open your eyes, dammit.* But it was hard . . . so tired . . .

The light turned green. She shot out into the street, dodging around the grown-ups. She liked running. She was fast, too. Her legs were long, and she could beat most of the kids in her class.

Sometimes it really helped, being able to run fast.

Sarita's big sister was going with Tom-Tom, so it would be safer to go with her, but she could take care of herself. She had to, didn't she? Mama wasn't well enough to take her to the park like she used to. Mama wasn't well enough to do much at all anymore.

The sky was gray all over, like it might rain or even snow. She really needed to get to the park today. Grown-ups talked about how great spring was with its new grass and flowers, but no one where she lived had grass, and the only flowers were in plastic pots at Thompson's up the street, where they went for groceries. Food stamps wouldn't pay for flowers, so they never got any of those.

Cynna liked fall. School started then, and school was almost safe. You had to watch out for some of the big kids, but she could hold her own with the ones her age. The days got cooler, too, and after a long summer with no air-conditioning those first cool evenings were heaven.

Most of all, she liked when the leaves fell. After hanging on way overhead all summer, they turned loose and joined her on the ground.

For sure it was better to go to the park today than stay at home. Mama was passed out again.

Her mama was sick. She couldn't help herself. That's what Mrs. Johnson said, and maybe she was right, but Cynna couldn't help her, either. She'd tried and tried, but she couldn't. She used to think she could—that if she took better care of her she'd get her real Mama back, the one who used to read to her and fix supper every night and take her to the park and push her in the swing.

When she got home from school today Mama had been sprawled on the couch, out cold and stinking of Jim Beam. She'd been so mad. All-over mad. She'd shaked her and shaked her, but Mama wouldn't wake up.

Cynna had wanted to hit her. Mama wouldn't even know. She could punch her right in her stomach, and Mama wouldn't know. It made her own stomach knot up to feel like that. Better to go to the park and kick around the dead leaves.

The problem with the park wasn't the number of blocks you had to walk. It was the big kids who hung out there. Kids who'd started wearing colors, like Tom-Tom and Raphael and Derek. The park was their turf, and you had to pay a toll.

Cynna didn't have any money of her own, so she stole a five and three ones from the coffee can where Mama kept her cash. Might as well. Mama'd just drink it or smoke it. The five could go for supper, 'cause the refrigerator was empty except for some mayonnaise and pickles and something in an old butter bowl that was green on top. The ones were for her toll.

If she was lucky, Derek wouldn't be there. Tom-Tom was okay, and Raphael wasn't too bad. But Derek scared her. He got bored easy, and he liked to pick on whoever he could when he was bored. Unless he was using. Then he just got mean. If Amy had been with her to get kissy with Tom-Tom, she wouldn't have needed a toll, but she wasn't.

Cynna did not know why Amy liked to kiss Tom-Tom . . .

Wait, wait. I do know. I like kissing now. I just kissed someone. Cullen. Yes. He fried me but good, and I'm . . . I'm . . .

This time she got her eyes open. Dark. It was very dark, but there was a sliver of light . . . drapes, yeah, the drapes weren't closed tight. She was in a hotel. Which one? Where?

She tried to care, but she was so tired. The dream pulled at her, dragging her back down. She didn't want to go there. Not again. But her eyes wouldn't stay open, wouldn't . . .

. . . she waved her arms and the leaves crackled and crunched all around her. She was lying right in them, in the pile she'd made. Usually there weren't enough for a pile, but today . . .

Had there been a pile of leaves that day? She stopped, confused. That part was different, but the rest was the same. Something bad was going to happen—had happened, was happening again . . .

A pair of black high-tops stopped near her face. "What you doin' on Angel turf, little girl?"

Derek's voice. Derek's sneakers. Her heart thudded in fear. "I paid the toll." She started to scramble to her feet, but one of those great, huge shoes landed on her belly, holding her down.

"Didn't pay me."

"I paid Raphael."

Suddenly there was something wet in her ear. A tongue. "Miss me?" a woman's voice said. "You're a cute little thing with your skin all bare."

Jiri? No, it couldn't be. Not here, not now. Jiri was . . .

Hunkered down beside her, grinning that wide grin. She had big, flat teeth, very white and straight. Her skin was so dark, like she'd been dipped in night. Her hair was super-short but her head wasn't shaved, so this was an early Jiri, before . . . before . . .

"Hey, I can show up however I want to. It's your dream, but it's my body, isn't it? More or less. Watch out. He's about to—"

The big foot slammed into her side. She cried out and curled around it, pain blocking everything else—sight, sound, and Jiri. Who couldn't be here. She didn't meet Jiri until . . .

The big foot landed in her side again. Again. Pain exploded. *No! This isn't how it happened! He kicked me, but then I got away.*

"That was then," Jiri said. "This is now. This time you didn't get away."

I will. She twisted away from the sneaker and pushed to her feet, and she was her right size—an adult, not a little girl. Her own foot flashed out in a sideways kick, and she broke Derek's kneecap. Derek howled and fell to the ground.

"Listen to that pop," Jiri said, straightening to her full height, which was almost exactly Cynna's height now. "You really want this to end the way it did before?"

No. No, she didn't. "What are you doing here?"

"You can change it, you know."

Can't change the past.

"But this isn't the past. This is now, and you're dreaming. Dreams can change."

Dreaming. Yes, she was—but Jiri was really here. That was wrong. There was something terrible that could come of talking to Jiri in her dreams. She couldn't remember what, but she began to fight, willing herself to wake up. Wake up.

"God, you're stubborn," Jiri said, and grabbed her arm. Cynna tried to pull free, but it was one of those molasses moments, when all the will in the world didn't affect your dream body, and you couldn't move.

"Keep this for me." Jiri pressed something in her palm.

Cynna looked down. A dead leaf. Jiri had given her a dead, brown leaf. She clenched her fist around it, crunching it into scratchy specks, and yanked her arm free, and she was—

Opening her eyes on darkness.

Her head ached, and so did her side, and in the first, nauseous confusion, it wasn't clear which was real and which was a hangover from the dream. She shoved the covers back and swung her legs off the bed, then just sat, leaning her forehead into the cradle of her palms.

God. Hadn't had that one for a while.

At least she'd managed to wake before the final sequence . . . hurrying back to her apartment with her side hurting, wondering if something was broken inside. Finding the ambulance out front. Watching them carry her mama out on a stretcher.

Cynna stood. Her head wasn't happy, but her side didn't hurt. That had been memory, of course, and her head wasn't as bad as she'd expected. The Rhej had done quite a job on her, and if she was still uneasy at the idea of stolen or borrowed magic, she couldn't argue with the results. A couple ibuprofin ought to fix her up pretty well.

The light leaking through the imperfectly closed drapes was

dingy gray. Either it was really early still, or the day had woken up in the same mood as her. Either way, she might as well stay up.

She padded over to the window and peeked out. Daylight, but not enough of it. Looked like it would be one of those grizzled days when Mother Nature was feeling the ache in her knees and was pissy about it.

Another discomfort made itself felt and she headed for the bathroom, unclothed but not feeling bare. Magic coated her skin like invisible fur, and the intricate patterns holding it there were a shield of sorts, too.

She didn't bother with a light, knowing her small space too well to need one. She emptied her bladder and washed her hands, then splashed water on her face. It didn't help. The dream clung like cobwebs, sticky strands of memory and emotion.

The more things change . . . No one got away with kicking her these days, but the adult Cynna still lashed out too quick, too hard, trying to stop a beating that had taken place twenty-five years ago. And she hadn't been able to save her mother. After a couple years of meetings she'd accepted that it hadn't been her job, but the anger still slunk back at times, growling.

Old news, all of it. She didn't know why she kept revisiting it.

As for Jiri . . . her unconscious wasn't exactly subtle. She was scared of her former teacher, but she was going to have to suck it up and go after Jiri anyway. No surprise if her dream jumbled those fears together with even older ones.

What time was it, anyway?

She was heading back to her bed and the clock beside it when her phone chirped. She veered, bending to dig into the tote she'd dropped at the foot of the bed. It was buried under the clothes she'd stripped off before falling into bed last night.

Caller ID told her who was calling. "Hi," she said. "Listen, if I'm late I'm sorry, but—"

"It's 8:42 on Saturday. I was afraid I'd wake you," Lily said.

"Oh. No, I'm up. Not exactly wide-awake yet, but I'm up." Three steps took her to the bedside table. She clicked on the lamp and stood blinking in the sudden light.

"How's your head? Are you up to driving? Grandmother has something she wants to tell us."

Cynna frowned. She was still groggy, but . . . "You called because you want me to meet your grandmother?"

"Sorry. I forgot that you haven't met her, so that sounds peculiar, but Grandmother is hard to explain. If she says she has something we need to hear, though, we'd better listen. I've briefed her on what's been happening, and—"

"You briefed your grandmother."

"Ruben won't object. Grandmother has worked with the Unit before, unofficially. She . . . ah, she stays below the radar. Can you be here in an hour or so?"

"Sure, I suppose." Cynna's jaw cracked in a huge yawn. Curiosity was beginning to rouse a few brain cells. "My head's a lot better, so I could drive, but I'm without a car. Cullen's got yours."

"He didn't stay there? Somehow I got the impression . . ." Lily let that trail off delicately.

"We're working our way up to that."

"I'll have him pick you up, then. Oh—Rule says not to worry about breakfast. He's doing something with eggs. We've so many to feed already that a couple more won't make a difference."

They told each goodbye and disconnected. Cynna put the phone down, wondering about this grandmother who was hard to explain but worked with the Unit unofficially. She reached up with her other hand to scrub her face. And froze, staring at her palm.

Her naked palm—or it should have been. But it wasn't. Scrolled across the fleshy mound at the base of her thumb was a new *kilingo*, a delicate tracery that looked like the veins of a dried leaf.

One she hadn't put there.

Jiri had.

TWENTY-FIVE

THE kitchen smelled of onion, parsley, paprika, and people—people Rule knew and loved, people who mattered. Lily was chopping the potatoes she'd peeled; Benedict leaned against the wall near the door, watching; and Toby sat at the round table, reading. Rain drizzled down outside as it had, off and on, all night.

Rule was happy.

"What did you say this was called again?" Lily asked.

"A frittata." Rule looked over his shoulder. At Lily's insistence, he'd begun teaching her basic kitchen skills. It wasn't that she'd developed an interest in cooking. She just got twitchy if he did all the work.

At the moment she was dicing potatoes . . . slowly. Meal preparation took longer with her help than without it, though he had hopes she'd pick up speed eventually. "Would you like a measuring tape?" he asked politely as he whisked the eggs.

"That's sarcasm," she observed without looking up. Another careful slice. "You said you wanted a half-inch dice."

"It's okay to be off a millimeter here and there."

Toby looked up from his book. "Is it almost ready?"

"No. You can get out the bread and slice it, however. We'll use the two round loaves in the pantry."

"But I'm—"

"Toby."

His son sighed heavily, turned the book facedown, and went to the pantry.

Lily's contribution to the influx of relatives were in the front room. Lily said that Li Qin would happily help out if asked, but she wouldn't offer. To offer would be rude, implying that her hosts weren't able to handle things without her. She hadn't had to explain that her grandmother was incapable of helping. Madam Yu could take over. She couldn't assist.

The two older women had gone to bed very early last night, so they'd been up early. Li Qin had come down to the kitchen to prepare tea for the two of them and asked that Lily attend her grandmother. Rule hadn't been present for that conference, but he assumed Lily had told Madam Yu everything.

The exchange hadn't been mutual. Madam Yu wanted a larger audience for her explanations, whatever they might be.

Lily brought the cutting board over, piled high with precisely cubed potatoes. Voice low, she said, "Are you sure he ought to do that? He doesn't have super-duper healing yet."

"He'll do fine. The bread knife is serrated, and he'll saw with it, not slice. It takes a remarkable degree of inattention to saw through your own finger."

"If you say so." She tucked her hair behind one ear and gave Toby a quick glance—checking for blood, probably. "What next?"

"You could grate the cheese."

"How much?"

He had no idea. He cooked by guess, based on experience. But she needed to measure everything, or she wouldn't know if she'd done it right, so he gave her a firm number. "Three cups."

"Okay." She went to the refrigerator.

He carried the potatoes to the range, turned the burner on under the skillet, and added a healthy chunk of butter. He looked at her for the sheer pleasure of being able to do so. Yearning twisted through him.

Ah, hell. Damned, spoilsport wolf.

He'd begun his penance that morning at six A.M. He'd expected Changing back after only ten minutes to be difficult, and not only because of the magical strain. Wolves had little use for clocks. For them, the time was always now. So he'd fixed in his mind an image of the clock reading six ten, and reminded himself of the Lady's wishes.

The Change hurt. It always did, but it hurt more when he wasn't grounded, and he'd chosen to Change in their bedroom on the second floor, where he could see the clock. And Lily. As wolf he'd lain on the wooden floor and watched her sleep. And even as he'd looked at her, breathing in their mingled scents, he'd grieved.

Foolish wolf. He scraped potatoes into the hot skillet. The Lily who had been with him in Dis wasn't gone. She lived on in this Lily . . . though this Lily didn't remember. She didn't know what the sky looked like in Dis, or the beauty of dragonsong, or what she'd done when she first woke, naked and frightened, sundered from memory and alone in a terrible place . . . alone but for a demon and a wolf.

She'd reached for him, burying her fingers in his fur. She'd known him. When she hadn't known herself, she'd known him.

Rule shook his head and grabbed the onion he'd gotten out earlier, and a knife. The wolf didn't understand, but he wasn't only wolf. He could remember for both of them, and Lily was here, right here with him. He hadn't lost her.

He began slicing the onion, his knife working a great deal faster than hers had.

He opened the oven and heat rolled out, parching his face.

Rule froze. Then, carefully, he slid the pan onto the rack inside the oven. He straightened, closed the oven door, and set the timer.

It had happened again.

"The bread's all sliced," Toby announced.

He found a smile and turned. "Very good." Had Lily helped the boy? She was getting plates down now, but she might have assisted him earlier. The slices were unnaturally even.

He didn't know. Apparently he'd finished assembling the frittata, but he had no memory of it. Better not comment on the bread, or . . . or she'd know what had happened.

That was when he realized he wasn't going to tell her. Not this time.

The doorbell rang. "I'll get it."

Benedict straightened away from the wall. Rule shot him an annoyed glance and received a bland one in return. He wouldn't be answering the door on his own—or eating, sleeping, or pissing, he thought.

A large, silent, older-brother shadow trailed him through the dining room. He did his best to ignore that.

He couldn't have lost much time. He'd been slicing the onions;

the green peppers would have been next. Five minutes. When the potatoes finished browning he would have . . .

"Your food arrives slowly," Li Lei Yu announced from her temporary throne in the front room, an armchair that could have held two of her. She wore western clothes today, black slacks with a severe gold shirt buttoned firmly at the throat. Both were silk.

"I've had help."

Li Qin looked up from the magazine she was reading and smiled. Harry was sprawled across her lap, purring. "Good morning again."

Benedict gave her a nod and a smile. Rule smiled, too. One couldn't help smiling at Li Qin. Even the bloody cat liked her. "Excuse me a moment, ladies. I need to get the door."

"Your well-armed brother will answer the door," Madam Yu told him, and, to his surprise, slid off the chair and stood. "You will come here."

Rule kept his voice polite. "Madam, I adore you, but sometimes I'm at a loss to know why."

"You do not like being—what is it? Ah—bossed around." Her rare smile flashed, and for a moment a much younger woman peeped out. "I do not like it, either. But I am much older, so you will indulge me."

"I think a great many people have indulged you over the years." But he gave Benedict a nod, and while his brother went to the door, he crossed to the old woman. He lifted his eyebrows: *Here I am. Now what?*

She wasn't smiling anymore, but neither did she wear the imperious mask she so enjoyed. Solemn and assured, she stretched up both hands and placed them on his cheeks.

"Li Lei!"

Li Qin's startled exclamation had Rule turning his head. The other woman had dropped her magazine and looked distressed.

"Hush," Madam said, but her voice was gentle. Firmly she turned Rule's face back toward her.

He frowned. "What are you up to?"

"Nothing that can hurt you." Her eyes were that extraordinary dark brown that looks black, the whites almost invisible. He found himself staring at that darkness, fascinated.

Her palms grew warm. Very warm. He heard Cullen's voice, and Cynna's, and the timer going off. None of it seemed to matter. He floated . . .

Her hands fell away. He blinked.

"Madam." Li Qin's voice reproached her.

"What did you do?" Cullen demanded. He stood a few feet away, glaring at the old woman. Cynna was beside him, a frown tucked between her eyebrows.

"I cannot fix it." Her voice was crisp on top, but underneath he heard sadness.

Rule shook his head, dispelling the traces of whatever she'd done to him—but not the anger. He'd been taken over in some fashion, and he didn't like it. "If you're talking about the demon poison, neither can a Wiccan high priestess nor a Catholic arch-bishop, among others."

"Bishops, monks, priestesses—bah. They are good with questions, not so good with doing." With that opaque comment, she reseated herself. "You may introduce me. Cullen, I know. This other—"

Li Qin, amazingly, interrupted her. "You risked much."

The old woman gave a small shrug. "Some secrets will not remain secret so much longer, I think."

"That is not what I meant."

"I want to know what you did," Cullen said. "And what you tried to do."

"So do I," Lily said from the arched entry to the dining room, her face pale. Rule couldn't tell what had drained her color—anger or fear.

Madam Yu's eyebrows rose imperiously. "We do not always get what we want."

Li Qin folded her hands in her lap, placid once more. "I am sorry. In my distress, I brought confusion. The risk was not to Rule, but to Madam. She attempted—"

"Li Qin," Grandmother snapped.

"—to absorb the poison into herself," Li Qin finished, untroubled by the scowl directed at her. "At times, she mistakes herself for indestructible."

"Bah." Madam Yu rose. "I am hungry. We will eat now."

LI LEI YU didn't often indulge in sentimentality, but as she looked around the dining table she felt quite tender. Her granddaughter and namesake had assembled an interesting family for herself.

Rule Turner sat at the head of the table, as was proper. He

wasn't entirely over his anger, of course. Cage a wolf—or a strong man—and you could expect snapping teeth. He owed none of his current cage to her, but she had suppressed his will, however briefly and benevolently. He was wary of her.

She didn't object. It was well for the strong to respect the strong.

Li Lei approved of Rule Turner. Her daughter-in-law did not. While bewailing Lily's choice of mate, Julia Yu had shown enough sense not to harp on the man's ability to turn wolf, since shapeshifting was hardly a flaw in Li Lei's eyes. Instead she'd made much of the fact that the man wasn't Chinese.

Julia was prone to shallow thinking. Li Lei had pointed out tartly that if she'd wanted her children and grandchildren to marry only Chinese, she would not have left China.

Cullen Seabourne looked up from his plate, which he'd cleaned without, she suspected, at all noticing what he ate. He saw her looking and winked.

Cheeky. She shook her head at him, but he would know she was not offended. She had a soft spot in her heart for a beautiful rogue. What woman did not? She did not allow this to blind her. Cullen was a dangerous man. He possessed both power and obsession, and if those had helped preserve him during his years as a lone wolf, that existence had also driven great cracks through him.

She liked him very much. Li Lei took another bite of the frittata, which was excellent. She was glad her granddaughter's lover was teaching her how to cook. Her mother had certainly failed in the attempt.

Cullen was flanked by two she did not know. Lupus bodyguards. They would eat quickly, then replace the other two guards, who were still outside, so they could eat. It was sensible for Rule Turner to be guarded, though she knew he experienced their presence as part of his cage.

At the moment, Rule Turner was more dangerous than his sorcerous friend because his own danger was so much greater. Li Lei wished her attempt to help him had not failed.

She frowned. Li Qin should not have spoken as she had. The risk had not been great. Li Lei's body would have thrown off the poison. Probably.

Of course, Li Qin also disapproved of her using her gaze as she had. It had been years since she had done so, at least to that extent. But she did not regret using it today. Why ask for what you knew would be denied? Rule Turner would not have agreed to let her try to take his poison into herself.

On Rule's right, his warrior brother ate quickly and efficiently. She had great respect for Benedict. He'd made of tragedy a forge, attaining the purity of a weapon. Not that she knew the nature of his tragedy—one did not poke into the painful places of a man one respected—but she recognized its effects.

She knew tragedy. And survival.

Benedict turned to smile at Toby, seated on his other side and chattering away. Li Lei's heart filled. Children were life's greatest gift. They were not, as many silly people claimed, the hope for the future. True, they carried the future around as if it held everything yet weighed nothing, but that was their own gift from the Creator, not one they could share. Nor was it the easy love they offered that made them precious; like most sweets, that was a keen but fleeting pleasure. Their true blessing lay in the way they opened numb or embattled hearts.

This boy shone brightly. It spoke well for Rule Turner that his son possessed both courtesy and curiosity, along with a fierce and brimming well of intention, as yet largely unrealized.

A pang stroked through her. She missed her own son. Edward's passion for the ordinary had been a frustration, even a disappointment at times, but she understood that it arose from his own disappointment. The magic in her blood had passed him by, choosing instead to alight in his middle daughter.

Who sat now on Rule Turner's other side, doing an excellent job of hiding her fear. She'd eaten very little, but aside from that was carrying on well.

Lily hadn't asked her grandmother to help her lover. She hadn't fluttered over her, either, after Li Qin's ill-judged revelation. Lily did not flutter. She'd offered neither reproaches nor questions, a restraint that earned her many points. She'd simply kissed her grandmother on the cheek and looked into her eyes.

Spoken thank-yous were all very well, but Li Lei preferred the unspoken sort. She was very proud of her granddaughter. If the fear was great, also . . . ah, well. She had yet to learn the trick of living without fear.

Li Lei's gaze moved to the last person at the table. Cynna Weaver sat at the foot, which was not proper, but Lily needed to be near Rule. Her hair was absurd: a stiff, bleached mane cropped too short for any grace or beauty. Her skin was extraordinary. Quite beautiful, if considered without bias. But to wear one's isolation so flagrantly . . . that spoke of great strength, great anger, or great pain.

Not that the three didn't often travel together. Cynna's accent and clothes—she wore a hideous gray suit—spoke of her origins from the lowest rung of society. Li Lei did not hold that against her, but she was not an egalitarian. The poor were not the same as the rich—for which one should thank God, since the rich were often boring, their minds and souls stultified by privilege. But poverty was more likely to birth meanness of spirit than nobility.

Lily had told her that Cynna Weaver went to Dis with her and Cullen to save Rule. Lily trusted the woman. Li Lei reserved judgment but thought that, of all those present, Cynna was most like Benedict. But Benedict had passed through his fire. The flames still licked at Cynna; many of her choices still lay ahead.

Cynna was stiff and worried now, watching the others or her plate, speaking little. She'd shown them the new mark on her hand, which she believed came from her old teacher. None of them—not even the sorcerer—could tell what the mark was meant to do, but Cynna was certain she would know if the spell became active.

Li Lei was extremely curious about Cynna Weaver.

Some of what Lily had disclosed earlier had come as a shock. A blow, even, she thought, sipping her cooling tea. Her granddaughter had been in acute peril, her soul sundered, half of her trapped in a hostile realm. And Li Lei hadn't known, being on the other side of the world, seeking ghosts.

She should have known better. She did know better. Ghosts were never the least help to anyone.

Oh, her son had called to inform her of the externals, the parts of the story visible to everyone. Edward was not so foolish as to try to keep such things from her. But neither he nor Julia knew exactly what had happened to Lily—only that she'd been wounded, that her Gift and her lover had been missing for a time . . . and that she had somehow brought dragons back to the world.

Emotion clutched her so tight and fierce it tore her breath away for a moment. But only for a moment. So much had changed . . .

So much was changing, and would continue to change. She

looked at Li Qin seated next to her and obeyed a rare impulse. She reached for the other woman's hand and squeezed it.

Li Qin looked up, surprised. Her cheeks flushed faintly with pleasure. She gave Li Lei that sweet, serene smile.

Love arrived in so many guises. Though it had taken her years, Li Lei had learned not to spurn any of them. She nodded at Li Qin and released her hand.

It was time. "I will speak now."

TWENTY-SIX

"*I cannot fix it.*"

Until Grandmother spoke those words, Lily hadn't realized how much part of her clung to the idea that Grandmother could, indeed, fix anything. That she would know what to do for Rule.

Childish. If her fear had redoubled after that failed effort, it was her own fault. She'd hidden her hope from herself and was paying the price. Add guilt to that for the way Grandmother had risked herself, and what little she'd been able to eat rested unhappily in her middle.

"By all means," Rule said, "speak."

Grandmother was amused by Rule's sharp tone, but she didn't stop to fence with him. "I wish your word that what I say does not go beyond this room, save for whatever you choose to tell your father. Your pledge will bind the lupi here."

Rule considered that a moment, then nodded.

Grandmother looked at Lily. "You will feel it your duty to report to your FBI. I ask only that you speak of this to no one except Ruben Brooks and those on this—what is the silly name? Task force. Yes. You may tell them." She looked at Cynna. "I do not know you. I do not know what moves you, what your word means to you."

Cynna stared back at her. "I'm not the one who tried to ensorcell someone."

Grandmother snorted. "I did not try. In that much, I succeeded. Do I have your word you won't repeat this except to your FBI people?"

"Yeah. Sure."

If Grandmother objected to the casual phrasing, she didn't say so. She looked them all over one more time, then began. "I tell you a tale I believe is true. It was told to me by one who knows, and it begins in times so ancient the suns have since changed. I will skip most of that beginning," she added dryly. "Or we would be here a very long time. The part that matters today concerns those you call Old Ones."

"Like the goddess?" Lily asked. "The one we don't name?"

"Her, and others. Many others. We call them gods, angels, devils—they are none of these, and all. Their true nature is beyond us. Many of them . . . call them guardians, though what they guard is hard to say. Reality, perhaps. They are those who remained when the last Great Cycle ended and the universe died and was reborn."

Rule made a small noise. "Tell me you aren't talking about the big bang."

"Scientists name it that." She shrugged. "I tell you only that some from the last Cycle lingered into this one, though whether they stayed from duty or love, avarice or failure, karma or choice, I do not say. Perhaps only part of them stayed behind. Our words do not stretch to encompass such as they. Some of them took as their purpose the balance between the realms."

She paused to sip her tea and made a face. "Cold tea," she announced, "is an abomination. Perhaps three thousand years ago, those who tend the balance saw it was in danger. Others disagreed. There was much conflict, much devastation."

"The Great War," Rule said slowly. "You're speaking of the Great War."

She nodded once. "It touched our realm but was fought in many. Your Lady played a part, as did your people. In the end, those concerned with balance won. They . . . moved things."

Lily licked dry lips. "Uh . . . the realms?"

"Yes. Such a feat is difficult, even for them. But enough of them chose to work together to do this much: our Earth was closed to most of the other realms. Magic here dwindled—slowly at first, so that for centuries little seemed different. Then faster. And they—even they—were forbidden to enter here or to meddle in our affairs."

"That's why the Great Bitch can't cross?" Cullen said sharply. "Because she's forbidden by others of Her kind?"

Li Lei shrugged again. "*Forbidden* is a human word. I do not know what laws or bindings act on such as they."

"The task force," Lily said suddenly. "Fagin, the guy in charge, believes that magic began dwindling about four hundred years ago, not three thousand."

Grandmother looked at her. "His guess is not so bad. By then, the remaining magic was not enough to . . . hold things together. That is when the dragons left, and the last of the elves, and many others of the Blood, and their leaving made a hole. Magic poured out faster than ever. And the Book of All Magic—"

"Was lost," Cullen broke in. "Or was it?"

Grandmother fixed him with a severe stare. "You," she announced, "are going to be a problem." She folded her hands on the table. "The shift in the realms, the closing of ours from the others, was not meant to be forever. The story I know calls the moment when the realms return to their previous state the Turning. Two nights ago, I felt it happen."

No one spoke for a long moment. It was Cynna who broke the silence. "Excuse me, but are we supposed to just, you know, believe that? We'd already figured out that the realms are shifting, but the rest of this . . . are you claiming that, of all the people on the planet, *you* felt this Turning and knew what it was?"

For whatever reason, that made Grandmother smile, as if at a good joke. "Yes."

"What you're saying," Lily said, leaning forward, "is that magic isn't going to return to the level of four hundred years ago. It will go back to what it was three thousand years ago."

"Yes. Though not right away, I think."

"And the Codex Arcanum?" Cullen demanded. "The Book of All Magic. You started to say something about it."

She looked at him and sighed. "Yes. According to legend . . . theory . . . a good guess," she decided. "We will call it a good guess, made by the one who told me this tale. He believes that what you call the Codex was taken away and hidden when the magic failed. He believes it will return at the Turning, or be returned—or even that the Turning is a sign it has already returned. As do others," she finished grimly. "Including She we do not name. That is what She wants: the Codex Arcanum. The Book of All Magic."

"Don't tell them," Cullen said.

Lily stared at him. His eyes were glazed, his face tight with emotion. "What?"

"Don't tell the FBI about the Codex. I'm not sure I trust me with the knowledge that it's back—that *maybe* it's back. I for damned sure don't trust anyone else."

"I have to," she said. "They have to know."

His eyes flashed with such anger she almost reached for her weapon. He shook his head sharply, thrust his chair back, stood, and strode for the door.

Lily pushed to her feet. "Cullen—"

Rule laid a hand on her arm. "Let him go. He'll come back when he's ready."

TWENTY-SEVEN

HE wasn't ready for three days.

While Cullen was gone, Toby did indeed learn to play mah-jongg. So did Timms, who came to see Cullen the day after he took off, then returned at Madam Yu's regal invitation.

Madam Yu also became a student, or perhaps collaborator was the better word. Or guinea pig. She received a *kilingo* of Cynna's pain-blocking spell, and when she was able to make it work, Cynna imprinted the spell on two of the guards, who had less success. She didn't know if the spell lost potency from being copied or if the guards simply weren't able to work a spell of that sort. They decided to wait for Cullen's return before imprinting it on anyone else.

Rule's wound healed completely, though the scar remained. And he continued to lose time.

Early Tuesday morning, Cullen turned up at the door, unshaven and looking like he'd slept in his clothes. Which Rule assumed he had, for however little time he'd spent sleeping. "Have you eaten?" he asked, holding the door.

"Yes." Cullen frowned. "Not lately, though, now that you mention it."

"The kitchen, then." Rule headed that way.

They met Lily winging through on her way to the back door. She wore one of her pretty suits, this one with a dark blue jacket and a black pencil skirt. The coat he'd given her wasn't back from the cleaners yet, so she was shrugging into the Lands' End jacket.

Her face went blank. "Cullen."

"Like the proverbial bad penny, here I am once more." He sank into one of the chairs, a subtle lessening in his usual grace telling Rule exhaustion rode him hard. "Miss me?"

She scowled. "I was worried."

"That I'd absconded with your secrets and gone off to pursue the you-know-what?"

She rolled her eyes. "I've got to go," she told Rule, and came to him for a quick kiss . . . which didn't turn out to be so quick. He handed her the umbrella she kept forgetting. This was the third day of drizzle, but Lily hadn't adjusted to the notion of consistent wetness. She frowned at it, patted his arm, and sped out the door without looking back.

Normal. They both worked at keeping things as normal as possible. Rule knew she was afraid for him—he smelled it on her—but they both pretended otherwise. It helped.

Cullen was looking him up and down. "It's stronger. Not by much, but . . . stronger."

Rule kept his expression even. "So Lily says, also. Do you want eggs or meat?"

"Meat." Cullen propped his elbows on the table and leaned his head into his hands, scrubbing his face. "Where's Cynna?"

"Albuquerque." They'd eaten deli food last night. Rule took what was left of the rotisserie chickens from the refrigerator. "She left last night."

"Albuquerque?" Cullen straightened. "What the hell's she doing in Albuquerque?"

"Did you think you could set her down, go away, and find her still where you put her when you came back?" Rule poured a glass of milk. "You know women better than that. Here."

"I didn't think—" Cullen began indignantly, then broke off and grinned. "All right. I didn't think, and that's going to bite my tail, isn't it? But really—why Albuquerque?"

"She's interviewing one of Jiri's former students. So is Lily, though her target lives much closer, in Baltimore."

"Ah." Cullen lost interest.

Lily—via Ruben—had pried open the Secret Service's files on those in Jiri's inner circle. One was in prison; three had vanished beyond the ability of the Secret Service to locate; two were dead.

Of the remaining four, Lily had spoken with two, sent Cynna to talk to one, and was supposed to meet with the last one today.

Fortunately, the mate bond was in one of its more elastic periods, and Baltimore was less than forty miles away. Even if her target lay on the far side of the city, it shouldn't be a problem.

Cullen had gone back to scrubbing his face, probably trying to stay awake long enough to eat. Rule sliced off a drumstick and thigh, put it on a plate and set that, a fork, and the plastic tub of potato salad in front of his friend. "Eat," he said, and sat opposite him.

Cullen needed no encouragement, tearing into the chicken as if it had been days since he's eaten. That was unlikely. He might delay sleep more than was wise, but he kept himself fueled. It was one of the few good habits he'd developed while clanless. Lone wolves couldn't afford to get too hungry.

With the chicken reduced to bones, he started on the potato salad. "I wasn't off sulking, you know. At least, not the whole time."

"I realize that. Lily, however, has known you during one of your more stable periods," Rule said calmly. "Her expectations are different."

Cullen looked up, his eyes dark with anger—then gave a bark of laughter. "Women and expectations. Go together, don't they?" He sighed, pushed the empty container away, and picked up the glass of milk. "I'm feeling a tad volatile. You may have noticed. I should probably go burn something."

Rule let his eyebrows express astonishment. "You mean you haven't?"

Cullen's grin was easier this time, less edged. "No. Haven't been laid in far too long, either." He broke off to yawn hugely. "Lord, I'm tired. I did spend some time four-footed. Have you?"

"Every day." Ten minutes, as he'd been set to do.

"I don't mean penance. I mean running, being wolf as wolf is meant to be."

Anger licked at Rule's insides. He suppressed it. "Nag later. Did you learn anything?"

"Not much." Cullen slouched back in his chair. "I was in New Orleans. You'll be getting a Visa bill for the trip."

Rule nodded, accepting that for the explanation it was. Cullen's financial morals were peculiar, but within their bounds he was quite straitlaced. If Cullen had billed the trip to him, it was clan business, which meant he'd gone in search of help for Rule's condition. "You went to see a Vodun priest or priestess?"

"The one I hoped to consult hasn't been seen since the hurricane, but I talked to a couple others. One let me use her workshop." He lifted his butt enough to dig into his pocket and pulled out a small, silk-wrapped bundle. "Don't say I never gave you anything."

Rule unfastened the black silk gingerly. The contents were unremarkable: a single white feather. It looked like it had come from a chicken. "I hope I'm not supposed to eat this."

Cullen snorted. "No, you wear it next to your skin. Just a sec . . ." He dug into another pocket. "Here." He passed Rule a thin strip of leather. "This has been purified. Use it, not silver or gold. The original charm wards off evil spirits—not exactly your problem, but we tinkered with it."

"We?"

"The priestess whose workshop I used helped me work out some of the changes. The original charm was Vodun—got it from the guy who's missing—so I needed advice on the modifications. If it works, it'll stop the demon stuff from growing."

"And if it doesn't?" Rule picked up the feather. There was a small silver cap on one end with a loop to run the leather strip through.

"I suppose it could cause a rash." He grimaced. "Hell, Rule, I don't know. It's the strongest charm I could make. I think it will work, but I don't know. Even if it does, it won't last more than a week. Maybe less."

Rule turned the charm between his fingers. It felt like just a feather, no zing or punch at all. He wondered what it would feel like to Lily. "Blood magic, Cullen?" Most Vodun magic involved blood, or so Cullen had once told him. And most blood magic came with an expiration date.

Cullen scowled. "It's not black."

But it was probably gray. Rule suspected that any moral penalties from the charm wouldn't redound to him but to his friend. It was probably too late to object. The charm was made. Refusing it wouldn't lessen any price Cullen had agreed to pay.

But he didn't like it. He didn't like it at all. "Our friendship is getting unbalanced. You went to hell for me. Now you've taken on God knows what kind of burden to—"

"Shove it. First, you were my friend when it cost you—and don't tell me it didn't. Second, you're now my Lu Nuncio. What happens to you affects the whole clan. I'm allowed to protect the clan."

Rule turned away abruptly and grabbed the chicken carcass. He yanked open the refrigerator. "Do you have any idea what that's like? People guarding me, protecting me, paying for my safety with their lives—do you know what that's like?" He grabbed the milk, spun, and hurled it across the room.

The carton splatted against the wall. Milk went everywhere.

"Feel better?" Cullen said cheerfully.

"No." What a mess. What a goddamned mess.

"Funny. It usually brightens my day to break things. Oh, well." He shoved back his chair. "Let's get it cleaned up. Where's your brotherly shadow?"

"You," Rule said, incredulous, "are going to help clean up?"

"I'll hand you the sponge and point out any spots you miss." He looked around. "Where *is* the sponge?"

Rueful, Rule shook his head. "That's going to take more than a sponge." He went to the pantry and took out the mop. "Benedict's upstairs with Toby. I promised not to leave the house without him."

"I'm surprised he agreed to put a whole floor between you."

"The warden cut me a deal." His brother had probably heard everything—Rule's temper tantrum, much of their current conversation. Benedict's hearing was uncanny, even for a lupus. Rule picked up the burst carton. "Throw that away, will you? I'm supposed to spar with Freddie later." Methodically, he began mopping. "For some reason everyone thinks I'm strung a little tight."

"If you start acting as erratic as me, we're in trouble." Cullen dumped the carton in the trash and added quietly, "You've had more . . . incidents, haven't you? Blackouts, I guess we could call them."

"Four." He carried the mop to the sink, rinsed it, and brought it back to finish. Three times in the last two days his memory had simply ceased working. "The gaps are short—between ten and twenty minutes. So far, no other symptoms. Lily knows about one. I haven't told her about the other three, so don't mention them."

"Jesus, Rule! And you accuse me of being an idiot with women!"

"No, you're thoughtless, but when you bother to think, you're bright enough." Rule finished mopping and carried the mop back to the pantry. The wall still had to be washed. "Don't bother giving me advice. I'm not going to worry her more than I have to."

Cullen shook his head. Another yawn hit.

"You'd better get to bed. Take my room—the others are occupied."

Cullen managed a tired grin. "Think Lily will object to my sleeping in her bed?"

"No, but she'll hate the way you'll bring it up at whatever moment irritates her most." He retrieved the sponge Cullen had pretended not to see earlier. It was hiding on the shelf above the sink.

"Couple of things I need to tell you before I crash, if I can keep enough brain cells operating to do it." Another yawn. "About Timms—"

"I told you I wasn't keeping him for you."

"I know that." Cullen was irritated. "I called him, told him I had to be out of town awhile. I . . ." He stopped, eyes narrowing. "You knew that."

"He's come over every day. He's on medical leave because of his arm, so I guess he's at loose ends. Madam Yu," he said, "is teaching him mah-jongg."

"Good God."

And that, Rule thought as he stooped to wipe down the wall, was both typical and brand-new. Cullen hadn't called Rule after he vanished—typical. He'd expected Rule to understand. He also hadn't wanted to give Rule a chance to object to what he meant to do. He hadn't called Lily or Cynna because it hadn't occurred to him. But he'd called Timms.

Cullen had always collected strays—often, though not always, human. People as hungry in their way for belonging as he was. But he'd never tended to them himself for long, instead finding someone else to assume responsibility.

But he'd called Timms.

"Might as well call him, tell him I'm back. Can't tell him everything, of course," Cullen said. "Especially about the Codex." He paused. "I suppose Lily has already passed that bit on."

Rule finished the wall, straightened, and nodded.

Cullen's fists clenched, then relaxed. "I guess the ones we most wish didn't know about it already do. I've an idea about the Codex. That's the other thing I wanted to tell you before I crash."

"I'm listening." He put the sponge back and returned to the table, where he picked up the feather and the leather strip. He might as well wear the damned thing. Maybe it would help. He threaded the leather through the silver loop.

"The report Lily gave me. Putting it together with what I can remember or reconstruct—does that make you as mad as it does me?" he asked suddenly. "Having your memory messed with?"

Since he'd just finished cleaning up the evidence of his temper, Rule's voice was dry. "Yes. It does."

Cullen nodded. "Anyway, the FBI detected what they call a nodal disturbance down in Galveston. Their reader's estimate was so high—in the neighborhood of sixty thousand fyllos—they assumed it was a glitch. That kind of nodal energy just doesn't happen, and if it did, there'd be other disturbances . . . kind of like what we've seen lately, as a matter of fact. But they sent someone to check it out anyway. Regular FBI guy from the local office, not the Unit, but he had some Wiccan training. He talked to several people who lived near the node. Including Molly Brown."

Rule tied the leather around his neck and slipped the feather under his shirt. He didn't feel different. But then, he didn't feel different when he lost time, either. "Molly's your succubus friend."

"Right. She had another friend with her—a woman named Erin DuBase. Registered Wiccan, rumored to be a priestess or high priestess. Also present was someone they claimed was Molly's nephew . . . named Michael."

Rule saw where he was going. "The same first name as the sorcerer who visited you. The one you think tampered with your memory."

Excitement burned off Cullen's exhaustion. He began to pace. "Next thing you know, there's an APB out for Molly and Michael, who've left Galveston—only no one knows who issued it. Molly calls me at some point, then she and Michael fly out to see me. We're together for hours. I don't remember it clearly at all, but it doesn't occur to me for a long time that there's anything wrong with my memory. Aversion spell," he said, stopping crisply. "I found the damned thing in my head."

"Did you get rid of it, then?"

Cullen's grin was fierce. "I did. Learned a few things in the process, too. But back to my story. My next clear memory is waking up with Molly and Michael gone. I'm not alone long. The Azá come calling, looking for Michael, though they settle for me.

"Lucky me. At some point before their arrival, I acquired shields. Shields so good no one, not even the telepathic Helen with that damned staff augmenting her power, can break through. We're talking the Rolls-Royce of shields, Rule, when no one on this planet today knows how to build a goddamned Model T."

Rule felt cold. "But that sort of spell might well be in the Codex."

Cullen licked his finger and drew a *one* in the air. "Your point, ace. Both the shields and the tampering with my memory took skills that haven't existed since the Codex vanished." When Cullen's fists clenched this time, he didn't relax them. "He's got it, Rule. The original power reading was no glitch—it takes ungodly amounts of power to open a gate. That's when the Codex returned. And the son of a bitch who messed with my mind has it."

It made sense. It made too damned much sense. "You think this Michael tampered with your memory, then kindly equipped you with shields?"

Cullen waved that away impatiently. "He needed something from me. I wish to God I could remember what, but it's gone. The shields were my payment—which suggests he's not a complete son of a bitch, or at least that Molly wouldn't let him kill me. But he forgot to take away one thing. I know what he looks like."

And if Cullen had been hot to find the man before, now the need was burning him up. "Maybe," Rule said slowly, "we should let the Codex stay hidden."

"Make like an ostrich, you mean? If we pretend nothing bad's coming, the boogieman won't get us." Cullen was disgusted. "*She's* after it. How can we not do our damnedest to get hold of it first?"

He was right, yet—"The Codex is the biggest Pandora's box the world has ever seen. If it contains the kind of knowledge you believe it does—"

"That *She* believes it does, too."

"Then who can be trusted with it?"

Cullen ran a hand over his hair. "If you're thinking I can't be, you're probably right. Oh, not that I want to set myself up as world ruler. I don't have time for that. But better to have it in Nokolai's hands than the government's."

The government. Lily. "What are you saying?" Rule snapped.

"Don't tell Lily. Not yet. She'll been dead-set on telling that damned task force, and—"

"I have to tell her. The last time I kept things from her—" Rule gave a quick, harsh bark of laughter. "That's when she ended up in hell. So did I."

Cullen shook his head. "What you withheld was clan business and had nothing to do with what happened to the two of you."

"I can't hold back on her."

"You already are."

LILY grabbed her purse and her computer, slammed the car door, and headed out of the garage at a good clip. Automatically she scanned the backyard, but she couldn't spot the guard.

It gave her the willies, frankly. She was glad the guards were there, but she didn't like the idea of anyone being so well-hidden.

The back door opened just as she reached for it. She jumped, then stepped through. "That's damned disconcerting," she told Benedict, who was holding the door for her.

He smiled. Benedict was a man of few words—often no words.

"Rule!" she called, setting her laptop on the table, then digging her phone out of her purse before tossing the purse there, too. She hit the speed dial for Cynna's cell.

"Things are popping," she said, glancing at her watch as Rule came into the kitchen. "Come on, Cynna, pick up," she told the ringing phone, continuing to Rule without a pause, "I've got a lead. I'm going to have to go to Chicago, so I guess some of the guards will—damn." Cynna's voice mail invited her to leave a message.

She did, telling her to call back ASAP, then explaining to Rule as she slipped off her bulky jacket. "The woman I talked to in Baltimore was scared—Jiri's done quite a number on her followers—but she finally gave me a name. This one's new—the Secret Service didn't have it. Hamid Franklin joined the movement well after Cynna left. Apparently he was one of Jiri's favorites, so . . ."

His stillness and lack of expression finally sank in. "What is it? What's wrong?" Dumb question, when so much was wrong—but there could always be more.

There was.

"I can't go to Chicago," he told her. "Paul's body is being released to me today."

TWENTY-EIGHT

THE hearse ahead of them was black and shiny in the late afternoon sun. For this, the sun had finally deigned to come out. That just pissed her off.

Lily was hungry, tired, worried . . . all right, not worried. Scared. She was scared on so many levels it was hard to keep track of them all. Rule was infected with demon stuff. Her mother wasn't speaking to her. Her older sister was, unfortunately. The world was set up to be blasted with repeated doses of magic, changing everything, probably killing people. Demons were popping up all over, and an Old One who'd been around since before the big bang wanted to destroy the lupi, seize the Book of All Magic, and rule the world.

Her feet hurt.

She'd found Alexia Morgan, but she'd had to walk over half of Baltimore to do it. The woman hadn't been at home, at work, or at her favorite bar. Lily had finally tracked her to a laundry center. But she'd struck gold once she found her, and now . . .

Now Cynna was handling the Chicago trip, she reminded herself. Cynna was perfectly capable of doing that while she, Rule, his brawny brother, and his sorcerous buddy followed a damned hearse whose driver thought it respectful to go fifty in a seventy-miles-per-hour zone.

Rule had just finished telling her Cullen's theory.

"You waited on purpose." She tried to keep her voice low. She really did. "You didn't tell me about this Michael character and his possible connection to the Codex until we left. You wanted to keep me from telling Ruben or the task force." This couldn't be reported over the phone. No line was sufficiently secure to discuss the Codex Arcanum.

He didn't deny it, which did nothing for her temper. "Goddammit, Rule, we can't just sit on this! Admittedly it's only a theory, but it fits. I have to—"

"Think," he said coolly. "You need to stop and think before you do anything, which is why I waited. I wanted you to have time to chew over the options."

She threw up her hands. "I'm an FBI agent. My *option* is to tell Ruben."

"That's one of them. He'll have to tell the president, of course, who will need to speak of this with a few trusted advisers. Who will all advise her to get her hands on the Codex without delay."

"And your point is?"

"What might the Pentagon do with the Book of All Magic?"

That stopped her for a moment. "What else can we do? Assuming it is here, and that we find it—pretty big assumptions, but let's go with them for now. It isn't up to us to decide."

"Passing on what we know *is* a decision, and makes us culpable, in part, for what happens later . . . if your faith in the authorities turns out to be misplaced."

"I trust Ruben."

He thought that over, then nodded. "I do, too. I might even be willing to trust him with the Codex, if he, in turn, were willing to tell no one he had it. But whoever possesses it must be not only honorable but able to defend it against everyone who wants it. Which will include much of the rest of the world, once word gets out."

"Other worlds, too," Cullen put in from the backseat.

She drummed her fingers on her thigh, counted to ten, and said to Rule, "Why don't you yell when you get mad?"

"I prefer to throw things," he said dryly.

Cullen snorted.

She turned to glare at him. "And why are you here, anyway? I understand why Benedict's with us." And was damned glad of it. Benedict had agreed to leave the other bodyguards at the house—Toby needed protection, too—but he'd flatly refused to let Rule travel to Leidolf territory without him. "But you don't serve any purpose on this little outing."

That amused him. "Sure I do. Decoration. I may be useless, but I'm pretty."

"You're not useless. Annoying, infuriating, arrogant, but not useless. But I don't see why it's okay for you to accompany Rule if other Nokolai can't."

He shrugged. "Leidolf may object, but I'm not seen as a threat. They'll probably shrug and let me in."

"But they know you're a sorcerer."

"Most lupi disdain magic, aside from the Change."

Benedict's deep voice came as a surprise. It often did, both because of the bass rumble of it and because he so seldom spoke. "Cullen will try to learn the extent of Victor's illness."

"You sound like you already know what his illness is."

"There aren't many possibilities," Rule said, slowing as the hearse did. They were nearing the turn-off for Nutley. "Cancer is the most likely."

"Cancer? But I thought lupi healed malignant cells along with everything else."

"Normal malignancies, yes," Cullen said. "But there's a form of cancer peculiar to our species. It only occurs at two points— early adolescence, when puberty and the first Change make wild alterations in the body, or in old age."

Adolescence? She thought of Toby, and glanced at Rule.

He was watching the road or the hearse or maybe listening to his own thoughts, but he must have felt her looking at him. "It's much more rare in adolescence than old age, fortunately. Nettie says that at the first Change our magic seeks a balance between rapid healing and cellular immortality. Since the only truly immortal cells are cancerous—"

"Cancer is immortal?"

"On a cellular level, yes," Cullen said. "Do you want the geneticist's explanation, or the simple one?"

"Simple, by all means."

"Cells replace themselves through division. Cellular senescence—old age—is basically the loss of information needed for the cell to divide. Normal cells have what's called a Hayflick limit. That's the number of times they can divide to reproduce themselves, and it more or less determines how long an organism can live. Cancer cells duck this limit through an enzyme called telomerase. Telomerase keeps adding six-letter units to the telomeres—that's the bit at the end of the chromosomal chain— so the cell can continue dividing, which means—"

"You're sure this is the simple explanation."

"Simplified to the point of absurdity. I haven't even mentioned cross-linked proteins, AGEs—"

"Don't."

"Okay, okay. The point is that cancerous cells can divide indefinitely; regular cells can't. We can't study lupus cells in the lab to determine how they manage to duck the Hayflick limit, of course."

"Cells from those of the Blood produce wacky test results."

"Right. Separated from its organizing principle, our magic reverts to chaos. So, with no clinical tests possible, all we can do is theorize, but the most likely theory is that magic does what the telomerase enzyme does. It allows our cells to divide without losing information."

Lily thought she followed his reasoning. "And that's what you said cancer does, only it uses this enzyme instead of magic. So if something's a little off with the magic, you get cancer instead of mega-healing."

"Bet your teachers loved you. Yep, our magic works great as long as it conforms to its organizing principle. When it doesn't, we sprout cancers. Multiple, systemic cancers."

She considered that as they followed the hearse in a stately procession. "There seem to be a lot of cars headed for Nutley."

"I noticed," Rule said grimly. "I think we're arriving with half of Leidolf. Randall's memorial will follow Paul's tomorrow. The clan is coming for that, both out of respect and because Victor will call the naming then."

"You mean he'll name the new heir tomorrow?"

"No, that's when he sets the date for the ceremony. Traditionally the Rho calls the naming, then speaks the names of those of the blood—the ones who potentially could carry the mantle."

"But it always goes to a son of the Rho."

"Almost always," he corrected. "The blood is strongest in a son of the Rho, but others in the clan will have founder's blood, too. We're hoping like hell Victor breaks with that particular tradition."

"But could he name Brady? I thought the heir had to have at least one son."

"Brady sired twin sons several years ago. One was stillborn, but the other lived a few days. Technically, that qualifies him, but the clan won't like it. I'm not sure they'd accept him."

"Do they have a choice?"

"There's the testing. It's part of the ceremony. Victor names his heir, then he's tested."

"Challenged, he means," Cullen put in. "That's one of the reasons for the wait between calling the naming and holding it. It gives the clan time to talk over who will handle the Challenge. When Rule was named, of course, there wasn't any question about that. Benedict Challenged."

"What?" She swung around to stare at the big man. "You Challenged Rule? Fought him?"

It was Rule who answered her. "If the heir can't command the most powerful fighter in the clan, he can't be Rho. I wouldn't call Benedict's Challenge a formality," he added with a thread of amusement, very dry. "He made me work. But if he hadn't been willing to have me as heir, I wouldn't have won."

"There's always at least one Challenger," Cullen said. "No matter how popular the choice of heir. But there can be more. If Brady is named, I'm betting there will be plenty."

"Is he likely to win a Challenge? Is he a good fighter?"

Cullen sighed. "He's good. Rule could take him. So could Benedict, but that goes without saying. I'm not sure who within Leidolf—"

Benedict spoke in his deep, quiet voice. "Victor will not name Brady unless he wishes his son dead. Alex Thibodaux is a good fighter, and he has honor. If Brady is named, Alex will Challenge and kill him."

That notion seemed to brighten everyone's day.

THE little town of Nutley looked worn but not worn out—lived-in, Lily decided, mentally comparing the streets they passed to the map she'd studied. She liked to know where things were, just in case. They were second in a small line of vehicles behind the hearse, whose driver held to his principles and drove below the speed limit.

She returned to the cancer question, turning her head to ask Cullen, "What's this organizing principle you mentioned?"

"If you figure that out, let me know."

Benedict spoke quietly. "Some say it's purely physical, that the magic takes its template from our bodies. Some say our will or intent shapes it. And some believe the Lady creates a pattern for each of us."

She twisted further to look at him, sitting directly behind her. "Which do you believe?"

"If it came from the Lady, it would work all the time. No one would develop cancer. If it came from our bodies, we'd all be about thirteen years old, physically—the age of our first Change, when the magic arrives. If will or intent formed it, old bastards like Victor would live forever. He's got the will for it."

He'd just eliminated every theory he'd mentioned. "But what do *you* believe?"

"That the adolescent cancer arises when a lupus's body tries to reject the magic, and the two battle instead of melding. That we live to a certain age because we're supposed to. That some suffer cancer in old age because sin has twisted their magic."

"Sin?" she repeated, startled. It was the last thing she'd expected from Benedict. "That's . . . very biblical of you."

And it was all he intended to say, apparently. He didn't respond.

"Benedict can be downright Old Testament at times," Rule said, "for someone who was raised to follow traditional Navajo beliefs."

They were climbing now, leaving Nutley behind. Lily tried to set her mind on the case, on what their options would be if the Chicago lead didn't pan out. But she was so damned aware of Rule she couldn't concentrate.

It still hit her at times, this physical draw. Mate bond or love? She wasn't sure—was no longer sure it mattered. But it embarrassed her to feel this physical acuity with others present. It wasn't arousal, precisely, but it led that way.

Still, she found herself watching him. Warm afternoon light slid over his face, marking the strong cheekbones. She loved his eyebrows, those winged slashes so much more expressive than her own. His hands on the wheel drew her gaze. Strong hands, long fingers . . . gold glinted at his wrist. He'd worn a watch today; he'd didn't always. The cuffs of his dress shirt looked very white against his skin and the dark wool of his suit jacket.

Like most of the Western world, lupi wore dark colors for funerals. But they wore them for all important ceremonies, also.

Black, deepest blue, and charcoal represented the depths through which the moon moved.

At least, that's what they wore when they wore anything at all. Lily was glad this wasn't one of the skin-only ceremonies. Not that she'd have had to strip—nudity was required only of those who might Change. But where do you look in a crowd of naked men?

She was pretty sure where her eyes would be drawn.

Since nudity was, thankfully, not called for, Lily had packed her best black slacks and jacket; she'd wear a dark blue shell beneath. Funeral colors weren't necessary until the memorial tomorrow. Though Paul would be buried tonight, only his closest kin would be present for that. Lupi considered burial a private business.

The coat Rule had given her was slung over the back of the seat. The cleaners had delivered it just before they left. She wished they'd been a few hours slower. Paul had bled into that coat.

The hearse was slowing. Its turn signal came on. Nearly showtime, she thought as they, too, slowed for the turn.

The hearse bumped off down a dirt road. They turned—and stopped abruptly. Three men wearing blades much like Benedict's had stepped in front of their car. Lily glanced at the others. They seemed calm, as if they'd expected this.

One of the men stepped up to the window, which Rule opened. "Nokolai isn't welcome here."

"I'm accompanying the body of Paul Chernowich—as you know."

"He isn't." The guard jerked his chin toward Benedict in the backseat.

"If there is a ceremony, Nokolai must witness it as well as Leidolf. My brother accompanies me for that and because of the threat of demon attack, not from any lack of respect for Leidolf. My Chosen is with me," Rule added. "It would be odd if I—or Leidolf—refused her the protection my brother can provide."

The guards discussed it among themselves, then consulted someone via cell phone while four cars behind them waited. The hearse waited up ahead, too, its driver having realized his escort was detained. Eventually the guards announced that Benedict would be allowed onto Leidolf land if he surrendered his right to Challenge.

Benedict refused. He made a counteroffer: he would avoid all Challenges if possible and would bind himself not to Challenge someone named Alex.

"That's his counterpart," Cullen explained while the guards consulted some more. "Head of their security, and their best fighter. He'd have to accept a Challenge if Benedict issued one."

"The others wouldn't?"

Rule took up the explanation. "Benedict's reputation makes it unlikely that anyone but a young fool would accept a Challenge from him. It would be an embarrassment to refuse a Challenge, but no real loss of status in this case. Everyone knows Benedict would win. But Alex's position makes him a sort of placeholder for the Lu Nuncio the clan currently lacks. His refusal of a Challenge would reflect upon the entire clan. If Benedict Challenged, Alex would have to accept."

"So they aren't just being pissy with their conditions."

Cullen snorted. "Oh, they're being pissy. If Benedict gave up his Challenge right, they'd feel free to offer insult."

"Our notion of insult," Rule added dryly, "might strike you as a trifle violent."

The guards came back, having obtained agreement from someone to Benedict's terms, which he then had to state for the record. There was one more brief delay. They wanted to search the car and remove all guns. Apparently Benedict's blades were acceptable; firearms were not.

Lily was fed up. "There are several weapons in the trunk," she said coolly, addressing the guards herself for the first time. "They're mine. I'm an FBI agent, as I imagine you know, investigating the demon attacks on lupus heirs. I'm not handing them over."

They didn't believe her. In their world, little bitty women didn't shoot AK-47s. Lily got out, marched around to the back of the car, pulled out the weapon, set her feet, and shouldered it. "Anyone in those trees?" She nodded at a thick stand of oak.

"I—no," the tallest guard said.

She fired a blast, decimating several innocent branches. "Good stopping power, even on demons," she announced, unable to hear herself speak. Served her right, she supposed, for showing off. She knew from experience her hearing would return in a moment.

They let her keep the guns.

When they pulled away from the checkpoint at last, she asked Rule to tell her about Leidolf.

"What do you want to know?" Rule asked.

"You said I wouldn't like some of their ways. Do their ways have anything to do with what Cynna told us? Their Rho apparently thought it was okay to hump the barely legal mother of his late son's child in the hall of his home."

"Nokolai and some of the other clans don't like the way Leidolf treats its female clan. They haven't exactly come into this century where women are concerned."

Cullen snorted. "They had to be dragged, screaming and kicking, into the last century, and I'm not sure they ever made it. Victor and his merry band believe women really do only have one purpose, and that's what they teach their female clan."

Lily's lip curled. "They want them barefoot and pregnant?"

"Or on their knees, their backs—whatever. Which is why Rule's great-granny extricated herself and ten others from the clan."

"What?" She swiveled, staring first at Cullen, then at Rule. "Your great-grandmother was Leidolf?"

He nodded but didn't answer right away. Rain plus all the recent traffic hadn't been good for the dirt road; the ruts were deep, the potholes deeper. "You should know the story," he said at last. "It's a large part of the reason for Leidolf's hatred of Nokolai. Iselda sought out my great-grandfather at an All-Clan. That's not unusual—a lot of trysting goes on at an All-Clan, and Rhos are— ah, an attractive partner to many women. This was especially true when the mores of the external culture were so repressive. When clan of either sex had the chance—"

"They snuck off into the bushes with like-minded souls. I can see how that would happen, but weren't your clans enemies?"

"Nokolai and Leidolf have never been friends, but there wasn't open enmity back then. More like residual distrust. Some of that came from events very long ago, but those might have been forgotten if not for a regrettable nationalism. Before the clans emigrated, Leidolf was German, Nokolai French."

"So you had a history of not getting along, but you weren't yet the Hatfields and McCoys. Did Leidolf get mad because Iselda snuck off with a Nokolai man?"

"No, that sort of thing was expected. But Iselda conceived."

"That must have been a shock."

A small smile touched his lips. "I'm told she claimed she'd planned it—though how anyone can plan conception, when it's so rare—"

"Not as rare with interclan couplings," Cullen put in, "as within a clan."

"Still, it would be like walking through the desert counting on rain for your water supply. We might say Iselda took her stroll during the rainy season, but the odds were against her. At any rate, her tryst shocked no one, and her pregnancy would have been a matter for rejoicing throughout her clan—if she'd remained Leidolf."

"But she didn't."

"No. She chose to leave the All-Clan with my great-grandfather and be adopted into Nokolai, making her child Nokolai. Leidolf's Rho—the whole clan, really—was furious. Still, had matters stopped there, Leidolf might have forgiven."

"What happened?"

"She bore my great-grandfather a son. My grandfather. As a boon, she asked him to free ten women of her former clan. He agreed."

"Free them? But—they weren't slaves. They could have left if they wanted to. Even back then—"

"Actually," Rule said, "they were slaves."

"What?"

"This happened in 1848. Slavery was still legal in the South." Right. She'd tripped over assumptions based on human life spans. Rule's father looked a hale sixty, but he'd been born nearly a century ago. "But Leidolf was German. Though I guess if they got slave women pregnant—"

"That happened, too, but Leidolf took it a step further. In most of the old South, possessing any trace of African blood legally rendered you black. Leidolf . . ." Rule's lips tightened. So did his hands on the steering wheel. "Leidolf arranged to have some of its female clan declared black whether or not they had African blood. Legal trickery, arranged through a corrupt judge, that allowed them to own their women outright."

"Sick. That is . . ." She didn't have words for it. "Sick. But why go to such extremes? Women were pretty much chattel anyway back then."

"Compared to slaves, women had many rights. Slaves couldn't own anything. They had no rights to their children or their bodies, and they couldn't marry. That was Leidolf's main goal, according to Iselda. Leidolf didn't simply disapprove of marriage—they considered it an abomination."

"Your great-grandmother left. She wasn't forcibly returned to her owners."

"Not all of their female clan were declared slaves, only those whose ancestry could be sufficiently muddled. Those with brothers near their age were usually safe, since they couldn't take a chance on the males being suspected of having African blood. Iselda had a younger brother. Victor Frey."

"It's a family name?" she asked.

Rule just looked at her.

"It's not the same man. It . . . he . . ." Oh, Lord. Rule's expression made it clear that the Victor Frey she would soon meet really was the younger brother of a woman who'd lived in 1848. Lily did the math, did it again—and still couldn't believe it. "You're saying that Victor Frey is your great-uncle, and he's—"

"About to hit the big one-six-oh," Cullen said cheerfully.

TWENTY-NINE

THEY didn't meet Victor Frey that day, after all.

Leidolf Clanhome was bursting at the seams. The large, dormitory-style building across the clearing from Frey's frame house was full, and the ground had sprouted tents everywhere except the central field. Nokolai Clanhome had a similar field, used for important ceremonies.

Not that the entire clan was present. Though Leidolf was concentrated in Virginia, West Virginia, and North Carolina, it had members in other parts of the country, too. And some clan were staying at hotels in Harrisonburg, but the vast majority of those who would attend tomorrow's ceremonies had crammed themselves onto their clanhome however they could.

Benedict's counterpart, Alex, met them at the house. He and Benedict stared at each other for a moment, then each gave a small nod, and Alex vanished into the house. He was replaced by a middle-aged woman in a brown dress—Sabra Ewings, Victor's daughter.

Sabra invited them in, told them their car would be moved to a parking area once they'd gotten their things from it, and apologized for having only a single room for the four of them. "We weren't expecting to need more, you see, and with the memorial and the naming, we have no empty rooms." She managed a strained smile. "Victor isn't up to leaving his room yet, I'm afraid, but he bids you welcome."

Lily thought they should turn around and head for Harrisonburg, where there were hotels. That, apparently, would be a major insult. "They can try to kill your father, but you're not supposed to insult them?" Lily said dryly when they reached the privacy of their single, cramped room.

Rule set their suitcase on the bed. "From this point on, it's wise to assume that anything we say is overheard."

Lupus hearing. Great. They had to be diplomatic in private, too. Pity she didn't have his hearing. They could have insulted their hosts by subvocalizing—speaking under the tongue, they called it. They did it without moving their lips, speaking so softly only another nearby lupus could hear.

At one point, she'd been able to hear it. The mate bond had briefly blurred the lines between his Gifts and hers, but it hadn't lasted. Nor had it happened again. Rule thought it might have been a one-time deal; the bond had been brand-new, and a new mate bond was powerful.

Lily looked around the room. They lacked privacy visually as well. The single window had lace curtains, no shades. The bed was a four-poster covered by a faded chenille spread; there was a small chest of drawers but no nightstand. Though the furniture was minimal, so was the room. There was barely enough floor space on either side of the bed for a pair of sleeping bags.

If they'd had them. "You didn't bring sleeping bags, did you?"

"Lily." Cullen's voice was reproachful. "Are you saying you won't share? And after I spent most of the day in your bed, too."

"What the hell are you—" But he was grinning, pleased with himself for having gotten a rise out her. So she stopped talking and threw a pillow at him.

He fended it off and plopped down on the bed, still grinning.

"Get your feet off the bed," she told him.

Rule was more direct, swiping Cullen's feet to one side. "Don't get comfortable yet. We still have to unload Lily's arsenal."

"I feel sure the rest of you can . . ." Cullen's voice trailed off.

Everyone but Lily looked at the door. A few seconds later, someone knocked on it. Rule gave Benedict a nod, and he opened it.

"I came to see him. I'm Roland Miller, Paul's father, and I came to see him."

Benedict stood aside.

The man who entered was smaller than anyone in the room except Lily. His hair was black, his eyes dark brown; he wore the ubiquitous lupus uniform of jeans, but he'd dressed them up with a faded blue work shirt. He held himself stiffly.

He looked very much like Paul—older and weary with his grief, but much like Paul. Impulsively, Lily moved forward. "Mr. Miller, I'm so sorry. Paul was very brave. I don't know if that's any consolation, but . . ." Her voice trailed away.

He was looking right past her. She might have been a mosquito buzzing in his ear for all he noticed. No, he might have swatted at a mosquito. His attention was all for Rule. "You submitted to my son."

"I did, to save him from being shot by an overly zealous police officer."

"Didn't save him for long, did you?" He looked Rule up and down. "I'll accept a son's duty from you tomorrow. Eight o'clock, in the meeting field, north end." With that he turned and left, closing the door behind him.

"Did he ignore me because he's grieving?" Lily asked the room in general. "Or because I'm female?"

"Got it in two, luv," Cullen said from his sprawl on the bed. "You'll find that most male Leidolf ignore you unless you badge 'em. Or unless they're propositioning you."

"They'll be polite," Benedict said. He'd taken off his suit jacket and was hanging it in the tiny closet. "I'll be there. Rule will be there. They'll be polite."

But they wouldn't see anything wrong in hitting on her with Rule standing right beside her, and they'd ignore her otherwise. "Paul wasn't like that."

"You met Paul in the outside world. You're in their clanhome now," Rule said. "Consciously or not, many of them will fall into the old ways."

"Are they going to expect me to eat in the kitchen with the womenfolk?"

The total silence that met her made her jaw drop. "You're kidding," she said. "Tell me you're kidding."

"You won't have to accept," Rule said. "But Sabra will invite you to join her and a few of the women . . . ah, in the kitchen."

Oh, this was going to be fun. She could hardly wait to see what tomorrow would bring.

* * *

DAWN broke cold and clear. Lily learned that by twitching aside the bedspread Rule had draped over the curtain rod for privacy. The window was cold to the touch; the sky was wiped clean of the clouds that had drizzled on them for days.

It was also quiet, for which she thanked any gods who might be listening.

They'd ended up eating in their room. If that offended Sabra, Lily figured she could live with it. She'd had this irrational certainty that she shouldn't let Rule out of her sight, and maybe he'd felt the same way, because he hadn't argued. After dinner, Cullen had taken off—planning to listen to gossip, he said. Needing to get rid of the fidgets, she thought.

The rest of them had played poker. Neither of the men had been concentrating on the game. She was up $10.75 and Cullen was still gone when they turned out the lights.

She hadn't slept well. Cuddling with Rule generally soothed her, but generally they cuddled after making love. That hadn't been an option with his brother sleeping on the floor beside the bed, and her body hadn't appreciated the neglect.

Funny how fast her body had turned greedy on her. Not long ago it was entirely used to that sort of neglect. She'd given it a stern lecture and done her best to relax.

The lupi camped outside had other ideas about how to relax. For them it was party time.

Oh, not with alcohol. It was possible, Rule said, for a lupus to get drunk if he really worked at it, but since the effects wouldn't last more than ten or fifteen minutes, it wasn't worth the effort. But the clan had been glad to get together, and they'd expressed that loudly—fighting, singing, yelling, laughing, dancing around a huge bonfire . . .

Yipping. Howling.

Cullen had returned about two A.M. She'd still been awake.

Hygiene got a bit of a pass that morning; people, people, everywhere, and only two bathrooms in the house. She and Rule dressed first. Beneath jacket and shirt, he wore the charm Cullen had made for him. It may have been working. He hadn't had a blackout since putting it on.

She went into the hall so Benedict and Cullen could dress. Not that any of the men would object to her remaining, but she felt better not knowing what Rule's brother looked like naked. Rule chose to wait out there with her, mostly so he could offer an opinion on whether she should leave her weapon in the room.

It was a short discussion. No way in hell was she stirring out of their room unarmed. She slid her phone in her jacket pocket and changed the subject. "Is that charm Cullen made helping?"

He gave her a sharp look. "I didn't tell you about the charm."

"You didn't tell me about your other blackouts, either, but I'm a detective. I detected them. And you don't usually wear a chicken feather around your neck, so I deduced that it came from Cullen."

He was silent a moment. "No memory gaps. Not since I put on the charm. I, ah, expected you to be angry that I didn't tell you about the blackouts."

"It was stupid, but I understood. You need to protect me just like I need to protect you."

"You make me feel better and worse at the same time."

She smiled. "Good."

Benedict came out, looking like a well-dressed mountain in new jeans and a midnight blue shirt with a gray sports jacket. Then Cullen emerged.

She'd been surprised to learn that Cullen owned a suit. She'd never seen him make any effort with clothes, and God knew he didn't have to—he was eye candy in his usual ratty jeans and T-shirts. Even so, once she knew he was going to dress like an adult, she should have been prepared.

Or maybe not. Maybe the sight of Cullen Seabourne in a black, custom-tailored suit with a black tuxedo shirt was more than any woman with a functioning heartbeat could prepare herself for.

It was just as well Cynna wasn't here to see him. She'd trip him and beat him to the ground, and Lily was far from sure the tangle those two were headed for would end well.

He grinned. "What do you think?"

Her dumbfounded stare had already told him, which she thought was more than enough ego food for the man. She opted for damning with faint praise. "Nice. Sort of Johnny Depp meets Johnny Cash."

"Johnny who? Cash I've heard of, but the other guy . . ."

She rolled her eyes, put on her coat, and they set off for the field.

The sky was pinking up in the east. Dawn looked different on this side of the continent, less prone to the vivid hues she was used to. Pretty in its way, but she preferred the desert. There, beauty wore barbs so you'd know where to step.

Their destination was obvious. No one else seemed to be awake yet, save for the small cluster of people—all male—at the north end of the field. They headed that way. The grass was wet, the dampness promising to soak through the thin leather of her shoes. The air was cold enough to make her glad she wore a coat . . . she just wished it wasn't *this* one.

They weren't quite the only ones up. As they started across the field, so did a woman in a long white dress. She came from the south end, where the chimney of a small stone house leaked a thin plume of smoke. White meant that was the Rhej, the only one who would wear the moon's color today.

Not a dress, Lily realized after a second look—a long white robe that seemed to glow in the early light. "The Rhej is part of the ritual?" she asked. Her breath puffed white in the still air.

"She'll observe, not participate. She's the clan's memory. Her presence at the ritual is rather like recording a document at the courthouse."

Lily nodded at the men waiting at the far end. "Are any of them Victor?"

"No, and I'd expected him to be present for this. He's not needed, strictly speaking, but it's the sort of thing a Rho generally attends. Either he was hurt worse than the Rhej indicated, or he's avoiding us."

"Didn't smell right," Benedict put in briefly.

"Meaning?"

Cullen picked up the explanation. "I didn't smell illness on him before. Admittedly, he took care not to come too close, but I'd have picked up the scent if the disease was out of its earliest phase."

"He was injured," Rule said, "which means his body kicked into healing mode. That can accelerate the course of the disease."

"And this matters to Nokolai because . . . ?"

"With a healer like the Rhej on call, the disease can sometimes be arrested for years in its earliest phase. No scent then. Once it crosses into the next phase, though, little can be done. If that has happened, Victor has a year at most."

Cullen added, "Many don't care to hang around once the disease goes into that phase. The magic is no longer following its organizing principle, and the results aren't pretty. Multiple tumors, bizarre growths—"

"Brain tumors," Benedict said. "Uncontrollable rage. Hallucinations."

All of which would be very bad news for Leidolf. For Nokolai . . . "I guess you need to know what's going on with your enemy."

Rule nodded, but lowered his voice even more. "We're getting too close to discuss this further."

Lily squelched the question quivering at the edge of her tongue. She could see why they couldn't talk about Victor's illness when members of Leidolf might overhear, but there were things she needed to know. What did Cullen hope to learn from seeing Frey that he hadn't been able to see a few days ago?

As they drew near, the waiting men—there were five of them—turned to watch them approach. Lily saw faces for the first time. She recognized Paul's father but none of the others.

"Shit," Cullen said. "That's Brady."

Rule was calm. "With the Rho not attending, it makes sense for his son to be here."

"Let's hope he's in a sane mood today."

"Hush," Rule said softly.

When they reached the others, no one spoke. Lily took her cue from Rule, but the thick, nervy silence bugged her. She occupied herself studying the others, especially Gunning.

Brady Gunning was all angles, as if he'd never filled out after his last growth spurt. His dark blond hair made her think of her mother's old stove—harvest gold, that's what they called it. His face was narrow, with a long nose and a short forehead, and his pretty blue eyes were watching her study him.

He didn't look like a sociopath. Neither had the guy she'd arrested a couple years ago for killing his neighbor over some daylilies.

The Rhej arrived, and still no one spoke. Silently they formed up in two rough semicircles. *Them versus us,* she thought, standing between Rule and Cullen, with Benedict on Rule's other side. They faced the Leidolf clan members while the Rhej stood apart, her dark face expressionless.

"Leidolf," Brady said suddenly. "Brady Gunning."

"Leidolf," said the man on his right. "John Ellis."

And so it went, with each of them naming his clan, then himself. Rule kicked it off on their side; Benedict spoke next, and that's when she learned his surname: Two Horses, the same as his daughter. Which sparked a flash of curiosity. He wouldn't have been married to Nettie's mother, so how did they come to share a name?

One more question she couldn't ask. She spoke her part: "Nokolai. Lily Yu." Then Cullen spoke his.

The ritual itself was brief. That seemed to be the case with most lupus ceremonies. Roland Miller walked to the center of their not-quite circle and spoke in a quiet but clear voice. "I am Roland, father of Paul. Those with me know this to be true. Let the one who was *en susmissio* to my son when he died meet me."

Rule moved to stand in front of Paul's father. He was a full head taller than the older man, strong and straight. "I was *en susmussio* to Paul and was present when he was killed. I failed to protect him. I offer you a son's duty."

Lily waited, her breath catching in her throat. Rule thought it quite possible the older man would refuse the offer—likely, even, since it made a tie between Leidolf and Nokolai that neither clan wanted.

Roland Miller inhaled suddenly, loudly, as if he, too, had forgotten to breathe. His voice was louder than before. "I accept."

If Rule was startled, he didn't show it. Swiftly he flowed to one knee, bowing his head. This was conditional submission, she'd learned. Rule's bared nape indicated respect, not personal submission, as well as his willingness to be bound by what was said next.

Not that she understood what was said next. Roland Miller spoke, then Rule, but they used the Latin that lupi had been using for centuries as a common tongue among the clans. Kind of like the Catholic Church had done during the same period, uniting its many parts through a single tongue.

She knew the gist of it, though. To receive a son's duties, Roland had to offer a father's duties in return: financial support, if needed; advice, if requested. Rule would promise much the same: financial support, if needed; attendance at certain clan functions, if requested.

Listening to the formal cadence, since the words meant nothing to her, she looked at the men opposite them. And caught an expression on Brady Gunning's face that worried her.

The hate she understood, based on what she'd been told about the man. But why was the Leidolf Rho's crazy son so damned happy?

THIRTY

CYNNA supposed this was one of God's little jokes. How else to explain the way the investigation had brought her here?

The deli was gone, she noted, striding down the cracked sidewalk, her heavy trench coat flapping around her ankles. A Vietnamese take-out joint had replaced it. But the laundry was still there, and the buildings looked the same—old, dingy, gray. Everything on this street was gray. When you spoke of color here you meant skin or gangs.

There were more white faces than there had been in her youth—integration coming to the ghetto at last; she'd really stood out as a kid. But most were some shade of brown.

The street had changed, Cynna decided, but not enough. She hoped the same wasn't true of her.

The weather was bitter as only a Chicago winter could be. Funny, that, because she'd been in colder places, but something about Chicago in December went right to the bone.

Mounds of filthy slush made crossing the street an adventure. Cynna survived that, keeping her gloved hands jammed in her pockets for warmth . . . and to keep from worrying at the mysterious *kilingo* Jiri had placed on one of them. It hadn't woken yet, but it would. Jiri hadn't planted it for laughs.

She needed to get it off. For that she could use some help, she admitted. Cullen's vision, to be specific. Removing a spell she knew, one she'd placed on her skin herself, was tricky. She didn't know how to get rid of a mystery spell.

She'd have to let a whisper of power slip into the spell for him to see it. That ought to be safe enough; a spell as complex as this one looked was bound to need more than a whisper to work. He'd be able to see how the magic moved through it, and the two of them could figure out how to undo it.

Once he deigned to show up.

When he first took off she'd been pissed. She admitted that. Rule said that cutting out was a survival skill Cullen acquired when he was a lone wolf. When his temper flared too high, he left—right that second, no discussion. He was out of there until he cooled down. Now that he was Nokolai he probably didn't have to do that anymore—being clan moderated things somehow—but the habit was ingrained. When he got mad, he walked out.

Apparently he'd stayed mad. As for her, she'd gotten over it. She should have known better than to get bent out of shape in the first place. Yeah, they were working up to doing the wild thing, but what did that mean? Sex could happen quick. It hadn't happened for them yet because life kept interfering, but it would. But friendship was a slow build. You started out with some reason to like each other, you got some respect going, then you let it simmer until you'd brewed up some trust.

It might take a lot of simmering for either her or Cullen to hit trust.

She headed across the street. A car shot through the yellow, splashing her with icy slush. Automatically she offered the traditional one-finger salute . . . Huh. The driver was Chinese. No, probably Vietnamese—a cluster of immigrants from that country were turning a pocket of former slum into a decent area a few blocks east of here.

That made her think of Lily. Wonder what she'd make of Chicago weather? She seemed to think it was cold in D.C.

Cynna snorted, but thinking about Lily while she moved down this street depressed her. The China doll might have patrolled in hoods like this, but she hadn't lived in one. She'd grown up clean. Cullen, now . . . she had a feeling he knew the bad spots in every city he'd ever lived in. He'd knocked around a lot while he was clanless. But she was pretty sure he hadn't grown up in this kind of place. Lupi didn't let their kids grow up poor and desperate.

Cynna glanced to her left. *Three blocks over,* she thought. If she walked three blocks west and two north, she could see the place she'd grown up.

Fat chance.

The address Lily had given her belonged to an ancient apartment building that seemed to lean tiredly into its neighbors. She checked the scraps of cardboard that passed for nameplates in the tiny vestibule.

H. Franklin was on the fifth floor. Figured. The building didn't aspire to anything like a security system, so she started up the stairs.

The lights were forty-watt, bare bulb, which was just as well. No one wanted to see what they were stepping on here. Trash collected in corners of the stairwell, and the treads were sticky. And the smell—the smell hit her right in the snake brain. Cabbage, piss, burnt meat, onions. A whiff of pot as she passed the second floor.

You didn't notice the smells so much when you lived here, she reflected, shoving her coat back so she'd have quick access to her weapon. Familiarity deadened the senses. It was nice, in a way, to know her nose wasn't numb to the stink.

People were arguing in shrill Spanish on the third floor. On the fourth, a screaming baby competed with rap on one side, the drone of a television on the other. She was halfway up the last flight when the clatter of footsteps said someone was headed down, fast.

Quick, heavy steps—a man, probably. Definitely not a kid. She readied her stun spell.

He stopped when he saw her—a man about forty with medium brown skin and curly hair. Probably some Latin and Caucasian in the mix, but he'd call himself black. He wore a do-rag, jeans way too big for his skinny butt, and a scarred leather jacket over a dirty T-shirt. Everything was black or gray. No colors, gang-related or otherwise.

His eyes widened. That's what tipped her. He saw her face with its tattoos, and he was afraid. "Hamid Franklin?" she said, coming up a step.

"I'm dead," he said in a thin voice. "Oh, God. I'm a dead man."

"Cynna Weaver." She reached into her pocket and pulled out her shield. "I'm with the FBI."

He didn't bother to look at her ID, shaking his head. "You're

FBI? Yeah, sister, an' I'm with the Pentagon. Listen." He came a step down, his hands held out to show they were empty. "I din't talk. I don't care who say so, I din't say a word, ever. Jus' give me a chance. You can spell me, find out for sure I'm tellin' the truth."

"I'm not with Jiri," she said quietly. "Not anymore. I'm with the FBI, like I said. Listen, man, if Jiri wanted you dead, she wouldn't send a *person* to do it. You've got to know that."

He was still a moment, then his head bobbed. "Yeah. Yeah, you're right. It'd be one of her pets, wouldn't it? But you—wait a minute. What you say your name was? Cynna? I heard of you." He looked around, as if someone might be lurking in the narrow stairwell. "You was her favorite, yeah, long time ago. You walked."

"Not her favorite. Her apprentice. But I walked, yeah."

Truculence crept in as fear receded. "What d'you want?"

"We'll talk in your place. You don't want anyone listening in."

It took some persuading, but she got him back upstairs and into his apartment. It was about what she'd expected—a mattress on the floor in one corner, food wrappers scattered around, a couple chairs.

He didn't invite her to sit, which was just as well. No telling what substances had left the stains on those chairs, or what might be living in their sagging cushions. He was jittery as hell. Coming down off something, probably.

His most common drug of choice, however, was tobacco. The place reeked of cigarettes, and he lit one as soon as he got inside. "I don't know nothin,'" he said, inhaling some degree of courage along with the smoke.

"A minute ago you were claiming you hadn't talked. What's to talk about if you don't know anything?"

"So I'm paranoid." He exhaled quick so he could draw in another drag. "I see you, I think Jiri's decided I know somethin', but I don't."

She eyed him. He might be using, he might be none too clean, but he kept himself up—the shoulders and chest said he worked out regularly. A hardbody, she thought, with a face that used to be pretty before it got so used up. Jiri's type, all right, and not for spellwork.

Lily hadn't gotten much in the way of facts from her contact—just this guy's name, that he'd been tight with Jiri, and roughly when he left the movement. Cynna made a guess and went with it. "I'm told you do know things. A lot of things. You were her favorite, weren't you?"

"For a while." He puffed like he couldn't suck the cigarette down fast enough. "You know Jiri. She do love variety."

"She kept you around for a couple years, though. Right up till she did her last fade. No one's seen her since."

"Who told you? Who told you that?"

"The way it works is, I ask. You answer. Did you get mad when she nudged you out of bed for someone else?"

"Hunh. You forget what it's like? She don't mind having more'n one in bed, when she's in the mood."

"But she kicked you out. You didn't leave because you were ready. What's the matter? Did she wring you so dry you couldn't get it up anymore?"

"Bitch." He said that without rancor.

She needed him mad or scared or both. Hadn't pushed the right button yet. "Who'd she put in your place?"

A twitch—small, but she caught it—under his eye. Like a nervous tic. "How'd I know? I was gone."

Cynna pressed him on it, but she knew better than to spill. So she switched tacks, wandering idly around the filthy room. "Guess you won't miss this place too much. You given any thought to where you'll go?"

He glowered at her. "Whatcha mean? I ain't going nowhere."

"No?" She stopped, turning to face him in surprise. "And here I thought you were a survivor. You just going to hang here, wait for her to send one of her pets?"

"She ain't gonna do that. I ain't' told you nothing—'cause I don't have nothing to tell."

"Wonder if that's what she'll think? I mean, she's going to hear that I came around. My face is kind of hard to mistake. People saw me headed here, so—"

"I din't tell you nothing," he insisted.

"Yeah, and we both know how she likes to give the benefit of the doubt, don't we?" She came closer and looked him in the eye. They were almost exactly the same height. "See, the mistake you're making, Hamid, is you're looking so hard at Jiri and what she might do that you can't see what's right in front of you."

"Like what?" His lip curled. "You? You ran off. Things got too mean and scary, and you took off."

She flipped her left hand over, and the Burger King wrapper near his foot burst into flame.

She watched, pleased, as he yelped and grabbed a half-empty liter of Coke, upending it over the flames. She'd been practicing that. She couldn't call fire directly the way Cullen did—even a few poky little flames drew down her power too much to be practical, and she had to use a spell. But fire did impress people.

Hamid rounded on her. "Crazy bitch! You crazy!"

He was mad, but he was sweating now. She sauntered up and put her face near his. "I wasn't her favorite, Hamid, like you were. Sex doesn't mean that much to her. Power does, and she shared some of that with me. She taught me things she didn't teach anyone else. You're right that I'm not as scary as she is . . . but I'm here. She isn't. You want to keep me happy."

"Christ on a crutch! You know what she'll do if I tell you anything!"

"You might as well, because she'll assume you did. She knows me. She knows you. She'll know which of us came out on top here."

When she left the dirty room, Hamid was scurrying around, snatching up his few belongings. He was scared enough to use the money she'd given him to relocate instead of squirting it up his nose.

Out on the sidewalk she took a deep breath. Car exhausts smelled great after that place.

She hadn't crossed any lines, she assured herself as she started back the way she'd come. Burning people was a big no-no, but intimidation was okay. And she'd gotten what she needed, hadn't she?

According to Hamid, Tommy Cordoba had started out in Jiri's bed, but he'd gone on to join a much more exclusive club. She'd made him her apprentice.

It was possible Jiri wasn't behind the murders, after all. If Cordoba had learned enough . . . not likely, she reminded herself. Jiri didn't share well. Cordoba would have had a hard time learning everything he'd need to know to pull off multiple bindings. It was more likely Jiri had reached a point where she needed an apprentice to handle some of the lower-level demons for her.

But Cynna's step was lighter as she left the old neighborhood. The air had the heavy, wet feel of snow on the way, so she lengthened her stride. She made it to the Hampstead intersection before the first big flakes started drifting down. She was trying to flag a cab when her palm started itching. Absently she pulled her hands out of her pocket, scratching at one through the glove—

God, you idiot! Her palm—the one with Jiri's spell! Cynna tried to run a protective spell, but it was too late. A swirl of red misted up over her eyes.

Then she wasn't there at all anymore.

"**MUST** be close to a thousand people here," Lily whispered.

"Something like that." Rule wasn't usually bothered by crowds, but this wasn't a comfortable crowd for a Nokolai. Especially for the Nokolai heir. Especially when, according to Lily, Brady had been so pleased when Rule took on a son's duty to Roland Miller . . . and the first duty Roland had required of him was attendance at the memorials for both his son and Victor's.

Paul's memorial had been well attended, but not on this scale. It had been followed by a barbecue for which Rule, Lily, and Cullen had adjourned back to the house. Victor had apparently eaten in his room.

Randall's memorial had begun at one. For that the field was crammed elbow to elbow with Leidolf. The smell of them made him stand very still.

Lily whispered again. "Doesn't Leidolf have more female clan, though? There must be five lupi present for every woman I see."

"The women are tending the children," he said dryly, his voice very low. Traditionally clans included all their members, even the children, in such ceremonies. Leidolf had abandoned that tradition by the early sixteenth century for more human behavior. In fact, much of what he disliked about Leidolf had been taken from the larger culture around them, yet now that human norms were changing, they clung to their male-centric ways.

That could change. A clan took on some of the character of its Rho, and Victor had been Leidolf Rho for a very long time.

Someone on the eastern edge of the field was recounting a story from Randall's childhood. That was a relief—it meant the memorial was finally nearing an end. Lupus memorials moved backward through the deceased's life; the first to speak were those present at the death.

Rule hadn't been asked to speak of Paul's death. Lily had.

That had been a calculated slap at Rule, but if it was the worst that happened today, he'd be pleased. And Lily had done well. After a moment's frozen horror—she was not used to speaking in front of so many people—she'd handled the situation with her usual good sense. It probably helped that the custom was for each to speak where he or she stood, since there was no platform or podium. Rule had suggested she pretend she was giving a report to a nearly deaf police captain.

Maybe she had. Her account had been stark by lupus standards, but perhaps all the more moving for that. She'd finished by saying, "He acted with great courage. I will honor him always."

Thunder rumbled off in the east, still distant. He glanced that way and saw big fists of clouds piling up, the knuckles puffy and bruised. As he watched, lightning stitched a line from sky to ground.

He glanced at Lily and almost smiled. Back in San Diego, people got excited when it rained. They stopped working to look out the window, comment on their lawns, maybe claim credit for nature's behavior through the mysterious alchemy of car-washing. It hadn't taken long for that attitude to wear off for Lily. She was as affronted as her cat by so much rain.

Behind him he heard Benedict's rumble, speaking under the tongue so softly the Leidolf man nearest them wouldn't be able to hear: *Brady's headed this way. Coming up from your rear.*

Since Benedict, contrary to all accepted norms, had chosen to stand back-to-back with Rule, his rear was thoroughly covered. *He see you?* Rule asked the same way.

Yeah.

Probably won't try anything, then. Cullen—

I heard, Cullen said. *Hope he does try something.*

You're insane. Rule left it at that, but the last thing he needed was for Cullen and Brady to try to kill each other here. He'd wanted to leave Cullen in their room, actually, knowing that the crowd, the stillness, all would wear out his friend's small store of patience. But Cullen was determined to guard him.

As if one man—even a lupus, even a sorcerer—could stop a thousand or so lupi if they decided Nokolai could do without its heir.

And that was intolerably paranoid, not to mention stupid. The majority of Leidolf were honorable. He'd been granted guest status by their Rho, and his vows to Paul's father made him *Leidolf ad littera* for the duration of this ceremony. *Ad littera* was a legal fiction, of course, like calling a corporation a person under the law, but he was a guest, and *ad littera* for the next hour or so— this would surely end soon—and in danger only from those like Brady. The loose cannons, not the entire clan.

The speaker finished. There was silence for a moment, then Victor's voice rang out. He stood in the center of the clearing, of course, with the Rhej and two of his councilors. "I thank all of you who shared my son's life with me. I thank those who today shared their memories of him. We remember."

"We remember," a thousand voices echoed back.

"We didn't only lose a friend, a son, a lover when Randall was killed," Victor went on. "We lost our Lu Nuncio and our heir. I call the naming."

A female voice spoke—the Rhej. "When do you call the naming?"

"Now."

Rule went from bored and edgy to barely breathing. Everywhere people were exclaiming, talking, reacting.

"Rule," Lily's voice was low, but no longer a whisper. "What's he up to? What does this mean?"

Only two possibilities he could see. Either Victor hoped to slide Brady in immediately, with no time for a proper Challenge . . . or he was dying.

Neither of which he could say aloud in this crowd. "I don't know. Let's start moving toward the edge of the crowd . . . just in case." Maybe it was his touch of claustrophobia, or maybe a genuine hunch, but he had a strong need to be elsewhere. He grabbed her hand, catching Cullen's gaze with his and giving a jerk of his head toward the road.

"Rule," Benedict said.

Rule stopped edging past the two men closest to him to look at his brother. Benedict jerked his head to one side, directing his attention that way.

Brady stood ten feet away with only a couple people between them. His grin held triumph. His hand held a gun. "Don't leave now," he said. "Party's just starting."

THIRTY-ONE

SHE wasn't in Chicago anymore. She wasn't in her own body anymore.

The disorientation was short but severe. It was like closing both eyes, then opening all four of them. Like having the axis of your body shift while gravity took up hip-hop.

It was like riding. Exactly like riding. Long-unused reflexes took over, lining her up properly with the new body as he/she/they strode up the street.

Big. That was her first clear thought. This was the biggest son of a bitch she'd ever ridden. She guessed that her/their eyes were about ten feet off the ground, but it was the sheer massiveness of him she felt most keenly.

Out of his peripheral vision she saw houses on either side of him/them—houses in red, gold, pale gray, seen through eyes that processed color differently. Where were they? She turned her/their head—or tried to. The muscles didn't answer.

Panic hit—real, yet oddly distant and quick to evaporate.

Because he didn't feel it, she realized, and without a bodily response, her emotions thinned. His body responded to his feelings, though. She knew what he felt.

Eager. Hungry.

And if she felt him and he didn't feel her—if his muscles wouldn't answer to her—she was purely a passenger, not a rider, which shouldn't be possible, but she was here. She had to get out, get back to herself. Mentally she shouted words that should have sent her back.

Nothing. Those words were meant to be spoken, and this throat, these lips wouldn't respond to her. But intent—she had that, and some knowledge. Desperately she tried to wrench herself out. Nothing happened.

Trapped. She was trapped.

Part of her felt as if she were panting from fear and effort. Part of her—no, it was the demon who felt that lick of excitement as he observed the houses around him, watching with a sense no human has. Demons called it *üther*. Cynna thought of it as their life sense, for that's what it picked up. The demon sensed the lives around him—most clearly the one in the shrubbery, thin but tasty; more dimly because of walls and distance, the thicker lives inside those homes . . .

He couldn't eat them. Wouldn't. She reminded herself of that. Demons ate almost anything living, except humans. They consumed something of the life along with the flesh, and souls drove them mad. That's what they believed, or remembered—demon memory being enough to drive a human crazy, because they also ate each other and retained something of the consumed within their own consciousness . . .

Oh, God. Had she been eaten? Was that why she couldn't make the body respond, or escape back to her own body?

This time the fear was so great it swallowed her, embodied or not. She sank into it, into a vortex of fear and flailing—

And the demon stopped. And spoke. "Cynna. Be still. You can't get out until I release you, and you must pay attention. You'll want to take control from me. You can't, but you won't even be able to try unless you know the body. Pay attention."

The demon's voice was an impossibly deep bass. It sounded . . . vexed. That yanked her out of her panic long enough for her to start thinking again.

It hadn't been the demon who spoke to her, but Jiri. Jiri who rode, Jiri who'd made her a passenger. She'd been forced into his body, but she hadn't been consumed.

And Jiri was right, damn her eyes and every other stinking part of her. Cynna had to pay attention. If she were to have any chance of gaining control of the demon . . . and she didn't need all of his body. The throat and mouth, that's what she needed, to speak the words of release. But she had to learn his body first, know how to operate it. He was too different from any she'd ridden back in her bad old days.

They traveled another block, with Cynna paying close attention to his/her center of gravity, the kinesthetic knowledge of his/their muscles as they strode silently down the street. The peculiar colors of demon vision were a distraction; the area looked familiar, yet so distorted in the glimpses she caught that she couldn't place it. He was a safety-conscious demon, watching out for cars, avoiding those that cruised by—the drivers never saw him, of course, but dogs barked frantically as they passed, not looking closely at the houses.

What she glimpsed, what she heard, said city. And familiar. She'd been down this street, or one much like it.

He was older than any demon she'd ever ridden. Older by far. The mass told her that, an indescribable sense of heaviness, density . . . he'd been eating lives a long, long time. Old meant strong, powerful—that scared her enough that it took a second for her to catch on to the pronoun she'd automatically been using. *He?*

Yes, she realized as massive legs carried him/her/them along the cold pavement. Definitely this one was male. Though most of the demons she'd ridden in her misspent youth had been hermaphrodites, she'd hitched on an incubus once, so she knew: male felt different. It wasn't just the lack of breasts, or the sensation of an extra organ at the crotch—the younger demons came equipped with both kinds of genitals. And strength damn sure wasn't a sex-based characteristic, not with a demon.

But male felt different.

He stopped. He was looking at one house, a house she knew, even painted as it was in the lilac and beige of demon vision.

Washington. They were in Washington, D.C., and he/she/they were looking at Rule's house.

RULE hadn't taken his eyes off Brady. The man had obviously expected Victor's announcement, which gave weight to the "slide Brady in quickly" theory. But what did he hope to achieve by holding Rule here at gunpoint?

"Brady." Lily raised her voice. "Unless you're planning to shoot all three of us, you'd better put that up. I'm a cop. I don't take it well when someone draws on me."

"Draws what?" Brady's eyebrows flew up in a parody of innocent confusion. "I didn't draw anything. Did I?" He looked around, grinning.

Most of those nearest were melting back, leaving a small open space between them—except for a knot of about ten clustered around Brady.

"Been collecting a pack, Brady?" Cullen made sure that sounded like the insult it was.

Rule took the smooth, deadly slide into combat mode, where wolf and man melded. His thoughts were crisp, his goals clear: keep the others alive, kill Brady. "He has backup," he observed dispassionately, "and the others, even the ones who hate him, won't act. Not during the naming."

"I can take his toy away from him," Benedict said. "Little boys shouldn't be allowed to play with guns."

"Best if none of you move at all," Brady said. "Don't wave to a friend or scratch your nose. I might mistake it for a threat."

Rule switched to subvocal, pitching so low only Benedict and maybe Cullen could hear: *Give me a second to get in front of Lily. If he gets a shot off—*

Lily seemed to be reading his mind. She edged back—and with his peripheral vision he saw her reach inside her jacket.

"Uh, uh, uh!" Brady sighted down on Rule's forehead. "Unless you want to see how well your sweetie heals brain tissue."

Benedict considered that, gave a tiny shake of his head. *He'd get you before I could stop him. We need him distracted for a second. Seabourne—*

"Leidolf." Victor's voice rose over the clamor, addressing his clan. "If you wish to hear, be silent."

Cullen's voice, barely audible even to Rule: *I can't throw fire without a gesture.*

Victor cried out, "I name Alex Thibodaux as Lu Nuncio."

A many-throated roar rose from the crowd. Rule noted it without looking away from Brady—who, damn it, wasn't distracted. So this, too, he'd expected—but it made no sense. Thibodaux didn't carry the blood, couldn't hold the mantle, so unless Victor had lost his mind—

"Leidolf!" Victor shouted. "Silence! Alex is to be your new Lu Nuncio—not your heir."

What the hell—?

"I break with tradition, yes," Victor was saying. "But there is precedent. The heir does not have to be Lu Nuncio. I consulted our Rhej and my councilors. Etorri has no Lu Nuncio—"

"We are not Etorri!" someone shouted. Others began chanting, "Leidolf! Leidolf!" Still others shouted names: Reese. Thomas. Max. Phillip.

No one called out Brady's name. Why was he so damned smug?

Victor had to shout to be heard. "Twice Leidolf has separated the positions—when the blood had grown thin and there was no suitable heir strong enough to act as Lu Nuncio. It was temporary! Temporary," he repeated, his voice dropping as they quieted. "The blood has grown thin, Leidolf. And I am dying."

This time, he got silence. "You need a Lu Nuncio you trust. I give you Alex. If I still live after six months, I will call you here to invest the heir as Lu Nuncio. If not . . . you will need a Rho and a Lu Nuncio."

They listened now, intent and unmoving. Rule knew what they were thinking as clearly as if he'd been suddenly gifted with telepathy: that Victor meant to name Brady heir and hoped to make him more palatable by denying him the Lu Nuncio's authority.

If so, Victor's strategy had already failed. This was not the silence of assent, but that of a thousand hunters uncertain of their prey.

"We have several who may be able to carry the mantle," Victor went on. "I know—it grieves me, but I know—some of you do not want to see it go to my son. My only living son." His voice caught briefly. "So I bring to you another tradition. Though we have not followed it for many years, it is an ancient and honorable path. Rather than naming my heir, I will loose the mantle and let it choose."

That brought a buzzing of whispers and subvocalization. Leidolf was shocked, but this way, while very old indeed, was understandable to them. Though who would have thought Victor could surrender control to such a degree?

All at once Rule knew. His mind didn't leap from fact to fact, connecting them; he simply knew what Victor meant to do. Calmly he said to Benedict, *Get Lily out of here. Now.*

"Forget it," she said. "I'm not going anywhere."

His head swung toward her. "You heard me?"

"Of course I . . ." Her eyes widened. "Uh—you weren't talking out loud, were you?"

"Let those of the blood," Victor called, "all those of the blood, for two and three generations back, come forward!"

"That would be us," Brady said, grinning like a cat about to torment the mouse in its paws. "Cousin."

LI LEI had not been born patient, but she'd had sufficient lessons in patience that she understood waiting. Best to ignore it. Having done what was necessary, she now paid attention to the present, and the things that mattered.

Such as winning. Toby looked very much like his father when he frowned that way. "You did well," she assured him. "You do not enjoy losing, but you played well. You may take the mah-jongg set upstairs now, to my room."

He grimaced, but obediently he began to gather the tiles, though he slid her the kind of look she used to see on her own son's face . . . and still did, at times. "At my house we have a rule that the winner puts the game up."

She didn't allow her mouth to smile, but knew her eyes were. She compensated by lifting both brows. "You are not in your house now, I believe."

He grinned but didn't argue. *A good boy,* she thought as he sprinted for the stairs. Spirited enough to push a little, to test, as the young should. Strong enough within himself that he didn't have to push.

"I almost had you," Steven Timms said. He leaned forward, careful of his cast, which was supported by a sling. "If I'd drawn—"

"Very little is won on 'if.' You held on to the red dragon too long."

Timms scowled. Like most men, he disliked being corrected. Li Qin said something soothing, so he turned to her and began telling her things she already knew about the game they'd just played. Not stupid things—simply unnecessary. Li Lei stopped listening.

Steven Timms had come to play mah-jongg every day after the beautiful Cullen left. True, she had told him to return; mah-jongg was better with four. But that was her reason. He thought he was protecting them, and he wanted his new friend to return and appreciate this.

On the surface, it was an odd bond. She had wondered if

Timms were a man lover who had conceived a passion for the beautiful Cullen but soon decided he was simply lonely. He was one of those who are very bright, but people blind.

Not in an evil way. True, he liked to shoot things—he was very boring on the subject—but he was not what Lily called a stone killer. He simply did not understand how to behave. He couldn't fathom the rules, how to be close to others instead of pushing them away.

She had read somewhere that doctors had a name for this problem. Doctors always felt better once they'd named things; it was an obsession with them. Li Lei couldn't recall the name, and didn't care. Neither did Timms interest her greatly, but Cullen Seabourne did, and he—

An orange blur skidded into the kitchen, claws scrabbling for purchase on the wooden floor. Dirty Harry raced to the back door and yowled, demanding that it open. His bristled fur made him look like a tattered marigold.

Li Lei sprang to her feet. "We are about to be attacked. Harry thinks the demon is out front. I trust his judgment. Li Qin, go with him. Tell the other guard to come in *now*, then get help. Telephone the police."

Timms shoved his chair back and stood, closing his hand around Li Qin's arm. "Wait a minute. You can't think that cat knows—"

"A great deal more than you," Li Lei snapped. Or her, in this instance. Cats were uncannily sensitive to demons. "Go. And hurry," she said to Li Qin, and removed Timms's hand.

That startled him, of course. He had no idea of her strength. "Go upstairs and make sure Toby hides," she told him. "I'll—"

"Calm down, calm down. If you think something's wrong, I'll check—though I think our werewolf guards would hear or smell a problem before I could see it." He gave her what he no doubt thought was a soothing smile and pulled his big gun from its holster, which he'd hung on the back of his chair.

"Do as you're told. Toby will not want to hide, but he must." She drew hard on the energy in her gut. *Fast. This one must be fast.* Harry feared very little—not Rule Turner, German shepherds, or wolves. Not even her. For him to flee meant that what was coming was bad, very bad.

Heat slapped through her body, vicious in its greed. She spoke the rest with difficulty. "You may come down and shoot things after the boy is hidden, but do not shoot me. I am going to Change."

"Change what?"

But she already was. And even as her cells burst and her body slid into otherness, she heard gunfire out front.

To his credit, Timms didn't drop his gun—or fire it—when the Change finished and ten feet of tiger stood before him. Nor did he stand staring for more than a second when she leaped out of the kitchen, heading for the foot of the stairs. She took her position there, to guard the boy. A moment later, Timms raced past. He was halfway up the stairs when the guard out front screamed.

Seconds later, the front door splintered.

IF there had been a moment she could have acted, Lily had missed it. She had no time to play Monday-morning quarterback over any possible missed opportunities, though, as she, Benedict, Cullen, and Rule were marched through the crowd, courtesy of one gun held by a madman and a dozen thugs.

Lupus thugs. Her heartbeat was going crazy. "This is crazy," she muttered. "What do they hope to accomplish? I'm arresting all of them. They have to know I'll do that." Unless they planned to kill her—right after they killed Rule.

"They believe the clan will speak as one," Benedict said calmly, "to discount your testimony."

Rule's damned brother was always calm. He'd charged a dozen gang members with guns—calmly. *After* putting her forcibly out of the line of fire. "But why are they doing this? They don't want Rule to be heir."

"*They* don't think he will be." Cullen's abbreviated gesture indicated the clan members parting for them as they headed toward the center of the field. "They think this is Brady's little joke on Nokolai, a way to humiliate Rule."

Lily caught the glance Rule gave Cullen. The two of them knew or guessed more than they were saying. "It isn't a joke, but it doesn't make sense, either. Rule can't be Leidolf heir. He's Nokolai heir."

"Technically," Benedict said, speaking very low but not subvocalizing, "it's legal for him to be both. One of his ancestors carried the Leidolf founder's blood, and he's *ad littera* clan."

"But why would Brady do this?"

"He wants to kill me," Rule said, as calm as his blasted brother.

"Brady and Victor," Cullen said viciously. "Victor's behind this. We won't stop this without crisping the son of a—"

"No," Rule said sharply. "Victor must live a bit longer. Death shock in such a crowd would send too many over the edge. You'd never get Lily out alive."

Lily stopped moving. "Rule." She reached for him. "You are not getting me out without—"

"Hush." He wrapped his arms around her, holding her close, pressing kisses into her hair, which covered any movement of his lips as he said, *You can hear me?*

She nodded.

The mantle. Victor isn't going to allow it to choose. He'll try to force the heir's portion on me, which would be . . . bad. Murder, most likely, but done in a way Nokolai couldn't claim as murder. But the mate bond is active. The last time this happened, I also gained. If your immunity to magic stretches to cover me, he won't be able to force the mantle on me.

"Move along, now." Brady was all good cheer, but the thug at his side gave the two of them a rough shove.

Rule spun, growling.

"Be nice to the lady, Merrick," Brady said, gun raised to point at Lily's forehead. "Or I'll have to shoot her."

"You're dead, you know," Cullen said.

"Me?" He laughed. "Oh, no, I don't think I'm the walking dead man here."

HE/SHE/THEY studied the house. A life burned brightly in the car parked in front; no driver was visible, but the guard couldn't hide from the demon's *üther* sense. The lives inside the house were visible in the same way, their presence muffled by walls and distance, but the demon *saw* them well enough for Cynna to count.

Five lives were in that house. Five people she cared about.

He/she lumbered toward the car, though. Not the house. Cynna screamed inside, trying desperately to seize just one bit of the demon, make a noise, something! But he/they reached the parked car, then reached inside in an indescribable way, bringing more of their mass into this realm.

He/they punched through the car window.

The guard reacted fast. He had his rifle ready and he fired point-blank. The bullets hit, too—three of them—hot stings that annoyed the demon as they reached inside and seized the man's shoulder. He screamed, which excited them. They dragged him out through a window too small for his body.

The blood excited them even more.

THE last few people parted in front of them, and Lily saw Victor Frey for the first time. He looked like hell.

Cynna had described him as dapper and academic, looking about seventy. She saw a military martinet, not an academic—a very old martinet. He sat in an armchair, incongruous in its floral print on the winter-dead grass. He sat very erect, but his skin sagged in the runneled folds of very old age. How he'd summoned enough wind to outshout his clan earlier, she couldn't imagine.

Behind him stood ten well-armed lupi. Four of them immediately surrounded Benedict; though they kept a healthy distance, the rifles they trained at his head would keep even him from acting. Two flanked Cullen, guns drawn.

The Rhej stood beside Victor in her white robe, her face impassive. On his other side stood a man who must have been related to her—same eyes and skin tone, plus the proportions between their chins and mouths matched.

"Alex," Benedict said. "Did he tell you that he'd name Brady heir if you didn't agree to be Lu Nuncio?"

Victor turned cold eyes on him. "Nokolai is not welcome here. Be quiet or be muzzled."

"Nokolai," Rule said dryly, "was brought here at gunpoint. Is this normal for those who guest with Leidolf?"

"But you aren't—entirely—Nokolai today, are you?" The twitch of those pale, desiccated lips was probably meant for a smile. "Today you are Leidolf as well. And by blood and my sister's great folly, you are also my great-nephew. How could we leave you out?" He gestured at the others as he raised his voice again. "Our candidates are assembled."

Seven other men stood in front of their Rho. They were giving Rule the kind of looks a butcher might give a mongrel that's eyeing his roasts . . . or that a wolf might give another wolf intruding on its territory.

A single wisp of magic, feathery light, tingled across Lily's face. A sorcéri, she realized. Cullen had said there was a node in the central field. They often leaked a bit. She tried and failed to think of some way to take advantage of that.

She still had one weapon. A SIG Sauer wasn't proof against a thousand lupi, but she need only train it on one. "You must be Victor Frey," she said, stepping forward. "I'm Lily Yu with the FBI's Magical Crimes Division. You're in a lot of—"

"Stop her," Victor said.

Whatever the mate bond had done for her hearing, it hadn't granted her lupus speed. She got her gun out, but it clattered uselessly to the ground when two guards grabbed her, one on each arm.

Rule jolted but didn't move. "You're putting hands on a Chosen," he said softly, and looked at the Rhej.

"She won't be hurt," the woman said. Though her face remained impassive, trouble edged her voice. "Will she, Victor?"

"Of course not. But she can't be allowed to shoot me." He pushed to his feet and stood stick-straight, but it cost him. She saw the tremor in his hand, the way his face tightened. Yet he found that carrying voice again. "The candidates will kneel."

The seven who'd given Rule such unfriendly looks dropped to their knees. So did Brady, she saw when she twisted in her captors' grip to check.

Rule didn't.

Victor smiled. It made his face a gargoyle's mask of wrinkles. "You will," he said softly, "before we are through." He closed his eyes and said something in Latin. He spoke the words three times.

Lily waited, her heart trying to knock its way through her chest. They were gambling everything on the mate bond, the capricious, do-what-it-wants bond she'd never understood, much less controlled. "Lady," she whispered, "if you're around, if you're in charge of any of this, help him. Help him."

The Rho held out his hands, palms forward as if he were pushing something. He swayed. One of the kneeling men made a small sound, maybe of astonishment. Another toppled over in a silent heap.

And Rule . . . like the Rho, he swayed. His eyes were wide, unseeing, his hands limp at his sides.

And the power wind blew in.

THIRTY-TWO

NOT *a wind,* Lily thought in the first split second as magic gusted across her face, prickled up her nose, and burned her hands.

A gale. Stronger than the first one, horribly strong.

Reality splintered. Here—here—here—everywhere the vortex of the Change seized men and spun them into other shapes. Screams sounded. One of Lily's guards dropped his hands or lost them to the Change.

It was all she needed. Her elbow rocked into the other guard's ribs, distracting him from his battle with the Change. He howled and bent, and reality splintered even as she spun away, diving for a rifle dropped by one of Benedict's guards.

She got her hands on the rifle, rolled, and flowed to her feet.

Wolves. Wolves everywhere, with a scattering of women uncertainly upright in the sea of fur. None near her were two-legged except the Rhej, who stood motionless, her eyes closed and her lips moving; the Rho, equally unmoving where he lay on the ground, unconscious or dead, his skin blooming with dark lesions . . . and Rule.

Rule was on his knees as Victor had wanted, his head thrown back, his face contorted. Screaming. And bleeding. Even as she stared, more blood sprang out in drops on his skin like sweat.

She threw herself into motion only to jerk to a halt, nearly falling. Benedict's hand had closed over her arm and stopped her. She rounded on him and would have hit him—or tried to—if that hand had been free instead of full of rifle.

That flashback to sanity brought with it a full-fledged thought: his *hand* had stopped her. Benedict wasn't wolf anymore, but he had been. His clothes were gone. How could he have Changed back so quickly?

"No!" he shouted over the howling. "You can't touch him now. The mantle has him."

The power wind still rushed over her skin, but silently. The howling came from lupus throats—a dozen, two dozen, more. As Rule fought some terrible internal battle, Leidolf howled.

"Why doesn't he Change?" she cried.

Benedict's voice was hoarse. "He can't."

The Rhej moved. Only four steps, but each taken with such ponderous care she might have been treading quicksand or crossing a minefield. She knelt between Rule and the prostrate Rho, stretched out her arm, and seized Victor's hand. With her other hand she gripped Rule's shoulder.

Lily jolted, instinctively wanting no one to touch Rule if she couldn't, but Benedict's grip held her fast. The Rhej's eyes rolled back. She held there, motionless in the dead grass, a white-robed bridge between the two men—one unconscious at best, the other . . .

Rule stopped screaming. Slowly he straightened, swaying, though he remained on his knees. The blood drops began to dry on his skin. His eyes were open but it was obvious he saw nothing as tremors snaked up his spine in quick succession. The Rhej released him.

Growls rumbled up from a throat far too close. Her head swung. Most of the wolves howled or watched the tableau of Rule, the Rhej, and their Rho, but two didn't. Two gray-black wolves the size of small ponies watched them, ears flat, heads lowered, hackles raised. Then another one moved, this one with reddish fur, and smaller—Great Dane instead of Shetland. She shouldered the rifle.

"Don't shoot the little one," Benedict said, his own rifle ready. "It's Cullen."

Suddenly the air lost its rush of power and was just air, cold and still. Then the magic returned, but quieter now, brushing her skin in an ebbing rhythm until it tickled her face like dandelion fluff.

The howling died, but the growling increased as more wolves focused on her and Benedict and the red wolf standing between them and the rest. The ground was littered with clothing. Shoes, jeans, slacks, belts, shirts—all had fallen to the ground when the form they belonged to whistled into elsewhere and came back re-shaped.

Rule slumped forward suddenly, catching himself with one hand so that he didn't quite land on his face in the dirt. But that arm trembled, and his chest heaved as if he'd run for miles and miles.

"Goddamn it." She couldn't go to him, not with wolves surrounding them, wolves with little that was human shining in their dark eyes. Dozens now watched her and Benedict with hackles raised, their growls a rumbling chorus.

"Leidolf! He lied to you!"

A woman's voice, rich and loud: the Rhej. Lily spared her the barest flick of a glance. The woman had moved closer to Victor, rolling him onto his back. She held his hand in both of hers as she spoke. "Your Rho lied. He didn't let the mantle choose. He tried to force it on Rule Turner, and it cost him. Look at Victor. Smell him. Your Rho has the cancer, and he damn near killed himself tryin' to find a legal way to kill someone he'd granted guest rights. He'd die now, be dead in seconds, if I let go of him. And I will let go if you attack our guests. I will let go, and the Rho will die."

Some of the growling faded. Not all.

"Women," the Rhej called, "your brothers know you. Pet them, touch them, help them remember who they are." She looked at Lily, and her voice dropped. "Go to your man. Move slow, but go to him. Get him on his feet. He's got the heir's portion now. He was winnin' the fight till the node burst open and damn near the whole mantle was just sucked right up into him. I forced most of it back, but he's heir. Leidolf won't like that, but they have to feel it, smell it on him."

Lily did fine on the "go to him" part, not so well on moving slowly. But she made it without inciting a lupus riot, knelt, and got her free arm around Rule.

He raised his head to look at her, his eyes bleary with pain. Barely aware.

Benedict moved to Rule's other side, and the red wolf posted himself in. Lily shifted, getting Rule's arm over her shoulder as Benedict did the same. They got him to his feet.

He swayed, shook his head. "Lily."

"Here. I'm right here."

"You got to get out of here," the Rhej told them, her voice hoarse. "All of you. The ones that ain't back yet—you don't smell right to them. The ones that're coming back, they'll be thinking Challenge soon, as much as they think at all."

One of the biggest wolves tipped his muzzle toward her, ears forward. His coloring reminded Lily of Rule's wolf form—black, barely tipped with silver.

"That's right." The Rhej addressed the wolf as if it had spoken. "If they start in on the Challenges, he's dead." A jerk of her head indicated Rule. "And so is Leidolf, 'cause if they kill the heir the mantle will snap back into Victor. I'm barely holding life in him now—that mantle rebounds on him, he's dead. I need you two-footed, Alex. I need your voice with mine, and so do they. Try. You're Lu Nuncio now. For the Lady's sake and Leidolf's, try."

The wolf whined unhappily and closed his eyes. Reality pleated itself, but slowly. For the first time Lily could almost follow the Change as it happened . . . almost, for some of it was simply *other*, too far outside what the senses could report or her mind absorb.

Fur folded into skin, legs kinked, lengthened; there blinked into not-there, into somewhere, into . . . a man, a big man, almost Benedict's size, naked, his dark skin gleaming with sweat in the cold air, his face tight with pain. "Shit," he said. "Shit."

"Buck up." That was his sister, unsympathetic. "Talk to them."

He straightened. After a moment he spoke, projecting his voice strongly. "Listen. I am Lu Nuncio, and you will listen. Does Leidolf kill those with guest rights? Do we remember the price of dishonor? Listen. Listen, and remember. In the days when Eiriu fought with Trath, when gnomes dwelled beneath the Earth and elves still walked its forests . . ."

A story. He was telling them a story, one from their oral history, one of the legends they'd been raised on. And it seemed to work. He had their attention.

"Girl," the Rhej said quietly, "bring your man here. Ah can't let go of Victor, but Rule Turner's bad muddled. No one's built to hold two mantles, an' he had damned near all of Leidolf's shoved in on top of the Nokolai heir's portion."

Lily exchanged glances with Benedict, and they did as she asked.

Rule had forgotten how to walk. He tilted to one side, then the other. He thrust one leg forward twice instead of alternating, realized that was wrong and stopped, rearing back so fast he nearly dragged Lily down. Benedict righted him.

The Rhej lowered herself to sit cross-legged on the cold ground, keeping her grip on Victor's hand. The Rho was a sight to frighten small children . . . hell, big, tough federal agents, too. Mottled skin sagged off his bones like congealed wax, skin mottled like a toad's by the cancers that had sprung up like mushrooms after a rain.

So fast. How could the tumors have grown so fast? "Can you help Rule?" she asked the Rhej, fear roughening her voice. "If you're keeping Victor alive, how much can you spare for Rule?"

A grin, unexpected and fierce, flashed across the dark face tilted up to them. "Damn near anything, right now. Ah've got more power to draw on than any Rhej since the dawn times." She looked at Rule. "Two-mantled," she said softly, making the term sound like a title. "Will you let me help you?"

Rule stirred as if trying to take more of his own weight, but sagged again. "Could use . . . help, serra."

"Ah need his hand." She reached up with hers.

Carefully Lily unwound Rule's arm from her shoulder, trusting Benedict to keep him upright. Rule managed to stretch out his hand himself. The woman took it in hers, frowned. "You've got some funny stuff in you."

Rule didn't seem able to answer, so Lily did. "Demon poison. He was wounded by one, and it got into him." Her voice wasn't steady. With all that had happened, she'd actually forgotten the demon poison.

"Don't think Ah can help with that. But with the other . . ." She closed her eyes, and began to hum . . . "Rock of Ages," Lily realized, the incongruity of hearing the old gospel hymn in this setting almost shocking her into a giggle.

Or maybe that was hysteria trying to blossom. She squelched it.

Alex was still speaking, telling a tale of some ancient Rho and his enemy . . . and a few feet away, reality did its splinter dance once more. Where there had been a red wolf, a naked Cullen stood bent over, hands on his knees, gasping.

Alex glanced that way. Without losing his storyteller's cadence, he said, "Eric. Reese. Can Nokolai do what Leidolf cannot? Change now. I need you two-legged. Now, Trath agreed to speak of truce with Eiriu," he went on, "and both would guest with Leidolf. But Trath had taken . . ."

Cullen moved more slowly than usual, bending to retrieve something from one of the piles of clothing. Not his slacks, however. A necklace. Sunlight glittered on the diamond he rehung around his neck.

Off to her left, two wolves fractured into pieces of otherness and began re-forming.

Rule straightened. His breathing evened, slowed. He turned his head, met her eyes . . . and he was back. Exhausted, his hair sweat-soaked, but back. He smiled at her, then at the Rhej. "Serra," he said, and did a very Rule thing. He raised the Rhej's hand and bent to place a kiss on it. "I thank you."

"Thank me later," she said tartly. "Get moving now."

". . . agreed that Eiriu's power must be broken," Alex said, "for it had turned rancid with bloodlust. Reese, Eric, go with them. Get my keys from my pants. They'll take my Suburban; their own car is too far away. Now, Leidolf didn't want to break the bonds of . . ."

And so Lily was escorted through a field of wolves by five men, every one of them except her lover as bare as the day he was born. She now knew exactly what Rule's brother looked like naked. Clothes didn't do Benedict justice.

A few wolves growled as they passed, but none opposed them. She kept the rifle ready. Rule walked on his own, but his exhaustion was obvious—not that any of Leidolf were going to notice, because they wouldn't look at him. Their escorts kept track of her and Benedict and Cullen without once glancing at Rule. The wolves they passed through scented them—noses lifted, nostrils twitching—but none looked directly at Rule.

They could deal with the purely Nokolai Benedict, she supposed, or her own female self, but the one who was both Nokolai and their heir must have made them uneasy. Though maybe *uneasy* wasn't the right word.

Still, they made it to the road and across it, to a green Suburban parked in front of Victor's house. One of their escorts—Reese or Eric, she had no idea which—held out a set of keys. She reached for them, but Benedict was faster.

"Don't you think the one who hasn't Changed twice should drive?"

"No."

If he was still fast enough to beat her to the keys, he was probably up to driving. He was also still naked. "Maybe . . ." She glanced at the house, thinking of the AK-47 upstairs, but also about pants.

"No," Benedict said again. "We don't retrieve our things. We leave now."

She didn't argue.

Lily climbed in back with Rule. He held her hand and leaned his head back as they took off, the tires spitting dirt. "You're okay," she told him softly, but it was also a question.

He got that, turning his head to smile at her wearily. "Mostly. Things are still . . . a bit jumbled inside. What the Rhej did got the circuits uncrossed, so the new mantle's settling in, but it . . . makes words difficult right now."

She squeezed his hand, telling him words weren't needed.

Benedict was driving too fast for anyone but a lupus over the rough road. She approved, lowering the window so she could fire out if necessary. Lord knew there was plenty of cover if someone wanted to stage a last-minute ambush, and the way the road wound around, a party of wolves cutting straight through might be able to cut them off. She rested the rifle's barrel on the open window. "I'm going to come back and arrest Brady once he and the others are two-legged again."

"No need," Cullen said. "He's a dead man." He gave his head a shake. "I think I'm power drunk. If that's what the magic wind was like before—"

"This was worse. A lot worse. If it was this bad everywhere . . ." Reminded of the outside world, Lily released Rule's hand just as they took the turn up onto pavement, tires squealing.

It was probably safe to put the rifle down. She did, then got her phone from her pocket to call Ruben. She'd had three missed calls: her parents, the ever-popular Unknown, and Cynna. "Brady isn't dead," she pointed out. "In spite of everything, no one died."

"He meant that Rule will kill him," Benedict said.

"Um . . . no." Cynna first, she decided and punched the call button. It rang and rang, though, without Cynna or her voice mail picking up. She frowned, checked that she had a connection, then called her own voice mail. "You're integrating more with the human world, remember? Killing people who piss you off is not the way to do that." She fast-forwarded past the first two messages.

"Lily." Rule squeezed her shoulder. "I am sorry, but they are right. Brady must die."

She turned startled eyes on him, but Cynna's message started, and her voice was one breath short of panic. Lily listened to the disjointed words with horror pooling in her gut. "Benedict," she said, and could not understand why her voice was so steady. "Have you got plenty of gas?"

"Yes."

"Hit it, then. Open it up. We need to get to D.C. We need to hurry. I . . . I'll get us an escort." Yes, an escort, a cop car with its cherry light clearing the way—they needed that. She turned to Rule and gripped his hand. "Jiri attacked the house. She got to Toby."

THIRTY-THREE

MARIO Andretti in a Formula One couldn't have gotten them to D.C. quickly that day. What was normally a three-hour drive took them . . . well, four. Benedict did floor it when he could.

Lily had hoped the force they'd experienced from the power wind had been due to the node. They'd been right on top of one, so it made sense that they'd been hit hard.

But the world was full of nodes.

There were rumors of a meltdown at a nuclear reactor in Poland. The Middle East was exploding—literally. Stores of munitions had exploded spontaneously in Palestine, Israel, Syria, and Egypt. In the United States, two planes had crashed when flight control at LAX went out; another had crashed in Milwaukee. There were many fires, but the worst was in Houston, where twenty city blocks were burning. Witnesses claimed fire had fallen from the sky like rain. A power failure hit the Northeast when computers controlling the grid went wacky, trapping thousands in subways, offices, traffic jams. Wall Street shut down; there were brownouts as far south as Charleston.

A flock of griffins had popped into the air over Washington. The capital went Code Red, scrambling jets—which weren't much good, it turned out, at chasing mythological creatures when their computers kept malfunctioning.

The power wind had lasted only twelve minutes, but magic was still leaking from nodes everywhere. Not strongly, but enough to continue to mess up computers intermittently. The Internet was down in many places; individual computers suffered, too—in planes, cars, trains, homes, offices. People were urged to stay home or at work, not to drive. Traffic pileups were common with traffic lights malfunctioning and vehicles stalled.

They learned some of this from Ruben, once Lily was able to reach him. Most of it came from the radio. Radio signals weren't affected, though the stations with computerized playlists were off the air. Cell coverage was spotty, but Lily managed to reach the D.C. police shortly after getting Cynna's message. They said two units had already been dispatched to the address but wouldn't tell her anything else. She couldn't get through to the house or Cynna.

They stopped in a Wal-Mart in Harrisonburg. Benedict was firm that the men, at least, needed to eat, so Lily got take-out chicken plus jeans, sweatshirts, and flip-flops for Cullen and Benedict. Also some wet wipes so Rule could clean off some of the dried blood. The automated cash registers weren't able to log onto the network, so Lily's Visa didn't work, and she didn't have enough cash. That's when the threatened storm hit, naturally—when she raced back out to the Suburban to get money from Rule.

Twelve minutes later, Li Qin called.

"Your grandmother lives, Lily. Harry was not hurt. Is Rule Turner there? I would speak with him."

So she passed the phone to Rule and had to wait, hearing only his short responses while the others in the car no doubt caught every word.

Rule disconnected abruptly. His chest moved in a sudden, sharp inhale, as if he'd forgotten to breathe for a moment. He stared at the phone blankly, then handed it back. "Lost the signal."

"Rule?" She put a hand on his arm.

He nodded once, jerky, as if to say, *I'm here—give me a moment.* She could see the effort it took to pull himself together enough to speak, but he managed it. "Toby's alive and has no obvious injuries, but he's in a coma. He's been transported to Washington Hospital Center. One of the guards is dead—Freddie. The others are injured, two of them seriously. Your grandmother . . ."

He covered her hand with his. "She sent Li Qin for help but stayed to fight. She's hurt, but Li Qin says she'll heal. She's at the hospital, too. Along with the other guards. And Timms."

Lily swallowed. "What happened?"

"A demon. Not one of the red-eyes. Li Qin didn't see it—Madam Yu got her out before it broke down the door—but she got a description from someone. Upright, humanoid but very broad, maybe ten feet tall, with tusks and a tail. Reddish skin, hairless, and male."

They hashed it over, though there was little to be concluded from such limited information. It did seem that the demon summoner needed the power wind, but none of them could explain why the first set of attacks had targeted heirs so precisely and this one had missed.

Unless Toby had been the target.

At New Market they had to leave the interstate, detouring through Luray and Sperryville. A highway patrolman told them that three woolly mammoths had appeared on the I-44, causing a pileup it would take hours to clear.

They spent a lot of time trying to call various places. It took Rule seven tries, but he reached his father and told him about Toby. Isen didn't know of any other attacks, but he'd only been able to reach two other Rhos so far. Even landlines weren't working consistently, especially with long distance; computers controlled the switching. Rule kept trying reach the hospital but couldn't get through. He gave her phone back.

She listened to her messages and heard her mother's voice: "Your father bumped his head when his car died and the one behind hit him, but it's nothing. He's well, I'm well, your sisters are well, but what about you? Where are you? Call. Call. It's not right to leave me so worried."

Her mother was worried. Her mother was speaking to her again, and it had only taken worldwide calamity to bring her to that point. Something tight inside Lily uncoiled fast, snapping back like a released spring, and stinging. Stinging.

Rule put an arm around her. She leaned into him, blinking fast to clear the tears, and tried to call her mother back.

No luck. She had service, but those at the other end didn't. She tried her parents' home phone, her mother's cell, her father's business number, her father's cell phone, and finally her little sister's cell. The last one at least rang, but Beth didn't pick up; Lily left a message. She still had a signal, so she tried Cynna again—nothing—then the hospital.

Progress. She got a "lines are busy" recording instead of blank air.

Finally she listened to the last message, the one from Unknown. It was probably some annoying huckster, but she couldn't stand to delete messages without hearing them.

"Lily Yu." A woman's voice, low and musical with some hint of accent she couldn't identify. "This is Jiri. You are looking for me, and I am ready for you to find me. I will call again with instructions for you. Tell no one official of this call—none of your FBI or police friends—oh!" She chuckled. "Except for Cynna, of course. I forget sometimes that she is official these days. But tell no one else, or Rule Turner's son will never wake up."

WHEN they reached the hospital, Cynna was waiting for them, pacing up and down on her long legs in front of the drop-off area. When she saw them, she motioned at a young thug leaning against the building, arms crossed. He sauntered up, all tough-guy swagger, gangster pants, and attitude.

"Jo-Jo will park it for you," she said. "I already paid him half. He gets the rest when he brings us the keys."

Lily looked dubiously at Jo-Jo.

"It's okay," Cynna said. "Jo-Jo here brought a friend in to get stitched up, and his friend's got some sense even if Jo-Jo doesn't."

They took Cynna at her word and climbed out; the homeboy slid behind the wheel, his lip curling. No doubt Suburbans weren't his style.

"How'd you get here so quick?" Lily asked as they hustled inside. "I thought planes were still grounded."

"Commercial flights, yeah. I hitched with the Air Force."

They'd finally managed to reach Cynna by phone just as they hit the outskirts of D.C. Traffic had been amazingly light after that. Either everyone had already emptied out of the city, or they were following instructions and staying put.

"Toby's in CCU," Cynna said, adding quickly, "Not because he's critical. His vitals are good, except that his heart rate is real slow. It's a trance state, so his heart *would* beat slowly, but doctors turn hard of hearing when you start talking magic. Even with the *kilingo*—"

"What?"

"Jiri marked him." Cynna closed her hand tightly as if hiding her own mark. "Like she did me, only this spell's different than the one she stuck me with. I . . . he's there, inside. I checked. He's not been forced to ride, or anything like that."

Lily's breath caught. She hadn't thought of that possibility.

They lucked out—the elevator was emptying just as they reached it. They refilled the little box; Cynna hit the button for the third floor, and the doors closed.

Lily reached for Rule's hand, though she suspected he was too eaten up with worry about Toby to notice the small, closed space this time. But she needed the contact, too. "My grand-mother?"

"She's back from surgery," Cynna said. "She's good. She's amazing. I just checked on her."

"Surgery?" Lily said, alarmed. Grandmother healed even faster than lupi. If she'd needed an operation—

"She was gored."

Bile rose. Lily swallowed. Swallowed again.

"She's good," Cynna repeated hastily. "The worst was her lung, but she never lost consciousness. And she couldn't be anesthetized—Li Qin explained to me about that—but she used my spell. It shut off the pain so they could operate. I'm told she gave her surgeon instructions while he was working."

A little bubble rose up and popped inside her. Not laughter, not quite, but relief. "She would."

"Her surgeon's stunned. He's planning to write her up in some medical journal. Your people . . ." She looked at Benedict. "I'm sorry. Stan Carlson died. They didn't have a shaman on staff to put him in sleep, and he couldn't make the pain-block spell work. He died on the operating table.

"The other two are doing fine," she went on. "Brown, he needed some surgery because of his ribs being so bad, and he couldn't get the stupid spell to work, either, but he passed out, and his condition's good now. Lincoln just had a couple broken bones, and once the doc got the ends lined up right and casted, he was okay. They're sharing a room on the second floor."

"Timms?" Cullen asked.

"Post-op. He's, uh, critical."

Minutes later Lily and Rule stood in CCU looking down at Toby. She'd tried to prepare herself for the intrusive technology, for the way the boy would look—small and fragile, his color bleached to a terrible pallor.

Machines beeped, tubes were everywhere, but Toby didn't look ill or broken or pale. He looked like a kid who'd played hard and was catching up on his sleep. His cheeks held their usual color. His nail beds were pink and healthy. Only he wouldn't wake up. Couldn't wake up.

The *kilingo* was on his forehead. It was small, the size of a large postage stamp, the complex lines as fine as spider silk. She brushed his hair away from the mark and let her hand rest on his forehead.

Orange. Slick and somehow complex this time, but the orangey sense of the magic was unmistakable. "Demon magic," she said quietly. "Not exactly like other kinds I've touched. There's a layered quality to it, as if—"

"As if it had been crafted." Cynna stood in the entry to the cubicle. "The demon magic you've touched before came straight from the source, and demons don't use spells the way we do. But a *shetanni mwenye*—a demon master—does." Cynna looked down at the sleeping boy, her voice tightening as if she had to force the words out. "Jiri is *shetanni mwenye*. She did it. She did this to him."

Cynna would know. In some fashion she'd been there when it happened, propelled by the mark on her palm. That much she'd told them on the phone.

"Can you—no, of course not. If you knew how to remove the spell, you already would have."

"I can't remove a spell I don't know," she agreed, her voice heavy with regret. "But Cullen has a sleep charm. I'm hoping it's enough like this that between us we can figure out how to get rid of it."

THEY tried. Rule and Lily had to go to the CCU waiting room to keep the number of visitors within approved limits, but they didn't have to wait long before Cullen came in. He shook his head.

"Dammit, Cullen!" Rule was ready to explode. "You have to be able to do something!"

"Maybe . . ." He took two quick steps, stopped, and ran a hand over his hair. "Maybe if I have long enough to study it, but . . . hell, Rule. By putting it on his skin, she's tied it to him. It's got threads running everywhere, woven deep into him. If I tug on the wrong one, I'll stop his heart."

GRANDMOTHER was one floor up. Unlike Toby, she looked awful—shrunken and fragile and pale.

After Cynna's cheery words about how well Grandmother was doing, Lily couldn't quite hide her reaction as she bent to kiss the old woman on the cheek. If this was amazing, what kind of shape had she been in before? "Grandmother," she said, her voice wobbly. "Fighting demons? At your age?"

Grandmother gave a one-shoulder shrug. Her other arm was in a sling. "He would not look in my eyes. If he had, I would not have needed to fight." She looked at Rule. "The boy. They tell me he is all right, but he sleeps."

"Yes. He's all right physically. He's enspelled."

Madam Yu gave a single nod. "So. I couldn't stop them. I tried, but . . . bah," she said when her eyes sheened suddenly.

Lily knew better than to notice the tears. "Them? Was there more than one?"

"The demon and whoever controlled him." She was testy. "He didn't want to go upstairs. He wanted to finish killing me and enjoy the blood. Someone prevented that." She looked away. "I tire. Go away now."

Li Qin moved up beside Lily. She'd come with them to see Grandmother while Cynna stayed with Toby, Cullen checked on Timms, and Benedict went to see the two surviving guards. She spoke softly. "You may go, Lily, if you wish. I will stay with her."

Grandmother glared at her. "I do not need my hand held."

"Of course not." Li Qin settled in the chair next to the bed and held out her hand. "I do."

Grandmother stared at her. The corner of her lip tucked down, but it was the kind of down-tuck that hid amusement. They left the two women holding hands.

"I didn't realize they were lovers," Rule said as the door closed behind them. "I can usually tell."

"I'm still not sure," Lily said, "though I've wondered. There's love there, but what kind? Not my business, I guess—which is the least of what Grandmother would say if I went insane and asked her. I did say something to my mother once—"

"I know she took that well."

Lily's laugh surprised her. It was brief, but she hadn't thought she could laugh at all right now. "You could say that. I wouldn't, but you could."

"We'd better go get Toby now."

"Go get . . ." She stopped and spoke carefully. "You don't mean take him out of the hospital."

"There's no reason for him to stay here." He was reasonable. Calm. "Hooked up to a bunch of machines that can't do a thing for him . . . of course we'll take him home with us. That's where he should be. At home. It will be easier for Cullen to figure out how to undo the spell there."

In the hall, in the elevator, she gently pointed out why Toby needed to stay in the hospital. Yes, he was physically fine, and could probably be moved out of CCU. But they didn't know if he'd stay fine. He needed to be where they could keep an IV in him, at the very least. Besides, they didn't have a home to take him to; Nokolai's house was boarded up. There was blood all over.

Rule continued to sound reasonable. Home was wherever they were—a hotel, the borrowed Suburban, it didn't matter. If she thought Toby needed an IV, they'd leave that in. But it would be easier for Cullen to study the spell and undo it away from the hospital.

He hadn't touched Toby, she realized as they approached the doors to CCU. He hadn't touched Toby's face or reached for his hand as he lay there sleeping amid the beeps and tubes of critical care. She should have known he'd slipped around some inner corner. He and Toby touched often, easily . . . a hug, a pat, a snuggle. She'd envied that sometimes. Her own family didn't touch that way.

She'd thought he was dealing. He'd clamped down hard on his anxiety to keep functioning, she'd seen that, but he'd seemed to be dealing with the situation okay. She looked at him closely as they approached the cubicle that held his son.

He still looked okay. But he wasn't.

Visitors had changed places again. Benedict and Cullen were with Toby now. The CCU nurses wouldn't let them all in at once, of course, so Lily told Benedict and Cullen to come with her and give Rule a few minutes alone with Toby. He was talking to his son when they left . . . but not touching him.

Touching him might make it too real.

On the other side of the swinging doors, she told them about Rule's determination to take Toby out of the hospital. Her voice broke.

Benedict just nodded. "I'll talk to him. Outside."

"Talk isn't working." She felt frantic, close to tears, and she hated that, hated the utter uselessness of crying.

"Hey." Cullen put an arm around her, startling her. He gave her shoulders a squeeze. "We'll talk a little differently than you have been." He looked at Benedict. "You're the best, but Rule's not bad, either. I'll go with you. I'm fast enough, and we don't need any more injuries."

Benedict nodded and pushed on the CCU door.

"You're not talking about talking," Lily said stupidly.

Benedict paused. "We'll talk. Then he'll hit us. It's what he needs. He's too exhausted to do much damage, but Cullen's right. Two of us can make sure of that without damaging him."

THIRTY-FOUR

THERE were no chairs in CCU. Lily stood by Toby's bed, holding his hand and wishing she believed in prayer.

Death wasn't the end. Souls existed. She knew that beyond any doubt, but she didn't know if anyone was in charge—but if so, He or She wasn't doing a very good job. The inmates were running the asylum and had been for a long time.

But it couldn't hurt to ask. Even if she wasn't sure who or what she prayed to, it couldn't hurt to ask. *Please. Please help him. Help us.*

"He looks okay, doesn't he?"

She turned. Cynna stood in the open entry, sipping from a steaming cup. Lily smelled coffee. "You don't like coffee."

"Tastes like crap," she agreed, stepping into the glass-walled cubicle. "Where's Rule?"

"Getting some fight therapy, I think. He . . ." She chewed on her lip, uncertain how much to say. "I thought he was dealing. I didn't look closely enough. I guess a psychologist would say he was repressing, or in denial, or something like that. Benedict said he needed to hit someone. He and Cullen took him outside to talk, lupus style."

"Fight therapy. Huh. I could use some of that."

Beneath the inky filigree, Cynna's face was tight. No, Lily realized, she was tight all over, as if she were made of overwound springs ready to snap. "I guess I'm more like Timms. I'd rather shoot than punch."

"You know how to fight, though."

"I'm too mad to fight well right now." Lily hadn't known that was true until she said it, but she was aware of the anger now—a hot, hard knot of it in her belly. "You make mistakes when the anger's in charge."

"Guess that's why you're black belt and I'm just brown. When I'm mad, I like to fight. When I'm not mad, I don't see the point, so I don't practice." Cynna sipped from her cup, grimaced. "Here. You might as well drink this."

Lily accepted the cup. Milk had turned it to a paler shade of sludge she wasn't desperate enough to drink. "How much did that mess you up?" she asked softly. "What Jiri did, I mean. Making you ride again, having to witness everything."

"Witness." Cynna's voice was ripe with bitterness. "Riding's not like that. It isn't just watching."

"You've never talked about it."

"Not going to now, either."

"You didn't do this, you know. You didn't attack the others or do this to Toby."

Cynna took two steps as if she wanted to pace, but there was no room for it. "She kicked me out before I could see what she did to Toby. Didn't want me getting a clue about how to undo it. But for the rest . . . I might as well have done it. It didn't feel like the demon's hands reached in and dragged Brown out of the car. It was *our* hands that killed him. *We* broke down that door. *We* were pissed when the tiger attacked and . . ." She swallowed and raised miserable eyes to Lily's. "A rider doesn't just get the physical stuff. You get the feelings, too. Not thoughts, but I felt what the demon felt."

"It wasn't your will, your intent, in charge."

"Yeah, intent matters. I know that, but . . ." Her gaze jumped from Toby to the IV stand to the heart monitor. "Why did she do it that way? Why force me to ride? That's what I don't get. It didn't give her any advantage. Hell, it took some of her advantage away. I've got her pattern now, a current pattern."

"Vengeance. Threat. I—" Lily broke off. She felt Rule approaching. A moment later the doors to CCU opened and Rule, Cullen, and Benedict came in.

They were a bit worse for wear.

Cullen was limping. Benedict had a cut over one eye. Rule was the worst mess, though, with his jacket gone, his shirt torn, and a doozy of a black eye. It had already aged to the greenish yellow phase, but was still swollen.

He came straight to Lily. One of the nurses darted out from their central station, telling them they had to leave—they couldn't have this many in CCU at one time. Rule didn't seem to notice, but Benedict spoke politely to her.

Rule stopped in front of Lily. For a long moment they just looked at each other, each seeking something too large to fit neatly into words. Then the corner of his mouth kicked up and she reached for him, or he reached for her, and they were holding on. Holding on tight.

Benedict told her the rest of them would be in the CCU waiting room. She nodded without stirring. Rule loosened his grip just as the CCU doors opened. Cynna had paused in the doorway, looking back at them. And for a second Lily saw too much in her face. A hard sorrow. Longing. Envy.

Then Cynna turned. The door closed, and Rule went to Toby's bed and took his son's hand.

THEY stayed at the hospital another three hours. Toby was moved from CCU to a room in pediatrics. He didn't stir. Timms was upgraded from serious to stable. Cynna told them about her interview in Chicago and Jiri's other apprentice, Tommy Cordoba; they filled her in on events at Leidolf Clanhome.

Jiri didn't call.

Ruben did. The Bureau's computers were still wonky, so they couldn't run a trace on Cordoba, but Ruben promised he'd put a priority on it.

After some discussion, they settled that Benedict would take the night shift with Toby. Or rather, Benedict settled it—he told Rule and Lily to go away and get some rest. To Cynna's amazement, they listened. Then they had to almost drag Cullen out. He seemed to feel responsible for Timms.

They adjourned to a hotel near the hospital, where Rule got a two-bedroom suite for him, Lily, and Cullen, with an adjoining single for Cynna, and ordered room service hamburgers.

Not that anyone seemed hungry. When the food arrived, all of them except Cullen sat at the round table and tried to eat. Cullen slouched in the big armchair in front of the TV with his plate, absorbed in CNN or his own thoughts.

"But what does it mean?" Cynna asked Rule, dragging a fat home fry through ketchup. "You've got two mantles, or part of two mantles. What does that do to you?"

His expression was odd. Baffled. "I can't describe it, but . . . I'm okay."

Lily grimaced. "The mate bond didn't do us any good, after all. I guess with the power wind—"

"No," he said. "It did help. It's still helping. I don't know how to explain, but it helped the two mantles settle in together."

"Two-mantled," Cullen murmured.

Cynna looked at him, surprised he'd followed their conversation. He was frowning at the TV.

"The Rhej used that phrase," Lily said. "She made it sound like some sort of title."

Cullen didn't look at them. "It's from a legend. A very old legend."

"I never heard of it," Rule said.

"It's an Etorri tale."

"What's Etorri?" Cynna asked.

There was one of those silences, like when someone farts and everyone pretends not to notice. At last Cullen answered. "My former clan. The one that kicked me out."

Oh.

"Power's back on up North," he said in an obvious change of subject. "And some asshole's decided to let commercial flights resume."

"You don't think it's safe?"

He snorted. "More like an extreme solution to overpopulation. There's too much loose magic for computerized systems to be dependable."

Lily and Rule joined him in front of the television. Cynna paced but listened. Fire still raged in Houston. An earthquake in Italy had left thousands homeless. The nuclear meltdown in Poland had been confirmed, but details were sketchy. Wall Street expected to reopen in the morning. And phone service remained problematical, but landlines worked better than cellular.

Jiri had Lily's cell number.

Cynna couldn't sit. She paced, swerving by the table that held her food every so often to grab a fry. Her skin felt as if she'd washed it in hot water and it had shrunk. Or like the last-year's clothes she used to start school in. As if she might bend or move wrong and rip something open.

At last Lily clicked the remote and the TV went dead. "We've heard from the world. Now we need to deal with our corner of it—sort out what we know, what we guess." She looked at Cynna. "We never got the whole story on the attack."

"You want details? Like who bled where?" She reached the wall. Turned. Kept moving.

"Tell us about the demon. It wasn't a red-eye, like the others. Li Qin said it was male."

"That's right." Cynna made an effort to strangle her jitters so she didn't jump down anyone's throat. "They don't settle on a sex when they're young. This one isn't all that bright, but he's old, strong, powerful. We . . . *he* wasn't bothered by the bullets. They hurt, but it was like being poked with a pin over and over. Infuriating, but no biggie. Of course, he didn't have all his mass pulled out of dashtu. If he had, he'd have busted those stairs instead of climbing 'em. The older ones are heavy. Dense."

"You mean their mass is dense? Not their heads?"

Her mouth turned up in an attempt at a smile. "Sometimes their heads are pretty dense, too. But I meant mass."

"So she's riding a powerful demon. What does that tell us?"

"Not exactly riding. She's a demon master, not a rider. It's . . . a different level of control." *And defilement.*

"But what does it mean?"

"That she's got mega-oomphs of power and an old, not-too-bright demon who'll do whatever she wants."

"What can you tell us about her?" Rule asked.

"I've already told Lily—"

"You've given her facts, what few you have. You haven't said what makes Jiri tick. What she wants. She wants something, wants it bad."

"I don't know! God, if it were that easy . . . When I first knew her, she was okay. No," she corrected herself. "She was good. A good person. She started out wanting to change things, make them better for people who needed change. That's what the movement was, at first. Sure, we talked tough. We were street kids—that's what we knew. But we pulled together to make things work for people who needed hope."

"What happened?"

"Demons happened." Cynna made a noise between laughter and tears. "You ride 'em, you feel what they do. She warned us, all of the ones she brought into her . . . I guess you'd call us the inner circle. She warned us to be careful, or we'd lose track of the line between us and them. And that's what happened, exactly what happened, with her. I watched as those lines got erased in her. That's why I left. I could see what I'd end up like."

"Then you must be able to guess what she's after," Rule said.

"You," Lily said.

"She missed, then, didn't she?" Bitterness coated his voice. He pushed to his feet and then stood there, looking like he needed to hit something again.

Lily stayed in her chair. "You weren't there, so she enspelled Toby. It's a way to get to you."

"Goddamn her. It could be. It could be true. Cynna, there must be something—"

"Rule." Cullen uncoiled from his chair. "Enough. She's had enough."

"It's okay," Cynna said. "It's his son in danger, his men she killed."

"And if you could do anything to change that, you'd have already done it." He walked up to her, no particular expression on his face . . . and that was odd. Cullen was always *something*—smiling, teasing, angry, laughing—some emotion always seemed to be burbling up in him. "Just cut it out, will you?"

"What?" She tried a laugh. "Cut what out?"

He gave his head a half shake, just to one side and back, his lips thinning as if she were the slowest student in the class. "Never mind." He grabbed her face in his two hands and kissed her. And kissed her. And went on kissing her.

Stars collided. Whole universes. Neurons burst in her brain, dying a violent but beautiful death. She sucked his tongue into her mouth and bit it.

Eventually that luscious, lovely, talented mouth left hers. She noticed that her eyes were closed and considered opening them. Her body was held tight against his. It was very happy about that.

"Cullen," Lily said sharply, "I don't think—"

"Glad to hear it, since this isn't any of your business." His eyes were hot, and some of that heat was temper. "She needs this. And by God, so do I." He ran one hand down Cynna's arm to take her hand, and tugged. "Come on."

She did, though it was hard to say who led who to the connecting door to her room.

"Cynna?" That was Lily again, worrying.

"It's okay," she said without looking back. "He's a jerk, but he's right. After all, I didn't get any fight therapy, did I?"

He pulled her through the door, closed it behind them.

The room was small, the walls a neutral green, the bed a tidy rectangle a few feet away. Her heart pounded madly in her throat. Why didn't he just grab her? She was expecting that—the quick heat, a rough climb, maybe some ripped clothes. She wanted it.

Instead he put his hands on her arms. "They don't get it," he said softly. "You hit your biggest fear today, didn't you? This time the demon swallowed you."

"Hey." She jerked away. "If I'd wanted talk, I'd have stayed in the other room."

He ignored that. "Blood, sex, power. That's the price demons ask of a rider, isn't it, *shetanni rakibu*? One or all of those things."

He knew too much. That's why she wasn't going to do this. She remembered that now. She didn't want anyone knowing those things about her. She fumbled for the door.

"Cynna." His hand on her arm stopped her. "You didn't pay for the ride, so it wasn't yours. You couldn't have stopped him from doing what he did. You didn't pay. You are not responsible."

She shuddered, rounding on him. "You don't get it, either! It wasn't him smashing Freddie up against the wall, it was *us*! *We* slurped his blood until she—the master—made us stop. I felt it all; not just the physical parts, but everything he felt—and he liked doing that. It was—it felt good!"

"You felt what the demon felt." His hands on her cheeks weren't gentle or soothing. They trapped her, making her look at him. "But you felt other things, too. Horror—fear—"

God. Oh, God. She squeezed her eyes closed. "I tried. I tried so hard."

"You didn't pay. You weren't in charge, so you couldn't change things." His hands left her face—and closed over her breasts. "You won't be in charge now, either."

"What?" Her eyes popped open. "I don't need some macho bullshit—"

"Yes. You do." He ran his thumbs over the tips of her breasts.

"What you called fight therapy . . . We didn't take Rule outside because we like bruises, his or ours. We took him out there to lose it. He has formidable control, but control is a two-edged blade. He was bleeding inside from holding on to it too tightly."

His thumbs were making her dizzy. Or maybe his words were. She shook her head, certain there was a flaw in his logic.

"Sometimes you have to lose control to get it back. And it's okay to turn loose with me. You can't hurt me."

Memories squeezed inside her, so tight it was hard to breathe. "You can be hurt. You'd heal, but you can be hurt."

He shook his head. "Not by you, not here and now. I'm too much stronger. Faster. You won't hurt me, and God knows you won't shock me. Want to go for a little bondage?"

Quick as a thought, he gathered her hands and pinned them behind her with one hand. His other hand was busy with her breast. She sucked in a breath. "No." Her voice came out harsh. "I just want to fuck. Hard and fast."

At last he quit talking.

His mouth was full of demands. He scooped her up and carried her to the bed, his mouth making those demands the whole way. Then he dropped her. She hit the bed, bounced, and was reaching for the buttons on her shirt before she finished bouncing.

He stripped quickly, efficiently—and she had one pang of regret, because she'd love to see him take his time with that.

But not tonight. Tonight she didn't want to think. She wanted to—was desperate to—feel human, to forget what she'd experienced as a silent rider in a demon's body.

He came to her naked and fully aroused, which was a major distraction, because then she needed to get her hands all over that stunning body. She needed to taste the skin he brought to her.

He needed her clothes off. And he was right. He was a lot stronger, and she wasn't in charge.

Buttons popped as he yanked her shirt off. He shoved her bra up out of his way and lowered his head to suck. And that was good, that was incredible, the slow liquid tugs in her belly making her moan.

She put her hands in his hair to hold him there, but the perverse man immediately decided to wander across to her other breast, then down the center of her body to her navel, where the band of her trousers stopped him.

"Damn," he muttered. "You've still got clothes on."

She laughed. It just struck her as terribly funny, and she laughed when she would have sworn she couldn't—but he caught the laugh with his mouth, his hands busy now with her bra, unfastening it. "Get the rest of it off," he told her. "I want to see. You smell fantastic, but I want to see, too."

So she wiggled out of slacks and panties, and he looked and smiled, dazzling her. "You've got an incredible body, Wonder Woman, but I'm not a patient man." He crawled on top of her and kissed her, put his hand between her legs. And was still kissing her when he thrust inside.

She felt that all the way to her scalp. It had been a long, long time since a man came inside her naked like this, but with a lupus lover she didn't need a condom. She was on the pill, and he couldn't catch or transmit a disease.

She was safe, he was safe. It felt wonderful.

She dug her fingers into his shoulders and pushed back with her hips, and he gave her the fast and furious ride she'd asked for. They found each other's rhythm quickly, as if they'd done this a dozen times, and lust shot off skyrockets in her belly. Her body burned with it, the wonderful living heat of passion. When she felt her climax coming, she almost wanted to stop, to wait, to make it last—

Too late. She bucked once and smashed through a blinding orgasm.

He was still going. "Not . . . patient," he panted, and he even grinned. "But I've been . . . practicing . . ." He punctuated that with a rolling thrust that made her gasp. ". . . awhile."

Over the next several minutes he showed her how good an impatient but well-practiced man could be. When he finally came, she was on her third climax and he was on his knees with her legs hooked over his shoulders. She damn near melted.

He did collapse, right on top of her, his chest heaving. And that was lovely, she thought once a few of those destroyed neurons regenerated enough to rub up a thought. Lovely to know he was wrecked, too. Lovely to lie close like this, all sweaty and limp, their legs tangled together, her hand free to stroke his back . . .

A jolt went through his body. He jerked his head up, staring at her with—what? Shock? Horror? Something awful, because . . . God, those were tears. Tears filling his eyes.

"What is it?" she whispered, terrified without knowing what could possibly be so wrong.

Slowly his expression changed, though she still couldn't read it. He raised up on one elbow and ran his hand down her body, his gaze following it, until hand and gaze both rested on her belly. "Lady," he whispered. "Oh, Lady. Thank you."

This was getting weird. She'd had men thank her for sex, but not like this. "You're freaking me out here, Cullen."

"I'm . . . pretty freaked myself." He raised his head, looked her in the eyes. His were all shiny and wet. "You're carrying my baby."

She heard the words, but for a long moment they stayed stuck on the surface of her brain. She couldn't attach any meaning to them.

All at once they sank in. "Get off." She shoved at him.

Obligingly he rolled off and just lay there, grinning at her. Blissed. The asshole was blissed out, and she was—"You're nuts," she told him, getting off the bed. Grabbing up clothes with hands that shook. "I'm on the pill. I'm not pregnant, and even if I were, you wouldn't know. Not—"

"It's given to us to know." He sat up, and Lord, he made her breath catch in her throat with that simple movement. And he was happy, damn him. So happy.

It terrified her, that happiness of his.

"I'd given up," he said. "Years ago, I gave up thinking I'd ever . . . But you're carrying my baby."

The knock on the door made her jump. "What?" she called. "We're a little busy here."

Rule's voice: "Jiri called. We have to go. Now."

THIRTY-FIVE

THE Suburban shot through a yellow light to the blare of car horns. Lily ignored that. Her thoughts were harder to ignore.

She'd learned long ago to cram the personal stuff in a box and sit on the lid when she was working. Cops had to be able to do that, or they couldn't do the job. But the personal was so tangled up with the job this time there was no way to separate them. Rule's life was at stake. Toby's life was at stake. And Cullen and Cynna had picked this time to turn weird on her.

"I'm getting a hint of direction," Cynna said from the backseat. "East and a bit north."

Cynna had done a cast before they got in the Suburban and found that Jiri was blocking her. Apparently that was possible, given enough knowledge and power. Jiri had the knowledge and a demon to draw on for power, but she couldn't block her former student completely. Cynna knew roughly how far away she was, and was beginning to pick up her direction.

"That matches," Cullen said crisply. "The park's northeast of us."

Rock Creek Park. That's where Jiri said she'd meet them, at a stone bridge in the park. She must have read the kidnappers' tip sheet: tell the victims not to contact the cops or the FBI. Give them a tight time limit to respond to your demands. They had twenty minutes to get there.

Cullen knew where the park was. He wasn't sure about the bridge, but they'd find it . . . and her. They had Cynna for that.

"Right at the next light," Cullen said.

And there was one of those personal cords tugging at her. Something was going on with Cullen and Cynna. Not the sex—that had been inevitible, and if it had made Lily uncomfortable for them to go at it in the next room, that was probably her problem. But Cullen was behaving strangely. When they came out of the bedroom he'd grabbed Rule and told him something—speaking under the tongue, dammit, and the stupid mate bond was not giving Lily that kind of hearing anymore. Whatever he'd said, it had made Rule grab Cullen and hug him hard.

Cullen's years as a lone wolf had made him less easy about touch than most lupi, and Rule's position as Lu Nuncio and heir had done something of the same for him. And men might give a buddy a backslap or punch on the shoulder for scoring, but a hug?

Besides, Rule wasn't a scorekeeper. She hadn't thought Cullen was, either. And Toby's life was at stake, dammit. So it hadn't been about sex.

"I still think we should stop for ammo." She'd lost the argument about stopping at a cop shop to pick up reinforcements. If Jiri was a farseer, that was too dangerous. But they hadn't been told to come unarmed. They had the rifles they'd brought with them from Leidolf, but no reloads.

"If Jiri's there on her own, we won't need extra ammo," Cynna said. "If she's got her overgrown friend with her, rifles won't help."

"Only if we can't separate them." That was the plan, such as it was.

If Jiri did offer them a deal, they'd hear her out. Cynna said a demon master had enough demon stuff inside her that she could be bound by her word, just like a demon, if you knew how. Cynna knew how.

But Lily was expecting an attack, not a deal. If they were attacked, they couldn't use deadly force on the demon unless they could be sure of not killing Jiri along with it. She'd know that. She'd be counting on it. But Cynna could hit the demon with her spell—which, it turned out, stopped demon hearts. This one had multiple hearts, so the spell might not kill it, but it would probably go dashtu. If it did, it would be physically separated from its master. Cullen could throw mage fire at it while Rule and Lily went after Jiri.

An optimist might say the plan left them room to improvise. A pessimist would call it full of holes.

"Too late to change our minds now," Cullen said. "That's it on the right."

The place was closed, of course. It was nearly nine. They parked the Suburban in the empty lot and climbed out.

The temperature had plunged after the sun set. The air was raw with cold and damp, with just enough of a breeze to make things worse. Lily shivered and zipped her jacket, settled the rifle comfortably on her arm, and started for the gate with Rule and Cynna.

Cullen was already there. "What do you know—they forgot to lock it." The gate swung open at his touch.

That was another way Cullen could be handy. He was good with locks. Lily had never asked how and why he'd aquired that particular sorcerous talent. Some things it was better not to know.

She looked up at Rule. "You okay?"

The overhead lights of the parking lot picked out the sharp blades of his cheekbones and limned his mouth, but his eyes were shadowed, no more than a liquid gleam in the darkness. He slid a hand over her nape and into her hair, answering her with his touch and a smile.

"I've got her," Cynna said suddenly. "I've got a Find on her now. She's here physically, not just riding her demon."

"And the demon?" Lily said.

"He's around, but . . ." She shook her head. "I think he's dashtu and not too far from Jiri, but I'm not sure. I'm sorry. Holding two Finds is tricky."

"Quit apologizing," Cullen snapped. "Most Finders can't do two Finds at all."

Sex didn't seem to have turned them into lovers. Not in any conventional sense, at least. But what about either of them was conventional?

They passed through the gate into the park.

They'd debated splitting up, but in the end decided they were too small a party for that, especially since demons were hard to sneak up on. Rule or Cullen might have managed it in wolf form, but both needed to remain two-footed. Rule had to be able to speak if Jiri did want to make a deal, and Cullen couldn't throw fire in his wolf form. So everyone kept together and on two legs as they set off down the path.

Lights on poles made to resemble old-fashioned gas lanterns were spaced at intervals just wide enough to be useless while still ruining her night vision. The path itself was crunchy with gravel and leaves crisped by frost, and Lily's breath plumed white when they entered the circle of light under the first lantern. Overhead, a few stars struggled to penetrate the city haze. The moon hung low, just over the trees to the east, looking like a lump of orange sherbet. It was still a week from full.

Their path turned before reaching the creek to run parallel to it, separated by a fringe of small trees. Lily heard it lapping against its banks, slapping around the rocks in its bed. She thought she could hear her heart pounding, too. God knew she could feel it.

She was terrified.

Rule would know that, as would Cullen. They'd smell it on her. That bugged her, but it fell on the list of things she couldn't do a damned thing about. Not that she was ashamed of being afraid; that was a sane response to facing a demon. She acknowledged the feeling and put it away. Worse by far was the fear she couldn't speak.

What if Jiri wanted to trade Toby's life for Rule's? Would he agree?

Would she try to stop him?

Don't fight a battle that isn't joined, she told herself, and moved ahead as silently as she could.

"Wards ahead," Cullen said softly.

Rule stopped. "What kind?" he asked in a barely there voice.

"Not the keep-us-out sort, but she'll know we're here. I can disable them without her knowing, but it will take time."

"How much?"

"Ten minutes, maybe."

Which would put them over the time limit. Lily didn't think Jiri would kill Toby if they were a few minutes late; he was too valuable to her. But it wasn't a chance she wanted to take.

Neither did Rule. "Then we'll ring her doorbell before entering." He moved on.

They didn't bother being quiet after that. Their path veered slightly away from the creek, skirting a large, rocky outcropping. Trees had just closed in overhead, their branches scratching each other in the breeze, when Cynna spoke quietly. "She's just past those evergreens, about ten yards away."

Rule held up a hand. They stopped in the shadows beneath the trees. He tilted his head up—scenting the air, Lily realized. But the wind blew the wrong way.

After a moment he shrugged. "We may as well keep our appointment." He moved forward.

Their path had led them true, right to the stone bridge. A tall woman dressed in black sat smack in the center of the bridge's arch. Her skin was so dark it blended into her clothing—a leather catsuit, black and form-fitting. She was easy to spot, though. No trees arched out over the bridge to block the moonlight, and one of those fake gaslights was on the other side of the bridge.

She stood. "You may as well come out of the trees. As you see . . ." She gestured widely. "I am alone."

"Not entirely." That was Cynna, her voice hard. "Your familiar is on the other side of the creek."

"Cynna," she murmured. "How you hate me. I am sorry for that. In so many ways, though, you wouldn't be here if not for me, would you? Yes, Tish is near, but I had him wait at enough of a distance that you would know you could escape him, if necessary. I need your help."

Rule's laugh was harsh and brief. "You've an odd way of asking for it."

"I'll admit," she said, walking slowly to the near end of the bridge, "that I wanted to control the situation. I trust you no more than you do me. You think I'm behind the attacks on the heirs. Cynna has no doubt convinced you I am evil."

"You killed my men. You enspelled my son. What do you call yourself?"

"Desperate." That came out flat and oddly convincing.

"What do you want?" Lily asked, her own voice as expressionless as she could make it.

Jiri looked at her. Lily felt the unmistakable tug of a shared gaze and knew the woman saw better than average in the dark. Better than human? Cynna said she had a fair amount of demon stuff in her. "Lily Yu. Do you love your lover's son?"

The question rocked her out of her professional detachment—as, no doubt, it was intended to do. Did she love Toby?

She'd only begun to know the boy, so some of what she felt for him was more readiness to love than a feeling centered on

Toby himself. But she thought of an eager young voice, quick footsteps racing up or down the stairs, the stubborn set of a small chin in a young face both like and unlike the older face she loved. "Yes." Her voice came out hoarse. "You have the control you wanted. We're here, ready to do just about anything to have the spell lifted from Toby. What do you want?" she asked again.

"Your help. I haven't hurt the boy. I won't hurt him. This much Cynna should be able to tell you—I don't harm children."

"Freddie had a son," Rule said.

"Freddie?"

"One of the men you killed today."

"Ah." For a second her face went blank, as if his death came as news to her. "I am sorry for that. Does the boy have a mother?" There was a curious intensity to the question.

"He does. That doesn't make up for the loss of his father."

"But children need . . . no, we aren't here for that. Never mind." She tilted her head up, and light shivered down over a face Lily saw clearly for the first time. An exotic face, the nose broad and flat, the forehead high and rounded. Sloe-eyed, thickly lashed. And skin not truly black, but brown. The filigree of tattoos over-laying it was so dense, far denser than Cynna's, that at first you saw only darkness.

"I've worked so hard for this," Jiri murmured, "for so long, and now that the time has come, I'm afraid. How foolish. But I've been afraid for so long . . . it becomes a habit. Well." She faced them again. "What do I want? I want you, Rule Turner, to lead as many of your people as you can summon. I particularly want your sorcerer friend. I want to attack a man who was once my apprentice."

"Tommy Cordoba," Cynna said.

Her eyebrows arched in surprise. "You found out that much? Yes, Tommy. He's behind the attacks on lupi, not me." Her lip curled in scorn. "He would say he's made a powerful ally. You know who I mean—She's your enemy. He has taught some of Her servants—you call them the Azá—to summon demons, but he is the master. You won't take my word for this, of course. Tish. Show yourself to our visitors."

Beside the fake gas lamp on the other side of the bridge the air grew fussy, like smoke swirled with a finger. Within seconds it had resolved into . . . a thing. He was humanoid, as Li Qin had said, but nothing about him made Lily think of a person. He was massive, like pictures Lily had seen of a troll: ten feet tall and twice as broad as the biggest man she'd ever seen. His neck was thicker than her hips. His skin was the color of dried blood and the texture of rock, and tusks a foot long curved out from either side of a wide, lipless mouth. His tail curled neatly around his feet, broad and sinewy like a boa.

And yes, he was male, in a gargantuan sort of way.

"Hold fire," Rule said softly.

Lily had snugged the rifle to her shoulder automatically. She kept it trained on the demon.

"I can still lie," Jiri was saying. "I admit that. But Tish cannot. I have taught him English. Ask him who is behind the attacks. He will answer."

"Cynna?" Rule said in a low voice.

"Demons can't lie, but you have to phrase your questions carefully and pay close attention to the answers. They'll make technically true statements that add up to a lie if they can."

"You've experience with questioning demons?"

Cynna took a long breath, expelled it. "Yeah."

"Then you do the questioning."

"Rule." Cullen's voice was sharp.

"From here," Rule added. "He can hear us from here."

Lily thought Cynna could have a career as an attorney if she decided to change professions. Her questions allowed no wiggle room: Is the woman standing on the bridge in front of me, whose use-name is Jiri, your master? *Yes.* Do you have any knowledge or reason to suspect or surmise that your master has summoned, aided in the summoning, or caused to be summoned demons other than yourself who have attacked lupi in this realm? *No.* Do you have any knowledge or reason to suspect or surmise that she has lied to us tonight? *No.* Do you know who summoned the demons who attacked various lupi four nights ago? *Yes.* Who? *You know them as the Azá.* Who mastered those demons? *Tommy Cordoba is their master.*

Cynna looked at Rule. "Best I can do. I think it's true."

"Tommy is behind the attacks," Jiri insisted. "If you kill him, they will end. The ones he taught would still be able to summon demons, but only a master can control them beyond the summoning circle."

Rule spoke coldly. "Do you expect me to believe you engineered all this to persuade me to kill someone who is my enemy?"

"No. I brought you here to kill my enemy. It's your good fortune that he's yours, as well."

"Why did you attack me?" Cullen asked.

"Why do you think? You're a sorcerer. I hoped to bring you back with me and avoid . . . all this. Had I been able to do so before the second shifting, when Tommy gained so much power . . . but I failed. You fought me off."

"Your demon defeated four lupi, one human, and . . . another fighter today," Rule said. "Why do you need us?"

"Tommy's warded his place against demons. Tish can't get through, and I can't get in by myself without setting off alarms. I hope your sorcerer will be able to undo the wards. And—and you and I have something in common." She drew a shaky breath. "He holds my daughter hostage. That's the other part of my price. I want you to get her away from him."

THIRTY-SIX

RULE inhaled deeply, his head cocked, testing the air for scents, listening. He'd moved all of them back down the path, far enough away that they could discuss Jiri's demand without being overheard by Jiri and the demon.

The air was chill yet rich with smells; it was almost like being four-legged, his senses were so keen. And the power . . . a bit intoxicating. His power hadn't doubled with the addition of a second heir's portion, it had tripled, or more.

His mind had almost broken when Victor tried to force the mantle on him. Even after the Rhej shoved much of it back into Victor, he'd hovered in some gray place, his mind dull and confused. But once the two heirs' portions were balanced . . .

Balanced, but not restful. They jostled still inside him, same and yet not the same. The Leidolf portion felt alien, as if he'd woken up with a third hand sprouting from his elbow. Still, unlike the clans they belonged to, the mantles seemed able to coexist.

"I'm accepting Jiri's terms," he said abruptly, "unless someone has a very good reason not to."

Lily shook her head. "We can't just go kill someone."

This was hard for her. Her culture, training, and profession opposed acting outside the law. "I believe her. I think Cordoba is summoning demons, working with Her to destroy my people. I agree that we have to be sure, but if he is, I don't think he'll let you put him under arrest."

"Being sure means gathering evidence, putting the case before a jury."

"And Toby?" He gave her a chance to answer. She didn't. "I'll go where Jiri sends me, but look before I leap."

"Or bite, or shoot." Cullen was striving for cocky. "I'm in, of course. But Cynna stays here."

Lily's eyebrows snapped down. "Have you morphed into a chauvinist pig?"

Cullen didn't answer. He was watching Cynna, his eyes hooded.

"Forget it," Cynna said. "I'm needed, and I'm not . . . you've got to get that idea out of your head."

"What idea?" Lily demanded.

"Oh, hell." Cynna hunched one shoulder impatiently. "He told Rule. You might as well know, too. Cullen has decided that, modern pharmaceuticals to the contrary, he got me pregnant."

Lily's jaw dropped. She closed her mouth, then opened it to speak, but Cynna talked right over her. "I don't know if he tells every woman that, or if I showed up at the peak of his lunatic cycle, but—"

"Cynna." Lily cut in sharply, then gentled her voice. "They know. Lupi know if a woman they've been with conceives."

"Maybe they do sometimes. This time, he's wrong."

Had she been this stubborn when they were lovers thirteen years ago? Rule only had to ask himself the question to have the answer: yes, every inch as stubborn. And just as wrongheaded at times. "We can't discuss this now. If Cynna is willing to go—"

Cullen rounded on him. "Goddammit, Rule!"

"It's her decision," he said softly. "You know it has to be her decision."

Cullen looked ready to burn something or someone. But he knew clan law—necessary because the temptation was so keen. Nokolai had been the first to make it criminal for a lupus to constrain a woman who carried his child, but most of the other clans had followed. Persuasion was fine, but the woman's life, her choices, had to remain in her hands.

Cullen turned away, paced a few steps, paced back. He didn't say anything, but Rule could see he had himself under control again.

Cynna scowled at all of them. "If all that means I get to choose—damned right I do. And I'm in."

"You can bind Jiri to what we agree on?"

She nodded grimly.

"Lily?"

She took longer than he liked, but at last she nodded. "I reserve the right to arrest him, if it's feasible."

"Then we'll give her our answer."

Jiri waited at the bridge, motionless and tense. A proud woman, he thought. Too proud to ask for help, to surrender that much control—and that pride had cost two men their lives. But if Cordoba held her daughter, her need was desperate. He thought she'd been honest about some things, at least. He'd smelled her fear when she spoke of her daughter being held by Cordoba, its acrid odor mingling with her own scent. Odd, that. She didn't smell like a demon, but she wasn't entirely human, either.

"You've decided," she said.

Rule stepped out of the shadows beneath the trees. "We will go after Cordoba and return your child to you—if she's there, as you've said. And if she is your child."

The tension remained. "Tonight. It must be tonight."

He shook his head. "We need time to plan. And," he added bitterly, "you've killed or wounded all of my trained fighters on this coast. With airplane travel undependable, it will take a few days to gather an attack force."

"It has to be tonight," she repeated. "Tommy gave me an ultimatum. Either I bind myself to him and the Bitch Goddess by tomorrow at midnight, or he . . ." She swallowed. "What little humanity he retains has much in common with Henry Lee Lucas or the BTK killer. If you won't rescue my daughter tonight, I'll go there now and bind myself to him and free my daughter that way. And Tommy won't care if your son ever wakes up."

Rule held himself still. He had to. The fury that swept through him at the threat to Toby carried him too close to an edge he couldn't afford to cross. After a moment he managed to speak evenly. "Cordoba will be expecting you to act tonight. He'll be doubly on guard."

She shrugged. "It can't be helped. If your sorcerer had been a bit less clever, I wouldn't have had to wait until the last minute."

"Or kill two men, wound others, and enspell my son." His rage was ebbing, but the strength and suddenness with which it had hit bothered him. This was not the time to lose control. "Very well. I will accept your terms if you will bind yourself to mine. You'll swear to release Toby from your spell whether I succeed or not."

Her lips quirked up, but the smile came nowhere near her eyes. "Cynna's been telling all my secrets, hasn't she? All right."

"**YOU'VE** lost it," Lily said flatly. "You can't mean to—"

"I can. I have to." They were in the Suburban, which Rule had started to get the heater going. He wasn't cold, but he knew Lily was.

After Cynna had performed the binding, Jiri had given him a computer disk with maps and the architect's plans for Cordoba's place at the northernmost end of the North Carolina shore. She planned to meet them there but she wouldn't travel with them or give them her phone number. Instead she would call Lily again at midnight to find out how they planned to storm a place guarded by demons.

When they reached the Suburban he'd filled the others in on what he intended to do, knowing Lily wouldn't like it.

"Is it even possible?" Cynna asked, obviously dubious.

Cullen answered for him. "Possible, yes. Likely?" He shook his head. "Rule, I don't want to argue, but—"

"Then don't." He took a deep breath, held it a moment before letting it out. His temper was unsteady. "According to Jiri, Cordoba has at least four of the red-eyes and several smaller demons at his place, plus four of the Azá. We need more fighters."

"The idea," Lily said with strained patience, "is to bring people along who try to kill the other guy, not you. There must be some Nokolai on this coast."

"They're not trained. An untrained lupus will do well against a few humans. Against demons, he's cannon fodder."

"Then we go it on our own. Cullen's mage fire—"

"Sorry," Cullen said. "Much as I'd like to agree with you, I don't have an unlimited supply. And it's hard to control well enough to use in hand-to-hand. I tend to burn up the good guys along with the bad."

Lily had a scar on her stomach from mage fire Cullen hadn't fully controlled. She didn't speak again until Rule pulled out of the parking lot. "I hate this. I really, really hate this."

So did he. He was going to need every bit of power from the two heirs' portions he carried.

The only clan close enough for him to call on for help was Leidolf.

THIRTY-SEVEN

THE moon was high when they pulled into the parking lot across from the Nutley courthouse. The location was Cullen's suggestion. It was neutral ground and open enough to discourage ambush on either side.

It was nearly two A.M. They'd made good time, but they'd had a couple of stops to make before leaving D.C.; first at the house for Lily's laptop and a few items from Benedict's arsenal, then to the hospital to check on Toby and get Benedict's help.

Benedict was rarely openly angry, but when he realized he couldn't come with them—they couldn't leave Toby unprotected—he cursed for two minutes solid. Then he sat down, studied the documents on Jiri's disk, and came up with a plan of attack.

There was only one other car in the courthouse parking lot. Rule's Mercedes. Alex Thibodaux and four other men waited beside it. One of them was Brady.

Brady had not been part of his arrangement with Alex. Rule parked and got out slowly. Cynna and Lily got out on the other side but followed instructions, saying nothing.

"You have a reason for bringing *him* to this meeting?" Rule nodded at Brady.

"He was Randall's brother," Alex said. "If the story you tell is true, he has a right to be in on the kill."

Rule had told Alex nearly everything when he called to set up this meeting. The Leidolf Rho was still deeply unconscious, unable to make decisions for the clan, which was one piece of luck. Victor would have found a way to turn this into a death trap for Rule. He didn't think Alex would, if he handled things right.

If he handled the mantle right, to be specific.

Rule seldom invoked the heir's portion of Nokolai's mantle. He didn't need to. The clan respected him, and they felt the mantle's presence even when it rested quietly within him. But he knew how. He knew, too, that once invoked, the mantle wouldn't let him leave what he began unfinished. That was its nature.

Lily, Cullen, and Cynna ranged themselves behind Rule, staying several feet back. Cullen knew what to do and, more to the point, what not to do. Lily and Cynna had promised not to interfere, but Rule wasn't sure he could depend on Lily's word if things went badly.

He'd have to make sure they didn't.

Alex straightened, his arms at his side, his face expressionless. "Why are you here, Nokolai?"

Rule reached inside with his attention, touching the more restless of the two mantles. Power flexed within him like a wild thing waking—flexed and rose, sending a physical rush through his body. And unbidden, the familiar mantle came roaring up, too, mingling with the new one, the twinned magics making every hair on his body bristle as the night turned sharp and achingly brilliant.

That wasn't part of the plan—but oh, the heady rhythm of it, like the moon's own song, but utterly physical. And his. His. It sang within him, the certain knowledge that he could not be defeated.

Not that the mantles bestowed invulnerability or some illusion of it. He knew he could die tonight. His plans could fail; he could meet with disaster. But neither death nor disaster was defeat to the mantles.

He walked up to Alex. The air was thick with *seru*, the scent of aggression and dominance. "I come, Alex Thibodaux, as heir of your clan while the Rho is incapacitated, unable to lead. I come to command you."

He sensed more than saw Brady's movement—and that the men on either side of him held him back. He ignored them. Brady was no threat at this moment. Everything depended on Alex.

If the heir can't command the strongest fighter, he can't be Rho.

Rule had no desire to become the Leidolf Rho, but he had to command this one man, whom the others would follow. And Alex had to know he could be commanded. Rule looked Alex in the eye and waited.

Alex was alpha. He didn't back down readily but stood stiff, his hands fisting, his own gaze steady. "Why do you come, Nokolai?" he demanded again.

"I come because the enemy of all lupi seeks to destroy us, and has killed the former heir to Leidolf. I come to call Leidolf to the hunt. You are Lu Nuncio. You know this is necessary. You know I have the right. You will accept my lead of the hunt."

A moment longer Alex met his gaze, then slowly his eyes dropped. Slowly he lowered himself to one knee and bent his head, baring his nape. "I accept your lead . . . heir of Leidolf."

Brady made a strangled noise. Rule looked at him, and Brady's gaze dropped, too. One by one he looked at the other three men. One by one they looked down.

Two-mantled. The power was heady . . . and a little frightening. These men weren't his clan and would normally be his enemies, yet at a glance from him they became his.

He was definitely going to ask Cullen about that Etorri tale.

The mantles were subsiding now that the others had acknowledged his dominance, but they jittered within him, uneasy. He soothed them the way he imagined a rider might calm a restless horse, then touched Alex's exposed nape, accepting the man's submission. "Rise."

Alex flowed to his feet. "I've loaded your weapons back in the trunk of your car, like you asked. Tank's full. Hennings brought his climbing gear, and we have our own weapons. You've got a map and a plan, you said. I'd like to see the one and hear the other."

THEY reached their rendezvous at ten minutes after four in the morning—the entrance to a trail with more ruts and overgrowth than road. The ocean was near and the sound and scent of it steadied Rule's heart. He thought Lily would find some comfort in the ageless rhythm, too. Even in hell, she'd been glad to have the ocean near.

Cullen had slept on the way to Nutley, then driven the last leg of the trip so Rule could sleep. Rule knew how to shut down before battle, and he'd done so, but he suspected it had taken Lily longer to fall asleep. Still, she did sleep; he woke her as they slowed.

The Suburban pulled up behind them. Alex, Brady, and the others got out. They'd travel the rest of the way on foot.

The trail struck out straight through scrubby trees for half a mile, then dropped steeply through rocky outcroppings to end at a narrow beach. Jiri was waiting there, as promised. Her demon familiar was nowhere in sight, though Cynna had told them he was near.

"This way," Jiri said abruptly and led them down the beach.

On their right, the ocean hushed itself ceaselessly, the wind from it steady and cold. Rule kept an arm around Lily while he could, willing some of his warmth into her. He wished fiercely he could have left her out of this.

She wouldn't thank him for that. She was a warrior, and both her skills and her Gift would be needed. But immunity to magic didn't render her immune to teeth, claws, or bullets.

He knew Cullen was finding Cynna's involvement every bit as difficult to face, though for a different reason . . . or perhaps not so different. Love had many forms, and Rule didn't doubt his friend treasured the life so newly begun.

On their left the land rose, rocky and rough, until they stood at the base of a cliff rearing fifty feet above. Jiri stopped, looked them over, and spoke for the second time. "You were late."

"I don't know how you travel these days," Cynna said caustically, "but we had to use cars. You knew we were here once the electricity went out."

The woman gave her a measured look, then dismissed her to speak to Cullen. "The wards start at the top of the cliff."

He tilted his head back. "I see them."

"Do you, now? And will you be able to disengage them?"

"I've got sorcerous vision, not eagle's vision," he snapped. "They're fifty feet up. I'll need to be a little closer to study them. But I expect I'll be able to shut them down and let your pet in."

"So confident," she murmured, looking up herself for a moment. The house wasn't visible from here, but the fence was—probably not to human eyes, but the moon provided plenty of light for him.

The house might be out of sight, but they knew it was dark. They'd stopped a few miles away at a transformer that supplied electricity to the area. Cullen had fried it, eliminating the regular alarm system. He'd deal with the magical one, too—the wards only he could see.

"It's time," Rule said. He didn't grab Lily for a last kiss. It wouldn't be their last, he promised himself. But he rested his hands on her hips and looked at her, just looked at her, for a long moment. "Lady's luck to you," he said at last.

She smiled, stretched up, and gave him a quick kiss. "And to you." She shouldered the AK-47 Alex had returned to them and melted off into the trees.

A sensitive couldn't be stopped by wards. Nor would she set them off.

Tonight was the only night Jiri could mount an attack, so surprise wasn't possible. Cordoba would be expecting someone to drop by. It was up to them to fulfill that expectation . . . in an unexpected way.

Lily would work her way around to the front and wait for Rule's call. When she got it, she'd go in alone. Cordoba had a security system but no backup power, so it would be inactive. In addition to the machine gun, Lily had a key to the front door and a small charm, made by the child's mother from a lock of her hair. It should lead Lily to the little girl.

The rest of them would climb the cliff and engage whatever demons took an interest. Jiri and her demon would join the action from a different point once the wards were down, creating all the distraction one might wish, giving Lily a chance to find the little girl before she could be used to stop the rest of them.

Rule's stomach clenched. It was Benedict's plan, and a good one. He hated it. "You ready?" he said curtly to Cullen.

Cullen finished blacking his face with the goo Benedict's light-skinned guards used for night duty. "Done." He tossed the small can to Rule and turned to Cynna. "Kiss for luck?"

She hesitated, then grabbed his face with both hands and gave him what he'd asked for. Thoroughly. Then she stepped back, frowning. "You're crazy, but watch your back anyway, okay?"

His grin flashed. Then he jogged to the cliff and began climbing. Alex followed him up. He would stand watch while Cullen worked on the wards and call Rule when they were down. Then Rule would call Lily.

Rule began spreading the goo over his own face and the backs of his hands. He passed the can to Cynna. "Slather up." He looked at the heftiest of the Leidolf men. "Hennings."

Not all of their equipment came from Benedict's hoard. The climbing rope Hennings brought was his own. He began hooking it to the harness Cynna wore. He would be her anchor.

Cynna grimaced. "I keep telling you I don't need that."

"You'll humor me."

She rolled her eyes and pulled on the black stocking cap they'd picked up at an all-night Wal-Mart along the way.

Eveyone still on the ground was fair enough to need to darken his face. Rule passed the little can around, getting a sense of how each man dealt with his fear. Alex had chosen well, he thought. He got no more than a whiff of fear scent from any of them. Even Brady.

Brady did sneer at him when he accepted the can. "If you've brought us out here on a wild-goose chase, I'll rip your face off and spit in it when I Challenge."

Rule didn't bother to answer. Brady meant to kill him regardless of the outcome tonight. He just hoped the man wasn't so mad for blood he'd try it before they killed their mutual enemy.

There was nothing left but the waiting. He hunkered down to do that, but glanced up at the top of the cliff. He couldn't spot Cullen or Alex, which was reassuring. The wind off the ocean would carry their scent toward the house, but demons didn't have a very good sense of smell. That had been one of the advantages he had over Gan, much resented by the little demon. But it had resented everything about Rule.

He shivered. Mostly he tried not to think much about the time they'd spent in hell, but tonight, looking up the cliff, the memories were suddenly fresh. There'd been a cliff there, too, higher than this one, rearing above their cave.

The cliff that killed Lily. While he lay useless, unconscious, she'd raced to the edge and—

His shoulders bunched as he pulled himself up, his left foot automatically finding a toehold in the stone. He froze.

God. It had happened again.

After a few seconds he looked up. The edge of the cliff lay about ten feet up. Cullen waited there; he caught a glimpse of his friend's face peering down. He checked to the side, then below. Several dark shapes were following him up. He had to keep moving.

Methodically he did, his mind racing. This was one helluva time for Cullen's charm to lose its potency. Even if it had quit altogether, though, he probably wouldn't have another blackout right away—the most he'd experienced was two in one day, and they'd been widely spaced.

But was he willing to bet everyone's lives on that assumption?

He didn't have a choice, he realized as he heaved himself up onto the thin strip of ground next to the chain-link fence. The Leidolf men wouldn't follow Cullen or Cynna, and Cullen wouldn't follow the Leidolf Lu Nuncio. Rule was only one who could hold their party together, and there was no way to call things off.

God. He hoped he'd done everything the way he'd planned. He didn't remember one second of it, but he had to assume he'd called Lily.

Cullen crouched beside him. "Problem?"

Alex was keeping watch; Rule saw him crouched beside the hole he'd cut in the fence a few yards away. "It stinks of demon here."

"They're around. None close right now, but a couple of red-eyes have been pacing the perimeter. Alex should smell them if they get close, even if they're dashtu." He added under the tongue, *What's wrong?*

Another blackout.

Cullen's startled face said more than he put into words. *Do you remember what you're doing here?*

I didn't lose that much time. The last thing I remember . . . He swallowed. His last memory had been a memory itself. *It hit shortly after you reached the top and cleared up while I was climbing.*

Fifteen or twenty minutes, then.

Rule nodded. *Don't speak of this.*

We're still going in?

Lily's probably already in.

Cullen nodded and moved away, making room for the next man to pull himself over the edge. It was Hennings. Cynna followed a few moments, later, winded and trying not to show it. Cullen went to unclip the rope and help her pull off the climbing harness. The others reached them quickly. Cynna had been slowest, of course; however fit, she couldn't climb as quickly as a lupus.

"The wards?" Rule said to Cullen—low, but not subvocal.

Cullen answered the same way. "I made a hole in them to match the one in the fence. We can cross there without setting off any alarms, but I couldn't shut them off entirely without alerting Cordoba. They're good," he said grudgingly, "damned good, with plenty of power behind them."

"Enough to stop Jiri's oversize pet?"

"I'm no expert on the pet, but probably."

"*Can* you shut them down?"

"Sure. I'll need to be close, though—within thirty feet or so. And Cordoba will know."

"We'll be more distracting if he knows we're here, but hold off until we're on the other side of the fence."

The hole wasn't large. Rule went first, staying low when he reached the other side. The others crawled through one at a time, their weapons held carefully; Rule was pleased by the way the Leidolf men moved; they'd been well trained. Cynna came last, and almost as quietly as the lupi.

The house was a long, low bungalow. It lay about half the length of a football field away with nothing but dirt and grass between them. On the left, trees climbed the slope toward the house, stopping forty feet from the south wall. To the north, as in front of them, there was only grass, dry and stubby from a late mowing. No cover, and dead grass was hard to cross silently.

Good thing they weren't really trying to sneak up. He wanted to get closer before engaging the enemy, though, if they could. He motioned for them to follow and started across the field, crouching low, his rifle held ready.

All at once Cullen straightened and sang out, "Incoming!" He flung out a hand.

Fire bloomed in the night. Something screeched in pain. In the sudden glow Rule saw what looked like darker masses of air speeding toward them from the north end of the fence line.

"Hennings—Robbins—now!" He fit his rifle to his shoulder and fired into the almost-visible demons charging them. The loud *crack* from his gun was followed quickly by others, even as the two he'd named Changed.

"Holy shit!" Cynna cried. Rule spared her a quick glance and saw her looking straight up—at a nightmare diving at them out of the sky.

The creature's wingspan was easily forty feet. It was fanged and leathery, the reptilian head made up mostly of jaws. It had a compact body and muscular hindquarters powering short legs that ended in huge talons, and Rule had seen its like before.

In hell. Gan called them Xitil's pets. "Hit it with your spell!" Rule yelled, aiming up.

"It's not a goddamned demon!"

Holy shit was right. "Hennings, Robbins," he called to the two wolves. "Keep the others off us. Everyone with weapons, fire at the big guy. Cullen—the wards." Rule shot at the creature's head, but it was diving so fast he missed.

At the last minute it swerved to the north. He tracked it with his weapon, firing again—and he hit it. He was sure he did, and the others were firing, too. It never faltered, swooping and grabbing one of the wolves in its talons.

The wolf's weight didn't bother it any more than the bullets had. The enormous wings beat strongly, and it soared up.

The red-eyes were almost on them, though Hennings ran in front, trying to draw them off. They popped into full visibility twenty feet away even as Robbins's dying howls faded overhead. Rule howled, too, in sheer rage and charged the red-eye in the lead. It checked, disconcerted, but only for a second. Then it leaped.

He fired right into the gaping jaws. The back of its head exploded.

He spun, rifle ready, but the other two red-eyes were circling, not attacking. He fired anyway.

"Stop! Stop, or she dies!"

That shout came from the house. Rule darted a glance that way—and froze.

A small man, dark-skinned and dapper in a brown suit, carried a bundle wrapped in a blue cloth of some sort over his shoulder. He led four other humans across the field toward them. Those four wore the hooded robes of the Azá and carried rifles . . . rifles pointed at Lily, who walked in front of them, her hands behind her back.

"He was waiting for me," Lily said. She spoke quietly, but he heard her easily across the twenty yards that separated them.

They'd been betrayed.

THIRTY-EIGHT

"**DROP** your weapons," the little man in the brown suit said, "or the sensitive is dead."

The flying nightmare swooped lower, releasing the bloody carcass in its talons. Robbins's half-eaten corpse splatted on the grass ten yards away. And Jiri's huge demon strode out of the trees with Jiri straddling his shoulders. Her supple figure swayed with the motion. She was smiling.

Lily was captured, and Toby—God, Toby! He'd failed his son, failed Lily, failed—

Rule was scarcely aware of raising his rifle, but there it was, fitted snugly to his shoulder, aimed at the dapper man's forehead, his finger on the trigger . . .

. . . he stood motionless, the rank odor of demon filling his nostrils, his arms twisted cruelly tight behind him—held there by the demon standing behind him, its breath audible and sour behind him. Jiri's demon.

Rage and fear flooded him, thick and noxious as smoke from a chemical fire. The emotions almost triggered the Change, but he fought it back, frantic to understand what had happened in the lost time.

Apparently he hadn't shot the little man . . . Cordoba? Probably. He stood directly in front of Rule but several feet away, talking to Jiri, with the two red-eyes sitting on their haunches behind them, their eyes glowing faintly.

That wasn't a bundle on Cordoba's shoulder, Rule realized. It was a child. A small child wrapped in a blue blanket.

Lily stood twenty feet to his left, still held at gunpoint by the two of the robed Azá. Rule's breath caught, broke, but he willed himslf to stillness. He had to stop reacting and think.

Where were the others? He was alive—why, he didn't know. But the others?

Cynna stood near Lily. One of the Azá was fastening her hands behind her back while another kept a gun at her temple. She was telling them things about their ancestry they might have taken exception to, but they ignored her.

Cordoba handed Jiri the child, a little girl maybe two or three years old, her rows of braids fastened with brightly colored rubber bands, her soft, round face slack with sleep. Jiri cradled her close and turned away, bending her head over the child . . . hiding her face from Cordoba, maybe? For it twisted suddenly, ravaged with emotion. Her lips moved as she whispered endearments, mixing English with a language Rule didn't know.

That much had been real, then—the desperation and the love.

He twisted to the right as much as he was able in the punishing grip and glimpsed the winged creature on the ground. The folded wings poked high into the air, like a bat's; the toothed jaws were closed, the eyes half-closed.

Two still forms were pinned beneath the talons: Brady and Cullen.

Brady he recognized mainly by the pale hair. He was farthest from Rule and facedown in the dirt, most of his body hidden by the talon imprisoning him. But Hennings was the only other blond in their party, and that motionless body was too slim for Hennings.

Cullen's face was turned toward Rule. Blood made a mask of it, but not so thoroughly that Rule didn't know him. But . . . yes, his eyes were closed. Relief rushed in. The eyes of the dead were always open.

What about Alex? And Hennings, and Bryan? The mantles stirred in him, urging him to take action. He was responsible for them. But he couldn't see them, couldn't look for them—couldn't remember, damn it all to hell. Maybe he'd known what became of them ten minutes ago. He didn't now.

"Is that the daughter we were supposed to rescue?" Lily asked in her cool, cop's voice. "Looks like you cut your deal with Cordoba before you talked to us, Jiri. Is that why Cynna's binding didn't work?"

"Very good, Miss Yu," Cordoba said. Though he spoke perfect English, there was a Spanish flavor to his voice. "You couldn't bind Jiri to her word, for she's wholly mine." He smiled. "I heard it all, of course."

Jiri straightened, her face smoothing until it held only a light, mocking smile. "Tommy's a far-hearer. A rare Gift in a rare man."

"Jiri." He shook his head. "Do they need to know that?"

"Why not?" She turned that mocking smile on Rule. "Almost everything I told you was true. I simply fudged a bit on the timing. When I was unable to recruit the sorcerer, I accepted Tommy's terms. I'm bound to him now."

Cynna made a small, choked sound. When Rule looked at her, though, her face was impassive. "It's not the same kind of binding I did. She means that she's his creature, just as the demon is hers. She's unable to act against him, or refuse to do what he tells her."

Cordoba ran a possessive hand up Jiri's arm. "She fought me, didn't you, *querida*? I knew she would. Just as I knew I would win in the end. But it's not so bad as you expected, is it? I let you have your way with some things—though I would like to know why you didn't want the unnecesary ones killed."

Jiri shook her head. "So wasteful, Tommy. You really must learn to plan ahead. A sorcerer—he *is* still alive, isn't he?—has obvious uses."

"Not if he's busy trying to kill us . . . though I suppose we might find a way to cure him of it. Or *She* may be able to. But why bother? She only needs the sensitive."

"It may be years before She locates the Codex and can copy it. In the meantime, She's shut out of this realm, and our power is limited."

They were after the Codex. No surprise that the Great Bitch was aware of its return, but what did that have to do with Lily?

Cordoba stroked her arm. "You hope to find something in the Codex to free yourself, don't you, *querida*? It's not possible, but you'll work so hard to find it. And when you do, you'll tell me."

"Don't gloat, sugar. It makes your eyes look beady." Jiri shifted the sleeping child gently, moving her to her other shoulder. She saw Rule watching and gave him a lazy smile. "Poor Rule. He's so confused. Why don't we explain it all to him? I think he deserves to know."

Cordoba cracked a small smile. "What did he do to make you so angry? If it amuses you, though . . ." His hand drifted to her ass. "You see how good I can be to you?"

She laughed low in her throat. "You're good for many things, Tommy. Maybe I will forgive you for the binding . . . eventually." She tilted her head, looking at Rule again. "You weren't surprised when I mentioned the Codex."

"You aren't the only one who knows about it."

"You see, Tommy?" she said without looking away from Rule. "There's information we wouldn't have had if we'd killed him right away. Do you want to know why we need Lily, Rule Turner?"

His mouth was dry. "Yes."

"It's the goddess who needs her, actually. Apparently the Codex is guarded in some way that will make it difficult to access once it's in Her possession. So She needs to make a copy, one without the built-in defenses. But it seems there's only one . . . what shall we call it? Receptacle. Only one type of receptacle suitable to hold the Codex Arcanum. A sensitive with her mind wiped clean—"

"—not going to tell you again, Turner," Cordoba was saying. "I've no pressing reason not to kill you now. Jiri may think *She* has some use for you, but I doubt it. I'd have her get Tish to do it. He likes to pull things apart."

The side of Rule's head, from crown to jaw, ached fiercely. His brain felt like mush, and his shoulders were on fire . . . because he was hanging inches off the ground, held up by the demon's grip on his arms.

He'd been struck, he realized through the fog of pain. He must have done something, tried to get at Cordoba.

And failed. They were going to wipe Lily's mind clean, and he'd failed her. Again. He closed his eyes and could have sworn he smelled the stale, dry air of hell. For a moment he was *there* in that moonless realm once more, and losing the moon's song was like losing breath yet still living. He hadn't died. He'd kept going, kept trying to breathe when there was no air for his soul—

"Rule?" Lily's voice was urgent.

He shuddered back to the present. "I'm . . ." His voice came out slurred. He'd bitten his tongue when he was hit, and it was swollen. He swallowed bloody saliva. "I'm okay. More or less."

Abruptly his feet hit the ground, landing hard enough that his knees started to buckle.

Cordoba looked at Jiri. "I didn't tell you to have Tish lower him."

Jiri wasn't looking at him, but behind Rule and his mountainous captor. "I saw something moving. I thought—"

He took two steps and slapped her hard enough to rock her back a step. "You didn't ask. Thinking is fine—I encourage you to think—but always ask, Jiri. Always."

Blood dripped from her lip, badly split from his blow. She looked at him without expression. The little girl in her arms never stirred. "Two of them got away. They could be circling back."

"Very well. We should make sure of them. But I want Tish here." He glanced over his shoulder. The two red-eyes rose and loped off.

The others weren't all dead. Two had gotten away. Hope stirred in Rule—and so did the mantles. Already restless, they seemed to be pulling at him as if they wanted something of him. Action, yes, they wanted him to take action . . . but it felt as if there was a specific action he should take.

"My arms are tired," Jiri said abruptly.

"Already weary of motherhood, *querida*?"

"My arms ache." She bent, placing the little girl carefully on the ground, making sure the blanket stayed wrapped around her.

"We'll be going inside in a moment anyway. I don't think the others are out there—the *tzmai* haven't found them, and I don't hear anything." Cordoba looked at the winged creature. "I suppose I should send Melli up to make sure."

"Best secure the sorcerer first. Make sure he isn't feigning unconsciousness." Jiri rubbed her arms, then sauntered toward Lily, Cynna, and their guards.

"I don't think I'll keep him," Cordoba said. "Too much trouble."

"As you wish, of course. But if the bindings I've been working on prove effective—"

"You think you can bind him, even without his cooperation?" That caught Cordoba's attention. "You've made some progress, but the woman used to be your apprentice. You've no such entry with the sorcerer."

"It will take awhile," she agreed. "You may not wish me to spend so much time on the project. But at least I won't have to work on him astrally, as I did with Cynna. And if we remove his hands and tongue, he shouldn't be too troublesome a guest."

"He'll grow them back . . . but we could keep removing them until you had him bound."

"Or until I find that I can't bind him." She stopped in front of Cynna. "Such loathing," she said lightly. "But aren't you happy to find you were right? Aside from a lingering case of maternal devotion, I *am* evil." She looked at Cordoba. "Shall we see if my binding works with this one? We can always shoot her if it doesn't."

Bile rose in Rule's throat, burning. So did rage: hard, red, and caustic. He needed to—had to—

Change. He had to Change.

He shook his head. It wouldn't help. He'd be free of the demon's grip, yes—nothing could hold on to him during the Change. But the disorientation was too strong for the first second or two immediately afterward. The demon would simply grab him again before he could move.

"Yes," Cordoba said decisively. "If it doesn't work, I won't bother keeping the sorcerer. If it does, though . . . go ahead. See what you can do with her."

"I'll need her hand." She held hers out.

"You're lying," Cynna said, her head high. "You can't bind me without my consent."

"I made you ride, didn't I?" Jiri looked at the guards. "Well? I need her right hand. Find some other way to secure her while I work."

"Do it," Cordoba said.

One of the guards held a gun to Cynna's head while the other one unfastened the handcuffs and jerked her left arm into a modified half nelson.

"Hold out your hand, Cynna," Jiri said.

"Go to hell, Jiri."

Jiri made an impatient noise. "Tommy, I need Beecher to hold her hand out and steady for me. Surely one guard is sufficient for the sensitive."

"No. By now she realizes we don't want to kill her. She might try something."

"She's handcuffed. Make her lie down on her stomach and threaten her lover if she moves."

Cordoba hesitated, but gave the orders. Rule was beginning to wonder . . . Jiri was bound to the man, but she was twice as smart. She seemed to be getting everything she wanted from him.

A few moments later Lily lay on her stomach in the dead grass. One of the Azá still guarded her, but the other fought to bring Cynna's arm forward. It took him a few moments, but he managed to hold her hand out, palm up.

"Good." Jiri rested her own hand on top of Cynna's. "Be ready to hold her up," she added. "She'll probably collapse."

"You didn't," Cordoba said.

"I consented." Jiri closed her eyes. She whispered something in that other language, the words soft and singsong. Cynna's eyes widened—then rolled back in her head. She went limp.

And the demon let go of Rule.

Pain roared from his shoulders down to his fingers in a white-hot sheet. But he didn't move his arms, though his abused muscles trembled and twitched with the strain of holding them back. He prayed desperately he was right—

"Did it work?" Cordoba demanded. "Wake her up. Make her . . . oh, make her kill the one Melli has pinned. Not the sorcerer. The other one."

The demon stepped out from behind Rule, but he moved clumsily, as if he'd forgotten how his muscles worked. A fierce joy seized Rule. He'd been right. He just had to hold on a moment longer, see which target—

Cordoba's back was to them, but one of the Azá saw. "Sir," a gravelly voice said, "The big demon—"

"What?" Cordoba snapped—but he glanced over his shoulder.

The demon lumbered into an awkward run. Straight for Cordoba.

Change.

Yes. Rule reached for the moonsong and threw himself into it. The pain in his shoulders vanished, subsumed by the familiar, rippling agony of the Change.

Cordoba's eyes widened. "Shoot her!" he cried, then slapped the barrel of the rifle pointed at Lily. "Not her, fool! Jiri! Shoot her!"

Jiri stepped away from Cynna. She was smiling, her eyes alight with triumph as one, two, all three rifles went off.

And the Change went on. And on. *Wrong,* shouted some yet-human pocket of him. Something was wrong. It was taking too long. The pain was huge, and the mantles—the mantles were—

Jiri was on the ground. Lily was moving, rolling into the legs of the man closest to her.

Lily! He tried to wrest back control from the mantles, but the Change had never been his to order. He could only—

Surrender.

He let go and blinked out, and then he wasn't.

And then he was. He stood and panted with his head hanging, remembered pain shuddering through him, though this body no longer hurt. But his front legs were weak, the joints throbbing. The scents of blood and demons were strong in his nostrils, but he couldn't think. He shook his head to clear it, but something was wrong. Different.

Never mind. He had to get to Lily.

But the demon already had. It tossed aside one of the Azá, then another—still clumsy, but moving faster, as if its rider was getting the hang of the massive body. Cordoba screeched and ran toward the house.

And the winged creature stirred.

Cordoba, Rule thought. He had to stop Cordoba, who controlled the creature.

But the wolf didn't want Cordoba. The wolf wanted the monster that spread its wings—not for flight, but for balance as it ran toward the two women and the demon defending them.

The demon was big, compared to a man. Not compared to the winged nightmare. And the demon's rider wasn't familiar with the body.

Rule snarled and threw himself at the beast. He wouldn't fail her this time.

It was fast. He was faster. It checked its charge when it saw him, stretching out one great wing, trying to sweep him away with it. He avoided it easily, so it tried to club him with the knobby bone at the hinge. He flattened, rolled, coming to his feet near the body. It tried stepping on him, but it was ungainly on the ground. He dashed around the taloned foot and darted beneath the belly to its other side.

The belly didn't tempt him. He needed the throat. He readied himself, haunches bunching, and leaped.

The head darted at him, jaws gaping. Rule twisted in midair so that his side smashed into the teeth rather than being seized by them. The impact stunned him, though, and he fell badly when he dropped. Pain shot up his left front leg when he stood, making him stumble. Those jaws descended on him, the breath rank and hot.

He'd learned how to run on three legs in hell. He did that now, racing beneath the belly, and spun the second he was shielded by the beast's body, darting between the legs to stand in front of it. And once more launched himself up—almost straight up, at its throat.

The man was screaming that this was wrong, he couldn't hang on to that leathery skin long enough to do any damage. But the wolf *knew*. If he could sink his teeth in that throat—

He struck, mouth gaping, and clamped his jaws shut through hide and flesh, holding on with every ounce of his strength. And hung there, fifteen feet from the ground. The creature snapped at him but couldn't reach him. It flung itself sideways, trying to throw him off. His body slapped to one side, then the other, but he hung on, his teeth meeting in sour flesh. And convulsed.

Huge, wrenching contractions seized him, spasms that pumped acid through his body—acid forced by the spasm up into his throat. He went blind with pain, blackness swarming over his vision, but he hung on as muscles he'd never felt before squeezed tight in his upper throat and jaw, pumping the acid out. Out of him and into the beast.

It howled. Then it, too, convulsed.

The contractions of those enormous muscles were too much for him. He lost his grip and fell, hitting the ground hard. He tried to scramble to his feet, but he was weak, so weak. When he accidentally put weight on the damaged leg, it buckled. Darkness flickered around the edges of his vision.

One of the taloned feet smashed into him, sending him skidding across dirt and grass. The blow knocked out his air. Consciousness wisped to a thin thread . . . He blinked. The creature was collapsing. The foot that had struck him had saved him from being buried beneath that great body as it crashed down, wings akimbo, head stretched out flat and motionless on the ground.

Eyes open and staring. Dead.

For several moments he just lay there and breathed. He was alive. He hurt everywhere, but he was alive. That seemed so starkly incredible he couldn't take it in. And Lily . . . Lily was coming to him.

He managed to turn his head so he could see her running awkwardly toward him, her hands still bound behind her. For a second—just a second—he saw two of her. Both Lilys were running to him: the one who'd known him mostly as a man, and the one who'd known him only as a wolf.

A joy so keen it blanked out all the pains of his body filled him. His head went light with it.

Then he simply passed out.

He came to with her kneeling beside him, crying and cursing the handcuffs and ordering him to wake up. He couldn't smile well in this form, but he tried.

"Rule! Damn these handcuffs," she muttered. "I can't touch you, can't check to see what . . . but you're alive. You'll stay that way," she told him. "Hang on a little longer, and we'll be able to get help. Cynna's back from wherever she was. I guess she was riding, but she's parked the demon now. He's just sitting there, not moving. Cordoba's dead."

How—?

She knew what he meant to ask. "The others got him. Hennings or Alex, I don't know which. They'd hidden inside the house, waiting for a chance to help. I think Jiri knew. She steered Cordoba's attention to the field, didn't she? To the cliff we came up and away from the house. She . . ." Her breath hitched. "She's dying."

He'd thought her already dead.

Alex limped up. Blood covered one side of his body, but Rule's nose told him it wasn't all his. "Three of the Azá are dead," he said. "The other's got a cracked skull, I think, but he might live. The other two demons, the overgrown hyenas, winked out when Cordoba died. I don't know how to tell if they're still around, though. How . . ." His voice caught. "How in the bloody hell did you kill that thing?"

Rule was in charge. He needed a voice and words for that. Drawing on the last of his power, he called up the Change.

And, seconds later, he lay gasping for breath in the cold night air. Normally cold didn't bother him, but he was too damned weak. He forced himself to sit. His left arm hung limp; the bone was broken just above the elbow. He hurt in places he didn't remember injuring. "Get the keys for the handcuffs," he told Alex. "The Azá who unlocked Cynna's cuffs probably has them. Where's Hennings? Robbins?"

Alex gave him a funny look. "You saw Robbins killed."

"My memory of recent events has some gaps."

"Hennings is hurt," the man told him, "but not badly. He'll probably be able to walk soon."

"All right. Bring us the keys, then see about our wounded. Cullen and Brady." Cullen had still been alive earlier. He was tough. Surely . . .

Alex nodded and took off at an uneven run.

"The girl," Rule said suddenly, remembering. "Jiri's daughter."

"Cynna has her," Lily said quietly. "Jiri . . . wanted to see her. She's still sleeping."

Toby. If Jiri died before removing her spell—Rule lurched to his feet, then swayed.

"Put your arm over my shoulders," Lily said.

"I don't—"

"Yes, you do need help," she snapped. "You've been a big enough hero for one night. I'm not injured. Lean on me so we can get over there and talk to Jiri."

He did. And she was right; it did help to lean on her a bit. Not just because of the physcial aid, but the peace of the mate bond eased through him.

He'd seen her. He'd seen both of her. The other Lily wasn't lost.

"How did you do that?" she asked softly. "How did you kill it? I thought . . ." She shuddered.

"The poison. The mantles." He shook his head, knowing he wasn't making sense to her. Though it all made sense to him now.

It was the wolf who'd hung on to the demon poison, the wolf's guilt over failing Lily that made it impossible to let go. And the man's need for control, he admitted, that made it impossible to understand. If he'd spent more time as wolf, he might have known, but the wolf felt he deserved to lose his memory, just as Lily had lost her memory of him.

Most of it, anyway. When she died. The part that lived on, her soul, remembered, but the Lily he spoke with and made love with had only brief flashes of memory from their time in hell.

It was the wolf who'd known how to expiate that guilt, but it was the two mantles that made it possible.

"Somehow the mantles affected the Change," he said slowly. "I don't understand it. I didn't know it was possible. Maybe it was the combination of mantles, demon poison, and the mate bond . . . I'm pretty sure there hasn't been another lupus with that mix acting on him before. I grew fangs. Real, hollow fangs, the kind a viper uses. I pumped the creature full of demon poison. It died, and . . . the poison's gone."

"You're sure?" Startled, she stopped. "Kiss me. I can't touch you because of these damned cuffs. Kiss me and let me check."

He smiled. "What an excellent idea." He bent, cupping her cheek with his good hand, and kissed her gently.

When he straightened, her eyes were wide. "It's gone. It's really gone."

Relief shivered through him. He'd been sure . . . almost sure. It helped to know Lily couldn't feel the poison anymore.

They started walking again. "It's beyond weird, but makes a certain bizarre sense. The poison was intended to kill other demons. That creature wasn't a demon, but it was from hell. It probably had a similar body chemistry."

Alex found the keys just as they reached the others. He unlocked Lily's cuffs, and she gasped in pain as her arms fell forward. Rule knew just how much it hurt, but she just shook her head at him and helped him over to Jiri.

The woman shouldn't have been alive. She had two bloody holes high in her chest and a much bigger one in her abdomen. An exit wound, he thought. One of the guards had shot her in the back. The dirt around her was wet and sticky with her blood.

Cynna sat beside her, holding the little girl, and Jiri held the girl's hand. Her eyes tried to find him as Lily helped him sit, but he could see death hazing them. He doubted she saw much.

"It's Rule," he said.

"Ah." Her voice was faint. Her eyes drifted closed, and she smiled. "Tommy's dead."

"Yes," Cynna said. Rule saw her throat work as she swallowed.

"Should've listened to you, Cynna, but I liked the power too much. Couldn't do what I wanted without an apprentice, but by then the only kind I could get were worse than me." Her voice faded, but she got her eyes open again, searching through what must be pure darkness to her. "Rule Turner."

"Here. I'm right here."

"Want you to take my Cece, raise her as clan. She needs protection. Damn that Tommy." Hatred momentarily strenghtened her voice. "Her own father, and he was ready to give her up to the Great Bitch."

"Cordoba was her father?" Cynna said, startled.

"Bastard. Thought he had me . . . damn near did. I couldn't disobey, but who taught him those bindings? I kept a little back. Not much, but it was enough. Rule." Her eyes shifted, sought his blindly. "You'll take my daughter as clan. The goddess wants her. You'll take her, or your son will never wake."

"I'd have seen to her welfare without the threat," he said evenly. "Even with it, I'll see she's adopted into the clan. I'd not let *Her* get Her hands on a child."

Her mouth twisted. "Habit . . . sorry. Your son woke before we attacked."

He jerked slightly in surprise.

"Told you—I don't harm children. Knew I wouldn't come out of this alive."

"Your daughter still sleeps."

"Cece . . . different spell. She'll wake at dawn." A tremor ran through her mangled body. "Tish can't hold me here much longer. More to say, but . . . Cece's Gift. You need to know about it. Same as mine, and strong."

"What's your Gift?" Cynna asked. "Are you a far-seer?"

Something like a chuckle shook her, sending another, harder tremor through her. "All of you always wanted to know, didn't you? I'm a patterner. One hell of a patterner. That's how I found your son, Rule," she added, her lids drooping over eyes that looked dead already, though she continued to speak. "Tweaked the patterns . . . tweaked the hell out of them tonight, too. Tish." Her free hand twitched. "Tish . . ."

The huge demon rose and lumbered over. Rule and Lily scrambled out of the way, but Cynna didn't move. The demon stopped inches from Jiri.

"Ah—did you bring him over here?" Rule asked Cynna.

Cynna shook her head. Her face was wet with tears she'd cried so silently he hadn't noticed. "She let me ride, truly ride this time. She couldn't order Tish to do things Tommy didn't allow, so she gave me control. But she's still master."

"Tish." Jiri's head turned and her free hand moved a few inches, coming to rest on the demon's huge foot. Her mouth turned up, and her face eased with what might have been affection.

Her other hand, which had held on to her daughter's so long, relaxed. Her body sank into the full stillness of death. And the demon vanished.

"It's gone?" Lily asked sharply.

Cynna nodded. "Back to Dis. When the master dies, the demon can't . . ." She shut her eyes, looking horribly weary. "Cullen? Is he . . ."

"Not too perky," Cullen said from behind Rule and several feet away. "But still around."

Relief flooded Rule. He turned to see his friend being carried by Henning, who'd Changed back to human at some point. Henning was limping, but not badly. There was so much dried blood on his leg Rule couldn't see the wound itself, but it didn't seem to trouble the man much.

It was obvious why he had to carry Cullen. One of Cullen's feet was missing, along with part of his calf.

"Jesus!" Cynna shoved to her feet.

"He's okay," Hennings said, sounding surprised. "Lost too much blood—that's why he passed out. Once his body got it scabbed over, he could start replacing the blood, though he needs some fluids. He's hardly scratched otherwise."

Cynna just stood there, shaking her head. She still held the child but seemed almost to have forgotten that.

"It's hard to get used to, isn't it?" Lily said dryly. "The way they are with injuries, I mean. But he'll grow everything back."

"It will take forever," Cullen said morosely. "And it hurts like bloody blue blazes."

"Take him in the house and find somewhere he can lie down," Rule said. "Where's Alex?"

"Looking for Brady," Hennings said as he switched course for the house. "After the creature let go, he apparently wandered off. Alex thinks he took a pretty good blow to the head. He may be confused."

Or a coward, Rule thought. Or just pleased to leave and let Cordoba handle killing Rule for him.

"Have you got your phone?" Lily asked. "We need to get some help here, and Cordoba took mine."

Automatically he felt at his waist. The movement sent a sharp pain through his broken arm, and he gritted his teeth, riding it out. Pity he hadn't gotten a copy of Cynna's spell.

"Rule?" Lily was there, slipping an arm around his waist, but carefully, as if she weren't sure where she could touch without hurting.

She was right. He winced as she accidentally pressed against sore ribs. "I'm okay. My phone's gone. I don't know when . . ." He looked around. Easier to find one in the house, he decided, than in the grass.

But his gaze snagged on the woman lying nearby, her dead eyes staring up. A deep sadness stole over him. What was evil? She'd caused the deaths of two of his men but saved his. And she'd given her life for her child . . . but she wouldn't have had to if she hadn't gone so far down the wrong path. Even at the end she'd fought to control everything and everyone, when she could have just asked for help.

He was aware of the lesson there. Learning it, applying it, wasn't going to be easy, but he could make a start. The pain from his arm was sweeping over him in dizzy waves. "I probably ought to sit down myself," he said abruptly, then looked down at Lily. "I could use some help getting to the house."

Her eyebrows lifted in surprise. She smiled. "Let's go."

He braced his bad arm with his good one, trying to lessen the jostling. If he didn't get it set soon, it would have to be rebroken so it could heal straight.

After a moment he raised the question that was bothering him. "I don't get it. Why did she get involved with Cordoba? She could think rings around him. He was so much less than her in every way."

"That's what she wanted. She wasn't looking for a partner, an equal. She wanted someone she could control."

That, Rule decided after a moment, was not a lesson he needed. He had a problem with trying to control too much—but what he wanted to control lay within him, not outside. And he much preferred having a partner and an equal. He smiled at the woman holding him, just as he was holding her. "Do you think—"

A gray streak raced out from the side of the house coming straight at them. Brady. In wolf form, and intending murder.

Automatically Rule pushed Lily aside so he could Change, but he was weak, his power exhausted by so much use and so many injuries. It took him precious seconds just to find the moon's song.

And Lily, damn her, put herself between him and the charging wolf. Rule snarled and grabbed at the wisp of power remaining—just as another wolf, this one jet-black with silver tips to his fur, leaped past them.

Alex. He collided with Brady, and they fell in a snarling, snapping tangle. Rule pulled Lily back several feet.

"A gun," she said when they stopped. "Come on. There are rifles back there."

He shook his head, holding her firmly so she couldn't act on her own. "Brady attacked without Challenge. Alex is Lu Nuncio. This is for him to handle."

Rule had seen Alex fight in human form, and he was good. As a wolf, though, he was brilliant. Brady was trained, and fought well—but he had no chance.

Brady might have submitted and sought mercy. He had to know he would lose. He didn't. Either he was too berserk with rage to stop, or he was sane enough to know he'd gone too far. Had he succeeded in killing Rule, the rebounding mantle would almost certainly have killed Victor. The death shock would have destroyed the clan.

Alex had no choice. In less than ten minutes, Brady was dead.

THIRTY-NINE

"I'VE been through a lot," Toby whined. "I really *need* to open a present early."

Lily paused in her frantic polishing of the mirror over the mantel. She smiled and reached out to tousle the boy's hair. "And I really need to finish cleaning the house before the house is too full for any of us to move. I think you'll survive waiting one more day."

It was two days before Christmas, and Toby's custom was to open presents on Christmas Eve. That didn't jibe with the way her own family did things, but Lily didn't care. Her parents might, but they'd jump that hurdle when it was in front of them.

After another crash and two near misses, the authorities had shut down the airports again for all nonemergency flights. The nodes were still leaking magic, and while the task force had come up with a few solutions, they were makeshift. Wall Street was functioning, and Houston had stopped burning, but the National Guard had been called out in Texas. Too many odd things had somehow crossed over during the last, and largest, power wind.

And so, unable to fly, Lily's father, mother, and younger sister were driving across the country to spend the holiday with all of them: her and Rule, Toby and Benedict, Grandmother and Li Qin and Cullen. Even Timms was invited, if he was released from the hospital in time. Lily's older sister, newly married, had, in a rare moment of rebellion, chosen to stay in California.

Lily was a nervous wreck trying to get everything ready. She was also happy.

Her mother had forgiven her and would sleep beneath Rule's roof. For her, that was a huge step toward accepting his place in Lily's life.

"But Lily," Toby said, "you get to open one early. It's not fair."

She thought of her coat and the night everything had changed, and her stomach clenched. So many had died.

"And you," Rule said from the doorway to the dining room, "are lousy about keeping secrets."

"I didn't tell!" Toby said, indignant.

Rule shook his head, but he was smiling. He looked entirely recovered, except for the sling and brace on his left arm. Lupi didn't bother with full casts unless it was a bad break, and his hadn't been. "Madame Yu wants to talk to you. She's in the kitchen."

The boy took off.

"Did Grandmother really say that?" Lily asked dryly.

"Not exactly, but she enjoys him. He's properly worshipful these days, in a pestering sort of way. Besides, she's been playing mah-jongg with Benedict."

"I take it Benedict's winning again."

Rule grinned.

Toby hadn't seen Grandmother Change, but he'd been told about it. Ever since, he'd been her happy slave. Lily understood. At his age, she'd spent all the time she could with Grandmother, too. The old woman was dictatorial, difficult, arrogant . . . and had been quite ready to die to protect a boy she barely knew. Her love for children shone with a purity they always recognized, however she tried to disguise it.

Rule came over, plucked the cleaning rag from Lily's hand, tossed it on the floor, and kissed her before she could finish forming her protest. So she didn't bother, settling into his arms as they turned to smile at the tree.

It had been delivered yesterday, fully decorated with toy drums and soldiers and such, along with hundreds of twinkling lights, just as Grandmother ordered. Presents had begun appearing under it immediately. There was a nice pile of them now.

"Grandmother wants to take Toby to the hospital tomorrow," Lily said. "She thinks a few games of mah-jongg will help Timms's recovery."

"The hospital doesn't allow children his age . . . but what am I thinking? She won't let that stop her."

Lily smiled. "How's Cullen?"

Rule had just returned from visiting his friend. They'd offered to put him up here, but he said it was too crowded. He was right. But he'd also turned down a hotel room, choosing to stay in Timms's apartment. That odd friendship seemed to be continuing; Cullen had been to visit Timms in the hospital twice, which Rule said was a record.

"Crabby as hell," Rule said. "He's especially pissed that it was his right foot, which makes it hard to drive."

"Drive? Rule, he can't be thinking of driving yet!"

"Has Cynna made up her mind about Christmas Eve?"

The change of subject told Lily that Cullen was probably not just considering driving, but doing it. She frowned, but decided not to argue. She'd inevitably lose. "I haven't heard from her, but she said she'd let us know by tonight."

They'd invited Cynna for the big family bash tomorrow night. Lily had stressed that she wasn't to feel obligated to come; it would be loud and crowded, and her family and Rule's weren't going to blend easily. But she hated to think of Cynna spending the night alone.

Or mostly alone. In a remarkable display of the power of denial, Cynna still insisted she wasn't pregnant. She wouldn't use a pregnancy test kit, either. But sooner or later, she'd have to come to terms with the fact that she and Cullen had, indeed, started a new life.

For the moment, though, she was avoiding him like crazy.

They stood there quietly, looking at the tree, soaking up the pleasure of a moment alone together. But Lily's mind wouldn't let her rest in the moment long. It picked at some of the still-tangled threads.

The leaking magic continued to cause problems, some minor, some major. Her father's predictions about the economy were dire. Lily's perspective was a little different; when the economy floundered, crime went up, and they were likely to be dealing with more Gifted criminals now. The power winds seemed to have woken Gifts in people who'd had barely a trace before. And the Unit was still stretched thin.

Then there was the whole two-mantled business. Victor was alive but comatose. He couldn't take the mantle back. The Rhejes of several clans were consulting their memories, trying to find a way to move the mantle without the Rho. If they couldn't figure something out before Victor died—he had, at most, a year left— Rule would become Rho of his clan's most bitter enemies.

Which made her think of Isen, who was all but cackling with glee at the prospect. Not the reaction she'd expected, or Rule either, from what he'd said. "It's a shame your father couldn't be here, too."

Rule looked at her. "You're a strong woman, but do you really think you're up to having your grandmother and my father beneath one roof?"

"Maybe not," she decided.

"But why?" came Toby's wail from the kitchen. "I was winning!"

Lily heard Grandmother's voice, but couldn't catch the words. Curious, she turned.

Grandmother came toward them, her figure as erect as ever. She'd already abandoned the sling, though Lily suspected she'd be more comfortable if she'd use it. Today she'd decided to wear her most traditional Chinese clothes, perhaps in honor of her son's imminent arrival: black silk pants and a silk tunic heavily embroidered in gold thread. "It is time to go," she announced.

"Go?" Lily's eyebrows shot up. "My parents will be here in less than an hour."

"A pity, but perhaps they can join us after they arrive."

Exasperated, Lily started to explain that they would not be going anywhere. "Grandmother—"

"Go where, Madam?" Rule asked softly.

"To the White House, I think." She tipped her head to one side as if listening. There was an odd softness on her face, an expression Lily didn't recognize. "Yes. We will wait at the White House."

LI LEI enjoyed her granddaughter's shock very much when her FBI person, Ruben Brooks, called to tell her which gate at the White House to use. Rule Turner was not as surprised as she would have liked, but that was a tribute to his opinion of her, so also pleasant.

Mostly, however, it was all she could do not to squirm like a child on the way there. But she managed to preserve her dignity.

Ruben Brooks had come to see her the day she was released

from the hospital. She had liked him right away and decided to confide in him, a little. Not that he believed her initially, but he was courteous and promised he would call if what she claimed would happen did, indeed, come to pass.

As of course it had.

We are nearly there, said the voice she had not heard in her head for nearly four hundred years. *You are sure they will not fire their weapons at me?*

I am told they will not, if the others do not come too close to their leader's home. She shrugged—and winced, for she was not entirely healed. *We are nearly there, too,* she told him, relieved to see the famous building drawing close.

Even with Ruben Brooks's help, there was still a great deal of security to be gotten through: guards, gates, and one who wished to search *her.* She did not allow that, which delayed things slightly, but she'd walked through their silly metal detector machine. That was enough.

Eventually, the secretary of state agreed that it would do, though the Secret Service people did not like it. Then she learned that the president herself would not come out for this first meeting.

Li Lei did not like the man who was secretary of state, but he was said to be a good bargainer. There was little challenge in dealing with a poor one, so she accepted his presence in lieu of the president's with fair grace. Then she had to explain it to Sun Mzou. He did not like it, but he, too, understood that they might fear exposing their leader to him.

In the end, Li Lei stood with Li Qin on one side and Lily on the other. She was sorry her son had not arrived in time but could not find it in her to regret her daughter-in-law's absence. Beside Lily stood Rule Turner with Toby, who was not behaving well. Too much excitement will do that to little boys. Behind them were ranged the secretary of state, Ruben Brooks, and many other official persons she did not know.

They did not have long to wait. The lights were bright all round the White House, making the sky a dead, flat black, as if the stars had hidden themselves. Out of that darkness another black shape gradually formed. He looked small at first, for he was very high. But as he descended in a beautiful spiral, his size became obvious.

As did his shape. The official persons made shocked noises,

as if they had not truly believed what their radar had told them until their eyes confirmed it.

"Oh, God," Lily whispered. "It really is him."

Slowly, as gracefully as if he managed only the weight of a butterfly on those huge wings, the black dragon, the oldest and most powerful of his kind, settled onto the South Lawn of the White House.

Li Lei's heart broke and sang, weeping joy through the pieces. She started forward, and somehow she forgot dignity, forgot her great age and all the official persons, and she ran to him.

She stopped near the huge head, which he'd lowered to greet her, his eyes glowing in a way she'd never forgotten. Though in those days, she'd been much larger . . . she rested her hand on the hard scales on his cheek. *You have a poor sense of time. You said you'd return. I did not expect to wait so long.*

You grew old.

Mortals do. Even one with dragon magic inside her.

For a long moment he said nothing, then: *Did you ever regret your decision, Li Lei?*

She felt his wistfullness, the echo of her own pain so many years ago . . . He'd wanted her to go with him, wanted it badly. She'd refused. *Every day,* she told him honestly. *And yet never.*

You had the child you craved.

Yes. The child she could not have had with him, for while he'd been able to give her much—even a form like his, for a time—he hadn't been able to give her that. *You brought my granddaughter home to me.*

She is strong and cunning. I like her. You bred well.

She swallowed and surreptitiously brushed the dampness from her eyes. *Well. We shall have time, if we wish, to talk about the old days later. Now, I think, we had best begin bargaining. That is why you wanted me here.*

That is only part of the reason, Li Lei, her first lover told her, amusement tinting the cool mental voice with rare warmth. *As you know very well. But let us begin.*

Lily turned to face the others: her family, those official persons, and the secretary of state. Pleasure suffused her.

This would be a bargaining session like no other. She would see that Sun and the others received everything they needed—gold, places to hunt, eyries of some sort. The usual things required by dragons. In return, the dragons would solve the world's crisis by doing what was as natural as breathing for them.

They would sop up magic.

That they needed the magic themselves to survive did not, in Li Lei's opinion, diminish their right to demand payment. "Mr. Secretary," she said in a clear voice, "if you will come forward, I would like to introduce you to Sun Mzao, whom some . . ." She couldn't resist a quick, undignified wink at her grandaughter and the man beside her. " . . . know as Sam."

Dear Reader,

Foxie, my fourteen-year-old Labrador retriever, is lying in the overgrown grass in the backyard, soaking up the kindness of September sunshine. She lifts her head to grin at me, doggie-fashion, then lurches to her feet.

Foxie is old. She wobbles as she makes her usual circuit of the yard, sniffing everything, scuffing up grass with a few strokes of her hind legs. As far as I can tell, her uncertain gait bothers me more than it does her. Today she has grass and sunshine. She isn't worried about her aging heart or some future day when her legs will no longer hold her. As long as I'm nearby, she's content. She trusts me completely—no holding back.

Trust is harder for us humans. By the time we're adults we've learned some of the many flavors of betrayal, disappointment, tragedy, heartbreak . . . and that's just from the nightly news. Chances are we've been force-fed a few bites of these poisons in our private lives, too. Maybe more than a few.

Cynicism comes easy. It also comes with a price.

In *Blood Lines*, Cynna and Cullen's world changed. Each of them played some part in the outward changes—the influx of magic after the power winds hit—but each is facing a personal cataclysm, too. However she tries to deny it, Cynna is carrying Cullen's child, and neither of them has any idea yet where their new reality will take them.

In the next book, *Night Season*, they find out.

An unusual messenger sends Cynna to another realm, one where magic is commonplace. Cullen goes, too—he isn't about to let her wander around Faerie without him. But their search for a missing medallion turns into a quest of another sort, and maybe these two world-class cynics aren't that surprised when they meet with betrayal in a world where the sun never rises. But what happens when their lives depend on their ability to trust?

Early in 2008, you'll find out.

Happy Reading,

Eileen Wilks

Dangerous, immortal, and thirsting for blood.
Like it or not, "they" are among us.
Laurell K. Hamilton
the Anita Blake series
MaryJanice Davidson
the Undead series
Christine Feehan
the Dark series and the Drake Sisters series
Diane Whiteside
the Blood series
Charlaine Harris
the Sookie Stackhouse series
Don't miss the best in vampire fiction from Berkley.
penguin.com

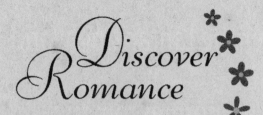